PENGUIN CLASSICS

NICK JOAQUIN

The Woman Who Had Two Navels
and Tales of the Tropical Gothic

Foreword by GINA APOSTOL

Acclaim for Nick Joaquin's
The Woman Who Had Two Navels and
Tales of the Tropical Gothic

"Manila was Joaquin's birthplace and his muse, yet the priests, social-
ites, and activists who populate these pages also evoke a globe-trotting
intellect and a wondrous universe all his own. This book brilliantly
captures the singular genius of Nick Joaquin, and will seduce readers
everywhere who are meeting this giant of Philippine literature for the
first time."
— Mia Alvar, PEN/Robert W. Bingham Prize–winning
author of *In the Country*

"One cannot overstate what Nick Joaquin is to Philippine literature.
Writing in English with the melody of Spanish and Tagalog, Joaquin
was the first Filipino writer to focus on the impossible contradictions of
a tribal civilization overlain by Spanish and American world views.
And because that tribal civilization was woman-centered, Joaquin's
heroines are as complex, romantic, and defiant as Madame Bovary and
Anna Karenina."
— Ninotchka Rosca, American Book Award–winning
author of *Twice Blessed*

"Nick Joaquin was both a brilliant poet and intense chronicler of doubleness that is a defining attribute of postcoloniality, in his case a His-
panicized Philippines complicated by Anglo American colonial rule.
Underneath his use of English one senses the patriarchal tone of Spanish and the feminist susurrations of Tagalog. Hence, Joaquin's world,
particularly in *A Portrait of the Artist as Filipino*, is one where remembering offers both solace and grief, and a subtle critique of empire. An
exemplar of postcolonial literature at its best, Joaquin moves us with
his empathetic depictions of a divided consciousness. Penguin's reissue
of his works is a benediction and cause for celebration."
— Luis H. Francia, PEN Open Book Award–winning
author of *Eye of the Fish: A Personal Archipelago*

"Nick Joaquin was such a presence in my childhood. I remember having
a collection of Joaquin's stories for children in my personal library.
They were large, beautifully illustrated volumes that provided commen-
tary to our culture in language so engaging for a child to understand. He
has been a beloved storyteller for the Philippines for generations and now
his memorable stories and play will be made available around the
world."
— Lea Salonga, Tony Award–winning singer and actress

PENGUIN CLASSICS

THE WOMAN WHO HAD TWO NAVELS AND TALES OF THE TROPICAL GOTHIC

NICK JOAQUIN (1917–2004) is widely regarded as the greatest Filipino writer of the twentieth century. Born on May 4, 1917, in Manila, Joaquin grew up in a household under the shadow of American rule but with material and familial ties to the late Spanish colonial culture and the turbulent legacy of the Philippine Revolution. Novelist, playwright, poet, journalist, historian, and biographer, Joaquin produced a body of work unmatched in richness and range by any of his contemporaries. As literary editor of the *Philippines Free Press* magazine in the 1950s and 1960s, Joaquin stood as an inspiration to generations of Filipino writers. His works include two novels, *The Woman Who Had Two Navels* and *Cave and Shadows*; three collections of short fiction; two volumes of poetry; and numerous works of nonfiction. His novel *The Woman Who Had Two Navels* (based on the short story) was first written on a Harper Publishing Company fellowship awarded in 1957, which brought him to the United States and Mexico. The book was published in 1962 and was awarded the first Harry Stonehill Novel Award. His play, *A Portrait of the Artist as Filipino*, has been widely performed in the Philippines, in both dramatic and film adaptations. His most celebrated short works and play written between the 1940s to the mid-1960s span the end of U.S. colonial rule, the Japanese occupation, Manila's near total destruction from World War II, and its uneven reconstruction in the post-colonial era. They show the height of Joaquin's craft as a storyteller. His stories, for which he coined the term "Tropical Gothic," were shaped by the spiritual pull of Spanish Catholicism, the violence and promise of American colonialism, the profound destructiveness of the Pacific war, and the turbulent beginnings of the post-colonial era. The recipient of numerous awards, Joaquin was honored as a National Artist of the Philippines in 1976 under the regime of late dictator Ferdinand Marcos. Joaquin accepted the award and requested the release from political detention of an imprisoned fellow poet and journalist Jose F. Lacaba, which was granted. In 1966, Joaquin received the Ramon Magsaysay Award for journalism, literature, and creative communication "for exploring the mysteries of the Filipino body and soul in sixty inspired years as a writer." On April 29, 2004, Joaquin died of cardiac arrest at his home in San Juan, Metro Manila.

GINA APOSTOL won the Philippine National Book Award for each of her first two novels, *Bibliolepsy* and *The Revolution According to Raymundo Mata*. Her third novel, *Gun Dealers' Daughter*, was shortlisted for the William Saroyan International Prize and won the PEN/Open Book Award. She lives in New York City and western Massachusetts.

VICENTE L. RAFAEL is a professor of history at the University of Washington, specializing in southeast Asian history. He has written widely on the political and cultural history of the Philippines, and his works include *Contracting Colonialism, White Love and Other Events in Filipino History, The Promise of the Foreign*, and, most recently, *Motherless Tongues: The Insurgency of Language Amid Wars of Translation*.

NICK JOAQUIN

The Woman Who Had Two Navels and Tales of the Tropical Gothic

Foreword by
GINA APOSTOL

Introduction by
VICENTE L. RAFAEL

PENGUIN BOOKS

PENGUIN BOOKS

An imprint of Penguin Random House LLC
375 Hudson Street
New York, New York 10014
penguin.com

The selections in this volume were first published in the Philippines.
"Three Generations" first appeared in *Graphic,* "Legend of the Dying Wanton," and
"The Summer Solstice" appeared in *Saturday Evening News;* "The Mass at St. Sylvestre" in the
Manila Post; "May Day Eve," "Guardia de Honor," "Dona Jeronima," "The Order of Melkizedek"
and "Candido's Apocalypse" in the *Philippine Free Press;* "The Woman Who Had Two Navels"
in the *Manila Chronicle Sunday Magazine;* and "Portrait of the Artist as Filipino:
An Elegy in Three Acts" in *Weekly Women's Magazine.*

LIBRARY OF CONGRESS CATALOGING-IN-PUBLICATION DATA
Names: Joaquin, Nick, author. | Apostol, Gina, writer of foreword. | Rafael,
Vicente L., writer of introduction. | Container of (work): Joaquin, Nick.
Woman who had two navels. | Container of (work): Joaquin, Nick. Tales of the tropical gothic.
Title: The woman who had two navels ; and, Tales of the tropical gothic /
Nick Joaquin ; foreword by Gina Apostol ; introduction by Vicente L. Rafael.
Description: New York : Penguin Books, [2017]
Identifiers: LCCN 2016040950 (print) | LCCN 2016045469 (ebook) |
ISBN 9780143130710 (print) | ISBN 9781524704544 (ebook)
Classification: LCC PR9550.9.J6 A6 2017 (print) | LCC PR9550.9.J6 (ebook) |
DDC 823/.914—dc23
LC record available at https://lccn.loc.gov/2016040950

Printed in the United States of America
1 3 5 7 9 10 8 6 4 2

Contents

Foreword

Nick Joaquin had the look of a dissolute emperor and the discipline of a monk. He lived, worked, and died in the city of his birth. He loved San Miguel beer, walking around Manila, and attending Mass. He spoke Tagalog, Spanish, and English, plus kanto-boy Tagalog and street Englishes. His style has a term: Joaquinesque. His command of voice, language, and form is absolute. Some of his sentences are like labyrinths that if you pulled a string through, you get this architectonic surety, a marvel. As a writer, I am always falling in love with him again. I study his sentences. Puns lurk in his precision. His favorite is "going for lost": inside the phrase is Tagalog, *nagwawala,* meaning both to lose and to go nuts. He likes gerundizing (Tagalog is verb based) and history puns. For Filipinos, Joaquin is sui generis. Almost maddeningly Manileño, subversively religious, pitch-perfectly bourgeois, preternaturally feminist, historically voracious, Joaquin's work has a fatality—*it simply is.*

I read him when I was a child in Leyte. MacArthur had landed on my island in 1944; and since May 1, 1898, when Spain's ships fell to American cannons in Manila Bay, the Philippines—condemned on that May Day to English—has made art in English from seeds of violence.

For the Philippines, an archipelago geographically fragmented, linguistically fissured, occupied by not one but two invaders heralding a fierce but frayed republic dominated by the oligarchic spoils of our split, postcolonial selves—in a land tectonically and climatically doomed to dissolution—for the Philippines, perhaps it is only through its fictions that it can conceive itself a unity.

These fictions are in multiple tongues. Some say the country is distinct because it was created by a novel—José Rizal's *Noli Me Tangere*. Joaquin is tonally different from Rizal not only because he wrote in English, Rizal in Spanish, and Rizal wrote before war, while Joaquin, like Aeneas carrying Anchises, bore war's effects. But Joaquin is equally oracular, with that slippery, ironic humor of the triple-tongued (or double-naveled) who writes in a conscious, resistant space between translation.

Rereading Joaquin, I feel ghosts, all of them women. Time-traveling Natalia in "Guardia de Honor," always about to lead the La Naval procession, the celebration of Manila that Joaquin loved. Child-heiress Guia in "Melkizedek," who undergoes metamorphoses: an array of freedom-hungry desires none of which guides her to liberation. The Grandmother in "Cándido's Apocalypse," soother of psychosis. Above all, those twin indelible figures, *desperada* and despot—Agueda of "May Day Eve" and my favorite, Lupeng of "The Summer Solstice." That searing moment in "The Summer Solstice"—when the husband Don Paeng "clawed his way across the floor, like a great agonized lizard . . . lifted his dripping face and touched his bruised lips to [Lupeng's] toes and grabbed the white foot and kissed it"—is stamped like a fever in my brain. I realize I was too young when I read that. And the scene in "May Day Eve" of Agueda staring at the mirror at her prophesied demon is an abiding portrait, since the Philippines still grants no divorce. I may not be the only Filipino for whom both empowered Lupeng and tragic Agueda embody two sides of one electrifying, inescapable Mother.

It is especially through his women that Joaquin diagnoses the spiritual horror of impassioned but truncated lives—his existential theme. His cure lies in the same women: they are daemons of the life-spirit—babaylan and Tadtarin and witches and supernatural powers that run through Joaquin's work. Joaquin is prescient and contemporary because he excavates what's ancient—women are vessels of transformative godhood: versions of Mary, animist, earthly.

But in "The Woman Who Had Two Navels," the eponymous woman is secondary beside the male ghost—the revolutionary

Monzon, exiled in Hong Kong since 1901, when he refused to pledge allegiance to America after the war for Philippine independence failed.

His trauma—that crippled independence—is at the heart of this collection.

The 1899–1904 Filipino-American war is a blind spot—we do not remember it. A brave, anti-imperialist war is the birthright of the Philippines: the nation was founded on revolt against imperial America in the aftermath of the so-called Spanish-American War of 1898, when the United States decided to occupy its ally against Spain rather than liberate it. The Philippines commemorates its 1896 war against Spain when it celebrates its revolutionary history; the Filipino-American war that succeeded the Spanish war is, oddly, forgotten. Joaquin once famously noted that he wrote to "bring in the grandfathers, to manifest roots." Some fault Joaquin for Hispanocentrism: but his gaze toward Spain is not nostalgic; it is a tool in his arsenal—a weapon in his critique of empire. That failed revolution, the wound of the American war, is the invisible scar in Joaquin's stories.

In "The Woman Who Had Two Navels," Joaquin recalls Monzon's past through the solipsistic babble of socialite Concha (that burlesque of the bourgeois voice is a Joaquin specialty): "She would always see her childhood as a page in an epic, brilliant with tears and splendid with heroes."

Through vapid Concha, Joaquin sketches the Revolution. Similarly, "Melkizedek" evokes the American occupation in one line about a charlatan, Melchior: "In March 1901, General Otis sent a Gringo infantry battalion . . ." to throw the cult into jail. In Joaquin's plots, war and resistance at first seem farce, barely drawn, and not foregrounded. Historical ellipsis, a recurring structural element in Joaquin, expresses his masterful understanding of his country. It marks hurt.

Nick Joaquin's father was a colonel under General Emilio Aguinaldo. The 1899 Battle of Manila was the eternal present of his father's generation: after that loss, to recall its acts was sedition. The 1945 Battle of Manila was Joaquin's: he lived through it. In Joaquin, a consummate Manileño, these two events, Manila's fall to Americans in 1899 and Manila's destruction by Americans in 1945, occur like doubled stereograph pictures, a history pun—as if, once refocused, they are the same trauma. Sketched most candidly in "A Portrait of the Artist as Filipino" and "Woman," this mourning—over ruined place, unsung heroes, lost hopes—perhaps comes from Joaquin's being an observant son. He took on with blithe sin the language of his father's enemy, mastering it to witness the paradoxical ways a nation survives.

His unapologetic, Calibanic choice of English is both rebuke to the occupier and revenge upon it.

Monzon the exile vows to return only when his country is free. In 1946, America "gave" the Philippines its freedom. But "it's not there anymore, your father's house," Concha reports, ". . . this last war had finally destroyed it."

In World War II, American artillery blasted old Manila to rubble in order to recapture it. The old city has never recovered. Among Allied capitals, only Warsaw was worse hit. Joaquin knew this destruction to the bone. In "Mass of St. Sylvestre," he summons it: "the city he knew has been wiped out by magic more practical and effective than any he had ever dreamt of." In Binondo, all that is left of Monzon's house is "a sad stairway in a field of ruin, going up to nowhere."

Joaquin "queers" history. His slant is invariably transgressive, questioning the norm—the revolutionary is catatonic, enslaved women are bosses, the virile are a mess, a GI, an ally, witnesses the destruction he made as if it were only illusion. Joaquin reads his country like the visionary madman in "Cándido's Apocalypse": people walk about exposing their truths, naked. But they do not know their own truths. Anachronism, psychosis, time traveling, fantasy, mirrors, ghosts: these are structures with which Joaquin sets the view awry in order to see it more right.

The past haunts Nick Joaquin. But as I reread him today, Nick Joaquin is more present than the world around me. His voice is vivid, idiosyncratic, sure, replete. Joaquin creates, as one reads him, his own precursors—his existence modifies the textual landscape.

My own whimsical list of precursors produced by Nick Joaquin includes Machado de Assis crossed with Holden Caulfield ("Cándido's Apocalypse"), shipwrecks in Melville ("Doña Jerónima"), neurotic women in telenovelas ("The Woman Who Had Two Navels"), Chaucer ("Mass of St. Sylvestre"), *bastos* conquistadors in Tagalog *komiks* ("Legend of a Dying Wanton"), García Márquez's Melquíades ("Order of Melkizedek"), a line in Dylan Thomas ("Three Generations"), Borges's magician dreamed by another ("Guardia de Honor").

In my mind, Joaquin alters his precursors. *Catcher in the Rye* is flat, after "Cándido's Apocalypse," because Holden has no Filipino grandmother. I start imagining Melville's harpooners passing unnamed wrecks of Manila galleons, and TV soap femmes fatales reciting Rizal's "Mi Último Adiós." The Romanism of Chaucer is archaic, but the Romanism of Joaquin is current: it's about grief under empire.

Of course, this amusing trick with texts I appropriate from "Kafka and His Precursors," a Borgesian joke about paradoxes of reading (and a fable on postcoloniality). Borges says, "Every writer creates his own precursors. His work modifies our conception of the past, as it will modify the future." Thus, in some stories, Joaquin reveals the Philippines as indigenously European, that is, grotesque and medieval; in others, Manhattan and Hong Kong are just flighty provinces of Manila. In all of them, women are central, casting healthy suspicion on all phallocentric plots that have come before Joaquin.

Joaquin wanted to be a priest. Instead, he wrote nonstop for seven decades. His journalism was as psychologically sharp as his fiction, his poetry as prized as his histories. He wrote his miraculous prose through terrible times with his integrity intact: a difficult feat. He had stature like no other. He lived like a hermit. Chosen National Artist of the Philippines by Ferdinand Marcos in 1976, Joaquin almost refused. In a jujitsu move, he accepted on one condition—that the dictator free the imprisoned poet Jose F. Lacaba. Thus Lacaba went home. Joaquin's gesture was long unknown. This tact occurs in Joaquin's stories: it's his characters' ability to live that matters. He is interested in vitality. Born of war and occupation, like his country, he sat every day in a monkish room with only books, a desk, and a manual typewriter, and he wrote. History is only precursor; the past is a ruin his prose survives. Writing is his triumph.

Reading him is ours.

GINA APOSTOL

Introduction

Telling Times: Nick Joaquin, Storyteller

I.

Just four years before Nick Joaquin's first story, "Three Generations," appeared in the Manila magazine *Graphic* in 1940, the great German critic Walter Benjamin writing half a world away remarked on the demise of the craft of storytelling. One reason for it had to do with the attenuation of experience. To the extent that stories consist of transmitting experiences— both the storytellers' and those of others—its waning had the effect of making it more difficult to tell and share them. In the midst of the Great Depression, the rise of fascism in Germany and Italy, and the growing threat of global war, storytelling was coming into a crisis. Conditions such as the spread of capitalism, inflation and economic depression, the commodification of everyday life, the mechanization of war, and the moral corruption of politics had in fact been going on for much of the modern era and had the effect of turning experience into private goods or public clichés, flattening their cultural singularity and historical specificity. "More and more," Benjamin wrote, "there is embarrassment all around when the wish to hear a story is expressed. It is as if something that seemed inalienable to us, the securest among our possessions, were taken from us: the ability to exchange experiences."[1]

Across the Pacific Ocean, in what was then the only formal colony of the United States, the deracination of experience, along with a crisis in the ability to communicate it, had long been taking place. The Philippines had been a Spanish colony for more than three hundred years, located at the western extreme of the first truly global empire since 1565. In 1898, the United States invaded and annexed the colony as part of its war against Spain.[2] Among the United States' new colonial possessions, only the Philippines vigorously resisted American designs. Filipino revolutionary forces, having fought and defeated Spain, declared independence and established a republic, launched a protracted guerrilla war that resulted in more than four thousand American casualties and about a quarter of a million Filipino deaths—one sixth of the entire population of the largest island of Luzon. Declared officially over by President Theodore Roosevelt in 1902, Filipino resistance continued in fits and starts until the 1930s. In the wake of revolution and war, and in the midst of the ever-present possibility of social uprisings, American colonial policy sought to reconcile Filipinos to the so-called benevolence of U.S. rule. Casting the former as "little brown brothers," Americans claimed to be benefactors and sincere philanthropists dispensing the civilizing benefits of the Anglo-Saxon race. These included elections, free trade, the rule of law, a public health system, a colonial military, among others—all designed to co-opt and entrench elites at the expense of the poor.[3]

The most effective counterinsurgency program, however, came in the form of the colonial public school system. Starting in 1899, the American regime established a network of public schools—what military governor-general Arthur MacArthur referred to as "adjuncts to military operations," needed to "expedite the restoration of tranquility throughout the archipelago."[4] A key feature of the public schools was the adoption of English as the sole medium of instruction. English was meant to supersede the staggering linguistic diversity that characterized the colony—a linguistic diversity that predated Spanish colonial rule and which missionaries, seeking to evangelize in the local languages, had further institutionalized.[5] More than one hundred distinct languages continued to be spoken then (and to this day) in the archipelago. Complicating this linguistic landscape was the limited knowledge of Spanish, whereby only about 10 percent of the most affluent and educated members of colonial society could claim to be fluent despite 350 years of Spanish rule. For the Americans, very few of whom knew Spanish, English was the only feasible language of instruction. It quickly became the dominant language of rule and education.[6]

II.

From the start, the decision to use English, like that of colonizing the Philippines, was fraught with contradiction. It had the effect of simultaneously incorporating Filipinos into the emergent colonial regime while keeping them at a distance from the metropolitan center. The goal of achieving mass literacy in English, meant to mitigate social inequalities and pave the way for a more democratic society, was short-circuited by the chronic shortage of funds, the failure to extend universal access to schooling, and the difficulty of retaining most of the students beyond the primary grades. But by the 1930s, an impressive 35 percent of the population could claim fluency in the language, making the Philippines the most literate in any Western language in all of colonial Southeast Asia.[7] Still, many remained with little or no familiarity with English depending on how much schooling they had. They continued to live in largely vernacular worlds below English and Spanish, both of which continued to be the speech associated with colonial elites. In other words, the colonial legacy of English, like that of Spanish, included the creation of a linguistic hierarchy that roughly corresponded to a social hierarchy.[8]

Philippine independence from American rule at the end of World War II further intensified this linguistic hierarchy. While Spanish fell largely out of use—thanks to the passing away of the last generation fluent in the language—the vernacular languages continued to be widely used among the majority of the population as the language of intimacy and informality at home and with friends and in commercial or "low-class" entertainment venues. Meanwhile, the prestige of English grew as a direct effect of colonial schooling where English was privileged while the vernaculars were repressed, endowing speakers fluent in English with a considerable cultural capital. The American victory over the Japanese further enhanced the position of English in the country. The postwar popularity of Hollywood movies and American pop music, the expansion of the military bases, and the extension of economic ties and cultural exchanges further deepened the hold of English in the postwar and postcolonial periods. Since 1987, the national language, Filipino—which is largely based on one of the largest spoken vernaculars in and around Manila, Tagalog—has sought to contest or at least mitigate the cultural dominance of English with little success. American English continues to be the language of authority, used in official state business and the dominant medium of instruction in higher education. The imperatives of globalization have meant that English has become the linguistic commodity par excellence, essential to the training of Filipinos as workers in the world of overseas caregiving and business outsourcing—the twin pillars of the current Philippine economy.

The historical role of English in consolidating structures of political, cultural, and economic power during and beyond the period of direct American rule helps to situate the significance of Nick Joaquin's literary legacy. His earliest stories were published during the Commonwealth, the Filipino state that governed the archipelago under American supervision starting in 1935 through a ten-year transition period toward independence. But as the literary historian Resil Mojares has pointed out, using the language of the Americans meant that Filipino writers had to willfully ignore the long and complex vernacular literary tradition that stretched back to the precolonial period and went through a remarkable renaissance during the early decades of U.S. rule. The growth of vernacular literature and journalism in the early part of the twentieth century came thanks to the cultural space opened up by the end of Spanish rule on the one hand and the yet-to-be-consolidated hegemony of American English on the other. The weakening of the linguistic hierarchy allowed for writing in the local languages to rise to the fore. Influenced by late-nineteenth-century Spanish modernist literature and Revolutionary nationalist writings, numerous novels, short stories, and poems in Tagalog, Cebuano, Ilocano, and other languages appeared in books and newspapers, while vernacular plays such as the Zarzuela were performed in most large towns and cities. These were often, though not always, nationalist allegories expressed through the prism of social problems such as class differences, gender politics, and the weakening of parental authority amid the influx of capitalism and American colonial rule. A few writers even espoused socialism as a way of dealing with labor problems and championed the cause of independence.[9] Yet, by the late 1920s, a new generation of Filipinos educated in English emerged who were roundly dismissive of vernacular writing. Their disdain for literature in the local languages was hardly surprising. It was a direct outcome of colonial education where fluency in English was acquired in and through the repression of vernacular languages.[10]

Indeed, the very identity of Filipino Anglophone writers emerged via their denigration of vernacular writings as mere entertainment and commercial fodder for the unenlightened masses. Informed by the racist claims of American colonial teachers regarding the inherent inferiority of the vernacular languages, Filipino writers came to regard serious "literature" as something that was possible only in English. Writing in American English also cut them off from the Spanish literature written by their revolutionary fathers. Instead, they saw their literary birthright to lie in the Western canon. They avidly read Cervantes and Dostoevsky (in English translation), Sherwood Anderson and Virginia Woolf, Ernest Hemingway and William Faulkner, e. e. cummings and Marianne Moore while setting aside Francisco Balagtas, Modesto de Castro, Lope K. Santos, Macario Pineda, Faustino Aguilar, and many other serious writers in the vernacular. Even the national hero José Rizal (1861–1896), who wrote in Spanish, was often read in English translation.[11]

Thus did Anglophone Filipino writers feel themselves to be a generation and a class apart: more politically advanced than their revolutionary forebears while far more aesthetically refined and intellectually accomplished compared with those who were still caught up in vernacular worlds. Among themselves, they epitomized the modernizing promise of colonial rule: the promise of eventual independence and cosmopolitan uplift precisely to the extent that they spoke and wrote in what they considered to be the very idiom of modernity itself. American English contained Philippine literature in the double sense of that word: not only did it function as the language of colonial valuation; it was also felt to be the privileged idiom for expressing the novel experience of a coming freedom. As Mojares wrote about the doubleness of English among the early generation of Anglophone writers, it became "a medium which put the writer at one degree removed from immediate experience . . . its use transfigured sensibility and vision in ways that did not only occasion alienation but also made possible unexpected illumination."[12]

One more context for understanding the unfolding of Filipino Anglophone writing was the relative absence of any serious American literary interest in the Philippines. No major piece of American fiction and no American writer of any consequence ever wrote about the Philippines under U.S. rule. No Conrads, Kiplings, Orwells, or Forsters ever emerged among the Americans with regard to their Philippine colony. It seemed that the burden of recording the colonial, and later on, the postcolonial experience fell to Filipino writers in English. But they, too, found themselves largely patronized and ignored by American literary critics in the United States. With rare exceptions— Carlos Bulosan and José Garcia Villa, for example—very few Filipino writers were ever acknowledged, much less validated, by metropolitan publishers, critics, and other American writers—again with very few exceptions.[13] As a result, Filipinos, despite seeking to enlarge their readership, ended up mostly writing for and reading one another within the Philippines. Thus arose a curious situation: despite working in a world language, Filipino Anglophone writers found their cosmopolitan outlook and modernist impulses dramatically provincialized, forced to stay within the boundaries of the emergent nation-state rather than be transported and disseminated into a larger

English-speaking world. They became, despite their earlier dis-
avowals, invariably vernacularized.

The promise of colonial modernity that English brought was
destined for further betrayal. The Japanese invasion and occupation of the Philippines brought U.S. rule to a sudden end
while bringing the Philippines within the imperial orbit of East
Asia. Nick Joaquin continued to write throughout the Japanese
occupation. The war's end saw a remarkable surge in his out-
put. During the first two decades of the postcolonial period
between 1946 and 1965, Joaquin published his most antholo-
gized works, eleven of which appear in this volume. Setting his
stories amid the bombed-out ruins of Manila—the second
most destroyed city after Warsaw—he sought to come to grips
with the turbulent and uncertain present by invoking the memory of the past. For Joaquin, one of the most devastating out-
comes of the war was the loss of what Benjamin refers to as the
"communicability of experience." Pressed between the Filipino-
American and the Pacific wars, three generations of Filipinos
struggled to survive, a task that required for Joaquin the capacity to recover what had been lost. It meant being able not just
to reconstruct a city destroyed beyond recognition; it also
entailed regaining the capacity of remembering itself in order
to reconstitute the remembering self. How to recall not just
what seemed beyond recollection, but the very faculty and
agency of recollection as such? How to tell the story of a nation,
let alone a city, now buried in the physical and moral rubble
that made up everyday life? And how to carry out the task of
recovery and recollection in English—that other tongue which
called for leaving behind the mother tongue? Who would listen
and who would respond? The task of the storyteller was thus
steeped in endless complications.

III.

Like many middle- and upper-class Filipinos in the post-
Revolutionary era, Nick Joaquin (1917–2004) grew up in a
household under the shadow of American rule but with

material and familial ties to the late Spanish colonial culture. His father was a lawyer and served in the Spanish colonial civil service. Along with many other Filipino nationalists of his generation, he joined the Revolution and rose in the ranks to become an aide to Emilio Aguinaldo. Nick's mother was a schoolteacher who early on learned English and was the first to teach her children the language. With the sudden death of Joaquin's father, the family's fortunes took a sudden downward turn. The large house in the wealthy Manila district of Paco was sold, and Nick was forced to live with his older brother Porfiro, or "Ping," and his wife, Sarah. At an early age, he took odd jobs and worked as a printer's devil for a local magazine. He had already quit school at the age of fourteen, claiming that he could learn more on his own by regularly going to the National Library and reading whatever he could get his hands on. His voracious reading of English-language texts was combined with a dedication to walking. Joaquin's sister-in-law recalls how he walked everywhere, frequently wearing out his shoes to see the city and talk to various people, listening to their stories, and exploring the spaces and archives of Manila's churches. Throughout his life, his walking and thinking went hand in hand, affording him the chance to explore high and low cultures, traversing the boundaries between the sacred and the profane, all the while living within the folds of two colonial powers and speaking their languages.[14]

After the war, he won a scholarship to study briefly at a Dominican seminary in Hong Kong, but, unable for various reasons to continue, Joaquin returned to Manila. By the 1950s, he began working as a journalist, writing lengthy features on crime and politics as well as assorted profiles on actors, visiting dignitaries, artists, boxers, and other social types in ways that highlighted the strange and ironic aspects of their lives. He reveled in popular culture, reading pulp fiction, working in theater, memorizing musicals, and watching all sorts of films.[15] From the 1960s to the 1970s, he also began to write insightful revisionary accounts of the nation's history, especially of its Revolutionary period, often swimming against the currents of ethno-nationalist and Marxist historiographies. But his most powerful works are arguably still the short stories he wrote between the 1940s and the mid-1960s. It was during those times that Joaquin's craft as a storyteller was at its height. As with other great storytellers, he enjoyed "the freedom with which [to] move up and down the rungs of [his] experience as on a ladder."[16] Such experience forms the substance of his stories. They were shaped, often to the breaking point, by the spiritual pull of Spanish Catholicism, the violence and promise of American colonialism, the profound destructiveness of the Pacific War, and the turbulent beginnings of the postcolonial era. How so?

IV.

In "The Mass of St. Sylvestre" (1946), for example, Joaquin tells a story about telling a story, foregrounding the most essential element of all: time. It recounts the Christianized version of the Roman god Janus, St. Sylvestre, the pope and patron saint "of doors and beginnings" whose feast day falls on the last day of the year. Carrying the keys of his office, St. Sylvestre "opens the gates of the Arch-episcopal cities" in all of Christendom, which, by the seventeenth century, included Manila. He then leads a celestial procession made up of numinous angels and various saints to commemorate the first Mass of the New Year: the feast of Christ's circumcision. Legend had it that whosoever witnesses this Divine Mass would be given the gift of time: a thousand years to witness a thousand more Masses. Hearing this, a native sorcerer and translator, Maestro Mateo, plots to see the Mass. He steals the eyeballs of the recently dead, screwing them onto his own eyes to shield himself from the blinding spectacle of the Mass. He hides behind the altar and forces himself to stay awake by using a knife to make cuts in his arms, reducing them into a bloody mess while sprinkling limes on the wounds to refresh the pain. But unable to resist the sublime sight before him, he turns into stone, only to awaken every year for the next thousand years to see again the cavalcade of divine beings marking the end of the old year and the coming of the new.

The narrator then reframes this story as a kind of cautionary tale that parents used to tell their children during Mass to keep them from falling asleep during the ritual. He passes it on to us, his readers, as something that was once passed on from one generation to the next. But the experience of the story as a kind of gift that circulates and which no one owns had been brutally shattered. World War II rained bombs on the city, bringing with it a magic "more practical and effective" than any sorcerer could ever conjure. Reduced to ruins, the city ceased hosting the holy procession of a host of angels and saints marking the arrival of the New Year. It could no longer furnish a site for ritually subsuming the mechanical tyranny of clock and calendar within the promise of messianic time. However, as Joaquin shows, one thing continued to survive amid the devastation: the story of St. Sylvestre's Mass and Maestro Mateo's plot to witness it. He recounts telling the story to a group of American GIs and is surprised when one of his American listeners tells him that one of the soldiers had actually witnessed St. Sylvestre's grand entrance into the city. Finding the soldier's address in Brooklyn, the narrator writes him a letter, asking him to tell him the story of what he, the latter-day Mateo, saw. The narrator reproduces the reply from the American. He did see the procession, he writes, but was unaware of the Christian references and names of saints. What captivated him, though, was the music and the vision of the city fully restored as the ancient parade passed by. Rather than the eyes of the recently dead, the American reached for a mechanical eye, his camera, with which to record the scene. But as he tried to take a photograph, everything suddenly vanished. "There was no crowd and no bishops and no altar and no cathedral," he wrote. "I was standing on a stack of ruins and there was nothing but ruins around. Just blocks and blocks of ruins stretching all around me in the silent moonlight . . ."

The time of the story shifts with each retelling. It begins in some unspecified moment of early Christianity when saints succeed pagan gods. It is then reset in the early period of Spanish conquest in the later sixteenth century. Finally it is recapitulated in the immediate postwar era. As a parable about the hubris of mortals seeking immortality by magical rather than liturgical means, the story does what stories are meant to do: provide counsel. At first glance, such counsel has to do with parents' warning their children to stay awake during the Mass lest they be turned to stone. But in the wake of war's catastrophe, there is a further twist. The storyteller retells the story by means of another source: a soldier's letter. By then the moral, as it were, of the story is of an entirely different sort. It is no longer about the need to stay awake, but of the need to endure the sense of loss amid the ruins upon ruins that remain. Such ruins become the occasion for both remembering the story and recalling its demise. The storyteller thus leaves off not with his own voice but with that of an American other.

While the city may be lost, something else remains: not just the ruins but, more important, the indestructible force of time that animates the capacity to remember and pass on stories, to become hearers ready to assume the position of tellers again from whatever distant shores and alienated circumstances. The story as a gift that passes from one time to another thus evinces the way by which storytelling allows us the experience of lingering on the ever-shifting threshold that divides and joins the old world with the new, the empty time of clock and calendar with the ritual time of messianic expectation.

V.

Displaced and decayed, the past seemed formless and forgotten in the postwar era. Yet the forgetting of history only meant that it was absorbed into the rubble of memory. Joaquin sought to call attention to the productive powers of the material traces of the past in his other stories. In his play, *A Portrait of the Artist as Filipino* (1951), he dramatizes the plight of the Marasigan family living in a grand house in Intramuros, the colonial core of Manila, which was steadily collapsing under the weight of unpaid bills, sibling rivalry, and paternal weakness. Narrated from the future perspective of the war's aftermath, when the house itself had already been leveled, the story relates the struggles of the family to rescue its legacy and cling to an older way of life even as the forces of modernity were busy tearing away its foundations. A central concern of the characters is the fate of an oil painting by the father that depicts him as a young man fleeing a burning city while carrying on his back an older version of himself—an allusion to Aeneas carrying his father Anchises as they fled Troy. Close to death, the weakened father imagines himself saving himself. The allegorical portrait is a gift that the father had given his two spinster daughters, Paula and Candida, in compensation for sacrificing their lives caring for him.

As part of the revolutionary generation, the father, like many other paternal figures in Joaquin's stories, is enfeebled by colonial and capitalist forces he could neither comprehend nor control. In need of money, yet unwilling to sell the portrait for which there is great demand, the sisters find themselves trapped in the house, besieged by American popular culture and its Filipino purveyors, by politically compromised politicians, and by their own feckless nostalgia for rapidly vanishing conventions. But by telling this tale from the future perspective of the near-total destruction of the city, Joaquin recalls the inter- and intra-generational struggles around historical legacy, private property, and the politics of conduct that enlivened even as it endangered late colonial families like the Marasigans. Condemned to perish, they are nonetheless redeemed in memory.

Indeed, Joaquin was obsessed with the masculinized struggle between and within generations—the Oedipal search for truth that came at the price of the violent exposure and displacement of the father's authority by sons and daughters immersed in, but guilt-ridden from, the desires of the flesh. His first story, "Three Generations" (1940), casts fathers and sons as if they were secret lovers as much as sworn enemies struggling to control their carnal desires amid their spiritual aspirations and worldly doubts. "Cándido's Apocalypse" (1965), written some twenty-five years later, takes up a similar thread, this time set in the new suburban developments near Manila where the father is a company man and the teenage son, Bobby, is thoroughly alienated from his parents' world. Seeking a way out of the hypocrisy of bourgeois life, he finds himself drawn to his alter ego named "Cándido," a Christian martyr who is also his calendrical namesake. As in "Three Generations," the son searches for a truth that would guide his conduct and allow him to live a "genuine" existence rather than, as Joaquin puts it in the teenage lingo of the 1960s, one who is constantly "over-acting." Possessed by Cándido, Bobby begins to see uncontrollably through the clothing and eventually the flesh of all those he encounters, driving him into a frenzy of embarrassment. Wanting to see the truth, he instead sees too much and is thus blinded to the very humanity of those whose inhuman behavior he seeks to disavow.

The figure of the weakened father also appears in *The Woman Who Had Two Navels* (1949). Once a widely admired doctor and officer in the failed Revolution, the older Monson chooses to go into exile in Hong Kong in the wake of the American occupation, swearing never to come back to his country until it is free even as he fills his sons with elaborate expectations of returning to the ancestral home. When the country is finally granted independence at the end of the war, he returns only to be greeted by the sorry state of their Binondo house, utterly destroyed except for the staircase. Thoroughly shaken, he quietly returns to Hong Kong and sits ossified in his room as his two sons take care of him. His failure to deliver on his promise of returning his family to their home leaves him in a state of emotional destitution. He can barely speak and retreats to using opium as his sons look on helplessly, unable to come to terms with the historical curse that they've inherited. Similarly, the two women in the story, the mother Concha and the daughter Connie, play out a more dangerous and violent generational conflict in Manila and Hong Kong. They seek to overcome the betrayals of corrupt politician-fathers and the desires of and for the same emasculated lover-musician who passes between them as they traverse two cities and two colonial eras—the late Spanish and the American, the two navels, as it were, of Filipino history.

The gendered and sexualized inflections of generational politics are similarly thematized in two of Joaquin's best-known works, "The Summer Solstice" and "May Day Eve" (both 1947).

In the former, set in the late nineteenth century, the patriarchal complacency of a wealthy Filipino home is shattered on the hottest day of the summer when one of the servants, Agueda, returns from an orgiastic fertility ritual with its roots in pre-Christian practices. Drawn to the erotic power suddenly palpable on the half-naked body of the servant, the properly feminine mistress, Doña Lupe, decides, with the encouragement of her much younger nephew newly returned from Europe and against the wishes of her older, more conservative husband, Don Paeng, to attend the ritual. Running off to join the frenzied dancing among women of all ages and classes, Lupe is transformed as she comes to absorb the repressed memory of pagan practices that elevated women's power of fertility over men's claims of ownership over that power. Back home, she triumphantly confronts her husband, forcing him to declare his adoration for her as her "dog," and "slave." In the unforgettable ending, he gets down on the ground like "a great agonized lizard," and crawls toward her outstretched naked foot, "kiss[ing] it savagely . . . the step, the toe, the frail ankle—while she bit her lip and clutched in pain at the windowsill, her body distended and wracked by horrible shivers, her head flung back and her loose hair streaming out the window—streaming fluid and black in the white night where the huge moon glowed like a sun and the dry air flamed into lightning and the pure heat burned with the immense fever of noon."

In "May Day Eve," we hear a story that's been passed down from one generation to the next: that holding a candle in a darkened room in front of a mirror will call forth the image of the one you will marry. But it might also cause the devil to appear. In Joaquin's telling of the story, a girl takes to heart the promise of the myth, rushes down to look at a mirror, and encounters the man who would be her husband, but who would also be her oppressor. Many years later, she recounts this tale to her granddaughter but says that what she saw was not her grandfather but the devil himself. Joaquin then retells another version of the story, this time from the man's perspective. Coming home from a political meeting, he is surprised to see his grandson looking at a mirror reminiscent of what his wife had done when they had first met. This unexpected encounter with the future generation reenacting the past triggers in the man a flood of memories about his wife, about the passionate love and miserable life they shared. Caught in the painful rush of images from the past, he looks out the window and hears the night watchman calling out the time as he had done at the beginning of the story, as if to synchronize the current telling and hearing of the tale with its earlier versions across three generations.

Intragenerational struggles figure prominently in Joaquin's only attempt at a murder mystery, "The Order of Melkizedek" (1966). It is set once more in the suburbs of 1960s Manila, where Joaquin retraces a series of crises that confront a Filipino expatriate returning from his job in New York with the United Nations. His siblings had asked him to help save their youngest sister from the clutches of an insidious cult leader seeking to resurrect an ancient order of pagan worshippers while passing it off as a revolutionary revision of Christianity. Precolonial and pre-Christian ideas about power and worship brush up against what Joaquin portrays as the ecumenical pop theology and pseudo-revolutionary politics characteristic of the Filipino reception of the Vatican II reforms in mid-sixties Manila. The Marcoses had just assumed power, the Beatles had just been summarily kicked out by thugs of the First Lady, and the descendants of the newly rich whose wealth came from the corruptions of their fathers mingle in sunken living rooms wearing Western suits and kitsch ethnic-designed dresses. A defrocked priest passing himself off as a new prophet employs thugs and theological mumbo-jumbo to cajole a rich, aimless heiress into his cult, while her hapless expatriate brother tries but fails to rescue her.

VI.

Alongside the obsession with gendered generational politics was Joaquin's concern with the temporality of the past—its *longue durée* that stretched into the future as it curved into the present.

In "Guardia de Honor" (1949), a conversation between a mother and daughter about a missing emerald earring worn by the latter's great grandmother takes place in the late 1940s but is overheard by that same great grandmother as she prepares to put on the set of earrings for a parade in honor of the Virgin Mary in the 1860s. As the point of connection across several generations, the lone earring is the remainder of a deadly accident borne out of passionate jealousy. The great grandmother's story unfolds as the tale of choice crashing against contingency.

Joaquin stages a conversation between the past and the future whereby the latter tells the former what it must not do, yet what it cannot help but do. Is the past made up of a series of accidents that, in hindsight, could have been avoided, or is everything a matter of fate, whereby events necessarily happen for a reason? Is the tragedy that brings death also the miracle foretold that gives birth to love and new life? Can the past learn from the future, or is the future condemned to play out the missed opportunities, the misplaced anger, the deceits and the shamefulness of the past? What can stories tell us of these confounded possibilities and tangled relationships across generations? How can we continue telling and hearing stories if all endings have already been foretold? Or is the point not the end of stories, like the end of life, but the afterlife of their telling, the possibility of their living on, spoken by another source, delivered to another recipient, who in turn tells it to someone else? Is this the lesson that the future offers to the past: not just the need to bear the inevitable passage of time but also the necessity of being alert to the coexistence of many other times?

Such questions persist in many of Joaquin's stories, inflected by and enfolded into the postcolonial dilemmas of memory making amid the social upheavals and surreal political violence and corruptions of his time. Just as the war reduced the city to its jagged, chaotic traces, so the inexorable but uneven process of reconstruction resulted in imposing upon the colonial past the architecture of anonymity and sameness. The result was a virtual lobotomy, wiping away awareness not only of the Revolution but also of the complexity of the Spanish legacy as well. Reaching back to the early period of conquest and conversion,

Joaquin dredged up legends from the nineteenth century that referred to the sixteenth for a mid-twentieth-century readership. Such a project, ranging far and wide in time, lent to his stories an epic quality frequently played out on the level of the sentence. Joaquin often resorted to long sinuous sentences that meandered like the Pasig River—the major waterway that links and divides Manila—overflowing into the many *esteros* of popular forgetfulness. There is, for example, the opening sentence of "Doña Jerónima" (1965):[17]

In the days of the galleons, a certain Archbishop of Manila was called to a council in Mexico but on the way there fell in with pirates who seized his ship, looted the holds, slew the crew, and were stringing up the Archbishop to a mast when a sudden storm ripped up and wrecked both pirate craft and Philippine galleon, drowning all that were on board, save only the Archbishop, who, being bound to the cross of the mast, was borne safely over the wrath of the waters and thus reached the shores of a desert isle, a dry isle that was but a tip of reef in the sea, where, for a burning year, he lived on fish and prayer, on rain water and meditation, crouched day and night in deep thought at the foot of the cross of the mast he had set up on the shore, all alone in that waste of ocean, until a passing ship, mystified by a reflection as of a giant cross shining in the air, tracked the mirage to the horizon and came upon the desert isle, and upon the cross of mast planted on the shore, and upon the bowed, mute, shriveled old man squatting motionless and cross-legged there, stark naked and half-blind and burned black as coal, all his hair turned white and his white beard trailing down to his navel, and hardly able to stand or move or speak or grasp, in which dismal condition he was carried back to his city, arriving there some two years after he had left in glory, having departed a fine blaze of a man, handsome and vigorous, and bidden farewell by all the city to a tumult of bells, banners, fireworks and music, and returning now in decay, terribly altered, terribly aged, mere skin and bone and wild eye, but still amid bells, banners, fireworks, music, and the tumult of the city, for news of his rescue had preceded him, the marvel of his sojourn on the island had grown into legend in the retelling, and he himself had become such a figure of miracle—the man twice saved by the Sign of the Cross; and fed on the desert isle, 'twas said, by ravens, like Elijah, and with manna from heaven, like the Israelites—that the folk who poured forth to welcome him dropped to their knees with a shudder as he was borne past, a frail wraith that, however, had power to stun the eye and seize the soul, that would, indeed, in those days, possess the popular mind, every traveling bard having but this one ballad to sing, and no print hawked at the fairs but carried the Archbishop's picture and a relation of his adventures, by which diverse manners the fame of him spread as a holy man on whom God had showered such mystical favors that when the Archbishop at last emerged from a long convalescence, firmer in fabric but never again to be in his prime, it was to find himself being revered in the land as a saint.

In this passage, certainty is carried away by the irresistible torrents of chance as space falls into the vortex of time. The Archbishop's life is condensed into a series of moments, each pregnant with other stories, other times, and other possibilities. This is a chronicle of accidents whose features emerge only after repeated recitations. One event comes after another, each as unexpected and unmotivated as the last and the next. What makes this tale arresting is its proximity to death. This is similar to an earlier story, "The Legend of the Dying Wanton" (1946), the tale of a rakish Spanish soldier in the seventeenth-century Philippines who, shipwrecked and near death from his wounds, suddenly witnesses the sublime apparition of the Virgin and Child and is subsequently found by another ship where a priest hears his confession before he finally expires. In both stories, death gives the storyteller a vantage point from which to see the unfolding of a life told in long, breathless sentences that pile up image upon image propelled by lush alliteration.[18]

In "Doña Jerónima," the Archbishop comes close to death but is saved by the very means with which he was to be killed, strung up on the mast like Christ hung on the cross. Swept toward a small desert island with nothing else but fish and prayer, he thrives in his new hermitage, finding another way to live apart from the political scheming and military adventurism of the colony. Cut off from the time of empire, he retreats into another time of isolation and meditation to become a different self. As luck would have it, he is rescued after a year. Back in the colony, he becomes a legend, his accidental history heralded as a miraculous event whose telling conveys blessings to those who hear and pass it on. His reputation for holiness is something he feels is undeserved but cannot escape, just as he cannot get away from public life once he is returned to Manila. Rather than redemption, rescue leads precisely to its opposite, subjecting him to the hell of public adulation that the island had sheltered him from.

Long sentences unfold in many of Joaquin's other stories. They do not represent real events so much as the possibilities of their taking place. As such, they convey the experience of remembering not what happened but what could have happened. One memory leads to another as if triggered by some involuntary process that distills the contents of an entire life into the space of a single sentence that, in its exuberant rush, delivers a series of shock effects to awaken the present to the past. Thickened with other times from other places, the past-present bursts open and becomes hospitable to other futures, beginning with the future retelling of the story. The storyteller thus conveys a particular kind of counsel: that each story is a kind of promise whose fulfillment lies precisely in its continual deferral with each successive telling and hearing. The meaning of the story is always yet to be determined, its lessons still to be applied, and its wisdom embedded in the very experience of hearing, then passing on the legend.

VII.

Walter Benjamin stressed the pragmatic nature of storytelling. Stories all convey something useful, whether "a moral . . . some practical advice . . . or a proverb or maxim. In every case the storyteller is a man who has counsel for his readers." Such counsel "is less an answer to a question than a proposal concerning the continuation of a story which is just unfolding. To seek this counsel one would first have to be able to tell the story. (Quite apart from the fact that a man is receptive to counsel only to the extent that he allows his situation to speak.) Counsel woven into the fabric of real life is wisdom."[19]

Nick Joaquin's stories provide us with such counsel. Swept by the catastrophes of colonialism and war, Joaquin, like St. Sylvestre, looked both ways. Lingering on the threshold of what had happened and what was yet to come, he found himself irresistibly drawn, like the Angel of History, to the debris of colonial catastrophes that just kept piling up around him. He sought to retrieve from the ruins of modernity the means for conveying experience—his own as well as others'—in stories about forgotten legends, repressed events, flawed fathers, two-naveled women, and the miracles of a merciful Virgin that continue to emerge from the ever-perplexing and vertigo-inducing history of a certain Philippines.[20] We, whoever we are, receive his stories told from a ruined world, hearing and perhaps sharing them as we would the shards of our own lives.

VICENTE L. RAFAEL

NOTES

1. Walter Benjamin, "The Storyteller: Reflections on the Work of Nikolai Leskov," in *Illuminations*, ed. Hannah Arendt, trans. Harry Zohn (New York: Schocken Books, 1968), 83–110. The quotations are from 83–84.

2. Histories of the U.S. Empire are legion. For a useful historiographic survey of the topic, see Paul Kramer, "Power and Connection: Imperial Histories of the United States in the World," *The American Historical Review* 116(5), (2011): 1348–91.

3. There is a vast literature on the Philippine Revolution and the Filipino-American War. See for example, Milagros Guerrero,

Luzon at War: Contradictions in Philippine Society, 1898–1902 (Mandaluyong City: Anvil Publishing, 2015); Reynaldo Ileto, *Pasyon and Revolution: Popular Uprisings in the Philippines, 1840–1910* (Quezon City: Ateneo de Manila University Press, 1979); Teodoro Agoncillo, *Malolos: The Crisis of the Republic* (Quezon City: University of the Philippines Press, 1960); Vicente L. Rafael, *White Love and Other Events in Filipino History* (Durham, NC: Duke University Press, 2000); and Paul Kramer, *The Blood of Government: Race, Empire, the United States and the Philippines* (Chapel Hill: University of North Carolina Press, 2006).

4. Quoted in Camilo Osias, "Education and Religion," in Zoilo M. Galang, ed., *Encyclopedia of the Philippines*, 20 vols. (Manila: E. Floro, 1950–58), vol. 9, 126. For a more or less critical look at the first thirteen years of colonial education, see Glenn A. May, *Social Engineering in the Philippines: The Aims, Execution, and Impact of American Colonial Policy, 1900–1913* (Westport, CT: Greenwood Press, 1980), 77–126.

5. For a history of the use of local languages for Christian conversion under Spanish rule, see Vicente L. Rafael, *Contracting Colonialism: Translation and Christian Conversion in Tagalog Society Under Early Spanish Rule* (Durham, NC: Duke University Press, 1993).

6. Vicente L. Rafael, "The War of Translation: American English, Colonial Education and Tagalog Slang," in *Motherless Tongues: The Insurgency of Language Amid Wars of Translation* (Durham, NC: Duke University Press, 2016), chap. 2. See also May, *Social Engineering in the Philippines*.

7. See Resil Mojares, *Origins and Rise of the Filipino Novel: A Generic Study of the Novel Until 1940* (Quezon City: University of the Philippines Press, 1983).

8. See Rafael, *Motherless Tongues*.

9. See Mojares, *Origins and Rise of the Filipino Novel*, 336–51. See also Caroline Sy Hau, *Necessary Fictions: Philippine Literature and the Nation, 1946–1980* (Quezon City: Ateneo de Manila University Press, 2000).

10. See Rafael, *Motherless Tongues*, chap. 2.

11. Mojares, *Origins and Rise of the Filipino Novel*, 336–51. See also Jonathan Chua, ed., *The Critical Villa: Essays in Literary Criticism* (Quezon City: Ateneo University Press, 2002); Soledad Reyes, *Nobelang Tagalog, 1905–1975: Tradisyon at Modernismo* (Quezon City: Ateneo University Press, 1982); and Bienvenido Lumbera

and Cynthia Nograles Lumbera, *Philippine Literature: A History & Anthology* (Mandaluyong City: Anvil Publishing, 1997).

12. Mojares, *Origins and Rise of the Filipino Novel*, 348. See also N. V. M. Gonzalez, "Moving On: A Filipino in the World," in Joseph Fischer, ed., *Foreign Values in Southeast Asian Studies* (Berkeley, CA: Center for South and Southeast Asian Studies, 1973); and Augusto Espiritu, *Five Faces of Exile: The Nation and Filipino American Intellectuals* (Palo Alto, CA: Stanford University Press, 2005).

Nick Joaquin himself espoused these views of the privileged role of print English in freeing the Filipino writer from the demands of and obligations to his readers versus the more "traditional" role of vernacular literature, which he considered not literature at all insofar as it was bound to oral forms and rooted in more parochial concerns. See Joaquin, "The Filipino as English Fictionist," *Philippine Quarterly of Culture and Society* 6(3) (Sept. 1978): 118–24. I disagree with Joaquin's and other Anglophone writers' insistence on the hierarchical distinction between "modern" print literature in English versus "traditional" oral storytelling in the vernacular. I am closer to the position of Resil Mojares, who argues that vernacular literature did in fact have a modernist aspect where experiments with form and content were just as vital as those going on in Anglophone literature, which writers in English, thanks to the workings of American colonial education, willfully ignored. I am also arguing for the deep historical affinity between vernacular and Anglophone literature, at least in Joaquin's case, where the practice of storytelling is concerned.

13. Here, the earlier generation of American literary critics such as Carey McWilliams, Leonard Caspar, and Roger Bresnahan come to mind. While a couple of Nick Joaquin's writings were published in American magazines, they were minor blips in the metropolitan literary scene, suffering a fate shared by most other Anglophone writers of being marginalized, then quickly forgotten. Whether or not this Penguin edition of Joaquin's stories that you hold in your hands will mitigate the relative invisibility of Filipino writing in the larger Anglophone world is, of course, something yet to be seen.

More recently, however, Filipino-American literary critics have begun to study Anglophone writing with great theoretical verve, including, among others, Martin Joseph Ponce, *Beyond the Nation: Diasporic Filipino Literature and Queer Reading* (New York: NYU Press, 2012); and John D. Blanco, "Baroque Modernity and the Colonial World: Aesthetics and Catastrophe in Nick

Joaquin's *Portrait of the Artist as Filipino*," *Kritika Kultura* 4 (Mar. 2004). See also the essays in Martin F. Manalansan IV and Augusto F. Espiritu, *Filipino Studies: Palimpsests of Nation and Diaspora* (New York: NYU Press, 2016).

14. For the most informative biographies of Joaquin, see Resil Mojares, "Biography of Nick Joaquin" (1996), www.rmaf.org .ph/Awardees/Biography/BiographyJoaquinNic.htm; and Marra PL. Lanot, The Trouble with Nick and Other Profiles (Quezon City: University of the Philippines Press, 1999), republished in bulatlat.com, www.bulatlat.com/news/4-13/4-13-nick.html.
See also two biographies by Joaquin's nephew and sister-in-law: Tony Joaquin (with Gloria Kismadi), *Portrait of the Artist Nick Joaquin* (Mandaluyong City: Anvil Publishing, 2011); and Sarah K. Joaquin, "A Portrait of Nick Joaquin," *This Week*, Mar. 13, 1955, 24–26.

 The first and so far only monograph-length treatment of Joaquin's work is Epifanio San Juan, *Subversions of Desire: Prolegomena to Nick Joaquin* (Quezon City: Ateneo de Manila University Press, 1988). See also Robert Vore, "The International Literary Contexts of the Filipino Writer Nick Joaquin" (PhD dissertation, Dept. of English, Northern Illinois University, 1997), which has the virtue of having one of the most detailed bibliographies of Joaquin's publications up to 1997.

15. Joaquin once wrote in a rare autobiographical vignette: "I have no hobbies, no degrees; belong to no party, club, or association; and I like long walks; any kind of *guinataan*; Dickens and Booth Tarkington; the old Garbo pictures; anything with Fred Astaire . . . the Opus Dei according to the Dominican rite . . . Jimmy Durante and Cole Porter tunes . . . the Marx brothers; the Brothers Karamazov; Carmen Miranda; Paul's Epistles and Mark's; Piedmont cigarettes . . . my mother's cooking . . . playing *tres-siete*; praying the Rosary and the *Officium Parvum* . . . I don't like fish, sports, and having to dress up." Quoted in Resil Mojares, "Biography of Nick Joaquin" (1996), www.rmaf.org.ph/Awardees/Biography/Biography JoaquinNic.htm.

16. Benjamin, "The Storyteller," 102.

17. For the background to this story, see Florentino H. Hornedo, "The Source of Nick Joaquin's 'Doña Jerónima,'" *Philippine Studies* 30 (1982): 542–51.

18. Hence, Benjamin: "Death is the sanction of everything that the storyteller can tell. He has borrowed his authority from death"; "The Storyteller," 94.

19. Ibid., 86–87.
20. The image of the "Angel of History," suggested in this instance by the image of the myriad angels surrounding St. Sylvestre as he leads his procession, is of course drawn from Paul Klee's painting *Angelus Novus* and discussed by Benjamin, "Theses on the Philosophy of History," in *Illuminations*, 257–58. I borrow the term "vertigo-inducing" from the great historical comparativist Benedict Anderson, who uses it to describe the conjunctural strangeness of the Philippines in world history. See Anderson, "The First Filipino," *London Review of Books* 19(20) (Oct. 16, 1997): 22–23. He, too, was an admirer of Nick Joaquin and Walter Benjamin.

Suggestions for Further Reading

STORIES OF NICK JOAQUIN

(And their original dates and places of publication. Note that the texts
for this Penguin edition are based on those published by Anvil
Publishing and not these magazines, as approved by the estate of
the author.)

"Three Generations," *Graphic*, Sept. 5, 1940

"The Legend of the Dying Wanton," *Evening News Saturday Magazine*, Oct. 5, 1946

"The Mass of St. Sylvestre," *Manila Post*, Dec. 29, 1946

"The Summer Solstice," *Saturday Evening News*, June 21, 1947

"May Day Eve," *Philippine Free Press*, Dec. 13, 1947

"The Woman Who Had Two Navels," *This Week*, July 10, 1949

"Guardia de Honor," *Philippine Free Press*, Oct. 1, 1949

"Portrait of the Artist as Filipino: An Elegy in Three Acts," *Weekly
Women's Magazine*, Sept. 28–Nov. 23, 1951

"Doña Jerónima," *Philippine Free Press*, May 1, 1965

"Cándido's Apocalypse," *Philippine Free Press*, Dec. 11, 1965

"The Order of Melkizedek," *Philippine Free Press*, Dec. 10, 1966

CONTEXT AND COMMENTARIES

Benjamin, Walter. "The Storyteller: Reflections on the Work of Niko-
lai Leskov," in *Illuminations*, edited with an introduction by
Hannah Arendt and translated by Harry Zohn. New York:
Schocken Books, 1968, 83–110.

Blanco, John D. "Baroque Modernity and the Colonial World: Aesthetics and Catastrophe in Nick Joaquin's *A Portrait of the Artist
as Filipino*." *Kritika Kultura* 4 (2004): 5–35. Web. Feb. 20, 2010.

Bresnahan, Roger J. *Conversations with Filipino Writers*. Quezon City: New Day, 1990.

Casper, Leonard. "Beyond the Mind's Mirage: Tales by Joaquin and Cordero-Fernando." *Philippine Studies* 31 (1983): 87–93.

———. "Nick Joaquin." *New Writing from the Philippines*. Syracuse, NY: Syracuse University Press, 1966, 137–45.

Cheah, Pheng. *What Is a World? On Post-Colonial Literature as World Literature*. Durham, NC: Duke University Press, 2016.

Chua, Jonathan, ed. *The Critical Villa: Essays in Literary Criticism*. Quezon City: Ateneo University Press, 2002.

Hau, Caroline Sy. *Necessary Fictions: Philippine Literature and the Nation, 1946–1980*. Quezon City: Ateneo de Manila University Press, 2000, 94–132.

Hornedo, Florentino H. "The Source of Nick Joaquin's 'The Legend of the Dying Wanton.'" *Philippine Studies* 26 (1978): 297–307.

———. "The Source of Nick Joaquin's 'Doña Jerónima.'" *Philippine Studies* 30 (1982): 542–51.

Joaquin, Nick. "The Filipino as English Fictionist." *Philippine Quarterly of Culture and Society* 6(3) (Sept. 1978): 118–24.

Joaquin, Sarah K. "A Portrait of Nick Joaquin." *This Week*, Mar. 13, 1955, 24–26.

Joaquin, Tony (with Gloria Kismadi). *Portrait of the Artist Nick Joaquin*. Pasig: Anvil, 2011.

Kintanar, Thelma B. "From Formalism to Feminism: Rereading Nick Joaquin's *The Woman Who Had Two Navels*." *Women Reading: Feminist Perspectives on Philippine Literary Texts*. Edited by Thelma B. Kintanar. Quezon City: University of the Philippines Press/University Center for Women's Studies, 1992, 131–45.

Lacaba, Emmanuel A. F. "Winter After Summer Solstice: The Later Joaquin." *Philippine Fiction: Essays from* Philippine Studies *1953–1972*. Edited by Joseph A. Galdon. Quezon City: Ateneo de Manila University Press, 1972, 45–56.

Lanot, Marra PL. "The Trouble with Nick." *The Trouble with Nick and Other Profiles*. Quezon City: University of the Philippines Press, 1999, 3–15, www.bulatlat.com/news/4-13/4-13-nick.html.

Lim, Shirley Geok-Lin. "Reconstructions of Filipino Identity: Nick Joaquin's Fictions." *Nationalism and Literature: English-Language Writing from the Philippines and Singapore*. Quezon City: New Day, 1993, 63–90.

Mojares, Resil B. "Biography of Nick Joaquin." Ramon Magsaysay Award Foundation. Web. June 7, 2010, www.rmaf.org.ph/Awardees/Biography/BiographyJoaquinNic.html.

————. *Origins and Rise of the Filipino Novel: A Generic Study of the Novel Until 1940*. Quezon City: University of the Philippines Press, 1983.

Oloroso, Laura S. "Nick Joaquin and His Brightly Burning Prose." *Brown Heritage: Essays in Philippine Culture and Literature*. Edited by Antonio G. Manuud. Quezon City: Ateneo de Manila University Press, 1967, 765–92.

Pablo, Lourdes Busuego. "The Spanish Tradition in Nick Joaquin." *Philippine Fiction: Essays from Philippine Studies 1953–1972*. Edited by Joseph A. Galdon. Quezon City: Ateneo de Manila University Press, 1972, 57–73.

Perkins, Elizabeth. "Crossing Culture as Identity: Nick Joaquin's 'Portrait of the Artist as Filipino.'" *Crossing Cultures: Essays on Literature and Culture of the Asia-Pacific*. Edited by Bruce Bennett, Jeff Doyle, and Satendra Nandan. London: Skoob, 1996, 225–33.

Rafael, Vicente L. *Motherless Tongues: The Insurgency of Language Amid Wars of Translation*, Duke Univ. Press, 2016.

————, "Mis-education, Translation, and the *Barkada* of Languages: Reading Renato Constantino with Nick Joaquin." *Kritika Kultura* 21/22 (Mar. 2014): 40–68.

San Juan, E., Jr. *Subversions of Desire: Prolegomena to Nick Joaquin*. Quezon City: Ateneo de Manila University Press, 1988.

Serrano, Vincenz "Wedded in the Association: Heteroglossic Form and Fragmentary Historiography in Nick Joaquin's *Alamanac for Manileños*." *Kritika Kultura* 18 (2012), http://journals .ateneo.edu/ojs/kk/article/view/1403.

Vore, Robert. "The International Literary Contexts of the Filipino Writer Nick Joaquin." PhD dissertation, Dept. of English, Northern Illinois University, 1997.

Acknowledgments

The family of Nick Joaquin would like to thank the individuals and institutions who have helped make possible this collection of Nick Joaquin's works by Penguin Classics: Anvil Publishing, Vicente Rafael, Elda Rotor, Maria Karina Bolasco, Andrea Pasion-Flores, Vincent Pozon, Billy Lacaba, Jose and Marra Lacaba. Through their generosity and that of many others, it is hoped that more readers throughout the world will appreciate his works that embody the Filipino soul. We are so privileged to witness up close the genius we call Tito Nick.

The Woman Who Had Two Navels and Tales of the Tropical Gothic

THREE GENERATIONS

The elder Monzon was waiting for his wife to speak. He had finished breakfast and had just put down the newspaper through which he had been glancing. Across the table, his wife played absently with a spoon. Her brows were knitted, but a half-smile kept twitching on her lips. She was a handsome, well-preserved woman and, her husband was thinking, a great deal more clever than she allowed herself to appear.

"It is about Chitong," she said at last. "He does not want to continue the law-course he is taking. The boy has a vocation, Celo. He wants to study for the priesthood."

"When did he speak to you?"

"About a month ago, the first time. But I told him to make sure. Last night, he said he was sure. Of course, you have noticed how devout he has been lately?"

Monzon rose. "Well, I would never have expected it of him," he said, but his wife shook her head.

"Has he not always been quiet and reserved, even as a boy?"

"Yes, but not noticeably of a religious temper."

"Only because he did not understand then. He has taken a long time maturing, Celo, but I think it is for the best. Now he knows what really calls him, and he is really very sincere. Are you glad?"

"It is a career, like all the others. Did he say what seminary?"

"We can talk that over later on. He was afraid you would refuse."

"What does he take me for? A heretic?"

The servant-girl came in to clear the table, and the señora rose and followed her husband to the sala. "Celo, when are you going to see your father? Nena called up last night. She was crying. She says she can do nothing with the old man. Your cousin Paulo is not there anymore to help her. It seems the old man broke a plate on his head . . ."

Monzon paused, his hand on the door-knob. He had put on his hat already. Suddenly, he looked very old and tired. His wife came nearer and placed a hand on his shoulder. "Why will you not let him have his woman again, Celo? He does not have very long to live."

He stared at her fiercely. "Please do not be vulgar, Sofia," he growled, but his wife only smiled.

For all the years they had lived together, he was still startled by a certain nakedness in his wife's mind; in the minds of all women, for that matter. You took them for what they appeared: shy, reticent, bred by nuns, but after marriage, though they continued to look demure, there was always in their attitude toward sex, an amused irony, even a deliberate coarseness; such as he could never allow himself, even in his own mind or with other men.

"Well," said Doña Sofia, withdrawing her hand, "he has certainly been wild since you drove that woman away. Nena says he refuses to eat. He takes what is served to him and throws it to the floor, plates and everything. He lies awake the whole night roaring like a lion. Yesterday, Nena said, he tried to get up. She was outside and did not hear him. When she came in, there he lay on the floor, all tangled up in his blankets, out of breath, and crying to the heavens. She called in Paulo to get him in bed again, and he grabbed a plate and broke it on poor Paulo's head."

Monzon did not look at his wife's face: he knew very well what he would see. He stared instead at his hands, huge, calloused, and ugly, and suddenly they were his father's hands he was seeing, and he was a little boy that cowered beneath them and the whip they held: "Lie down, you little beast! Lie down, beast!" "Not in the face, father! Do not hit me in the face, father!" "I will hit you where the thunder I want to. I will teach my sons to answer back. Lie down, you beast!"

"Your father never could live without women," Doña Sofia

was saying. "And now you have driven that one away. It is death by torture."

"You certainly can choose your words," Monzon retorted. "You know very well what the doctor said."

"But what does it matter since he is going to die anyway? Why not let him have what he wants?"

"You do not sound like a decent woman, Sofia." He turned his back on her and opened the door. "Tell Chitong to have the car ready this afternoon. He and I will go there together."

It was still early, only half-past seven; and when he came to the Dominican church, he went in. He knew he would find Chitong there. He did not know why he wanted to. But he went in and there were few people inside. From the high windows a many-colored light filtered in, drenching the floor violet, but in the side-chapel of the Virgin it was dark, with only the gold glow of candles: he saw his son kneeling there, near the altar, saying his rosary.

Monzon knelt down himself, and tried to compose his mind to prayer, but there was suddenly, painfully, out of his very heart, a sharp, hot, rushing, jealous bitterness toward that devout young man praying so earnestly over there.

He did not understand the feeling. He did not want to understand it. Enough that this thing was clear: that he hated his son for being able to kneel there, submitted utterly to his God. Yet why should he resent that so bitterly?

His own youth had been very unhappy, yes; but whose fault was it that he had suffered so much? The old man had really been no more heavy of hand and temper than most fathers of that time. He knew that. Those times gave to the head of the family absolute dominion over his women and children. He could not remember that any of his brothers had found the system particularly oppressive. They bowed to the paternal whip as long as they had to; then broke away to marry and breed and establish families over whom they had in turn set themselves up as lords almighty.

As for the women, he had suspected that they even took a certain delight in the barbaric cruelties of their lords. His father was never without two or three concubines whom he had whipped as regularly as he did his sons; but none of them, once fallen into his power, had bothered to strive for a more honorable status. If they went away, it was because the old man wearied of them; though at his bidding, they would return as meekly, to work in his house or in his fields, to cook his food, to wash his clothes, to attend to his children, and to bare their flesh to the blows of his anger or to the blows of his love.

Monzon had wept as a boy for his mother; but later on he had found out that she was only too thankful, worn out as she was with toil and child-bearing, for the company and assistance of these other women. If she fought the old man at all, it was in defense of her children, and especially of himself (for she had been quick to notice that he would not be so easy to break).

She had singled him out from among all sons to bear and fulfill her few childish dreams and ambitions; and in her last, long, lingering illness, this faith in him had shone in her eyes and trembled in her hands whenever he came near her, and it had frightened and terrified him. For, even then, he was beginning to realize that, though he might set himself against all those things for which his father stood as symbol, he, himself, would never quite completely escape them. Go where he might, he would still be carrying the old man's flesh along; and that flesh smouldered darkly with fires that all a lifetime was too short to quench.

Monzon buried his face in his hands. He felt strangely exhausted. Peace, he thought, peace of mind, of body: he had been praying for that all his life. Just a little peace. It was not possible that he was to go on forever and ever, divided against himself. But there was that little voice, as usual, that voice in his ears, mocking him: Your father could find peace in the simple delights of the body; but you thought yourself too good for that.

His bitterness leapt into active anger: Is this then what I get for having tried to be clean? But the voice laughed at him: When were you ever a lover of purity? All that solemn virtuousness of yours began as a gesture of rebellion against your father. And so it still is. If he had been a chaste man, your defiance would have taken a more perverse form.

And suppose I give up now, stop fighting, submit: would I be at peace? No, said the voice. You would be as miserable in your surrender to your body as you have been in your struggle against it. Besides, it is too late. Men like your father find their brief escapes in the whip, the table, and the bed. That rapt young man over there—your son!—is now groping for a more complete release. For him also there shall be peace. But for you . . .

Monzon rose. And just then his son looked around. Their eyes met. The young man stood up and came toward his father. He was still holding his beads, and his hands began to tremble. Why does the old man look so fierce? Has mother told him? He looks as if he hated me. As if he would do me a violence.

But as the boy approached, the elder Monzon turned away and walked rapidly out of the church.

"He was not angry at all," Doña Sofia said. "He was very pleased. You do not understand your father, Chitong. He does not speak much, but he is really concerned over what you are going to make of your life."

"But the way he looked at me . . ." Chitong began. He was having his breakfast and Doña Sofia sat across the table watching him.

"That, you probably imagined only."

"Oh no," insisted her son. "And suddenly, he turned away, without speaking to me." He pushed the plates away and propped his elbows on the table. "I could not pray anymore afterward. I felt empty and ridiculous. Mother, I said last night I was sure about this thing, and I still am. But have I any right . . . I mean . . . But how shall I say it!" He paused and considered for a moment, drumming with his fingers on the table. "You know, mother, he did have a hard time of it. It shows in his face. I often feel sorry for him. He had made it possible that I should not go through whatever he had to go through. But is such a thing right? And anyway, is it good for me?"

"What ever are you talking about, Chitong?

Her son sighed and shrugged his shoulders. "Nothing," he replied, and got up.

"You are to accompany him this afternoon to your grandfather. The old man is getting worse. You are to take the car."

Chitong was standing by the window. She had never seen his face look so grave. She was worried and, rising, she approached him.

"Son," she said, "if you are going to dedicate yourself to God, then nothing else should matter to you."

"But that is it, that is it precisely!" cried the boy. "I do wish there was something else that did matter. Something big and fierce and powerful. That I would have to fight down because I loved God more. But there is nothing." He made a gesture with his hand. "Nothing. And father knows it. And that is why he despises me. And he is right."

"Your father does not despise you. How you talk."

Suddenly the boy crumpled up on his knees, his face in his hands.

"I am not sincere, mother! I am a coward! I try to run away! I am nothing! And father knows it! Father knows it! He knows everything!"

She stooped and gathered him to her breast. She was terribly frightened. She was suddenly only a woman. Men were entirely different and alien creatures. Yes, even this one, whom she had borne in her own body. This one, also.

It was a good afternoon for a drive. The wind that met their faces smelled of the rain and earth, and in the twilight became vaguely fragrant. They were silent most of the way for, usually, when they were alone together, they felt embarrassed and shy, as though they were lovers.

Chitong was at the wheel. The elder Monzon sat beside him, smoking a cigar. From time to time, he found himself glancing at his son's profile. There was a difference there, he felt. The boy looked tense, tight-strung, even ill. When the darkness fell about then, they both felt easier and the older man began to talk.

"Your mother tells me that you want to give up law."

"Did she tell you why?"

"And I could hardly believe my ears."

"I know I am quite unworthy."

"Oh, as for that, I should say that no one can ever be worthy enough. I was merely wondering at the sudden conversion."

"It was not sudden, father. I had been coming to this for a long time without knowing it."

"Well, how *did* you know?"

"I simply woke up one night and said to myself: I belong *there*. And all at once, I knew why I had been finding everything so unsatisfactory."

"We all have such moments—when everything clicks into place."

"And becomes beautiful."

"It was though the appeal of beautiful things that you found God?"

"With the senses, yes. Certainly not with the mind: I am no thinker. Nor yet with the heart: I am not a saint. I guess that's why it took me so long to realize where I was heading."

"You should have come to me for information. I could have shared my experience with you."

"Your experience, father?"

"—of a vocation. I could have—But why do you look so shocked? I was young once myself, you know."

"But what happened, father?"

"Nothing. My mother wanted me to be a priest. I was quite willing. But when she died, I abandoned the idea."

"I never knew!"

"I never told anyone—not even your mother. Shall we keep it a secret between us?"

For a moment, the wall that stood always between them disappeared, and they could touch each other. I am an unclean man, the elder Monzon was thinking, but what was depravity in me and my fathers becomes, in my son, a way to God.

And the young man thought: I am something, after all, I am this old man's desire that he has fleshed alive. It sprang from him, began in him; that which now I will myself to be . . .

The evening flowed turgid with the fragrance of the night-flowers and of their thoughts; but the moment passed and they were suddenly cold and tired. They fell silent again, and shy, as though they had loved.

The house stood at the edge of the town. Monzon always thought of it as something tremendous and eternal. Each time he went back to it, he was surprised afresh to find that it was not very big really and that it would not last much longer; the foundations were rotting, the roof leaked, white ants were dis-integrating the whole structure.

Here, at the foot of the stairs, always, he must pause and gather himself together. A shrunken, rotting house. But here it was that he had been a little boy; and the roof seemed to expand above his head till it was as high and wide as the heavens.

At the sound of their coming up, a little harrased-looking woman came to the door to meet them. Monzon felt sorry for her. She was his youngest sister. All of them had managed to get away except this one. And she would never get away at all, he thought, as he took her fluttering hands in his. "How is he?" he asked. She merely shook her head and turned to Chitong, who bowed and kissed her hand.

It was dark in that sala; an oil-lamp on the table gave the only light. As they moved, the three of them cast huge, nervous shad-ows. The old man lay in the next room and they could hear his heavy, angry breathing punctuated with coughs and oaths.

"He is like that all the time," Nena complained, wringing her thin hands. "He has not eaten for days. He shouts at me whenever I enter. He tries to get up all the time and he falls, of course, and I have to call in someone to put him back." There was a pathetic pleading in the eyes she turned shyly on her brother. "He keeps asking for the girl, Celo. Maybe it would be much better . . ."

But Monzon refused to meet her eyes. "Go and prepare something, Nena. I am going to make him eat," he said. She sighed and went off to the kitchen.

The door of the old man's room stood open. When the two of them entered, the sick man, sprawled in the four-posted bed upon a mountain of pillows became silent. As in the sala, a single oil-lamp illuminated the room. The bed stood in shadow but they were aware of the old man's eyes, watching them intently.

Before those eyes, Monzon felt himself stripped, one by one, of all his defenses: maturity, social position, wealth, success. He was a little boy again and he bent down and lifted his father's enormous, damp hand to his lips, and at the contact, a million pins seemed to prick his whole body.

But Chitong came forward and kissed the old man on the

brow. The boy felt himself fascinated by those intensely hating eyes. He, too, was rather afraid of this old man; but with a difference. Even as a boy, he had felt the force of those eyes, lips, hands; but his grandfather had still been, then, in the plenitude of strength. But now, when he lay helpless, his legs paralyzed, the flesh gone loose about the bones, the face grown pale and shriveled, did he communicate all the more unbearably that pride, that exultation in simple brute power.

The boy felt himself becoming a single wave of obedience toward the old man. His lips lingered upon that moist brow as though they would drink in the old man's very brains. The feel of the wet flesh was an almost sensual delight, something new and terrifying to him and, at the same time, painful; almost as if the kiss were also a kind of death. It was a multitudinous moment for the boy. When he straightened up, he found himself trembling. And at the same time, he wanted to run away—to some quiet corner, to pray.

"Well, father, why have you sent Paulo away?" Monzon asked, speaking very loudly. The old man continued to stare at them in silence. He seemed to be checking even his breath. His thick lips were pressed tightly shut. Only his eyes spoke. His eyes hated them. His eyes sprang at their throats and wrung lifeless their voices. His eyes challenged this unafraid-pretending solid man that was his son; at the challenge, Monzon stepped nearer and abruptly stripped the blankets from the old man. For a moment they stared at each other.

Monzon had collected himself. Of you, I am not going to be afraid, his eyes told the old man. Not anymore. Often had he said that in his mind; now, he wanted to say it aloud because, almost, he believed it to be true. But he spoke to Chitong instead: "Your Tia Nena may want you to help her. If the food for your grandfather is ready, bring it in here."

When Chitong came back with the tray of food, he found that his father had taken off his coat and rolled up his shirt-sleeves. He had propped the sick man up to a sitting position and had changed his clothes.

The sick man's face had altered. He sat among the pillows, his face turned away, the eyes closed, the beautiful lips parted, as if in anguish. His hands lay clenched on his lap. He would not look at his son. He would not look at the food.

"You are going to eat, father," Monzon told him. He had taken the tray from Chitong. He did not speak loudly now. He knew he had won. This old man of whom all his life he had been afraid: had he not just dressed him like any baby? And now, like a mere baby again, he would be fed. "You are going to eat, father," he said again in his quiet voice.

The old man turned around and opened his eyes. They were fierce no longer. They were full of tiredness and the desire for death.

Chitong felt the old man's agony as his own. He could not stand it. He had an impulse to approach his father and knock the tray from his hands. He could not trust himself to speak.

The elder Monzon must have sensed this fury, for suddenly he turned to his son. "Chitong, you must be hungry. Better go and find something to eat."

Chitong swallowed the words in his mouth and turned away. At the door he paused and looked back. His father had laid a hand against the old man's breast; with the other he tried to push a spoonful of food into the tightly closed mouth. The old man tried to evade it, but now he could not turn his face away; his son had him pinned against the bed. At last he gave up, opened his mouth, and received the food. His eyes closed and tears ran down his cheeks.

Chitong glanced at his father. The elder Monzon was smiling . . .

In the kitchen, he found his Tia Nena, sitting motionless in a corner. She looked as if she had been struck down. Her eyes were full of fear and suffering. Chitong realized that what he had felt for a moment when he kissed the old man's brow, this woman had known all her life. That was why she could not leave the old man; why, of all his children, she had remained faithful. She was in his power; and like himself, Chitong thought bitterly, she was the kind for whom life is possible only in the immolation of self to something mightier outside it.

"Did he eat?" she asked and, when he nodded, began to cry. He stooped and took her in his arms and tried to still her sobbing, but he remembered how, this morning, he, himself, had cried in his mother's arms and was not able to find, nor in her bosom, nor in her words, the answering strength he sought . . .

Monzon, when he came out, found them sharing a scanty supper. For once, he looked quite happy. He kept rubbing his hands and smiling absently. He shook his head at Nena's offer of food.

"No, I am not hungry. And I have to go now." He took out his watch. "Is there still a bus I can take, Nena? Chitong, you are to remain with the car. Tomorrow I will come back with the doctor."

Chitong rose and accompanied his father to the door. The single lamp in the sala had gone out and they walked in darkness.

"Your grandfather is sleeping. If he wakes up, you can tell him I have gone."

They had reached the stairs. The elder Monzon paused and laid a hand on his son's shoulder. "Your mother has told you I am willing that you should follow your vocation, no?"

"Yes, father." Chitong could feel how in the dark his father's face had changed again. Even his voice had lost its momentary confidence.

"Yes. That is a good life," Monzon went on, "and it is, perhaps, the best for you."

He descended the stairs, opened the street-door below, and stepped out into the night. Chitong remained for some time at the head of the stairs, wondering just what those last words had meant.

In his grandfather's room, he spread a mat on the floor, undressed, and lay down. He had placed the lamp on a chair beside him and, now, he took out his breviary and began to read. The words that opened out to him were like cool arms into which he surrendered his troubled body. That had been a strange day, full of unrest and uncertainties; but as he read, an earlier sureness and peace came back to him.

". . . *my soul had relied on His word. My soul had hoped in the Lord. From the morning watch even until night, let Israel hope in the Lord. For with the Lord, there is mercy and with Him plentiful redemption. And he shall redeem Israel from all his iniquities . . .*"

In his bed, on the other side of the room, the old man was awake and restless. Chitong could hear him turning, now to one side, now to the other. His breath came in short gasps, as if in difficulty. He reached out with his hands. He clutched at the pillows. He tried to rise.

The boy rose from time to time to cover him up again or to pick up the pillows. The old man's hands sought and clung to the boy's arms but his eyes, Chitong saw, were closed.

Names poured from the old man's lips. He called on every woman he had ever loved. He wanted his women. He became angry and shouted for them as in the days of his strength. He commanded them to come near. He cursed and shook his fists at them. No one came. He tried to rise and fell back, moaning and beating on the bed with his hands.

Afterward, he became quiet. He must have realized that he was powerful no longer. Then he began to call on his women again, but softly, tenderly. He wooed them as a shy boy might; his lips shaped broken and beautiful phrases of adoration. But still no one came.

He fell into despair. He became furious again. He raged in his bed. He howled with all his might. He tore at the pillows. He tried to get up. The bed shook with his anger.

Chitong, lying on the floor, tried to deafen his ears to the old man's cries. He tried to read, but the words would not stand still. He closed the book and tried to sleep but, even in the intervals when the old man lay silent, he could feel him suffering, desiring, despairing, there in his bed in the darkness.

He got up and thought: I will pray for him. I will pray that he be delivered from temptation. I will pray that God quiet the fever of his flesh.

He approached and knelt beside the old man's bed, but a glance at that tortured face shot hollow all the prayers in his mouth. He felt again, as at Santo Domingo that morning, empty and ridiculous.

The sick man stared at him, yet did not see him. Those eyes saw only women and the bodies of women. Pain and desire had made him blind to all else. He stretched out his shriveled hands for the women that were not there. He had exhausted his voice; now he could only moan. Chitong could bear it no longer.

He rose and left the room. He was thinking of that woman— no, only a girl really—whom his grandfather had kept before his legs collapsed. The elder Monzon had driven the girl away, but she might still be living somewhere in the town. His Tia Nena was still up, ironing clothes in the kitchen; he would ask her.

But she was frightened when she learned what he proposed to do. Yes, the girl was living in the town. "But your father will surely find out, Chitong, if she comes here. Oh, do not ask me how. He will. He knows everything."

The words cut through the boy. "Then, let him!" he cried. "But I am going to bring the girl back. The old man needs her. Now, tell me where she lives."

It took him almost an hour to find the house, but only a few words to make the girl come. Chitong had seen her many times before, but when she came running down the stairs and stood beside him in the moonlight, he knew that he was seeing her really for the first time.

She was not very pretty, and still very young; but her body, her eyes, the way she moved, hinted at that attractive maturity which only physical love develops. She had wrapped an old shawl around her head and shoulders, and as they hurried through the empty streets, Chitong could feel her thoughts running ahead toward the old man. But his mind, sensitive in such things, was not repelled.

There was in her, he knew, as in his grandfather, that simple unity which he, himself, had been denied. It was not strange that two such people should desire each other, or that so young a girl, when she might have more youthful lovers, should prefer the sexagenarian in whose arms she had become a woman. They had had to drive her away when he fell sick.

Chitong had been there when it happened and he recalled his father's exquisite brutality and how this girl had seemed to him, at that time, incapable of either fear or shame. She had refused to leave the house; had stood before the elder Monzon, thrusting her defiant face into his; and Chitong remembered how his father's hands had trembled, though not a nerve in his face had twitched.

Monzon had released his belt on the sly, pushed the girl away suddenly, and given her a full stroke across the shoulders with the belt. And with the belt, he had pursued her out of the room and down the stairs, slamming the door in her face. She had remained down there, screaming and kicking at the door till the police came and dragged her away.

But she was not thinking at all of those things, Chitong saw, as he hurried beside her, glancing into her passionate face. She was going to her first lover. He had called her. He needed her. Young men were only young men: they could offer nothing in love to make her wiser than she had been in such things from the very beginning. And her nervous fingers, clutching the shawl across her breasts, spoke almost aloud the violence of her need.

A few steps from the house, a woman abruptly emerged from shadow. Chitong recognized his Tia Nena. She had been running; she could hardly speak.

"Chitong," she gasped, "your father has come back. He could not find a bus." She turned to the girl: "You must not come. Go back at once!"

The girl stepped back, but Chitong grasped her hand. "Do not be afraid," he said. "You are coming."

His aunt stared at him. "Chitong, you know how it is when your father gets angry . . ."

"I am not afraid."

"I think he suspects where you went . . ."

"So much the better then. Come on."

It was the first time in his life he had made a decision. He felt released.

The elder Monzon was standing in the sala when they entered. He had lighted the lamp and now stood watching it thoughtfully, his hands locked behind him. He glanced up as they filed in. When he saw the girl, he flushed darkly and he felt again the multitude of pins pricking his flesh. He dropped his eyes at once, but the girl's image persisted before him: the fierce eyes; the small, round mouth; the long, thin, girlish neck. She had drawn her shawl away and he had seen where her breasts began and how they rose and fell with her breath.

He had a sudden, delirious craving to unloose his belt and whip her again, to make her suffer, to tear her flesh into shreds, to mutilate that supple, defiant, sweet, animal body of hers. His hands shook and his desire became an anger toward his son who had brought this voluptuous being so near.

"Who told you to bring this woman here, Chitong?" He

tried in vain to make his voice calm. He doubled his fists: the nails dug into his flesh.

Chitong stared, open-mouthed. He realized now that what he had done was an action for which his soul would later demand reasons. It was not his father before whom he stood. It was God.

The girl was standing beside him and he felt her moving away. He sprang to life. "No, no," he cried. "You are not to go! He needs you! You must not go!" He held her back.

"A fine priest you will make!" snapped the elder Monzon.

Chitong came nearer. His eyes entreated the older man to understand. He stretched out a hand; with the other, he detained the girl. He had never found it so hard to make himself articulate.

"Father," he said at last, "if it is a sin to allow him this woman, then I will take the sin on my shoulders. I will pray that it . . ."

"Release that woman!" cried the older man. "Let her go away!"

The boy's face hardened. "No, father. She is not going."

They were standing almost face to face. Suddenly, the father lifted his clenched fist and struck the boy in the face.

"Not in the face, father!" the boy cried out, lifting his hands too late to shield himself; the blow had already fallen.

Monzon, horrified, heard the boy's cry through every inch of his body. He had never before laid hands on the boy. The impulse to strike had come so suddenly. He tortured his mind for an explanation. He had not wanted to hurt the boy, no. He had, the moment before, desired the girl evil, but it was not she, either, who had prompted his fist. Was it the old man, then? Was it his father he had struck?

No. No, it was himself: that self of his, inherited, long fought, which had, the moment before, looked on the girl with strange fury. It was that self of his, which perpetuated the old man, against whom he had lifted his fist, but it was his son who had received the blow—and the blow was a confession of his whole life.

Now he stood silent, watching the boy's flesh darken where his fist had fallen, and the gradual blood defining the wound.

They stood staring at each other, as if petrified, and the girl, forgotten, slipped swiftly away from them and into the old man's room, locking the door behind her.

A clock somewhere began striking ten. Nena sat in a corner,

crying. A late cock could be heard crowing. And from the next room came the voices of the lovers: the old man's voice, tired and broken; the girl's, sharp and taut and passionate.

"No," she was saying, "I shall never leave you again. I am not going away again. No one shall take me away from you again."

THE LEGEND OF
THE DYING WANTON

There lived in Manila in the year 1613 a certain Doña Ana de Vera, one of the principal ladies of the country at that time and a woman of great piety. This Doña Ana and her son, who was an official in the government, were from Madrid. At the Court and Villa they had enjoyed the patronage of Don Juan de Silva, in whose retinue—on de Silva's appointment as governor-general—they had come to the Philippines. Señor Vera had tried to dissuade his mother from coming along—she was over fifty and rather fragile of health but Doña Ana had mockingly feared he would degenerate into a savage in three days if she were not there to keep house for him. So, across two oceans and half the world she had come, one of the many spirited women who, hard on the heels of the conquistadores, sallied forth with kettle and skillet, with fan and mantilla, devoutly resolved that even in the heathen wilderness the rites for the altar and of the hearth should be performed with as much elegance as at the Court itself.

Now there was stationed in Manila at that time a wild young soldier named Currito Lopez, who was as evil as Doña Ana was good. This Currito was a lost soul, his every action being so public a scandal even decent people knew who he was and shunned him like a leper. Riding around the city in her carriage, Doña Ana often saw him in the streets: swaggering insolently if sober, reeling and howling if drunk—but his swart bearded face of a Lucifer never struck her with terror. Alone, perhaps, in all the city, she knew another side of this man's character.

Being in charge of the wardrobe of the "Santo Rosario"—the

fine Madonna whose shrine at the Dominicans the Dutch pirates were soon to make famous—she was often at that virgin's chapel when it was deserted, and at such times she always found the notorious Currito there, kneeling in an obscure corner, his head bowed and a rosary dangling from his clasped hands. She never disturbed him; he never disturbed her. She was Spanish enough not to be shocked at this commingling in a single nature of vice and piety. He was Christian enough not to be shocked that she was not shocked. So, without a word or a look between them, the virtuous old woman and the wicked young man became each other's friend. While she moved about her tasks at the altar, her face and hands gleaming like fine gold against the rich black of her skirts and mantilla, he knelt in his corner, red-shirted and black-bearded, praying and, sometimes, weeping quietly. From the blue dusk of her altar, the radiant Madonna smiled as lovingly on the wanton as on the saint.

One October day Doña Ana came down from the altar to find Currito waiting for her. Keeping a respectful distance away, he requested and was given permission to speak. Whereupon he asked if the señora would give him her blessing? When she looked astonished, he smiled gaily and explained that he was going away. The troops were being sent to Ternate. They were leaving for Cavite immediately and from Cavite would take ship. Ternate was, as the señora knew, a perpetual battlefield. Many who went there never returned. But he was glad to go, said Currito, with a toss of his tawny curls. He did not regret to leave the city. No doubt the city would feel equally unregretful! Alas, he had no friend to wish him well on this journey. And his mother, that saintly woman, was on the other side of the world, in Malaga. Would the señora do him a Christian favor? Would she take his mother's place and equip him with her blessing? It was not good that a man, however sinful, should leave on such a perilous expedition with no one to bless him, said Currito, smiling doggedly.

But Doña Ana, whom these words had moved to tears, approached and took him by the hand and led him to the altar.

And pointing to the Sacrament and to the Virgin, she reminded him that no man was so sinful he could not, by a sincere contrition, make God his friend and the Virgin his mother. And what were human solicitudes compared with those of Heaven? But if he wanted her blessing, said Doña Ana, she would gladly give it to him and would pray for him while he was gone and he must not think himself friendless on earth for she was his friend. So, he knelt down and she blessed him—and as she looked at his bowed head the sudden knowledge filled her that this man would soon die. Long after he was gone she still knelt before the altar, praying the Virgin to recall her promise that no one devoted to her and her rosary would suffer a death so sudden as to make impossible a last act of sincere contrition.

She was startled awake the next day by the sound of thunder—and of wind-whipped rain clattering on the roof. The walls trembled and a window she ran to pull shut broke loose from her hands and went whirling away on the wind. By noon the typhoon had flooded the streets and unroofed half the city. As she dispensed dry clothes among the families who had sought refuge in her house, Doña Ana found herself trembling for Currito, and for all the poor soldiers caught by the storm at sea. She pictured them on their teetering decks, hurtled now upward, now downward; the rain beating on their faces and the wild sea piling in from all sides. Shuddering, she whispered prayer after prayer for them—for the poor Currito, especially, upon whom (as she feared) the rain was indeed beating hard at that moment, soaking him to the bone as he lay, wounded and bleeding, not on a ship's deck but somewhere on the rocky coast of Mindoro. For the storm had caught the ship near that island; the ship had been hurled against the rocks and had shattered into pieces. A few men had saved themselves by swimming ashore, Currito among them and some other Spaniards, but the rest were natives who had been impressed to the service and who now turned against their cruel masters, pushing the Spaniards off the cliffs and hurling great rocks at them until they were all dead or dying, whereupon the natives fled to the wilderness.

So, the poor Currito lay on the flooded ground, unable to move; all his bones being broken and his whole body crushed to a pulp; the brute rain washing away the blood as fast as he shed it. And what with the cold, the pain, the exhaustion, and the loss of blood; he knew he must die in an instant. And straightway he fell to dwelling, not on the salvation of his soul, but on the things of earth his senses had enjoyed and would never enjoy again: thinking with anguish of food and drink and warm women, and of his home in Malaga, and of the fountains in Granada—and the intimate streets there: the families gathered on benches by the wayside, and girls' eyes flashing from behind grilled windows as he rode past with the muleteers to the market, while up on the Sierra Morena were the cypresses and bandits among them and an old, old, bearded hermit brooding naked in a cave, and down in Ronda the weeds ate the mute circus of the Romans and he had come upon some shepherds gathered in silence to roast a lamb but he was fifteen and had no silences, no stillness within him and so went sailing down the Guadalquivir on a raft with two boys, past Cordoba with its conquered Arabic ramparts, past the vineyards and the convents, past the orange and olive groves and deep at last into the shining marvel of Seville, its minarets swarming in the sky and spilling doves and hours—the gypsies everywhere, sailors and merchants everywhere, silks and spices everywhere, taverns and palaces everywhere, with tapestries gorgeous upon their windows, for the king was riding forth in a glory of gold flags and brocades, the jeweled majas crowding on the balconies to drop roses and wave their fans, and himself munching figs and boiled chestnuts and feeling happy, very happy, until in Sanlucar the river ended, the glory ended, youth ended among the whores, and he had gone to Cadiz where the ships were, their tall wings whispering of the flawless worlds in the West but the fishing-fleet had taken him to Palma, where it smelled of clams, and to Tarragona, where it smelled of goats, and he had ended up in Toledo, among the lazarillos, playing thief and pimp and beggar amidst the busy gloom of the wintry imperial city, not having cared to go home to Malaga where now—

alas!—he would never return again: nor to Palma, or Toledo, or Tarragona, or Seville: nor to the sweet wines of those places, whether cold in the cask or warm in the goatskin: nor to fish stewed in ripe lemons: nor to chicken boiled in thick olive oil: nor to buñuelos during the ferias: nor to puchero on Sundays; nor to the gypsy-girls and the majas and the snowlike blondes of the North since never again: never, never again would he sail homeward: never would feel under a ship's hull the boisterous Atlantic stop, its turbulence dissolving into the stately, historic rhythms of the Middle Sea: while the homing ship, Africa and the Pillars behind it, turned smoothly north and north again, its great sails tranquil: the winds being heavier now, smelling of tilled earth and oranges and noisy with gulls' wings: until there, in the thick mist, briefly appeared and vanished and appeared again, like enchantments of Arabian genii, vaguely glimmering at first, suddenly seen poised upon green hills and necklaced about with rivers: the white faery cities of the Andaluz.

And was it not a monstrous injustice (thought Currito) that, while the sun shone in those places and men ate and drank and were merry, he should be dying here in the mud, wracked by pain and cold, his bones broken and no part of his flesh unbruised? And he began to pity himself, lamenting himself as the most ill-used creature on earth, all the world against him now as from the moment of his birth. For surely he did not merit this punishment? Who was to blame for the evil he had wrought? Evil had been done him and he had merely repaid with evil. For an evil world had formed him; poverty had formed him; and greed; squalor; cruelty; hunger and suffering; the laws of the powerful; the insolence of the rich; the contempt of burghers; and the viciousness of the poor. Never, it seemed to him now, had he known a single moment of ease. The world had ground and ground him under its heels until here he lay in the mud, crushed and dying.

But the world should know that even a canalla had courage, had nobility, and knew how to die. He had always carelessly accepted whatever the Fates had given him: he would accept this death as carelessly. Sooner or later, anyway, one died. And the sooner, the better. But let the world witness how light-heartedly he performed this final business, thought Currito; such being human vanity that even at the hour of our death when, one might think, we would at last abandon the incoherent series of poses that we call the "self," we are still more concerned over the judgment of the world than of Heaven, persisting, whether on a public scaffold or in a private bed, to play our life out like an actor impressing an audience. And though even the Son of God could not face death without horror and wonder, we presume to know better in what manner a man should die, ignorant indeed of the awful mysteries and liabilities of our sojourn on earth to be able to think it somehow noble to be careless of dying. So, our poor Currito, instead of attending to his soul, set to posing himself in his mind (being unable to move), seeing himself as a sort of stoic, reclining gracefully in the mud, and defying the Fates (and the rain) with a smile.

He was sensible enough, however, to perceive in a moment the comedy of this pose and to find it so hugely amusing that, in spite of the pain and the flowing blood, he began laughing aloud at himself and had soon laughed away the bitterness inside him, laughter being the best purgative. And itemizing again his life's circumstances, he saw them as quite blameless in themselves, the evil being himself, and his indolence: his refusal to take any but the easiest way out, or that which most afforded him a selfish profit. He tickled to think he had lamented himself as a lamb among wolves. So easy to blame the world, or one's poverty, or your neighbor's wealth! The root of evil was always in money, or the lack of it, in power, or class, or position, or the laws, or in the lack of them—but never in oneself. The world was always going to be remade by people who were too busy to remake themselves first and who left the world twice as miserable as before. But what were earthly miseries if one chose to be above them? Christ had preached an indifference not to wealth only, but to both wealth and poverty—a total indifference, in fact, to one's status among men because you were intent on earning a status before God.

But he had loved to be talked about, thought Currito. He had loved to swagger and to be held in horror by the public and to be considered quite a devil. And it seemed to him that his wickedness had proceeded not from the heart but only from a childish taste for exhibition; that, essentially, he was a good man; and his evil, only a mask. God would surely forgive him. And, of course, the Virgin would intercede for him. He had been faithful to her in his fashion, saying her beads daily and saluting her at the angelic hours. She had always seemed near and clear to him; he had known her all his life. He had only to call on her and she would surely come and save him, thought Currito—whereupon he began praying her name aloud.

Straightway he was shaken to the bone by a terrific blast of lightning. The earth reeled and his senses blurred. Through stunned eyes he saw towering above him a woman robed in sunlight and crowned with the stars. But her face blazed with so fearful an anger she seemed the wrath of the storm made manifest. Seven swords plunged their cold steel in her heart but her left hand clutched a sword of fire. Silent she gazed at him, stern and beautiful—and he shook and sweated and shut his eyes against her, whimpering that he knew her not, that he had never known her, that it was not on her he had called. When he dared look again she was gone and the rain had ceased but the night was gathering fast all about him and the chilly winds whistled through the ruins of his bones.

And now did fear grip him in earnest: despair enhanced his torments. He was lost. He could almost hear the devils chuckling. So, had he known the Virgin all his life? But she had appeared before him and it seemed he did not know her after all and he realized how vast the mysteries were he had taken so lightly. He had felt too safe, too sure. Like so many Christians, he had depended too much on an old childhood familiarity with Heaven—and familiarity had bred presumption. He had dared to take Heaven for granted! And, meanwhile, he had followed his appetites wherever they had led him. And they had led him far indeed; they had lost him utterly. How could he presume to think his wickedness only a mask? It was his piety, rather, that was a mask, that was only a pose assumed to impress the Virgin and innocent old women like his mother and the Señora de Vera. He had dramatized himself as a weary wanton, a mystic Tenorio, torn between vice and piety, and weeping for heaven even while laughing among whores. His mother and Doña Ana, perhaps, he had deceived—but not the Mother of God. Alas, he had posed for the last time. Here at the ends of the earth, alone under the skies, he had been stripped naked to the bone and cracked open to the marrow, that the act of dying, at least, he might do honestly: knowing himself evil; knowing himself doomed to hell; and knowing the judgment just.

A great weariness possessed him. If he was damned, then damned he was! He felt no bitterness, only a desire to die quickly and perish in hell. And so exhausted was he in flesh and spirit he was sure he would die instantly if he but held his breath. But though he held it, though he relaxed his will, though he surrendered himself completely to dying—he could not die. Something seemed to stop him, to hold him back. He was not alone. The night was alive with presences. And with the clairvoyance of the dying, he knew what they were: people out in the world were praying for him. The night hummed with their voices, he could almost see their lips moving. Girls in school, old women by the wayside, priests at the altar, farmers in the field, and families gathered round the hearth—were praying, were praying for him, and for all sinners, now, and at the hour of their death. From the towns and cities of Spain, from Europe and from Africa, from the new worlds in the West and from the old worlds in the East—came the voices: choiring and clamoring and imploring God to forgive him his trespasses as they forgave those who trespassed against them.

And the poor Currito, though desiring intensely to die, found himself unable to do so, for the whole world seemed to have gathered around him, in choir upon choir of soft voices; determined to prevent him from dying. And now the serried choirs grew hushed and an old woman's voice trembled clear in the night. Currito shivered. It was his mother's voice: she was kneeling at the window of her shack by the wharves, looking out on the bay, and asking God to take care of her son. Then another voice rose tremulous—for Doña Ana de Vera was kneeling before the altar in her bedroom and begging the Virgin not to let him perish unshriven.

And how could he ever have thought himself alone, wondered Currito. Why had he ever supposed the world against him! It was he, rather, who had set himself against the world, against the human community of which he was part but had always rejoiced to play the outlaw and outside which he now desired to place himself eternally, by dying unrepentant, by dying in despair—the last gesture of utter egoism. And the world labored to save him now as it had labored to save him all his life. Monks were rising in the cold night to worship—because he had worshipped so little. They respected silence—because he had babbled so much. They enslaved their flesh—because he had been enslaved by his. Nuns went hungry (to atone for his greed) and were chaste (to atone for his lust) and humiliated themselves (to atone for his pride). For such is human solidarity that where any of us lack others may supply and the virtue of a single member nourishes the entire body.

And remembering how he had never done anyone good but rather had corrupted many by his infection, he marveled that the world should still care to save him, that its prayers should be clamorous about him, soaring in the night to the stars and to the very skies, knocking at Heaven itself on his behalf until he quaked to think how precious was a human soul and how shamefully he had wasted his own, and how full the world was of lovers, of God's lovers. His heart ached with love for them; his heart ached and glowed so warmly with love, contrition flamed aflower in it and, crying out in a loud voice, he prayed God to have mercy on him and to forgive him his sins.

In that instant the voices vanished, and looking down the still shore where ragged palms leaned wearily on each other, their long boles black against the moonlit sky and the shattered glass of the sea, he saw coming toward him a woman with a child. His heart leapt. He knew her at once: he had known her all his life. How many times had he sought solace at her shrine in Manila! Up the shore she hurried, her simple robes trailing in the mud and radiating the moonlight. And now she had arrived at his side; now she was kneeling down in the mud; and now the two holy faces were bending over him, warm and fragrant and luminous. But what poignant sorrow was in those lovely faces! What a world of grief! And knowing himself the cause, he burned with shame, he ached with anguish. Every sin he had ever committed seemed to become a fresh wound in his body and each wound separately pained, agonized, suffered death-pangs, died, grew bloated, putrefied, and sprouted worms—until his whole body seemed rotted and matted with worms.

But with each separate pain, with each separate agony and death, the sorrow diminished in the hovering faces and he seemed to perceive new beauties in them, and not only perceived but understood, and not only those faces but the moon and stars above them, and the leaning palms also, and the sea and the prone earth, and why he was lying there—the two faces growing ever more beautiful and still more beautiful, as each throb of pain seemed to multiply his sight and his senses, and not only more beautiful but nearer, clearer, more profoundly, more completely understood, for as poems or great music grow in beauty as we grow in wisdom—mere cut blossoms only, when we are young and have not suffered deeply, whose petals wither and fall apart in our minds, their seeds dropping on the soil of our minds where, as we grow older, they take root and project a stalk and some branches and more and more leaves until, in our old age, knotted with grief and suffering, we find in ourselves the complete poem or music; not the blooms merely but the leaves, the branches, the stalk, and the knotted root also, and the knowledge of how it grew—so, in the space of one spellbound moment, as he passed from pain to greater pain, and from rapture to greater rapture, each pain intensifying the rapture and each rapture intensifying the pain, and always with so increased a radiance of the understanding that he seemed every moment to tremble at the verge of total wisdom, the two faces that hovered ever nearer as he beheld them ever clearer seemed at last to pass into his being, to become a part of himself, to be growing inside him, filling his mind with a beauty so absolute, so vibrant, it throbbed aloud, it thundered aloud into music, flooding his mind with music as, already, it had flooded the night outside and the whole universe with music—a fragrant music that roared with the sea and whispered with the palms and in which the earth and moon and stars were being whirled in wild rapture; his own blood rushing, his own breath gasping in time to it; his frail mind creaking and quaking as the mighty chords roared and rose and swelled louder and louder and still louder: a monstrous typhoon of fragrance made audible, of beauty made eloquent, surging and straining against the weak walls of mortality until—alas!—at the very moment when he seemed no longer able to contain it: at the very moment when it seemed indeed he must break and burst and release it—that tempest of beauty— and releasing it be released himself: be destroyed utterly and dissolved and thundered out as pure sound or pure fragrance and be whirled in space as the earth and moon and stars, singing, were whirled; at that uttermost moment: that utterly agonized, utterly enraptured moment of being almost but not yet one with the beauty that was a total music, and with the music that was a total wisdom, and with the wisdom that was God— a human voice shocked his rapt ears self-conscious, whereupon the music perished; earth and sky stopped and were silent; and the two faces that now loomed immense, seeming to fill the whole sky, became unbearably radiant; dazzled and blurred with radiance; and vanished, glorious, in a keen heavenly blaze of light that, with infinite dismay he saw swiftly fading into the mere dull glow of the sun; seeing also—though without astonishment, without full consciousness, as if drugged—that it was night no longer but broad daylight and that the ground around him was not muddy but hot and dry and the air above murmurous and that the mere dim light of the sun was pouring down from a noon sky upon a dim sea out there, where a vague ship leaned at anchor, and upon the dim shore down there, where vague figures had jumped off a boat and were stumbling among the rocks and palm trees, cupping (now definite) hands to their mouths to shout halloo there, halloo there.

For the anchored ship (which was also bound for Ternate) being stopped on that coast by contrary winds, the commander had sent ashore some soldiers to see if the island be inhabited and food available, but they now found only corpses utterly decayed among the rocks and murmurous with flies. But one of the soldiers, a certain Gonzalo Salgado, amazed to hear his name being called, sought out the voice and discovered, with great horror, what seemed another heap of ripe carrion save that its eyes moved and sounds rattled in its throat.

But its body was bloated, its face horribly mutilated, and the entire carcass, from head to foot, a single enormous, grayly gaping, hotly odorous wound, swarming with flies and oozing pus and a foul oil and so thickly matted with worms you could scoop them out by the fistful, as the moist flesh seemed to have been scooped out indeed, having fallen away from the bones in so many places the skeleton already glittered triumphant through the last decayed rags of mortality. But this pile of rot moved its eyes and opened its mouth, calling Salgado by name; proclaiming itself Currito Lopez; and asking did Salgado not know him?

And Salgado, indeed, had known Currito in Manila; both of them had sailed for Ternate on the same day but on different ships; and how (asked Salgado) had Currito come to this mishap? And when Currito had related how his ship had been wrecked on the same day it set forth, Salgado cried out in amazement. For the troops (said he) had sailed on the seventh day of October but it was now the twentieth day of the month, wherefore Currito had lain on this shore for thirteen days, mortally wounded and without food or drink, and at the mercy of the elements. It seemed incredible, it seemed a miracle that he lived! On hearing which, Currito fell silent, and wonder, like a faint echo of that wondrous music he had heard, swelled in him. But he told Salgado how those thirteen days had seemed but a moment to him, for the Holy Child and His Mother had come and smiled at him, and their faces were so beautiful he seemed to have gazed too briefly, only for a moment but, behold, the moment had lasted thirteen days. Then he begged Salgado to go and fetch a priest from the ship that he might properly confess himself and be absolved, since for this reason had the Holy Persons sustained him alive these many days, but now he felt his hour upon him.

The priest being fetched (and with him a curious concourse), he confessed and was shriven, and turning to the soldiers about him he begged them to forgive him the former scandal of his example, urging them also not to despair if life be painful. For a lifetime (said he) was barely enough to educate us to the beauties of this world, which are but finite—and to educate us for God, whose beauty is infinite: could a mere lifetime, however long and however arduous, be deemed sufficient? And they, not understanding him, stared at each other, wondering was this Currito? But though he spoke to them, he seemed but dimly aware of them; seemed to be gathered away already; lifting his eyes from their faces to stare, calm and unblinking, at the sun; dying thus indeed: his lips parted, as if the last breath were a cry of wonder, and his eyes arrested, his eyes fixed in wild rapture at the noon sun; the priest crouched at his side and intoning the litany; the soldiers grouped around in awed attitudes—the palms ascending, the sea shimmering, the ship tremulous behind and below them—their armor and helmets golden and bristling with lightnings as the sun clashed hotly with the proud steel, clashing as hotly, and in the same moment, with the proud steel of soldiers poised on the young walls of faraway Manila, clashing as hotly indeed with the spires and red roofs of that city and flooding with molten pearl its crooked cobbled streets, empty at this hour of the siesta save for a carriage stopping at the Dominicans and Doña Ana descending, Doña Ana moving slowly across the patio, her head bowed and her face very pale and her skirts and mantilla vividly black in the hot whiteness of that hour—and her mood as black as her veils.

For she had had a fearful dream, a terrifying dream of Currito, whom she had seen kneeling in a dirty place, helmeted and armored, a rosary dangling from his clasped hands, when a blast of lightning had dissolved armor and helmet away, revealing a horrible leprous body, crawling with worms, the rosary dangling from cankered fingers, but another blast of lightning had dissolved the corruption away too, leaving only the pure skeleton from whose fingerbones the rosary continued to dangle until, at a final blast of lightning, the poised bones had collapsed and crumbled, the rosary dropping on mud, whereupon a crowd of people (and herself among them) had appeared on the scene and had picked up the soiled rosary and had prayed and wept over it, their falling tears washing away the mud until the rosary shone clean in their hands and gleaming like a pearl necklace: at which point she had woken up and found her cheeks and pillow wet with tears.

And she was sure the dream meant that Currito had died indeed, but whether in God's grace or in sin she could not tell—and the question tormented her. But it was a cruel world, cried Doña Ana as she entered the church, it was a horrid world if a single soul could perish in it. And there was no devotion in her heart as she ascended the altar and proceeded disrobing and attiring the Virgin in the fresh raiment she had brought. But she felt very bleak, she felt disconsolate. She would not lift her eyes, she would not lift her chin. But perhaps God would show her a sign, she thought suddenly, as she descended again, her arms full of the robes she had quitted from the Virgin and which she now spread out on a bench and was rolling into a bundle when, horrified, she noticed that the edges of the robes were stiff and stained with mud. And picking up the boots of the Child, she found them likewise covered with mud, and scraped and worn at the soles.

Straightway she forgot her gloom and bristled with spirit. For it was not she who had last attired the Virgin. She shared the privilege with another lady who, having a large family, was unfortunately not as devout at the task. And, obviously, this other lady had carelessly hung the robes in some muddy yard and they had fallen and been soiled. Or, more probably, she had left them lying around the house and the children had come upon and played with them, stamping the Child's boots and trailing the Virgin's skirts through the mud of some juvenile pageantry. And how impious, how sacrilegious a carelessness, cried Doña Ana. She would have to inform the prior, of course. She would go at once and show him the robes and the boots.

Wherefore, with eyes blazing and with chin thrust high, the soiled robes gathered up in her arms, Doña Ana departed in search of the prior.

THE MASS OF ST. SYLVESTRE

To open their doors to the New Year, the Romans invoked the God Janus, patron of doors and of beginnings, whose two faces (one staring forward, the other backward) caricature man's ability to dwell in the past while speeding into the future.

In Christianity, the post of Janus has been taken over by another Roman: St. Sylvestre, pope and confessor, whose feast falls on the last day of the year. At midnight of that day, the papal saint appears on earth and, with the Keys of his Office, opens the gates of all the principal archiepiscopal cities and celebrates the first Mass of the year in their cathedrals.

Manila has been a cathedral city almost from its foundation; for centuries it was one of the only two cities in the orient (Goa being the other) to whose gates the New Year's key-bearer made his annual visitation. For this purpose, St. Sylvestre always used the Puerta Postigo, which is—of the seven gates of our city—the one reserved for the private use of the viceroys and the archbishops. There he is met by the great St. Andrew, principal patron of Manila, accompanied by St. Potenciana, who is our minor patroness, and by St. Francis and St. Dominic, the guardians of our walls.

St. Sylvestre comes arrayed in cloth-of-gold and crowned with the tiara. Holy knights suspend a pallium above him; archangels swing censers and wave peacock fans; the Book, the Mitre, the Staff, and the Keys are borne before him by a company of seraphim; and cherubs flock ahead, blowing on trumpets. Below them swarm the Hours on fast wings. After them come the more sober Days—cryptic figures clad in silver above, in sable below—playing softly on viols. But behind the Pontiff himself, walking three by three, are the twelve splendid angels of the Christian Year.

The first three of these angels are clothed in evergreen and are crowned with pearls, and in their hands they bear incense, gold, and myrrh—for these are the angels of the Christmas Season. And the next three angels are clothed in April violets and are crowned with rubies, and they bear the implements of the Passion—for these are the angels of the holy time of Lent. And the next three angels are clothed in lilies and are crowned with gold, and they bear triumphal banners—for these are the angels of Eastertide. But the last three angels are clothed in pure flame and are crowned with emeralds, and they bear the seven gifts of the Holy Ghost—Wisdom, Understanding, Knowledge, Counsel, Perseverance, Piety, and the Fear of God—for these are the angels of Pentecost.

At the Puerta Postigo the heavenly multitude kneels down as St. Sylvestre advances with the Keys to open the noble and ever loyal city of Manila to the New Year. The city's bells ring out as the gate opens and St. Andrew and his companions come forth to greet the heavenly embassy. The two bishops embrace and exchange the kiss of peace, and proceed to the cathedral, where the Pontiff celebrates the Mass of the Circumcision. The bells continue pealing throughout the enchanted hour and break into a really glorious uproar as St. Sylvestre rises to bestow the final benediction. But when the clocks strike one o'clock, the bells instantly fall mute, the thundering music breaks off, the heavenly companies vanish—and in the cathedral, so lately glorious with lights and banners and solemn ceremonies, there is suddenly only the silence, only the chilly darkness of the empty naves; and at the altar, the single light burning before the Body of God.

Those who have been favored with glimpses of these ceremonies report that St. Sylvestre (like Janus) seems to have two faces—but these reports are too vague, too confused, and conflicting to be given credence. More respectable is the ancient belief that whoever sees and hears, in its entirety, this Mass of St. Sylvestre will see a thousand more New Years; and it is whispered that Messer Nostradamus succeeded (through black magic) in witnessing one such Mass, while most of Roger Bacon's last experiments (according to Fray Albertus Magnus) were on a prism that should make visible to mortal eyes this Mass of Time's key-bearer. They also speak of a certain magus of Manila who, like Nostradamus, intruded with black magic upon the sacred scene—and was punished for it.

This magus, who was known as Mateo the Maestro, lived in Manila during the early part of the 18th century and was feared by many as a sorcerer. He was equally famed as musician, artist, doctor, philosopher, chemist, and scholar; and in his bodega on the street of the Recollets a crowd of apprentices labored day and night at various arts and crafts—carving wood or chiseling stone, or narrating lives of saints on canvas, or conjugating Latin, or choiring together in rehearsals of a solemn Mass or chanted Rosary. The Maestro—a small, very shriveled ancient with white hair flowing down to his shoulders and a thin white beard—might look as frail as a mummy, but his eyes—and his temper—were still as sharp as a child's. Because no one could remember him young he was believed to be hundreds of years old, surviving (some said) from the days before Conquista, when, being a priest of the ancient cults, he wielded great power, wearing his hair long and affecting the clothes and the ways of women, but had hidden away from the Castilians in various animal disguises to plot a restoration of the old gods—those fierce and fearful old gods now living in exile on the mountaintops, and in dense forests, and out among the haunted islands of the south, but who steal abroad when the moon dies or when typhoons rage in the night, at which times you may invoke their presence by roasting a man's liver, and by other unspeakable devices.

The truth, however, was that Mateo the Maestro was not yet eighty years old and could not be remembered as a young man because he had spent his youth in incessant wanderings all over the country, thus acquiring his mastery of the arts, his command of a dozen tongues, and his profound knowledge of herb-healing and witchcraft. Like all magians, he was obsessed by a fear of death and the idea of immortality; but all the lore he had accumulated he found powerless to wrest the secret from life, though he had labored over countless experiments involving molten gold and pearls, the guts of turtles, the organs of monkeys, and the blood of owls. And after each vain experiment he would bitterly gaze out the window and reflect how, a few steps down the street, in the cathedral, there was yearly said a Mass which—had he but power to behold it—could increase his life by a thousand years.

He had consulted the dark deities in exile but was informed that the holy mysteries (except by divine dispensation) could be observed only by the eyes of the dead. Whereupon a monstrous idea had grown; the grave of a holy man was profaned; the dead eyes plucked out—and one New Year's eve Matco the Maestro hid himself in the cathedral, having grafted into his eye-sockets a pair of eyeballs ravished from the dead.

Just before midnight, he saw the dark naves suddenly light up and a procession forming at the high altar. Garlanded boys bore torches; flower-crowned girls carried lamps; acolytes pressed forward with the cross, the standards, and the censers; and a glittering angel lifted the great Flag of the City, its Lions and Castles embroidered in jewels. Behind a company of heralds appeared the mighty St. Andrew, attired in apostolic red and wreathed with laurel. Beside him walked the virgin St. Potenciana, robed in bridal white and crowned with roses. Behind them came St. Francis and St. Dominic and a great crowd of Holy Souls who had been, in life, illustrious citizens and faithful lovers of Manila. Down the aisle advanced the concourse, the cathedral doors swung open, and the Maestro followed the procession down the street to the Puerta Postigo. There the crowd paused in its chanting and, in a moment of silence so infinite you could hear the clocks all over the world intoning twelve, a key clicked audibly in the lock and (as in Jerusalem and Rome and Antioch and Salamanca and Byzantium and Paris and Alexandria and Canterbury and all the great Sees of Christendom) the gates opened and St. Sylvestre entered the city as the wild bells greeted the New Year, the two processions merging and flowing together to the cathedral.

Now, there was a fine retablo in our cathedral, carved in stone and representing the Adoration of the Shepherds, which at

Christmas time was lugged out from its side-chapel and placed upon the high altar. In this retablo, Mateo the Maestro now hid himself, since from behind the kneeling shepherds he commanded a superb view of the ceremonies commencing below. Having been warned that the Mass of St. Sylvestre cannot but prove unbearable to human senses, inducing (like the atmosphere of great heights) a coma in the mortal beholder, he had brought along a knife and a bag of limes, wounding his arms and steeping the wounds with the limes each time he felt sleep threatening to overcome him. But as the Mass progressed, it became more and more difficult, it became sheer agony to stay awake. His head swelled and swayed, the purloined eyes fought to squeeze loose from the sockets, slumber pressed down on him like an iron weight around his neck though he stabbed and stabbed his arms till both arms were bloody blobs of chopped flesh.

But at last the Mass drew to a close; the Pontiff rose for the final benediction. Writhing and sweating, bleeding and smarting, Mateo strained forward, leaning over the kneeling shepherds and forcing his agonized eyes open. St. Sylvestre was standing with his back to the altar—but had he turned his face or was that a second face that stared back at Mateo? Mateo retreated slowly but could not wrench his eyes away from those magnetic eyes below. He dropped down slowly, irresistibly, to his knees—still staring, still fascinated, his mouth agape. Then he ceased to move: his bones stiffened, his flesh froze. There he knelt moveless—one more kneeling and fascinated figure in a tableau of kneeling and fascinated figures.

Mateo the Maestro had turned into stone.

And there he has remained all these years—and, for generations, bad boys who drowse at Mass have had his crouching form pointed out as a warning. But every New Year's eve, at midnight, he returns to life. His flesh unfreezes, his blood liquefies, his bones unlock, and he descends from the retablo to join the procession to the Puerta Postigo; sees the New Year come in; hears the Mass of St. Sylvestre; and at the stroke of one o'clock turns into stone again. And so it will be with him until he has seen a thousand New Years.

Or has the spell broken for him at last? For his retablo is

broken, the cathedral is broken, and the city he knew has been wiped out by magic more practical and effective than any he ever dreamt of.

. . . And just as soon as the Liberation Forces opened the Walled City to the public, I went to see what war had left us of our heritage from four centuries. Nothing had been left—except the oldest and most priceless jewel of all: St. Augustine's. The Puerta Postiga still stands, but most of the city walls have been leveled to the ground and the cathedral is a field of rubble. Into what city (I wondered) would St. Sylvestre now make his annual entry? In what cathedral would he say his Mass? The retablo of the Pastoral Adoration has been smashed into pieces and dispersed into dust. Does that release Mateo the Maestro from his enchantment—or must he still, on New Year's eve, reassemble a living body from stone fragments to fulfill his penance of a thousand years?

Later, I told this story to some GI friends, who straightway clamored that a buddy of theirs, while stationed in the Walled City, had actually witnessed this entry and Mass of St. Sylvestre on New Year's eve, 1945. Unfortunately, the buddy had gone home to the States; but I took down his address and immediately wrote him, begging for a full account. His name is Francis Xavier Zhdolajczyk and he lives on Barnum Street in Brooklyn.

Here is the letter he sent me:

"... I didn't know all that about living a thousand years or I might have acted otherwise. If that stuff is true—what a chance I missed! We were camped just outside the walls—on the grassland between the walls and the Port Companies. That night—it was New Year's eve—I'd come back to camp early because I was feeling homesick. I was all alone in our tent, the other boys were still downtown celebrating. I lay awake a long time thinking of the war and of the folks back home and when was I going to see them. Around midnight I woke up from a doze and heard music. So I stuck my head out and I saw a kind of parade coming up the road. I wasn't surprised then and I wasn't surprised at anything afterward. I just told myself that you people must be having one *of your New Year's celebrations and wasn't it too bad your churches were all smashed up. But I turned my head just then— and there was the Walled City, and it wasn't smashed up at all. The walls were whole all the way and I could even see some kind of knights in armor moving on top of them. Behind the walls I could clearly see a lot of rooftops and church towers and they were none of them smashed up at all.*

I told you about not being surprised—I wasn't. I simply felt I should go and take a look. So I dressed fast and ran out. The parade had stopped at a gate in the wall and a bishop was open- ing the gate and bells began ringing. There was another crowd waiting inside and they had a bishop too and the two bishops kissed and then they all went through the gate and I followed. Nobody took any notice of me. Inside, it was a real city, an old city, and hundreds of bells were ringing and they had a park with fountains all around and beside the park was a cathedral. Everybody was going in there, so I did too.

You never saw such a sight! The bishops were saying Mass and it was all lighted up and the air swelled good like high mountain air and the music was so pretty you wanted to cry. Then I said to myself: what a picture you could take of this, to send home. But I hadn't brought my camera and I decided to get it. So I ran out and down the street and past the open gate and into our camp. Nobody was around. I got my camera and raced back. When I reached the cathedral I could see that the Mass was ending. I aimed for a nice view—but right when I was going to snap the shutter the bells stopped ringing and—just like that—it all disap- peared. The bright lights was only moonlight and the music was only the wind. There was no crowd and no bishops and no altar and no cathedral. I was standing on a stack of ruins and there was nothing but ruins around. Just blocks and blocks of ruins stretching all around me in the silent moonlight . . ."

THE SUMMER SOLSTICE

The Moretas were spending St. John's Day with the children's grandfather, whose feast day it was. Doña Lupeng awoke feeling faint with the heat, a sound of screaming in her ears. In the dining room the three boys, already attired in their holiday suits, were at breakfast, and came crowding around her, talking all at once.

"How long you have slept, Mama!"

"We thought you were never getting up!"

"Do we leave at once, huh? Are we going now?"

"Hush, hush, I implore you! Now look: your father has a headache, and so have I. So be quiet this instant—or no one goes to Grandfather."

Though it was only seven by the clock the house was already a furnace, the windows dilating with the harsh light and the air already burning with the immense, intense fever of noon.

She found the children's nurse working in the kitchen. "And why is it you who are preparing breakfast? Where is Amada?" But without waiting for an answer she went to the backdoor and opened it, and the screaming in her ears became a wild screaming in the stables across the yard. "Oh, my God!" she groaned and, grasping her skirts, hurried across the yard.

In the stables Entoy, the driver, apparently deaf to the screams, was hitching the pair of piebald ponies to the coach.

"Not the closed coach, Entoy! The open carriage!" shouted Doña Lupeng as she came up.

"But the dust, señora—"

"I know, but better to be dirty than to be boiled alive. And what ails your wife, eh? Have you been beating her again?"

"Oh no, señora: I have not touched her."

"Then why is she screaming? Is she ill?"

"I do not think so. But how do I know? You can go and see for yourself, señora. She is up there."

When Doña Lupeng entered the room, the big half-naked woman sprawled across the bamboo bed stopped screaming. Doña Lupeng was shocked.

"What is this, Amada? Why are you still in bed at this hour? And in such a posture! Come, get up at once. You should be ashamed!"

But the woman on the bed merely stared. Her sweat-beaded brows contracted, as if in an effort to understand. Then her face relaxed, her mouth sagged open humorously and, rolling over on her back and spreading out her big soft arms and legs, she began noiselessly quaking with laughter—the mute mirth jerking in her throat; the moist pile of her flesh quivering like brown jelly. Saliva dribbled from the corners of her mouth.

Doña Lupeng blushed, looking around helplessly; and seeing that Entoy had followed and was leaning in the doorway, watching stolidly, she blushed again. The room reeked hotly of intimate odors. She averted her eyes from the laughing woman on the bed, in whose nakedness she seemed so to participate that she was ashamed to look directly at the man in the doorway.

"Tell me, Entoy: has she been to the Tadtarin?"

"Yes, señora. Last night."

"But I forbade her to go! And I forbade you to let her go!"

"I could do nothing."

"Why, you beat her at the least pretext!"

"But now I dare not touch her."

"Oh, and why not?"

"It is the day of St. John: the spirit is in her."

"But, man—"

"It is true, señora. The spirit is in her. She is the Tadtarin. She must do as she pleases. Otherwise, the grain would not grow, the trees would bear no fruit, the rivers would give no fish, and the animals would die."

"*Naku*, I did not know your wife was so powerful, Entoy."

"At such times she is not my wife: she is the wife of the river, she is the wife of the crocodile, she is the wife of the moon."

"But how can they still believe such things?" demanded Doña Lupeng of her husband as they drove in the open carriage through the pastoral countryside that was the *arrabal* of Paco in the 1850s.

Don Paeng, drowsily stroking his mustaches, his eyes closed against the hot light, merely shrugged.

"And you should have seen that Entoy," continued his wife. "You know how the brute treats her: she cannot say a word but he thrashes her. But this morning he stood as meek as a lamb while she screamed and screamed. He seemed actually in awe of her, do you know—actually *afraid* of her!"

Don Paeng darted a sidelong glance at his wife, by which he intimated that the subject was not a proper one for the children, who were sitting opposite, facing their parents.

"Oh, look, boys—here comes the St. John!" cried Doña Lupeng, and she sprang up in the swaying carriage, propping one hand on her husband's shoulder while with the other she held up her silk parasol.

And "Here come the men with their St. John!" cried voices up and down the countryside. People in wet clothes dripping with well-water, ditch-water and river-water came running across the hot woods and fields and meadows, brandishing cans of water, wetting each other uproariously, and shouting, *"San Juan! San Juan!"* as they ran to meet the procession.

Up the road, stirring a cloud of dust, and gaily bedrenched by the crowds gathered along the wayside, a concourse of young men clad only in soggy trousers were carrying aloft an image of the Precursor. Their teeth flashed white in their laughing faces and their hot bodies glowed crimson as they pranced past, shrouded in fiery dust, singing and shouting and waving their arms: the St. John riding swiftly above the sea of dark heads and glittering in the noon sun—a fine, blonde, heroic St. John: very male, very arrogant: the Lord of Summer indeed; the Lord of Light and Heat—erect and goldly virile above the prone and female earth—while the worshippers danced and the dust thickened and the animals reared and roared and the merciless fires came raining down from the skies—the vast out-pouring of light that marks this climax of the solar year—raining relentlessly upon field and river and town and winding road, and upon the joyous throng of young men against whose uproar a couple of seminarians in muddy cassocks vainly intoned the hymn of the noon god:

> *"That we, thy servants, in chorus*
> *May praise thee, our tongues restore us. . . ."*

But Doña Lupeng, standing in the stopped carriage, looking very young and elegant in her white frock, under the twirling parasol, stared down on the passing male horde with increasing annoyance. The insolent man-smell of their bodies rose all about her—wave upon wave of it—enveloping her, assaulting her senses, till she felt faint with it and pressed a handkerchief to her nose. And as she glanced at her husband and saw with what a smug smile he was watching the revelers, her annoyance deepened. When he bade her sit down because all eyes were turned on her, she pretended not to hear; stood up even straighter, as if to defy those rude creatures flaunting their manhood in the sun.

And she wondered peevishly what the braggarts were being so cocky about? For this arrogance, this pride, this bluff male health of theirs was (she told herself) founded on the impregnable virtue of generations of good women. The boobies were so sure of themselves because they had always been sure of their wives. All the sisters being virtuous, all the brothers are brave, thought Doña Lupeng, with a bitterness that rather surprised her. Women had built it up: this poise of the male. Ah, and women could destroy it, too! She recalled, vindictively, this morning's scene at the stables: Amada naked and screaming in bed while from the doorway her lord and master looked on in meek silence. And was it not the mystery of a woman in her flowers that had restored the tongue of that old Hebrew prophet?

"Look, Lupeng, they have all passed now," Don Paeng was saying. "Do you mean to stand all the way?"

She looked around in surprise and hastily sat down. The children tittered, and the carriage started.

"Has the heat gone to your head, woman?" asked Don Paeng, smiling. The children burst frankly into laughter.

Their mother colored and hung her head. She was beginning to feel ashamed of the thoughts that had filled her mind. They seemed improper—almost obscene—and the discovery of such depths of wickedness in herself appalled her. She moved closer to her husband, to share the parasol with him.

"And did you see our young cousin Guido?" he asked.

"Oh, was he in that crowd?"

"A European education does not seem to have spoiled his taste for country pleasures."

"I did not see him."

"He waved and waved."

"The poor boy. He will feel hurt. But truly, Paeng, I did not see him."

"Well, that is always a woman's privilege."

But when that afternoon, at the grandfather's, the young Guido presented himself, properly attired and brushed and scented, Doña Lupeng was so charming and gracious with him that he was enchanted and gazed after her all afternoon with enamored eyes.

This was the time when our young men were all going to Europe and bringing back with them, not the Age of Victoria, but the Age of Byron. The young Guido knew nothing of Darwin and evolution; he knew everything about Napoleon and the Revolution. When Doña Lupeng expressed surprise at his presence that morning in the St. John's crowd, he laughed in her face.

"But I *adore* these old fiestas of ours! They are so *romantic!* Last night, do you know, we walked all the way through the woods, I and some boys, to see the procession of the Tadtarin."

"And was that romantic too?" asked Doña Lupeng.

"It was *weird*. It made my flesh *crawl*. All those women in such a mystic frenzy! And she who was the Tadtarin last night—she was a figure right out of a flamenco!"

"I fear to disenchant you, Guido—but that woman happens to be our cook."

"She is beautiful."

"Our Amada beautiful? But she is old and fat!"

"She is beautiful—as that old tree you are leaning on is beautiful," calmly insisted the young man, mocking her with his eyes.

They were out in the buzzing orchard, among the ripe mangoes; Doña Lupeng seated on the grass, her legs tucked beneath her, and the young man sprawled flat on his belly, gazing up at her, his face moist with sweat. The children were chasing dragonflies. The sun stood still in the west. The long day refused to end. From the house came the sudden roaring laughter of the men playing cards.

"Beautiful! Romantic! Adorable! Are those the only words you learned in Europe?" cried Doña Lupeng, feeling very annoyed with this young man whose eyes adored her one moment and mocked her the next.

"Ah, I also learned to open my eyes over there—to see the holiness and the mystery of what is vulgar."

"And what is so holy and mysterious about—about the Tadtarin, for instance?"

"I do not know. I can only *feel* it. And it *frightens* me. Those rituals come to us from the earliest dawn of the world. And the dominant figure is not the male but the female."

"But they are in honor of St. John."

"What has your St. John to do with them? Those women worship a more ancient lord. Why, do you know that no man may join in those rites unless he first puts on some article of women's apparel and—"

"And what did *you* put on, Guido?"

"How *sharp* you are! Oh, I made such love to a toothless old hag there that she pulled off her stocking for me. And I pulled it on, over my arm, like a glove. How your husband would have *despised* me!"

"But what on earth does it mean?"

"I think it is to remind us men that once upon a time you women were supreme and we men were the slaves."

"But surely there have always been kings?"

"Oh, no. The queen came before the king, and the priestess before the priest, and the moon before the sun."

"The moon?"

"—who is the Lord of the women."

"Why?"

"Because the tides of women, like the tides of the sea, are tides of the moon. Because the first blood—But what is the matter, Lupe? Oh, have I offended you?"

"Is this how they talk to decent women in Europe?"

"They do not talk to women, they pray to them—as men did in the dawn of the world."

"Oh, you are mad! mad!"

"Why are you so afraid, Lupe?"

"I, afraid? And of whom? My dear boy, you still have your mother's milk in your mouth. I only wish you to remember that I am a married woman."

"I remember that you are a woman, yes. A beautiful woman. And why not? Did you turn into some dreadful monster when you married? Did you stop being a woman? Did you stop being beautiful? Then why should my eyes not tell you what you are— just because you are married?"

"Ah, this is too much now!" cried Doña Lupeng, and she rose to her feet.

"Do not go, I implore you! Have pity on me!"

"No more of your comedy, Guido! And besides—where have those children gone to! I must go after them."

As she lifted her skirts to walk away, the young man, propping up his elbows, dragged himself forward on the ground and solemnly kissed the tips of her shoes. She stared down in sudden horror, transfixed—and he felt her violent shudder. She backed away slowly, still staring; then turned and fled toward the house.

On the way home that evening Don Paeng noticed that his wife was in a mood. They were alone in the carriage: the children were staying overnight at their grandfather's. The heat had not subsided. It was heat without gradations: that knew no twilights and no dawns; that was still there, after the sun had set; that would be there already, before the sun had risen.

"Has young Guido been annoying you?" asked Don Paeng.

"Yes! All afternoon."

"These young men today—what a disgrace they are! I felt embarrassed as a man to see him following you about with those eyes of a whipped dog."

She glanced at him coldly. "And was that all you felt, Paeng? Embarrassed—as a man?"

"A good husband has constant confidence in the good sense of his wife," he pronounced grandly, and smiled at her.

But she drew away; huddled herself in the other corner. "He *kissed* my feet," she told him disdainfully, her eyes on his face.

He frowned and made a gesture of distate. "Do you see? They have the instincts, the style of the canalla! To kiss a woman's feet, to follow her like a dog, to adore her like a slave—"

"Is it so shameful for a man to adore women?"

"A gentleman loves and respects Woman. The cads and lunatics—they 'adore' the women."

"But maybe we do not want to be loved and respected—but to be adored."

"Ah, he has converted you then?"

"Who knows? But must we talk about it? My head is bursting with the heat."

But when they reached home she did not lie down but wandered listlessly through the empty house. When Don Paeng, having bathed and changed, came down from the bedroom, he found her in the dark parlor seated at the harp and plucking out a tune, still in her white frock and shoes.

"How can you bear those hot clothes, Lupeng? And why the darkness? Order someone to bring a light in here."

"There is no one, they have all gone to see the Tadtarin."

"A pack of loafers we are feeding!"

She had risen and gone to the window. He approached and stood behind her, grasped her elbows and, stooping, kissed the nape of her neck. But she stood still, not responding, and he released her sulkily. She turned around to face him.

"Listen, Paeng. I want to see it, too. The Tadtarin, I mean. I have not seen it since I was a little girl. And tonight is the last night."

"You must be crazy! Only low people go there. And I thought you had a headache?" He was still sulking.

"But I want to go! My head aches worse in the house. For a favor, Paeng."

"I told you: No! Go and take those clothes off. But, woman, whatever has got into you!" He strode off to the table, opened the box of cigars, took one, banged the lid shut, bit off an end of the cigar, and glared about for a light.

She was still standing by the window and her chin was up. "Very well, if you do not want to come, do not come—but I am going."

"I warn you, Lupe; do not provoke me!"

"I will go with Amada. Entoy can take us. You cannot forbid me, Paeng. There is nothing wrong with it. I am not a child."

But standing very straight in her white frock, her eyes shining in the dark and her chin thrust up, she looked so young, so fragile, that his heart was touched. He sighed, smiled ruefully, and shrugged his shoulders.

"Yes, the heat has touched you in the head, Lupeng. And since you are so set on it—very well, let us go. Come, have the coach ordered!"

The cult of the Tadtarin is celebrated on three days: the feast of St. John and the two preceding days. On the first night, a young girl heads the procession; on the second, a mature woman; and on the third, a very old woman who dies and comes to life again. In these processions, as in those of Pakil and Obando, everyone dances.

Around the tiny plaza in front of the barrio chapel, quite a stream of carriages was flowing leisurely. The Moretas were constantly being hailed from the other vehicles. The plaza itself and the sidewalks were filled with chattering, strolling, profusely sweating people. More people were crowded on the balconies and windows of the houses. The moon had not yet risen; the black night smoldered; in the windless sky the lightning's abruptly branching fire seemed the nerves of the tortured air made visible.

"Here they come now!" cried the people on the balconies.

And "Here come the women with their St. John!" cried the people on the sidewalks, surging forth on the street. The carriages halted and their occupants descended. The plaza rang with the shouts of people and the neighing of horses—and with another keener sound: a sound as of sea-waves steadily rolling nearer.

The crowd parted, and up the street came the prancing, screaming, writhing women, their eyes wild, black shawls flying around their shoulders, and their long hair streaming and covered with leaves and flowers. But the Tadtarin, a small old woman with white hair, walked with calm dignity in the midst of the female tumult, a wand in one hand, a bunch of seedlings in the other. Behind her, a group of girls bore aloft a little black image of the Baptist—a crude, primitive, grotesque image, its big-eyed head too big for its puny naked torso, bobbing and swaying above the hysterical female horde and looking at once so comical and so pathetic that Don Paeng, watching with his wife on the sidewalk, was outraged. The image seemed to be crying for help, to be struggling to escape—a St. John indeed in the hands of the Herodiads; a doomed captive these witches were subjecting first to their derision; a gross and brutal caricature of his sex.

Don Paeng flushed hotly: he felt that all those women had personally insulted him. He turned to his wife, to take her away—but she was watching greedily, taut and breathless, her head thrust forward and her eyes bulging, the teeth bared in the slack mouth, and the sweat gleaming on her face. Don Paeng was horrified. He grasped her arm—but just then a flash of lightning blazed and the screaming women fell silent: the Tadtarin was about to die.

The old woman closed her eyes and bowed her head and sank slowly to her knees. A pallet was brought and set on the ground and she was laid in it and her face covered with a shroud. Her hands still clutched the wand and the seedlings. The women drew away, leaving her in a cleared space. They covered their heads with their black shawls and began wailing softly, unhumanly—a hushed, animal keening.

Overhead the sky was brightening; silver light defined the rooftops. When the moon rose and flooded with hot brilliance the moveless crowded square, the black-shawled women stopped wailing and a girl approached and unshrouded the Tadtarin, who opened her eyes and sat up, her face lifted to the moonlight. She rose to her feet and extended the wand and the seedlings and the women joined in a mighty shout. They pulled off and waved their shawls and whirled and began dancing again—laughing and dancing with such joyous exciting abandon that the people in the square and on the sidewalks, and even those on the balconies, were soon laughing and dancing, too. Girls broke away from their parents and wives from their husbands to join in the orgy.

"Come, let us go now," said Don Paeng to his wife. She was shaking with fascination; tears trembled on her lashes; but she nodded meekly and allowed herself to be led away. But suddenly she pulled free from his grasp, darted off, and ran into the crowd of dancing women.

She flung her hands to her hair and whirled and her hair came undone. Then, planting her arms akimbo, she began to trip a nimble measure, an instinctive folk movement. She tossed her head back and her arched throat bloomed whitely. Her eyes brimmed with moonlight, and her mouth with laughter.

Don Paeng ran after her, shouting her name, but she laughed and shook her head and darted deeper into the dense maze of the procession, which was moving again, toward the chapel. He followed her, shouting; she eluded him, laughing—and through the thick of the female horde they lost and found and lost each other again—she dancing and he pursuing—till, carried along by the tide, they were both swallowed up into the hot, packed, turbulent darkness of the chapel. Inside poured the entire procession, and Don Paeng, finding himself trapped tight among milling female bodies, struggled with sudden panic to fight his way out. Angry voices rose all about him in the stifling darkness.

"*Hoy*, you are crushing my feet!"

"And let go of my shawl, my shawl!"

"Stop pushing, shameless one, or I kick you!"

"Let me pass, let me pass, you harlots!" cried Don Paeng.

"*Abah*, it is a man!"

"How dare he come in here?"

"Break his head!"

"Throw the animal out!"

"Throw him out! Throw him out!" shrieked the voices, and Don Paeng found himself surrounded by a swarm of gleaming eyes.

Terror possessed him and he struck out savagely with both fists, with all his strength—but they closed in as savagely: solid walls of flesh that crushed upon him and pinned his arms helpless, while unseen hands struck and struck his face, and ravaged his hair and clothes, and clawed at his flesh, as—kicked and buffeted, his eyes blind and his torn mouth salty with blood— he was pushed down, down to his knees, and half-shoved, half-dragged to the doorway and rolled out to the street. He picked himself up at once and walked away with a dignity that forbade the crowd gathered outside to laugh or to pity. Entoy came running to meet him.

"But what has happened to you, Don Paeng?"

"Nothing. Where is the coach?"

"Just over there, sir. But you are wounded in the face!"

"No, these are only scratches. Go and get the señora. We are going home."

When she entered the coach and saw his bruised face and torn clothing, she smiled coolly.

"What a sight you are, man! What have you done with yourself?" And when he did not answer: "Why, have they pulled out his tongue too?" she wondered aloud.

And when they were home and stood facing each other in the bedroom, she was still as light-hearted.

"What are you going to do, Rafael?"

"I am going to give you a whipping."

"But why?"

"Because you have behaved tonight like a lewd woman."

"How I behaved tonight is what I am. If you call that lewd, then I was always a lewd woman and a whipping will not change me—though you whipped me till I died."

"I want this madness to die in you."

"No, you want me to pay for your bruises."

He flushed darkly. "How can you say that, Lupe?"

"Because it is true. You have been whipped by the women and now you think to avenge yourself by whipping me."

His shoulders sagged and his face dulled. "If you can think that of me—"

"You could think me a lewd woman!"

"Oh, how do I know what to think of you? I was sure I knew you as I knew myself. But now you are as distant and strange to me as a female Turk in Africa!"

"Yet you would dare whip me—"

"Because I love you, because I respect you—"

"And because if you ceased to respect me you would cease to respect yourself?"

"Ah, I did not say that!"

"Then why not say it? It is true. And you want to say it, you want to say it!"

But he struggled against her power. "Why should I want to?" he demanded peevishly.

"Because, either you must say it—or you must whip me," she taunted.

Her eyes were upon him and the shameful fear that had unmanned him in the dark chapel possessed him again. His legs had turned to water; it was a monstrous agony to remain standing.

But she was waiting for him to speak, forcing him to speak.

"No, I cannot whip you!" he confessed miserably.

"Then say it! Say it!" she cried, pounding her clenched fists together. "Why suffer and suffer? And in the end you would only submit."

But he still struggled stubbornly. "Is it not enough that you have me helpless? Is it not enough that I feel what you want me to feel?"

But she shook her head furiously. "Until you have said it to me, there can be no peace between us."

He was exhausted at last: he sank heavily to his knees, breathing hard and streaming with sweat, his fine body curiously diminished now in its ravaged apparel.

"I adore you, Lupe," he said tonelessly.

She strained forward avidly. "*What?* What did you say?" she screamed.

And he, in his dead voice: "That I adore you. That I adore you. That I worship you. That the air you breathe and the ground you tread is holy to me. That I am your dog, your slave . . ."

But it was still not enough. Her fists were still clenched, and she cried: "*Then come, crawl on the floor, and kiss my feet!*"

Without a moment's hesitation, he sprawled down flat and, working his arms and legs, gaspingly clawed his way across the floor, like a great agonized lizard, the woman steadily backing away as he approached, her eyes watching him avidly, her nostrils dilating, till behind her loomed the open window, the huge glittering moon, the rapid flashes of lightning. She stopped, panting, and leaned against the sill. He lay exhausted at her feet, his face flat on the floor.

She raised her skirts and contemptuously thrust out a naked foot. He lifted his dripping face and touched his bruised lips to her toes; lifted his hands and grasped the white foot and kissed it savagely—kissed the step, the sole, the frail ankle—while she bit her lips and clutched in pain at the windowsill, her body distended and wracked by horrible shivers, her head flung back and her loose hair streaming out the window—streaming fluid and black in the white night where the huge moon glowed like a sun and the dry air flamed into lightning and the pure heat burned with the immense intense fever of noon.

MAY DAY EVE

The old people had ordered that the dancing should stop at ten o'clock but it was almost midnight before the carriages came filing up to the front door, the servants running to and fro with torches to light the departing guests, while the girls who were staying were promptly herded upstairs to the bedrooms, the young men gathering around to wish them a good night and lamenting their ascent with mock sighs and moanings, proclaiming themselves disconsolate but straightway going off to finish the punch and the brandy though they were quite drunk already and simply bursting with wild spirits, merriment, arrogance, and audacity, for they were young bucks newly arrived from Europe; the ball had been in their honor; and they had waltzed and polka-ed and bragged and swaggered and flirted all night and were in no mood to sleep yet—no, caramba, not on this moist tropic eve! Not on this mystic May eve!—with the night still young and so seductive that it was madness not to go out, not to go forth—and serenade the neighbors! cried one; and swim in the Pasig! cried another; and gather fireflies! cried a third—whereupon there arose a great clamor for coats and capes, for hats and canes and they were presently stumbling out among the medieval shadows of the foul street where a couple of street lamps flickered and a last carriage rattled away upon the cobbles while the blind black houses muttered hush-hush, their tiled roofs looming like sinister chessboards against a wild sky murky with clouds, save where an evil young moon prowled about in a corner or where a murderous wind whirled, whistling and whining, smelling now of the sea and

now of the summer orchards and wafting unbearable childhood fragrances of ripe guavas to the young men trooping so
uproariously down the street that the girls who were disrobing
upstairs in the bedrooms scattered screaming to the windows,
crowded giggling at the windows, but were soon sighing amo-
rously over those young men bawling below; over those wicked
young men and their handsome apparel, their proud flashing
eyes, and their elegant mustaches so black and vivid in the
moonlight that the girls were quite ravished with love, and
began crying to one another how carefree were men but how
awful to be a girl and what a horrid, horrid world it was, till
old Anastasia plucked them off by the ear or the pigtail and
chased them off to bed—while from up the street came the
clackety-clack of the watchman's boots on the cobbles, and the
clang-clang of his lantern against his knee, and the mighty roll
of his great voice booming through the night: *"Guardia
sereno-o-o! A las doce han dado-o-o!"*

And it was May again, said the old Anastasia. It was the first
day of May and witches were abroad in the night, she said—for
it was a night of divination, a night of lovers, and those who
cared might peer in a mirror and would there behold the face
of whoever it was they were fated to marry, said the old Anastasia as she hobbled about picking up the piled crinolines and
folding up shawls and raking slippers to a corner while the girls
climbing into the four great poster beds that overwhelmed the
room began shrieking with terror, scrambling over each other
and imploring the old woman not to frighten them.

"Enough, enough, Anastasia! We want to sleep!"

"Go scare the boys instead, you old witch!"

"She is not a witch, she is a maga. She was born on Christmas Eve!"

"St. Anastasia, virgin and martyr."

"Huh? Impossible! She has conquered seven husbands! Are
you a virgin, Anastasia?"

"No, but I am seven times a martyr because of you girls!"

"Let her prophesy, let her prophesy! Whom will I marry, old
gypsy? Come, tell me."

"You may learn in a mirror if you are not afraid."

"I am not afraid, I will go!" cried the young cousin Agueda, jumping up in bed.

"Girls, girls—we are making too much noise! My mother will hear and will come and pinch us all. Agueda, lie down! And you, Anastasia, I command you to shut your mouth and go away!"

"Your mother told me to stay here all night, my grand lady!"

"And I will not lie down!" cried the rebellious Agueda, leaping to the floor. "Stay, old woman. Tell me what I have to do."

"Tell her! Tell her!" chimed the other girls.

The old woman dropped the clothes she had gathered and approached and fixed her eyes on the girl. "You must take a candle," she instructed, "and go into a room that is dark and that has a mirror in it and you must be alone in the room. Go up to the mirror and close your eyes and say:

> Mirror, mirror,
> show to me
> him whose woman
> I will be.

If all goes right, just above your left shoulder will appear the face of the man you will marry."

A silence. Then: "And what if all does *not* go right?" asked Agueda.

"Ah, then the Lord have mercy on you!"

"Why?"

"Because you may *see—the Devil!*"

The girls screamed and clutched one another, shivering.

"But what nonsense!" cried Agueda. "This is the year 1847. There are no devils anymore!" Nevertheless she had turned pale. "But where could I go, huh? Yes, I know! Down to the sala. It has that big mirror and no one is there now."

"No, Agueda, no! It is a mortal sin! You will see the devil!"

"I do not care! I am not afraid! I will go!"

"Oh, you wicked girl! Oh, you mad girl!"

"If you do not come back to bed, Agueda, I will call my mother."

"And if you do I will tell her who came to visit you at the convent last March. Come, old woman—give me that candle. I go."

"Oh, girls—come and stop her! Take hold of her! Block the door!"

But Agueda had already slipped outside; was already tiptoeing across the hall; her feet bare and her dark hair falling down her shoulders and streaming in the wind as she fled down the stairs, the lighted candle sputtering in one hand while with the other she pulled up her white gown from her ankles.

She paused breathless in the doorway to the sala and her heart failed her. She tried to imagine the room filled again with lights, laughter, whirling couples, and the jolly jerky music of the fiddlers. But, oh, it was a dark den, a weird cavern, for the windows had been closed and the furniture stacked up against the walls. She crossed herself and stepped inside.

The mirror hung on the wall before her; a big antique mirror with a gold frame carved into leaves and flowers and mysterious curlicues. She saw herself approaching fearfully in it: a small white ghost that the darkness bodied forth—but not willingly, not completely, for her eyes and hair were so dark that the face approaching in the mirror seemed only a mask that floated forward; a bright mask with two holes gaping in it, blown forward by the white cloud of her gown. But when she stood before the mirror she lifted the candle level with her chin and the dead mask bloomed into her living face.

She closed her eyes and whispered the incantation. When she had finished such a terror took hold of her that she felt unable to move, unable to open her eyes, and thought she would stand there forever, enchanted. But she heard a step behind her, and a smothered giggle, and instantly opened her eyes.

"And what did you see, Mama? Oh, what was it?"

But Doña Agueda had forgotten the little girl on her lap: she was staring past the curly head nestling at her breast and seeing herself in the big mirror hanging in the room. It was the same room and the same mirror but the face she now saw in it was an old face—a hard, bitter, vengeful face, framed in graying hair, and so sadly altered, so sadly different from that other face like a white mask, that fresh young face like a pure mask that she had brought before this mirror one wild May Day midnight years and years ago. . . .

"But what was it, Mama? Oh, please go on! What did you see?"

Doña Agueda looked down at her daughter but her face did not soften though her eyes filled with tears. "I saw the devil!" she said bitterly.

The child blanched. "The devil, Mama? Oh . . . *OH!*"

"Yes, my love. I opened my eyes and there in the mirror, smiling at me over my left shoulder, was the face of the devil."

"Oh, my poor little Mama! And were you very frightened?"

"You can imagine. And that is why good little girls do not look into mirrors except when their mothers tell them. You must stop this naughty habit, darling, of admiring yourself in every mirror you pass—or you may see something frightful some day."

"But the devil, Mama—what did he look like?"

"Well, let me see. . . . He had curly hair and a scar on his cheek—"

"Like the scar of Papa?"

"Well, yes. But this of the devil was a scar of sin, while that of your Papa is a scar of honor. Or so he says."

"Go on about the devil."

"Well, he had mustaches."

"Like those of Papa?"

"Oh, no. Those of your Papa are dirty and graying and smell horribly of tobacco, while these of the devil were very black and elegant—oh, how elegant!"

"And did he have horns and a tail?"

The mother's lips curled. "Yes, he did! But, alas, I could not see them at that time. All I could see were his fine clothes, his flashing eyes, his curly hair and mustaches."

"And did he speak to you, Mama?"

"Yes . . . Yes, he spoke to me," said Doña Agueda. And bowing her graying head she wept.

"Charms like yours have no need for a candle, fair one," he had said, smiling at her in the mirror and stepping back to give her a low mocking bow. She had whirled around and glared at him and he had burst into laughter.

"But I remember you!" he cried. "You are Agueda, whom I left a mere infant and came home to find a tremendous beauty, and I danced a waltz with you but you would not give me the polka."

"Let me pass," she muttered fiercely, for he was barring her the way.

"But I want to dance the polka with you, fair one," he said.

So they stood before the mirror; their panting breath the only sound in the dark room; the candle shining between them and flinging their shadows to the wall. And young Badoy Montiya (who had crept home very drunk to pass out quietly in bed) suddenly found himself cold sober and very much awake and ready for anything. His eyes sparkled and the scar on his face gleamed scarlet.

"Let me pass!" she cried again, in a voice of fury, but he grasped her by the wrist.

"No," he smiled. "Not until we have danced."

"Go to the devil!"

"What a temper has my serrana!"

"I am not your serrana!"

"Whose, then? Someone I know? Someone I have offended grievously? Because you treat me, you treat all my friends like your mortal enemies."

"And why not?" she demanded, jerking her wrist away and flashing her teeth in his face. "Oh, how I detest you, you pompous young men! You go to Europe and you come back elegant lords and we poor girls are too tame to please you. We have no grace like the Parisiennes, we have no fire like the Sevillians, and we have no salt, no salt, no salt! Aie, how you weary me, how you bore me, you fastidious young men!"

"Come, come—how do you know about us?"

"I have heard you talking, I have heard you talking among yourselves, and I despise the pack of you!"

"But clearly you do not despise yourself, señorita. You come to admire your charms in the mirror even in the middle of the night!"

She turned livid and he had a moment of malicious satisfaction.

"I was not admiring myself, sir!"

"You were admiring the moon perhaps?"

"Oh!" she gasped, and burst into tears. The candle dropped from her hand and she covered her face and sobbed piteously. The candle had gone out and they stood in darkness, and young Badoy was conscience-stricken.

"Oh, do not cry, little one! Oh, please forgive me! Please do not cry! But what a brute I am! I was drunk, little one, I was drunk and knew not what I said."

He groped and found her hand and touched it to his lips. She shuddered in her white gown.

"Let me go," she moaned, and tugged feebly.

"No. Say you forgive me first. Say you forgive me, Agueda."

But instead she pulled his hand to her mouth and bit it—bit so sharply into the knuckles that he cried with pain and lashed out with his other hand—lashed out and hit the air, for she was gone, she had fled, and he heard the rustling of her skirts up the stairs as he furiously sucked his bleeding fingers.

Cruel thoughts raced through his head: he would go and tell his mother and make her turn the savage girl out of the house— or he would go himself to the girl's room and drag her out of bed and slap, slap, slap her silly face! But at the same time he was thinking that they were all going up to Antipolo in the morning and was already planning how he would maneuver himself into the same boat with her.

Oh, he would have his revenge, he would make her pay, that little harlot! She should suffer for this, he thought greedily, licking his bleeding knuckles. But—Judas!—what eyes she had! And what a pretty color she turned when angry! He remembered her bare shoulders: gold in the candlelight and delicately furred. He saw the mobile insolence of her neck, and her taut breasts steady in the fluid gown. Son of a Turk, but she was quite enchanting! How could she think she had no fire or grace? And no salt? An arroba she had of it!

> "No lack of salt in the chrism
> At the moment of thy baptism!"

He sang aloud in the dark room and suddenly realized that he had fallen madly in love with her. He ached intensely to see her again—at once!—to touch her hand and her hair; to hear her harsh voice. He ran to the window and flung open the casements and the beauty of the night struck him back like a blow. It was May, it was summer, and he was young—young!—and deliriously in love. Such a happiness welled up within him the tears spurted from his eyes.

But he did not forgive her—no! He would still make her pay, he would still have his revenge, he thought viciously, and kissed his wounded fingers. But what a night it had been! "I will never forget this night!" he thought aloud in an awed voice, standing by the window in the dark room, the tears in his eyes and the wind in his hair and his bleeding knuckles pressed to his mouth.

But, alas, the heart forgets; the heart is distracted; and May-time passes; summer ends; the storms break over the rot-ripe orchards and the heart grows old; while the hours, the days, the months, and the years pile up and pile up, till the mind becomes too crowded, too confused: dust gathers in it; cobwebs multiply; the walls darken and fall into ruin and decay; the memory perishes . . . and there came a time when Don Badoy Montiya walked home through a May Day midnight without remembering, without even caring to remember; being merely concerned in feeling his way across the street with his cane; his eyes having grown quite dim and his legs uncertain—for he was old; he was over sixty; he was a very stooped and shriveled old man with white hair and mustaches, coming home from a secret meeting of conspirators; his mind still resounding with the speeches and his patriot heart still exultant as he picked his way up the steps to the front door and inside into the slumbering darkness of the house; wholly unconscious of the May night, till on his way down the hall, chancing to glance into the sala, he shuddered, he stopped, his blood ran cold—for he had seen a face in the mirror there—a ghostly candlelit face with the eyes closed and the lips moving, a face that he suddenly felt he had seen there before though it was a full minute before the lost memory came flowing, came tiding back, so overflooding the actual moment and so swiftly washing away the piled hours and days and months and years that he was left suddenly young again: he was a gay young buck again, lately come from Europe: he had been dancing all night: he was very drunk: he stopped in the doorway: he saw a face in the dark: he cried out . . . and the lad standing before the mirror (for it was a lad in a night gown) jumped with fright and almost dropped his candle, but looking around and seeing the old man, laughed out with relief and came running.

"Oh, Grandpa, how you frightened me!"

Don Badoy had turned very pale. "So it was you, you young bandit! And what is all this, hey? What are you doing down here at this hour?"

"Nothing, Grandpa. I was only . . . I am only . . ."

"Yes, you are the great Señor Only and how delighted I am to make your acquaintance, Señor Only! But if I break this cane on your head you may wish you were someone else, sir!"

"It was just foolishness, Grandpa. They told me I would see my wife."

"Wife? What wife?"

"Mine. The boys at school said I would see her if I looked in a mirror tonight and said:

> Mirror, mirror,
> show to me
> her whose lover
> I will be."

Don Badoy cackled ruefully. He took the boy by the hair, pulled him along into the room, sat down on a chair, and drew the boy between his knees. "Now, put your candle down on the floor, son, and let us talk this over. So you want your wife already, hey? You want to see her in advance, hey? But do you know that these are wicked games and that wicked boys who play them are in danger of seeing horrors?"

"Well, the boys did warn me I might see a witch instead."

"Exactly! A witch so horrible you may die of fright. And she will bewitch you, she will torture you, she will eat your heart and drink your blood!"

"Oh, come now, Grandpa. This is 1890. There are no witches anymore."

"Oh-ho, my young Voltaire! And what if I tell you that I myself have seen a witch?"

"You? Where?"

"Right in this room and right in that mirror," said the old man, and his playful voice had turned savage.

"When, Grandpa?"

"Not so long ago. When I was a bit older than you. Oh, I was a vain fellow and though I was feeling very sick that night and merely wanted to lie down somewhere and die, I could not pass that doorway of course without stopping to see in the mirror what I looked like when dying. But when I poked my head in what should I see in the mirror but . . . but . . ."

"The witch?"

"Exactly!"

"And did she bewitch you, Grandpa?"

"She bewitched me and she tortured me. She ate my heart and drank my blood," said the old man bitterly.

"Oh, my poor little Grandpa! Why have you never told me! And was she very horrible?"

"Horrible? God, no—she was beautiful! She was the most beautiful creature I have ever seen! Her eyes were somewhat like yours but her hair was like black waters and her golden shoulders were bare. My God, she was enchanting! But I should have known—I should have known even then—the dark and fatal creature she was!"

A silence. Then: "What a horrid mirror this is, Grandpa," whispered the boy.

"What makes you say that, hey?"

"Well, you saw this witch in it. And Mama once told me that Grandma once told her that Grandma once saw the devil in this mirror. Was it of the scare that Grandma died?"

Don Badoy started. For a moment he had forgotten that she was dead, that she had perished—the poor Agueda; that they were at peace at last, the two of them, and her tired body at rest; her broken body set free at last from the brutal pranks of the earth—from the trap of a May night; from the snare of summer;

from the terrible silver nets of the moon. She had been a mere heap of white hair and bones in the end: a whimpering withered consumptive, lashing out with her cruel tongue; her eyes like live coals; her face like ashes . . . Now, nothing!—nothing save a name on a stone; save a stone in a graveyard—nothing! nothing at all! was left of the young girl who had flamed so vividly in a mirror one wild May Day midnight, long, long ago.

And remembering how she had sobbed so piteously; remembering how she had bitten his hand and fled and how he had sung aloud in the dark room and surprised his heart in the instant of falling in love: such a grief tore up his throat and eyes that he felt ashamed before the boy; pushed the boy away; stood up and fumbled his way to the window; threw open the casements and looked out—looked out upon the medieval shadows of the foul street where a couple of street lamps flickered and a last carriage was rattling away upon the cobbles, while the blind black houses muttered hush-hush, their tiled roofs looming like sinister chessboards against a wild sky murky with clouds, save where an evil old moon prowled about in a corner or where a murderous wind whirled, whistling and whining, smelling now of the sea and now of the summer orchards and wafting unbearable Maytime memories of an old, old love to the old man shaking with sobs by the window; the bowed old man sobbing so bitterly at the window; the tears streaming down his cheeks and the wind in his hair and one hand pressed to his mouth while from up the street came the clackety-clack of the watchman's boots on the cobbles, and the clang-clang of his lantern against his knee, and the mighty roll of his great voice booming through the night: *"Guardia sereno-o-o! A las doce han dado-o-o!"*

THE WOMAN WHO HAD TWO NAVELS

When she told him she had two navels he believed her at once: she seemed so urgently, so desperately serious—and besides, what would be the point in telling a lie like that, he asked himself, while she asked him if he could help her, if he could arrange "something surgical"—an operation. . . .

"But I'm only a horse doctor," he apologized: to which she scathingly retorted that, well, if he could fix up horses—And she cried that it was urgent: her whole life depended on it.

He inquired how old she was and noted—while she replied that she was thirty—how her eyes turned cagey for the first time since she came into the room. He wondered, putting on his spectacles, if she might be knocking off a few years, but could not tell, for the stylized face with the black hat pulled low over it recorded no time in years, only in hours.

"But does my age matter?" she asked, turning coy.

"And are you married?" he primly pursued.

She nodded and, slipping off a glove, displayed her left hand, the thread of metal round the third finger not more polished than the flesh it bound.

"—with children?"

"No." Again she sounded cautious. "But I've not been married long," she quickly added; and more quickly still, defiantly, "The truth is," she rapped out, "I was married only this morning."

His face went blank, and she began to tell him about her life.

"When I was a little girl I thought everybody else had two navels. . . . Oh, *you* smile—you've never had to face a fact that was yours only, not general data. You were a nice boy—weren't you, doctor?—and lovingly sheltered. I can see that. You've always lived in the world where people have the right number of navels. But I shared—or thought I shared—that world only when I was very little. . . . I was the Eve of the apple at five years old: that was when I found out.

"I was walking with my doll one hot day in our garden and we came to a pond with goldfish in it. I decided that Minnie— Minnie was my doll—that she wanted a wash. So we sat down by the pond and I discovered that she had only one navel. I felt so sorry I cried, rocking her naked little body in my arms, try- ing to comfort her, and promising not to throw her away like the others. And then I became thoughtful. The day was grow- ing dark all around me, it was going to rain. But whom was I sorry for? Which of us was wrong? I sat very still by that pond, my tears flowing and the raindrops starting to fall. I carefully examined Minnie again and when I found that she had other parts missing I grew calmer—but I had grown crafty too. Nobody must know that I suspected. Poor Minnie would have to be sacrificed because I had torn her clothes off and could not put them back again. I hardly noticed the thunderstorm as I hunted around for a string and a big stone. I tied the stone to Minnie, kissed her for the last time, and dropped her into the pond. I threw in my bracelet too. Then I ran home soaking wet and told the grownups that a thief had grabbed me and had stolen my bracelet and doll. They didn't believe me of course— there are always armed guards planted all over our house: if you pushed a chair you bruised a detective—but everybody pretended to believe; nothing happened to me; except, that night, in my dreams, the goldfish ate up poor Minnie, and I was there in the pond, watching, and was not sorry. After that was like Eve after the apple. I was very careful about keeping myself well covered up especially when there were other chil- dren around being careless. I found out about them, they never found out about me."

"How about your family?" he asked.

She said she was an only child. "Mother knows, of course. I don't know about father. When mother or the maids gave me a bath they put on such matter-of-fact faces I was often tempted to point at myself and giggle. I knew that they knew that *I* knew, but we all pretended that I didn't and that *they* didn't. The setup was perfect for blackmail: I never had to threaten them aloud. If you beget a monster of a child it could prove you were rather monstrous yourself. I did what I pleased and was never punished. Can you imagine what kind of a childhood it was? If it was a childhood at all. . . ."

But once past the teens—"when you know how just one pimple can be such a torment: so think what I went through"—she had become indifferent. She had realized it was silly to squander thought and tears on so trivial an oddity; she stopped worrying. "My one big scare was when it became stylish to bare the midriff. Imagine! *They* would have been like pigs' eyes peering out. . . ." But she had taken ill and stayed in bed until the style staled. She had fallen in love with several boys who wanted to marry her but she had always drawn back: she dreaded a husband's eyes on her secret. "He might be horrified—I could never have stood that—or he might say I had cheated." So she had put off and put off marrying—until, suddenly, she was thirty, and she turned frantic.

"I could see myself getting older, painting myself thicker—a regular hard-boiled veteran, up to my neck in clubs and charities—having affairs with younger and ever younger men and sneaking off on 'combined-business-and-pleasure' trips abroad. . . . Ugh! That sort of freelancing may be slick but it's not everybody's bowl of rice. So I swept a most eligible man off his feet—and married him, this morning."

It was quite a wedding, the way she described it. She assured him it would be in all the papers—"and not on the society page either. On the *front* page."

"Are your people important?" he asked.

"Father's one of the sacred elders in the government, mother's a famous beauty, and my husband has four or five generations of sugar money behind him. But that's not why. About the front page, I mean. 'Bride of the Season Marches Off the Scene Too Soon.' '. . . *Running up the stairs in her charming Paris gown, the bride then laughingly hurled the bouquet at her husband's face, to the astonishment of a cosmopolitan crowd.* . . .'"

"Did you?" he asked uneasily, and she laughed at him.

"No—of course not. We were having a very noisy breakfast at my house afterward, with all those cosmopolitan people, and he looked at me and I looked at him and he said shouldn't we run over to his apartment and start packing because we were going off on an American honeymoon. I hadn't slept for nights worrying over that moment. I thought: he'll uncover and discover and everything will be over. And I remembered the little girl crying by the pond and Minnie naked and all the world suddenly dark. . . . But I smiled bravely and said yes to him, only I would have to run up and change first. So I ran up and changed and slipped down the backway and into a taxi and off to the airport where I took a plane. And here I am."

"Here" was Hong Kong, in midwinter, on Kowloon side.

And why *here?* wondered Pepe Monson, removing bewildered eyes from her face and looking rather dazedly around the room; feeling the room's furniture hovering vaguely—the faded rug on the floor; the sofa near the doorway, against the wall; the two small Filipino flags crossed under a picture of General Aguinaldo; the bust of the Sacred Heart upon the bookshelf, between brass candlesticks; the tamaraw head above each of the two shut windows . . .

Fog bulged against the windowpanes, as though elephants were wedging past. Hawkers, four stories below, sounded miles away—or whispering halfheartedly. Pepe Monson was grateful for the elephants and hushed hawkers but would have preferred the usual view at the window—of the harbor, gay with junks and ferry-boats; of the downtown buildings standing up in white ranks across the water, in the noon sun, the island's rock delicately ostentatious behind them, with toylike houses necklacing the various peaks or stacked like steps up the slopes or snuggling into private shelves and niches down the sides. But there was a fog and no view, and the lights were on in the cold room, but the cold was only a mist her mouth made to the woman sitting before his desk, insulated in black furs to her ears, her hat's brim cutting an angle of shadow across her face, and pearls gleaming at her throat when she leaned forward.

"But what on earth made you come here to me?" he asked. "Had you heard about me?"

"—from Kikay Valero. She said you did a wonderful job on her horse. So I thought I would look you up. Besides, you're a fellow-countryman. You are, aren't you?"

"My father is a Filipino, and so was my mother. I suppose I am too, though I was born over here and have never been over there."

"Did you never want to go?"

"Oh, most awfully. I wanted to study there but my father wouldn't let me. I went to England instead—and then to the Argentine, for the cattle stuff."

He understood her careless glance around the room. When she caught his eye, she flushed and he smiled.

"At home," she hurried to explain, "you would have an office that showed you had been abroad."

"Maybe I will, when I go there."

"Why wouldn't your father let you?"

"He was in the revolution against Spain and in the resistance against the Americans, and when both uprisings failed he came and settled here and swore not to go home, neither himself nor his sons, until it was a free country again."

"Well, it is now."

"And he did go back, last year. But he didn't stay long. Now we're trying to persuade him to make another visit."

"But why wouldn't he stay? Was he frightened?"

She had leaned forward and the pearls gleamed.

Her face blurred before him as, growing sad, he thought of his father in the next room, sitting in an armchair, a shawl around his shoulders and his feet propped up on a stool and no hope at all in the quiet eyes fixedly staring ahead. . . .

The girl's eyes were fixedly staring ahead too, and he drew back—though there was all the table between them—rather alarmed by the intensity of her regard and having fleetingly felt how odd that there should be in this room with him, making its furniture hover; that there should be seated before his desk, making its papers uneasy—in black furs and a black hat, with gray gloves on her hands and pearls at her throat—a woman who had two navels. But her eyes stopped short of him; the pause was hers alone; she had forgotten her question and was not awaiting the answer that he (the room having organized itself again around his old desk) was about to speak when she suddenly shivered and came to.

Sitting up and blinking away the tears while she fetched out her cigarette case, she remarked that her mother was in Hong Kong, too.

"Oh, does she live here?"

"No—just over on business."

The señora de Vidal said: "But she's not thirty, she is only eighteen—and she's been married almost a year now, not just this morning. And I'm quite, *quite* sure she has only one navel. . . ."

She paused—to bite off an involuntary smile; then begged him please to continue.

Pepe Monson disconsolately cleared his throat.

The señora was in furs too; she was belted up in a white fur jacket and wore a polka-dotted scarf round her neck and gold coins on her ears. She was smaller than her daughter, more neatly a piece—as though scissored entire from a style page and managed to look relaxed although vexed. She had refused the seat by the table—remained standing at the window, watching the ferry-boats (it was later in the afternoon and the fog had lifted) while she listened to his account of her daughter's visit that noon. The account, as he went on with it, began to sound more and more weird to him—and to her too, evidently, in spite of her vexation. She kept biting off smiles; kept glancing at him round the corner of an eye. Undoubtedly, she was laughing at him for having been taken in so easily and probably supposed him to have been charmed out of his wits. Actually, she was laughing because this pompous, pompous (and rather shabby) young man tickled her nostalgic bone. His bespectacled scrutiny reduced her to child size: repaired her skin; returned her into a schoolgirl's frock; and restored her old pigtails. . . .

Guessing only the laughter, he privately fumed. Quick to smell the weather, she was instantly all formality. She deplored the mis-use of his time but promised to see to it that a proper fee—

"But do you usually let your daughter run around telling indecent lies like that?" he cut in coldly.

"*I* don't let her run around, I'm not her husband—"

She stopped short, aware that she had almost snapped.

The pause snottily informed them that, childishly, they were venting their vexation with her daughter at each other. They both suddenly laughed—then smiled at each other for having laughed. He moved away from the door to share the window with her, while, with the plaintive intonations now of an old acquaintance, she continued:

"I've had cables from the poor Macho—Macho's her hus-band, Macho Escovar—and he tells me there's nothing at all the matter between them. Connie simply wandered away. He thought she might have joined me here but I never knew Con-nie was here until I ran across Kikay Valero and Kikay told me Connie had been hunting up your number. Did she say where she was staying?"

"She said she had just arrived. We arranged to meet in town this afternoon. I was taking her to consult a friend of mine."

"Then, would you please tell her—"

"But, of course, I don't mean to go anymore."

"No—of course not."

"I'm sorry."

She hung fire a moment. Then, turning around from the win-dow, swinging her gold coins, and tipping her face up to his male height, she radiantly announced that she knew his father.

He registered astonished pleasure.

His father's family (she continued) and her family were old friends. "And when I was in school your father was the school's physician. I remember that the older girls were quite in love with him and kept praying for fevers. He was such a handsome, a magnificent gentleman. Your father's family had a famous house in Binondo—Binondo's one of the oldest parts of Manila, the most labyrinthine—and your house was famous because our great men loved to assemble there—to talk, to dance, to quarrel, to plot revolutions. Mother took me there a few times.

I was just a child in pigtails and my eyes popped out with bash-fulness. . . ."

She was seeing—as she radiantly rattled away, her eyes never leaving his face, her gold coins dancing—the carriages filing down the cobbled street and pausing to let people out at the open doorway that had a great globe of light shining above it. Stepping out of their carriage, she had lifted her eyes to the balconies at the upper-story windows. Behind the curtains chandeliers blazed, fiddles were busy, and shadows of people came and went, gesticulating. Up there on the tiled roof that rose black and white in the moonlight but would glow red at noon she had seen pigeons roosting. "Make haste, girl," said her mother, standing under the globe of light. "Come, jump," said her father, holding out his arms. Walking up the stairs between her parents she had kept turning her face right and left to watch the sea-shells marching up in twos. . . . It was a courteous cordial house—an old, old house even then, and this last war had finally destroyed it, along with all the dear labyrinth of Binondo.

She said: "It's not there anymore—your father's house. . . ."

He nodded: they had heard it was gone. And because he had begun to like her: "It was waiting for us to come home," he added, and felt his father's bony fingers on his hair; saw his father on the beach, seated on the sand, and booming: *The house of our fathers is waiting for us to come home!*"

When his mother was still alive and they lived out Stanley way, they went swimming during the summers, the four of them that were all the family, to Deep Water Bay. He and his younger brother Tony wore trunks but their father wore an old pair of trousers and his pajama jacket while their mother wore a straw hat and sat on the sand and knitted. She did not at all care for salt water but was the most eager for these afternoons at the beach because the water always started his father talking about "home" and talking about home always relaxed his father who tended to brood. There was always a fleet of junks along the shore and the bathers were mostly dowdy family groups like their own: English, Chinese, Portuguese—Deep Water, in spite of its elegant white sand, is not fashionable; its currents and changing levels are too dangerous—but he and

Tony and their father could race each other all the way to an island across the bay that was an hour's fast swim going and coming back, although coming back they would feel so exhausted they could only crawl up the warm white sand to where his mother sat knitting beside the lunch basket and a rubber tire she always took along just in case she felt like a dip. While she handed the sandwiches around his father would tell them about the waters back home he had swum in when a boy. But what he most loved to talk about was the river that ran right behind their house in Binondo.

He would describe how their house in Binondo had a large stone azotea behind, with steps going right down to the water, and how you could go out on that azotea and buy everything you needed—rice, fish, honey, eggs, live poultry, feed for the horses, fruits and vegetables—from villagers rowing into town in small boats that looked something like American Indian canoes. The villagers' voices were what woke you up in the morning and his father would jump up from bed and run to the window and it would be just light enough to see the small boat down there on the river and the two people it carried: the husband sitting behind and rowing; the wife standing up in front, facing the river, her hands on her hips, and her body turning this way and that as, very clearly, very solemnly, her melodious voice lingering on each syllable, she described her wares to the sleeping houses. His father would snatch a towel and run down to the azotea. On other azoteas, on both sides of the river, other boys would be stripping for an early dip and hallooing at each other. The water was never very clean—"but that never stopped us," said his father, seated on the sand, eating a sandwich; and with one of his rare smiles he would add: "And I hope that a few dead pigs or dogs floating around will not stop you boys from enjoying that river when we go home."

Sprawled on their bellies on the white sand, at their parents' feet, he and Tony would ask: "But when are we going home, Papa? When are we going to see our own land?" And if his father was in a good mood he would smile and groan: "Only God knows. We must move Him with our silence. *Quomodo cantabo canticum Domini in terra aliena?*" But if troubled in spirit, a mild sarcasm would strain the fine skin tighter against the sharp bones of his face as he replied drily: "Soon, perhaps. The news is getting better and better." And his mother would quickly become very inquisitive about the house in Binondo: were its floors of good wood? how many bedrooms did it have? could the cousins be trusted to take good care of it until *they* came home?

She had never seen the house herself; she was much younger than his father—a ship captain's daughter whom he had met and married here in Hong Kong when he had begun to realize that the exile he had imposed on himself and had at first so confidently supposed would last only a couple of years might actually last all his lifetime. He had married desiring sons; quietly resolved that he should at least go home in the persons of his sons if—which God forbid!—it were his fortune to go home only as the dead bones and ashes that they, his sons, would carry back with them, to be buried in their own land, when it should at last be the free land for which, when a young man, he had fought so long and so bitterly.

Seated on the foreign sands of a foreign shore, beside a young wife, his two sons sprawled on their bellies at his feet, he had boomed, placing a hand on the head of each boy:

"The house of our fathers is waiting for us to come home!"

And as, awed, they stared at him he had lifted his eyes from their faces to the horizon and murmured:

"*Si tui oblivero, Jerusalem. . . .*"

But, now, a war had come and destroyed the house. It was waiting no longer. They might still go back, they could never go home now, thought Pepe Monson, more vividly remembering that house he had never seen (as he remarked to the woman standing beside him at the window) than any of the houses he had actually lived in.

"When my father was over there last year," he said, "he went to see what was left of it. There wasn't much—a piece of wall, a piece of the azotea—but the main stairway, which was all of stone, was quite intact; had even kept most of its balustrade. My father said it looked very sad: a stairway in a field of ruin, going up to nowhere. . . ."

But she saw it going up to the chandeliers and the noise of talk and fiddles.

"Whenever I see that broken stairway I feel your father waiting," she said, smiling, and saw *him* standing at the top of the stairs, a fierce young man with whiskers, with a guitar strapped round a shoulder, bowing over her mother's hand, whispering a word in her father's ear, crouching down to greet her, a shy child in pigtails, taking her hands in his and asking was she friend or foe. He had led her to the dining room and had fed her grapes and ice-cream while they discussed the hardships of school life.

Before that year had ended he was in the field with Aguinaldo, and the gay armies of the Republic were advancing in triumph through the provinces. A few more years, and he and his general were pale fugitives, fleeing up rivers, through jungles, over mountains; the Yanqui soldiery hot on their heels. But he had resisted to the end—he and so many other splendid young men—resisting with the spirit when, bound and jailed, they could no longer resist with arms. Their general might submit; their general might take the oath of allegiance; their general might call on all the still embattled caudillos to come out and surrender—but these hardheaded young men flung at the Yanquis their gesture of spiritual resistance, preferring exile to submission. A foolish gesture, perhaps, and a futile one—but a beautiful, beautiful gesture nevertheless—and during those days that saw the failure of the Revolution and the establishment of new masters; when her father went about tight-lipped and stern-eyed, and her mother wept continually and put on black, and wailing people peeping through cracks in shut windows beheld what was left of their armies being led into prison camps by the Yanquis; all through those bleak black days that were the early springtime of her girlhood, the proud gesture of all those hardheaded young men had burst upon the deep gloom like holiday fireworks. People began to wear their grief with a smile, their defeat with a fine air. The conquering Yanguis might jeer at the quaint architecture, the primitive plumbing, the ceremonious manners; behind impassive faces, people shared a secret pride, a secret exultation, and a lengthening litany of names.

She remembered the night the news came that Doctor Monson too, though wounded and gravely ill, had chosen exile. She remembered her father standing up very straight, her mother kneeling, as though the Sacrament were passing by, and how she herself, a mere child, had understood what they saluted. She had fled to her room and had wept behind the locked door for the magnificent young man with fierce whiskers who had fed her grapes and ice-cream and had so deeply sympathized with her difficulties in arithmetic. . . .

"How I would love to see your father again!" she exclaimed. She had learned, as a child, the feel of greatness. She would always see her childhood as a page in an epic, brilliant with tears and splendid with heroes.

"I'm sure he would be delighted to see you, too," said Pepe Monson. "Unfortunately," he added, lowering his eyes, "he's having a nap just now," and frowned, for it was more than a nap his father was having. When he went to call his father to tiffin that noon he had found the old man slumped forward in his chair, unconscious, although his eyes were open and his mouth smiled. The third time this year that sort of thing had happened. . . . He had still to find out where his father got the drugs—from the Chinese house-boy possibly, and this would make the third house-boy he had discharged this year—but he thought the stuff more probably a left-over from previous medical supplies that his father had hidden around somewhere, although they, he and Tony, had repeatedly ransacked the cabinets in vain.

"Of course he hardly knows me," said the señora, "but he would remember my parents."

The honest vehemence of the memory was fast ebbing from her face; had laid waste its delicate style. She looked old, and so tired that he again suggested sitting down. Side by side on the sofa they discussed his father and her daughter.

"When I was a little girl people like your father were my conscience walking around in elegant clothes. . . ."

—*When I was a little girl I thought everybody else had two navels,* said a second voice in his ear while the first voice went on:

"They were a reference, a dictionary that I always had open before me. I could never doubt how a word like 'virtue' for instance was spelled. I might spell it with a 'b' because I wanted to, or without the 'e' because I thought it superfluous—but if I did I knew very well what I was doing and that it was wrong. I had no excuse. But young people now, like my poor Connie—"

"They have an excuse?" he suggested when she paused.

"Where's the dictionary they're to believe in?"

"How about the old ones?"

"And on whose authority—mine? Oh, I should have been to poor Connie what people like your father were to me. . . . You think she's mad, don't you?"

'"Don't you think she might be sick?"

"Not more than everybody else."

"—or unhappy."

"Well, yes. She so wants to play the reckless sophisticate, but she has a conscience, poor girl, and it keeps her from doing the right things."

'"Still, she did marry rather young."

"Oh, she didn't do *that*. I did it for her. I had to."

And dropping her voice as she leaned intimately closer she began to explain why.

"Her father's in the government, you know, and when Connie was still in school there were some stupid charges against him—bribery, and using up the public funds, and having his daughter on the government payroll although she was just a schoolgirl who had never been inside an office. It was all just envious talk, of course, and soon blew over: you know how politicians love to play pranks on each other, they're such rogues. I never paid the matter any attention myself in spite of all the usual fuss the newspapers made. But the more sensational ones had carried Connie's picture as the girl who was gypping the public of its money so she could study in an expensive exclusive private school—just their usual brutal vulgarity, you can see—but poor Connie seems to have been upset. She suddenly turned up at home looking haunted.

"I was at my dressing table, I remember, having my nails manicured in a hurry—I was going out somewhere and I was late—and of course I felt a bit annoyed as well as surprised when

Connie popped up in the room. She was a boarder in that school and came home only on Sundays, but it wasn't a Sunday, and it was after dark too. But Connie would explain nothing with the maid in the room. To humor her, I sent the maid away; but to keep everything casual, I went right on doing my face while the girl raved. She said she had run away from school and didn't ever want to go back—that she absolutely refused to be educated on 'stolen money.' *Imagine.* I nearly swallowed my lipstick. I turned around on the stool to look at her: she was in that dreadful uniform of theirs, with clamps on her teeth and her hair sticking damply down her neck like an old mop. For a moment I was tempted to laugh at the little goose. But I made her sit down, and talked it over very solemnly with her, although I knew I was going to be ages late to wherever it was I was going.

"I told her that people who had our advantages must expect to be envied and reviled by people who were not so fortunate; and that there were many things grown-ups did which couldn't properly be judged by young people until the young people were grown-ups themselves; and that moreover it *wasn't* 'stolen money.' Do you know what she said? She said no, it wasn't stolen money, it was 'blood sucked from the people.' She had picked up all those frightful phrases from the newspapers of course but she insisted that they were insults the girls at school flung in her face. I immediately made inquiries—it's a very careful school—and I found that Connie was lying. Nobody had said anything. Most of the girls there are daughters of politicians too and are so used to hearing nasty things said of their fathers and mothers they don't think it's anything unusual, or to be ashamed of. So I told Connie she must learn their spirit, and packed her back.

"She went off—but not to school—simply disappeared. For a week we had the police looking for her. They finally found her, working as dishwasher in a chopsuey joint in the Chinese quarter. I had to go and fetch her myself, she wouldn't let the police touch her, she kept denying her name and actually seemed to have forgotten who she was, until she saw me. I don't think I have experienced anything so sordid in my life. The Chinese were screaming all over the place: they had heard what an important man my husband is and the panic had spread through the neighborhood. When I arrived the police had to club at the crowds to let my car pass through and when I stepped out at the chopsuey joint the Chinese who owned it came rushing out and began whining and groveling at my feet. They looked awful: the police had been beating them up and their heads were bloody. I was taken to the kitchen, and there sat my poor Connie, on a stool, in the center of the room, with the entire police department massed around her.

"She was wearing a repulsive dress that she had bought at some market and she had painted her face and had had her hair cut. I was raging with fury, you can imagine, but I couldn't help feeling sorry for the poor thing and I was afraid she might make a scene. *I* never make scenes. But the moment she saw me approaching she got up from the stool and hid her face in her hands. I told her she had been very naughty and should be grateful to all those nice policemen and I made her say thank you to them. Then I looked at my watch and said we must be going because it was lunchtime and I smiled around at everybody while Connie followed me out to the car. On the way home I said nothing and she said nothing. I had not kissed her nor taken her hand; I wouldn't touch her; I wanted her to feel my fury—but she seemed to feel nothing, sitting there with her hands folded on her lap and her painted face a blank and that repulsive dress making her look like a cheap taxi-dancer on a dull night.

"Neither her father nor I had ever punished her before but when we got home I made her father give her a good old-fashioned spanking. I was dreadfully frightened: she might have fallen into worse hands. I resolved to marry her off, after a long trip abroad. She still refused to return to school anyway and seemed willing enough to be married."

"Is her husband her age?" asked Pepe Monson.

"He's thirty—but a very young thirty."

"And she's happy with him?"

"She *was* happy with him."

"Oh."

"There's a bandleader here—Texaco or something."

"Paco Texeira?"

"Do you know him?"

"He's a Hong Kong boy. We were in grade-school together."

"Well, he was playing recently in Manila and Connie became very infatuated with him. If she's here now it's to chase him some more. . . ."

Her vexation had revived and she did not care who saw it. As she launched into a spirited account of her daughter's affair with the bandleader, Pepe vainly sought amidst the cold glitter of white furs and barbaric earrings the sentimental old woman he had almost begun to like.

When he protested: "But Paco's married—" she leaned away and her amused eyes considered him ironically, her gold coins swinging.

He thought of Mary Texeira, who was tall and brown-haired: a great walker and mountain climber; an expert water-colorist (she organized outdoor classes in drawing during the summers); and the devoted mother of three. Dear good Mary might have no chic but he could not imagine her just fading away beside women like the señora de Vidal and her daughter. He could not, in fact, imagine Mary beside those women at all; it seemed so improper his cheeks burned.

Smiling, the señora averted polite eyes from his blush. She said, "It's all very shocking, isn't it?" She added that she was glad some people still took marriage seriously. . . .

Still thinking of the Texeiras, he saw the clean table of their marriage being approached at the edges by ominous furs, pearls, and gold coins—as though a rustic altar were drawing pilgrimages. And what with pilgrims dropping in all day—the señora now, her daughter this morning—he had begun to feel like a wayside inn himself.

"I've had them pointed out to me," said Mary Texeira, "and, yes, they're both equally stunning. You'd think they were sisters if they ever appeared together. But it's the mother that's the real beauty—dead-white skin and dead-black hair and a glitter of ornaments—like one of those jeweled madonnas in Spanish churches. How could you ever have liked the daughter better, Pepe? Oh, I grant you she's more in the current idiom—but she looks rather cruel, don't you think? Although I hear there's no choosing between the pair of them. They're jewel thieves, people here say, or gem smugglers perhaps. I've asked Paco if it's true but he won't talk about them although he saw quite a lot of them when he was over in Manila and they've been writing him *such* letters. . . . Don't gape at me, Pepe. Paco himself gave me those letters to read. I didn't want to, but he insisted. You did, darling, didn't you?"

"I wish you'd shut up, Mary, and let Pepe drink his tea in peace."

"Am I being a bore, Pepe?"

"Absolutely not. I'm all agog."

"There, you see. Pepe's my own buddy boy and his mamma's going to cut him more cake. Which reminds me—Paco, will you see if the babies have finished their tea?"

"We'd be hearing them if they had. How's your father, Pepe?"

"Not any better. Tony thinks we ought to put him in a nursing home, but I feel rather sorry for the old man. He's been quietly going to pieces since he came back from that trip to Manila. I wish to God he'd never gone at all but it was the great dream of his life. . . . No, Mary—no more tea, thanks."

"Here, have a cigarette. It's just a Chinese brand, alas. We're very, very poor right now. That's why Paco had to go and work in Manila—and I wish to God he'd never gone either—"

"Do shut up, Mary."

"—and what did he get for it anyway? Just a Boris Karloff look in the eye. I don't mind doing my own cleaning and cooking besides looking after the babies; I don't mind this sardine can of an apartment—it's cute, Pepe, isn't it? Just pretend you don't feel my wash dripping over our heads—and we're grateful to have a place like this with housing what it currently is in Hong Kong even if we do have to climb up those four filthy flights of stairs very carefully because they're liable to break down any moment now. . . . Are you and your father still in that poky apartment on the waterfront?"

"Alas, yes. The stairs are just as dark and filthy: the rent's a king's ransom."

"But you were planning to move to Manila—"

"That was the idea when father went there last year. He was going to arrange about having our house there rebuilt, and I was to follow. But since he came back there's been no more talk of moving."

"How you and Tony used to lord it over us when we were kids because of that going home stuff—"

"We were brought up on the dream."

"Your poor father, Pepe—"

"I suppose he had to wake up sometime."

"Do you know—I've begun to wonder a lot what it's like in Manila. We all of us more or less belong over there, but only Paco here—and your father, Pepe—have gone back—and see what it did to them. . . . But when I went to see the lovely señora de Vidal she assured me it's quite a nice little place really— much warmer, of course, and rather dusty. . . . Why are you giving me that Karloff look again, Paco? Oh, you *didn't* know I'd been to see your señora de Vidal? Goodness, hasn't she told you yet? I was sure she'd let you know first thing—"

"Oh, *damn* it all!" gasped Paco, leaping so suddenly from the piano stool he bumped his head against the lines of washing strung across the cramped room, snapping them. He kicked aside the damp clothes fallen on the floor as he walked to the window, where he stood and trembled, his back to the room, his fists thrust into his pockets. He was lean and hard-bodied, with very black curly hair and a sharp swart profile; like Mary—who sat at the tea table, crumbling a biscuit into a cup—he was part Portuguese, part Filipino.

Hunched over the other side of the table, sadly knocking ash off his cigarette into a saucer, Pepe Monson noted again how like brother and sister the Texeiras looked (especially as they were at the moment wearing identical dark blue turtleneck sweaters)—like the stock twins of Italian romances, he was telling himself, when the dark twin faced around from the window and asked quietly:

"When did you go, Mary?"

"Monday afternoon," she demurely replied, not lifting her head, her soft brown hair swaying down her cheeks.

"And why didn't you tell me?"

"If we still told each other everything I wouldn't have gone at all. But we've started to hide, we've started to lie—so how could I tell you? I just went."

"But why, Mary—why?"

She looked up quickly and her dark eyes flashed.

"Because I was worried, because I was frightened. You've been so strange since you came back. And then those letters—Do you know, Pepe: he's hardly left the house since he arrived. He takes a very early morning walk and then shuts himself up in here, all day. You'd think he was a wanted man—"

"Use your head, Mary—use your head! If I haven't wanted to leave the house much, can't you see it's because I don't want to run into those women?"

"Well, why not? Have you been raping them? *both* of them?"

"You went to see them—or *her* anyway. Why didn't you ask?"

Her tense face altering: "We didn't talk about you," she announced haughtily.

"And what the devil did you talk about—nylons?"

"No—about my watercolors."

The two men burst out laughing, and Paco, as he shook with laughter, propped his elbows on the windowsill and slowly slid down until he was sitting on the floor. "Mary, you're *wonderful!*" he cried. "So you marched up there to ask that woman if I'd been raping her and she got you to talking about your watercolors instead—"

"Well, yes. She asked me what I did and seemed so interested when I told her that before I realized what was happening we were on our way to Rita's curio store so she could have a look at my stuff. And, Paco, she bought two pieces: the one of Yaumati Ferry in the noon rush, and my pink and brown study of a Chinese funeral. She wants me to do her a tint of Our Lady appearing to the children in Fatima—for her bedroom, she says . . . Oh, stop sniggering, Pepe, or I'll smash this pot on your head!"

"Oh, Mary, *don't!* I'm not laughing at you, honest—the joke's on me. What an absolute fool that woman made of me this afternoon! I sat there and let her pull and pull at my heartstrings—and she was only pulling my leg. And the way she talked about you,

Paco, I'd never have thought you knew her well enough to rape her. I gathered, in fact, that she didn't know you at all."

"Did she say so?"

"She couldn't even remember your name right."

"The *bitch*."

"But she doesn't look it," argued Mary with some warmth. "Even your cautious Rita, Pepe, was dazzled by her. She's every inch the great lady. Monday afternoon, she was wearing a Chinese dress of black wool, slit at the knee, with a stiff collar and a golden dragon prancing up in front, but her jewels were authentic Javanese. She had been reading about the apparitions in Fatima and was carrying the book clasped to her breast, one finger stuck inside the pages to keep the place, and while we talked she seemed rather moody and kept getting up and sitting down again and referring to the book until finally nothing would do but she must read me out some passages that she said she didn't understand. But what I heard in her voice was herself trying not to understand and denying that she understood and I felt really drawn to her, really sorry for her, and would have liked to rock her in my arms though I had on a shabby coat and my old beret, because her mild manner makes you forget what both of you are wearing—until afterward, and then you gasp. She's a very small woman really—but what a vitality. How old is she—forty? fifty? You don't notice her smallness, you're not conscious of her age. I didn't feel young or huge or shabby beside her—just my basic self. And I'm surprised you didn't notice it, Pepe, but she's deeply devout."

"—because she dresses up in dragons and pagan jewels to meditate on the Virgin?"

"—because she meditates, in spite of the dragons and the jewelry."

"I thought you were jealous of her, Mary."

"Oh, nonsense," she laughed, coloring a little. "Paco understands."

"Of course I do, darling," said Paco gravely, pushing himself up from the floor.

"—that I was frantic?"

"I'd feel worried if you weren't."

"And you haven't *actually* been raping anybody, have you, dear?"

"Well, not all the way. . . ."

"I'm sorry I was frantic."

"I'm sorry about your wash, Mary."

"Here, don't bother. I'll pick them up myself—" And she jumped up to help him.

"Oh. Let's just leave the whole damned mess," he cried, "and go take the children out to the park, shall we?"

"The sun won't last much longer."

"We've got, uh, about an hour—or should I junk this watch. Coming along, Pepe old boy?"

"If I don't make a crowd," said Pepe, twisting around to grin at them, stooped head to head behind his chair, their arms loaded with the wash.

"He must enjoy watching the sexes fight," said Mary.

"I'll go get your beret and our babies," said Paco.

When Paco Texeira took his band to Manila they had a contract to play at two night clubs there on alternate weeks for a minimum six months. His band, which was called "Tex's Tune Technicians," had been organized during the war and had done brisk business in occupation Hong Kong because, with the many cabarets that were still operating unable to import their musicians any longer from Manila, Paco's band, composed mostly of stranded Filipinos, was the freshest wartime Hong Kong could have of American jazz handled the Filipino way. The Tune Technicians were really expert technically and kept turning up, throughout those three years of the gnawed root and the rationed gruel, with witty variations of very tired prewar tunes—but their value was chiefly nostalgic; when the war was over and Manila orchestras resumed their monopoly of the orient's nightspots all the way from Calcutta to Canton and from Shanghai down to Surabaya, Paco found it harder to get prestigious engagements for his band, even in the restaurant and cabaret boom of postwar Hong Kong. He had been given the Manila contract because the two night clubs they were to play at were being opened by a Chinese millionaire (with Filipino fronts) who wanted to cash in on the swelling tourist trade in Manila by giving its night club set two places—the "Manila-Hong Kong" and the "Boulevard Shanghai"—which would be reminiscent of nightlife in those cities; and who therefore wanted dancebands fresh from Hong Kong and Shanghai to accentuate an atmosphere to be created by Chinese prints, lanterns, and mirrors on the walls, Chinese cigarette girls on the aisles, White Russian hostesses on the dance floor, and armed Bombay bouncers under the tables.

Paco, since late adolescence, had spent most of his nights listening to Manila stations on the short wave (to the great discomfort first of his mother and later of his wife, since Paco used an amplifier; although they had learned never to complain, because he was a fretful listener) and he could name all the major Manila orchestras of the last ten years; describe their present and past styles, and the intervening evolution; and could even remember the different night clubs they had played for and at what stage of their careers—but their music existed by itself in his mind and had no scenery behind it and few faces in front. The faces were of the bandleaders who had at one time or another played in Hong Kong and whom he had tried to congratulate for their ingenious re-creations of American jazz until he found that the bandleaders were quite unconscious of re-creating American jazz, of translating it for the oriental, which was what his ears told him they were doing but which they resentfully denied, preferring to consider themselves faithful approximations of their chosen American maestros. The general belief indeed that Filipinos alone in all the orient had an ear for American rhythms and could reproduce them with the least spiritual damage accounted for their monopoly of the orient's bandstands but did not explain how American rhythms had been made sufficiently comprehensible in the first place (even granting the effects of the movies as cultural bulldozers) to be understood by the Hindu, the Chinese, and the Malay, unless it could be proved—and Paco thought it quite obvious, merely natural, certainly inevitable, and all to the good—that even in Filipino hands and even when those hands were being most deliberately groovy (not using that term in its swing language sense, of course), the indigenous music of the modern world did suffer a sea-change—a sea-change that might make American aficionados wince but gave to their too fearfully Jules Vernish rhythms a homely bamboo murmurousness instantly recognizable to the Hindu, the Chinese, and the Malay; the Filipinos being in this department (as well as in a number of others) the agents between East and West, building the Harlem gods a bamboo habitation this side of the Pacific.

In spite of his obsession with Filipino jazz, however, and in spite moreover of his Filipino blood, Paco had never felt any curiosity about nor the least affection for the country of his musician father; and when he went to Manila, was stirred by no sentiments of filial piety. Unlike the Monson boys, who were always conscious of being Filipinos, exiles, and the sons of a patriot, Paco was a guileless cosmopolitan and would have felt at home—or rather, would have failed to notice that he was at the North Pole as long as he had his piano, his drums, a good radio, some people to play football with, and Mary. But then his musician father (whose name was De la Cruz; Paco carried his mother's name) had never lulled him to sleep, like the Monson boys' father, with stories of the old country, and was away from home so much of the time that when he finally died in Harbin, Paco, who was thirteen at the time and had not seen his father for the last five years, could remember his face only from a photograph hanging over the bureau in his room.

He had gone to look at the photograph when the news came, after having stood about awkwardly, unable to feel anything, while his mother sobbed against the door, clutching the telegram in one hand and her apron in the other, for she had been preparing breakfast. Now she was crying in a hurry; she must not be late to work. She was superintendent in a Chinese clothes factory—a dimly smallish woman with the alarming smiles of a polite person feeling seasick and trying not to show it—and was originally from Macao, where Paco spent his boyhood summers with her family. The first years of her marriage, when she had accompanied her husband in his dreary odyssey through the cabarets of the orient, had been a nightmare of dirty trains and cargo steamers, cheap hotels, hunger, the sluttish bickerings of vaudeville folk of all races, and the dishonesty of absconding managers. She had been a convent-school girl in peaceful, clean, and pious Macao and she never got over her horror of the company into which she found herself thrown by her marriage. After Paco was born she had refused to follow her husband anymore; she settled in Hong Kong, and went to work to bring up her child, since the boy's father seldom had any money to send and indeed had to be supported himself whenever, ill or without a job, he came to stay with his family in Hong Kong until the illness or the joblessness had been remedied. But she would not let Paco, when he was older, sell papers or shine shoes; he was going to school at the Christian Brothers and was always provided with good clothes and pocket-money; and in the squalid apartments from which they were always moving away because the drains stank or because the cracked walls crawled with bugs or because a prostitute had moved next door or because the apartments above had been raided for opium smokers, the single bedroom was always given to Paco, while she fixed up a corner in the living room, behind the piano, with a couch and a dresser for herself.

She endured meekly her boy's coldness and brusque temper because she thought it arose from shame of their poverty—but he bullied her from compassion. When he saw her hurrying home in the cold streets, in her wretched coat, a bag of groceries clutched tightly under each arm and her face feverishly working because of the wild schemes for making money that she was always turning over in her head, his child's heart would be so touched with pity that he would fall in fury upon the boys with whom he had been playing, provoke a quarrel and a fight, and arrive home even more savage than usual, barking at his frightened mother and reducing her to tears with some cruel remark, that she must be a crazy woman to walk about in public talking to herself. He had early hardened himself against her tears; she was always crying anyway, and over the silliest rot—but even when it was the death of his father that wrung her sobs he still could not bring himself to approach and console her; could only stand and watch her awkwardly until her sobs had subsided and she leaned limply against the door, hiding her face in the apron. Then he went to his room and sat down on the bed and looked at the photograph of his father hanging over the bureau.

The photograph had been taken when his father was still a vaudeville pianist in Manila and showed him in a tight striped suit of the '20s, sitting at a piano, his hands on the keyboard, his young face turned sidewise to grin at the photographer. The tunes that his father was probably playing at that piano began to jingle in Paco's ears—"Yes, Sir, That's My Baby" and "Somebody Stole My Girl" and "The Sheik of Araby" and "I Wonder What Became of Sally"—making him smile, because they were being played in the fast jerky style with corny flourishes that his father had long outgrown but liked to burlesque when at home, for his private fun and the nostalgia. Paco idly turned the piano into a bed and stretched out the grinning young man on it and then animated the studio backdrop into a raging Siberian winter storm—but even after he had told himself that his father had probably died more of hunger than of pneumonia (since the manager of the troupe he had last been working for had run away with an Hawaiian belly dancer and all the troupe's money) he still could stir up no feeling for the grinning young man in the tight striped suit dying on top of the piano. So he tried to remember what he could of his father talking but though he heard his father's voice very clearly no words were distinct until he remembered that he and a crowd that included Mary and the Monson boys and Rita Lopez had planned to go mountain climbing that afternoon and was wondering if it would still be seemly of him to go along with them with his father just dead when he suddenly heard his father talking very distinctly about mountains. He had asked his father if he might climb the mountains when he was bigger and his father had laughed and said that even a baby could climb these mountains in Hong Kong: they were so bald and wrinkled they looked like old dogs that had lost their hair, and so small you could climb up to their tops and down again in half an hour—not like the mountains back in the Philippines that took days and even weeks to climb and were thick with trees and shrubbery and dangerous with wild animals. Then he had begun to tell Paco about a range of mountains just across Manila Bay that looked like a woman stretched out in sleep.

That was about the only time Paco could remember that his father had told him something definite about the country he had come from, and he remembered it again when from the railing of the ship that was taking him to Manila for the first time, to play at the two night clubs, he had looked up and suddenly seen, with a shock of recognition, a range of mountains that looked like a woman sleeping. He had clutched the railing as he gazed at the mountains in astonished delight, thinking of himself as a boy, seated on the bed, staring at his father's photograph, and trying to stir up some feeling over his father's death, while out in the kitchen his mother whimpered and rattled a coffee pot, preparing breakfast. The astonishment had renewed itself all the time he was in Manila, every time he looked up and suddenly saw the sleeping woman outlined against the sky—and it changed the indifference with which he had come to his father's country into a stirring of clan-emotion—a glow, almost, of homecoming.

By the time he met the señora de Vidal he had become deeply interested in Manila and was ready to be interested in any woman who most piquantly suggested that combination of primitive mysticism and slick modernity which he felt to be the special temper of the city and its people: pert girls dancing with abandon all night long in the cabarets and fleeing in black veils to hear the first Mass at dawn; boys in the latest loudest Hollywood styles, with American slang in their mouths and the crucifix on their breasts; streets ornate with movie palaces and jammed with traffic through which leaf-crowned and bare-footed penitents carried a Black Christ in procession—and always, up there above the crowds and hot dust and skeleton ruins and gay cabarets: the mountains, and the woman sleeping in a silence mighty with myth and mystery—for she was the ancient goddess of the land (said the people) sleeping out the thousand years of bondage; but when at last she awoke, it would be a Golden Age again for the land: no more suffering; no more toil; no rich and no poor. So that when Paco first met the señora de Vidal (he had been playing in Manila over a month by that time, and had been learning the city block by block and street by street) he had felt the same shock of recognition as when, glancing up from the ship's railing, he had suddenly seen the range of mountains that looked like a woman sleeping.

Not that the señora looked as though she might be sleepwalking. She was fully awake, completely alive—but completely without flurry. Her poise was her verve: she did what she wanted without bravado attitudes. She called Paco to her table the first night she appeared at the "Manila-Hong Kong"—he was always being called to tables between numbers to be asked about Hong Kong personages—but the señora was not interested in establishing mutual acquaintants; she was interested in Hong Kong itself, where, she explained, she had spent her second honeymoon and many happy vacations before the war; she had been there several times recently, but always only for a few hours, passing through on her way to Europe or America; and she wanted to know: had the war greatly changed Hong Kong? But when he started to tell her she interrupted to ask what he looked so happy, so excited about—as she could not help noticing (she said) all evening. Paco laughed, and clicked into step: he told her all about his journeys of discovery through the streets of Manila—until it was time to return to the bandstand. She was with several young girls whom she had introduced as not her daughters; she danced a few times with the girls' young men but mostly sat alone at the table, nibbling salted watermelon seeds, and chatting with people round about.

Before she left, a little past midnight, she called Paco again and suggested that—since he was curious about Manila; and she, about Hong Kong—they should meet and trade information. He agreed; she gave him her card; and late the next morning—and every day after that—they met at her house, which was a white Spanish mansion in a suburb of tree-lined avenues, very prodigal with pavement, and of newly built mansion villas, whose terraced lawns were unfortunately cluttered with signs that warned: "DANGER—The Dogs Are Savage!" and "BEWARE—There Are Armed Guards Watching This Area Night and Day!"

Paco had no intention of snuggling up with a married woman old enough to be his mother—nor by the least flick of an eyelash did she ever indicate she had anything up her sleeve except a lady's arm. If he was Tex to her she was never Concha to him; though they were daily together they were seldom alone together. She was an active clubwoman: in the mornings Paco drove her to hospitals, orphanages, committees, conventions, cultural lectures, and mah-jongg sessions. In the afternoons she took him for tours through the slum barrios of the city, so he might savor the style and swagger of what she called *"los majos de Manila"*; or out to the country, so he might see carabaos and hear folk music; or to the homes of intensely nationalistic families, so he might catch—among the lavender and old lace; the ikons and family albums and interior patios; the elaborate baroque furniture and the framed daguerreotypes of mustachioed patriots— a feel of the country in the old days. In the evenings they met at whichever night club he was playing, where, arriving late with people picked up from the night's parties, not dancing much and remaining cool and composed while folk rioted, she sat and nibbled watermelon seeds until the club closed, when she would collect Paco and a dozen other persons for a midnight snack at her house.

Intimate with no one, she yet needed a crowd always around her; the door shutting at dawn on the last guest oppressed her like a coffin's lid. Locked in her room, she paced the floor and prayed, wringing her hands but unable to weep; and quietly rocked herself to sleep, crouched at the bedside or collapsed on the floor. She would wake up the next morning completely refreshed. She had bathed and breakfasted and had called up Paco to plan their day together when their companions of the night before still lay comatose in darkened chambers.

Paco liked her for her flat impartial sandpaper ruthlessness which, though harsh on first impression, did not leave rough edges on one's feelings but a tingling smoothness. The moist childhood with his mother had cloyed his loins with piteousness; he liked his women dry, and had found so congenial a wife in Mary because Mary too (though she might look so tender-hearted) hugged a thrift of sentiment as grim as his own. He and she had stepped over the prostrate bodies of their respective families to marry: she, abandoning a boozy father whom she had quietly supported since she was fifteen because he considered himself too hopelessly an artist to work; he, abandoning his uncomplaining mother to a pension and her relatives in Macao. He never had to feel his way around Mary: she was so much himself as to seem his twin; and in the first weeks of his friendship with the señora de Vidal he found no difficulty in writing Mary about it. Mary, reading the letters in Hong Kong, rather anxiously smiled at his ingenuousness.

He said that he found the señora a refreshing haven of neutrality but really meant that he liked feeling at home among her teacups and having her fine car to drive around as though it were his own. He did not think much of the people she ran around with but he enjoyed their collective sparkle and audacity. He had never met her husband nor any of her children—she had had four sons by her first marriage; a daughter by her second—but this absence of her family seemed natural enough since she spoke of them very freely and so often—her husband had made such-and-such a speech; her two sons that were killed in the war had been posthumously decorated; her daughter Connie, recently married, was learning to cook—that Paco sometimes felt they were all in the next room, awaiting a cue to come in . . . though they were never in the next room; and he realized that if she too had indeed stepped over her family, her duty to them fulfilled, to do some private living, she was not making conversational mountains out of her step for nosey people to climb and explore. Paco was not nosey; she could omit even the molehills: the ground was always clearing before them. Yet their relationship, which should have ranged unhampered over more and more cleared ground, since they had refused from the start all the dense hedging between men and women, became—as Paco grew aware of the eyes around them—increasingly stalled and static instead: an isolation on a desert island.

He fumed to find his private life becoming public jest.

—*Who's the son of a Turk?*

—*Oh, that's Concha Vidal's latest fancy boy.*

The moment he entered a room where she was, the movement of people knowingly stranded them together, but pruriently encircled. Even the members of his band had developed a special smile for him, which he could feel widening as he turned his back. Once, his nerves snapping, he swung a fist at the saxophonist, disrupting a morning rehearsal. His apology dropped like a pebble on the bandsmen; he had always been aloof with them: they were now frankly hostile. They complained that he skipped rehearsals to take his querida shopping.

Paco grimly broke off with the señora. He ignored her at the night club and eluded her over the telephone. She wrote to ask what was wrong: he did not reply. She came herself to his hotel: he was always out.

He had resumed his solitary explorations of the city but what he now saw increased his discomfort: the heat-dazzling panic-edgy streets darkened in his brains with doom, dirt, danger, disease, and violent death. Some venom was at work here, seeping through all the layers, cankering in all directions. The señora's world of mansions might sit uneasily on its avenues; the hovels of the poor squatted no less nervously on their gutters. The avenue matrons might not get up from a mah-jongg session for days and nights except to eat and relieve nature; the gutter matrons breakfasted, lunched, supped, and suckled their babies right at the gaming tables, and frequently relieved nature there too. And the young people who emerged each morning from the world of bugs in your bed, pigs and poultry in the rooms, and gutters sluggish with excrement and drowned rats, were no less brushed, polished, plucked, painted, perfumed, silk-shirted, nylon-hosed, wrist-watched, and bejeweled than the spoiled darlings in the world of the avenues.

Paco sensed an unreality in both worlds: the people who occupied them did not seem to be living there at all. They denied the locale—but their denial was not the asceticism of the mystic nor the vision of the reformer, but merely the aversion of the opium eater. They stepped over reality as they stepped across their gutters with the transient frown of the tourist, the neutral disgust of the foreigner. Their drugged eyes denied the garish imitation mansions no less than the patched-up tenements

where four or five families lived huddled together in each room
and did their cooking, eating, and washing in the foul passages;
where there were no lavatories and the people used the unspeakable roofless public outhouses—or any corner of the sidewalk.
They denied the heat and the dust and the rats as well as the not
quite authentic glitter of the downtown smart shops and the
swanky clubs—for in the world of their minds, they moved
with cool expertness, rich and poor, among marble halls and
ivory baths and luxurious wardrobes; through streets that were
all Park Avenues, where every building was an Empire State,
and every car a Rolls-Royce; where the men were all Pierpont
Morgans, and all the women unaging, unfading Betty Grables.
One might have to eat cold rice and squat on a pail in the out-
house and sleep on a bug-ridden floor: one sighed and pressed a
scented handkerchief to one's nose and invoked the vicarious
magic of one's wristwatch (just what all the Wall Street tycoons
are wearing now) or of one's evening dress (just what all the
New York hostesses are wearing now) against the cold rice, the
rank pail, the buggy floor. . . . One smiled and floated away,
insulated from all the drab horror of inadequate reality by the
ultra-perfect, colossal, stupendous, technicolored magnificence
of the Great American Dream.

But the strain showed in their faces—in their shifty eyes and
cold sweat and anxious smiles; in the way they tried to walk—
and the frantic way they danced; never for pleasure, never with
ease, one eye always on the audience, sweating from the violence
of their exertions and from sheer terror of not being up-to-the-
minute, of not making an impression, of not being able to do
what everybody else was doing. . . . So they jerked harder, and
laughed more naughtily, and sweated agonized—while, alone at
her table, the señora de Vidal sat and nibbled watermelon seeds,
remaining cool and composed while the room rioted, and chatting with people round about—until Paco began to feel that
though he fled her and she sat still, he never escaped, he never
moved at all: she was always there behind him, smiling at his
back, and nibbling watermelon seeds.

After only a week, he stopped fleeing and she tracked him down.

He was presently escorting her again everywhere, defiantly—for were he and she (she asked) the sort of persons to let wagging tongues wave them this way and that? But he had glimpsed the panic beneath her poise, and had felt the ground sway at his feet: their desert island was mined. Neutrals no longer, they fixed boundaries and could not resume the various commerce of the early days. He was sulky and nervous with her; she was more attentive, more deferential toward him; so that, without ever having been lovers, they looked more like lovers than before.

—*Pero mira que tio tan turco-turco!*

—*Cuidao, chica: es el nuevo* steady *de la Vidal.*

Paco suffered from the strain of the relationship—and from a feeling that he was being watched all the time, everywhere. He had stopped writing to Mary. The contract with the night clubs still had three months to go.

One hot afternoon he was waiting for the señora in her living room: she was out but was expected. He had drawn the curtains against the sun, for his head ached with the heat; and as he lay in the darkened room, sprawled on his face upon the piled cushions of a sofa, he suddenly had the feeling, more sharply than usual, of being watched. Looking up, he saw a girl standing in the doorway. He knew instantly that she was the daughter. As he rose she came into the room and said that she was Connie Escovar. She announced that her mother would probably not be coming home that afternoon: a dreadful thing had happened. Some friends of hers, ladies of great social importance, had been murdered by bandits in the provinces. Their bodies had just arrived, horribly mutilated, and her mother had been called to the morgue to help identify them.

While she talked Paco watched her face—they were standing very close in the dark room—and a smile appeared on the corners of his mouth. He was feeling more and more sure that it was this girl he had felt watching—not only just now but all the time before. He saw her coolly remarking his twitching mouth, his narrowed eyes. She asked if he were ill. Scooping the sweat off his brow, he swore at the heat. She offered to drive him out to the country where it might be cooler.

Her car was a yellow convertible. She drove while Paco smoked; they did not converse. They fled the broiling suburbs and emerged into open country. She jumped the car off the road and they rustled over grass till they came to a grove of bamboos and a river. The moment she stopped the car, at the river's edge, he shoved his arms around her and a wave of unspeakable relief convulsed his taut frame. He saw her eyelids swooning, her mouth soundlessly sighing open, as his face swooped down, as their bodies collided, gravitated. The shock of her mouth stunned his mind with such impact, abrupt tears scalded his eyes. But as, moaning, he moved his mouth over her chin, her ears, her tight throat, and felt the long-knotted ache in him sweetly easing, sweetly uncoiling at last, she opened her eyes and, groaning, pushed him away. He hovered in hunger, not quite conscious, blurrily baffled—the tears in his eyes and the moan in his throat—but she had sat up and fetched out her compact and was frowning at her face in the mirror. Bending, he pressed his mouth to her shoulder; she brusquely nudged him off. He grabbed her wrist so suddenly the compact shot out of her hands; whirling, she slapped him across the mouth. He toppled backward, hit his head on the car's door, and snapped out of the trance. He gaped in amazement at her vicious face. She said, spitting out the words: did he think she was as easy a job as her mother? As he tried to push himself up she suddenly started the car and burst laughing when he flopped down again. She continued to shake with laughter all the way back to the city; Paco was quiet. As the highway fanned out into streets she asked, controlling her mirth and turning her mocking face toward him: where would he like to be dropped?

That night she appeared at the "Manila-Hong Kong." Paco smilingly ignored her. She was there every night that week; he could locate her without turning around: wherever she was, the racket was loudest. She danced snatchily; she traveled among the tables: she laughed and chattered at the top of her voice— but whenever he turned around he caught her eye. His own smiling look stepped right through her.

The señora did not show up. Paco heard that she was ill and

was receiving no one: she had been deeply shaken by the tragedy of her friends. He did not visit her, he did not even call her up. He felt ill himself from the spiteful desire to get the daughter in his clutches—but in his dreams, restless with flying landscapes, the woman he hunted had two faces; and though he sweated to catch her he dreaded every moment lest she stop and turn her other face around.

When he shifted his band to the "Boulevard Shanghai" the following week, Connie followed—and she was there the night one young man shot another young man because they both wanted to sit on the same chair. The atmosphere, earlier that evening, had been tensed up by the appearance of two rival political bosses with their henchmen. The club's manager came running up and told Paco to cut out the intermissions, to keep right on playing—loud. The politicians occupied tables on opposite sides of the room. Timid folk fled; braver ones— Connie among them—remained and danced nervously, waiting for the shooting to begin. Nothing happened. The politicians kept getting up and crossing the room to offer each other drinks; they smiled and shook hands and thumped each other's backs; at midnight, they and their unsmiling constabulary very peacefully departed. But the few customers left behind, scared and disappointed, quickly developed ugly tempers. A quarrel over places, between two young men, ended with both of them whipping out pistols and firing—and with the unluckier one staggering headlong across the dance floor, doubled up and clutching his rent belly, and dropping down just a foot away from where Connie had flung herself flat on the floor. She screamed at the blood and Paco jumped up from behind a drum and ran to pick her up while people clamored and stumbled over chairs and tables in their frantic flight to the doors.

Paco dragged the girl out to the kitchen where he stood her up and shook her until she stopped shrieking. She swayed away from his hold and vomited all over the kitchen floor. He made her drink some water and she flung herself on his breast and sobbed wildly. He took off his coat and wrapped it around her and took her out to her car. A light drizzle was falling, blurring up the moonlight. He drove around the wet streets, one arm holding the girl to his breast, until she had sobbed herself out. Then he stopped the car and made her dry her face and gave her a cigarette. They smoked sitting apart; they felt rather shy of each other. He was ashamed, remembering her girlish terror, of his male spite; she shamefacedly remembered his tenderness. Then she threw away the cigarette and crept back to his breast and he put an arm around her and leaned his mouth on her hair. When she offered up her face he kissed her damp eyes and the rim of her nose and her quivery lips. He reached out with his free hand and started the car moving and she asked: where were they going. When he said that his hotel was just a few blocks away she put her arms around his neck and he could feel her mouth closing and unclosing against his neck as they sped through the gleaming streets. But when they arrived at his hotel she clung tighter to him and would not go down. Appetite collapsing from weariness, he agreed to drive her home but she asked him to take her to the Chinese quarter first.

They drove through the cramped slums where the Manila Chinese are kenneled: wet walls, wet cobbles, bridges arching over stagnant canals, craggy tenements dripping rain into tight twisting streets, a raggedness of black roofs and the arrowy silhouette of a pagoda soaring in the rainy moonlight. She bought a doll at a shop whose locked shutters she rattled until the owner opened up; she told Paco that she needed the doll for a thank-offering. She directed him through winding alleyways till they came to a small square, enclosed on three sides by buildings and on the other side by a muddy canal choked up with water lilies and spanned by the rickety wooden bridge over which they had come. She made him stop at the middle building, which was of stone and had an open balustraded porch in front, three steps up from the street, with a pair of stone lions flanking the top step. Paco saw it was a temple. In the open doorway, just clear of the rain, sat an old bearded Chinaman, sucking a long pipe; down the darkness behind him, candles remotely flickered. Connie got out with the doll—she would not let Paco accompany her—and ran up the porch, nodded to the Chinaman, and passed into the darkness. When she came out, in about ten minutes, she was no longer carrying the doll. She did not say where she had been and he did not ask. He drove her to her house where, alighting, she said he could take the car with him: she would send someone to pick it up the next day.

When she did not turn up at the club the following nights, he remembered that she had said goodbye, not good night, as he drove away, too fatigued by the night's emotions to take notice. He remembered the wistful shut, open, and shut again of the word in her mouth, and how she had turned away quickly when he dully looked up from the wheel. He remembered her tears in the moonlight and the wet wind in her hair and how tenderly she had brooded over the doll, cradled in her arms, and the shrewd peace in her face when she came out of the dark temple. He remembered her mouth closing and unclosing against his throat as they drove to his hotel and he knew now that she had been praying frantically all the time: those were prayers that he had thought were kisses. He felt no curiosity; he had forgotten his resentment and spite; he only knew that his bones were being borne helplessly flowing in a magnetic flood and that he must fight the currents; that he must not be dragged to her, but she to him—for the gravity pulled as suavely her way as his and must ultimately bear her swaying against him.

And when at closing time one night, two weeks after they had parted, he came out of the club and saw the yellow convertible waiting and her face at the window, the world around him swiftly lost impact; the babble of departing folk faded remotely; the moonlight turned fluid and he found himself being washed into her car, his every step the graduated motion of a figure in a delayed movie. While the car swam through the moonlight they sat and swayed, now touching, now apart—like two reeds in a stream—and could not talk, could not hold out arms, so heavily whirled the waters around them. But when the car stood still before his hotel, the tides stopped too; he turned around and she met him and they flowed into each other's flesh, their swarming arms entangled, their breath mingled. He opened the car's door to bear her out and she strained to follow but seemed rooted to the seat, and swooned and sweated from the effort while he tugged in vain. They broke away from each other, weeping with frustration and bewilderment, and he

groped and started the car and blindly, angrily drove through
the moon-white streets, not knowing and not caring where they
went, but when the black tenements of the Chinese quarter
closed in about them he knew that they had been headed that
way all the time.

They came to the shuttered stores and she bought her doll;
then they drove on to the temple and she went inside; after a
moment's hesitation, he followed. The old Chinaman glanced
up but did not stop him. He walked down the long dark corridor and came to a denlike chamber, strewn with straw mats,
where guttering candles and a saucerful of joss sticks smoked
before a warrior god. Connie was nowhere to be seen—but a
Hong Kong boy knows his way around Chinese temples: he
searched through the minor side-chapels until he found Connie, standing before a candlelit altar. She did not look around
as he entered. The small room reeked of the wasting wax and
the joss sticks. He stood behind her and looked over her shoulder at the god on the altar—an old fat god, with sagging
udders, bald and white-bearded and squatting like a Buddha;
and the sly look in its eyes was repeated by the two navels that
winked from its gross belly. Connie had laid her doll on the
idol's lap. As she turned away from the altar, Paco backed off
from her contact, feeling a furriness at the pit of his belly. Her
bleak smile accepted his shrinking.

They went back to the car but did not drive away at once.
The warm moonlight felt fresh after the musky gloom of the
temple. They lighted cigarettes and his pointed silence prodded
her to speak. When she told him she had two navels he believed
her at once, and felt—not repulsion—but the heat-lightnings of
a desire, feverish and electric, that charged his hands with eyes
and his eyes with mouths. While she talked—her bowed head
turned away; the cigarette glowing between her fingers—he
imagined her in the posture of the idol and he stripped her and
saw himself as the doll on her lap. Glancing up and catching
the look on his face, she asked, alarmed, to be taken home. He
smilingly informed her that she was coming back with him;
that she had played with him long enough; that he was deter-

mined to find out that night what sort of a monster she was. When she darted up in panic he started the car, and burst out laughing as she flopped down across the seat. He continued to roar with laughter all the way back to the hotel; Connie was quiet. When they arrived at the hotel he grasped her arm but she asked to be released: she would come quietly. Her eyes had slitted with the sly look of her god.

They went up to his room and he locked the door. He was merry no longer; this was going to be serious work, not play. He took off his coat, and she was waiting for him—in the darkness, for they had not switched on the light and the windows were shuttered. As he approached she swung out a leg and hit him on the loins. He sank down and she sprang upon him and they grappled but not a cry escaped their shut lips. They battled grimly, silently, rolling up and down the floor, oozing sweat and bleeding from bruises; the hiss of their breath and the clatter of a chair as they knocked it down the only sounds in the dark room. She broke loose and tried to stagger up but he was clutching her strap and the dress ripped across her bosom as she jumped on his face. He suddenly rolled away and she bounced onto the floor but as he dived at her she kicked up both feet at his face and scrambled under a chair. She grabbed the chair and hurled it at him as he was groggily kneeling up and the chair knocked him down flat again. But as, bolting for the door, she leapt over him he reached out and caught her ankle and down she went, hitting her mouth on the floor. She jerked her leg off and clutched at a table's edge to pull herself up but he was dragging himself up too over the other side of the table and they confronted each other, panting and dripping tears and sweat, but still game. He tipped the table over and she swerved but he was upon her before she could run, pinning her neck to the wall. She grabbed his hair and pulled; he tore free; she shot out a fist but he ducked; and when his fist exploded against her jaw she dropped to the floor and stayed there, stretched out stiff.

He groped round the wall to the washbowl and washed his face and drank some water. His shirt hung in tatters, his face

smarted with scratches; and he wanted to just lie down somewhere and die—but he groped back and stooped over her. She
did not move but was conscious, for her sly eyes gleamed up at
him, waiting for what he would do. Blood trickled from the corners of her mouth and her dress had been torn off her breasts and
shoulders. He had only to reach down and rip the dress some
more if he would discover her kinship with her monstrous idol—
but as he stood over her in the dark room, her sly eyes gleaming
up at him, his hot flesh went clammy with the feeling that there
were other eyes peering out at them, eyes avidly fastened upon
them, eyes that had been watching them all that night and all the
other nights before and he could not doubt whose eyes they
were. He felt the roots of his hairs straining tautly, his guts bloat-
ing; and as the warm vomit sourly flooded up his throat, the girl
on the floor saw him shudder and double up (like that young
man she had seen shot at the night club), one hand clutching his
belly, the other hand clapped to his mouth—and her own bloody
mouth smiled twistedly: she had won after all.

He staggered away and snatched his coat and ran out of the
room and down to the street, past her car that waited at the
curb, down white empty street after white empty street, fleeing
faster and faster—for the eyes had followed, the eyes were
everywhere; there was no escaping them in this evil city where
rich and poor alike huddled in terror behind their beasts and
their guns, where the crowds fled self-pursued and the teeming
streets might any moment become stark deserts as the latest
victim danced upon his blood: where ghosts were reported and
signs appeared upon doors and black headlines swarmed in the
air and apparitions waved warnings and a young girl whispered that she had two navels. . . .

But what was this horrible thing he had done? I've been
dragging her all along with me, he gasped, and shuddered. I've
been dragging her by the hair, he cried, and felt her hair in his
hands. But when he stopped, horrified, and peered down at his
hands he saw that it was his coat he clutched. It's only your
coat, you bloody fool, he shouted, laughing, and began to kiss
the coat in relief. And noticing the ocean coolness around him,
he realized that he was standing on the sea-side. He was alone,

he had escaped; and as he faced his fever to the cold wind he knew a moment of sobbing relief. But looking up and seeing the mountains, his heart stopped, his eyes started out of his head, his throat screamed soundlessly. He had not escaped, he had not fled at all—for there she still was, stretched out under the sky, the sly look in her eyes and the bloody smile on her lips, and her breasts and shoulders naked. He wheeled around to flee, but his legs had liquefied and, as he flailed the air with his arms, the ground suddenly seesawed and slammed against his face; the moonlight blacked out: stars blazed; sand swelled in his mouth and waters roared in his ears—but the next moment there were no more stars, no more sand, no more waters, only a total stillness, a total void. . . .

Two days later he was on a ship, sailing back to Hong Kong.

"I left without seeing either of them again," said Paco Texeira, lying on the grass in King's Park, Pepe Monson sitting beside him, and the winter night settling like soup in the bowl-shaped park. All around the bowl's brim, where twilight still glimmered, Pepe Monson saw the international clubhouses, each one packaged in fog, waiting in locked-up loneliness for Sunday's exiles.

"It was damned hard," Paco was saying, "to break with the band. The club's manager wouldn't release me from the contract and the men naturally thought I was doing them dirt. I couldn't blame them. But I had to get away or go nuts. So I just bolted— and they can sue me if they want to. I didn't even wait for the money I still had coming to me. I came back poorer than I left. Nastier, too. I felt as if I had sneaked off. It's not a nice feeling: gives you what Mary calls the Boris Karloff look in the eye."

"So that's the end of the Tune Technicians," said Pepe.

"—and of Tex the Bandleader," said Paco, his forehead wrinkling. "Nobody's going to trust me again after what I did. I'll have to teach me another trade. . . ."

"I wonder what drives her to tell a lie like that?"

"Connie?"

"—about the navel stuff."

"Oh, just to shock, of course, and to corrupt. She's not after one's body, she wants to ruin your soul."

"Oh, come now, Paco."

"They're both agents of the devil—she and her mother. They work as a team: the mother catches you and plays with you until you're just a bloody rag; then she feeds you over to her daughter."

"I'd say they were working against each other, not with each other."

"They work *for* each other. Whenever I was with one of them I could feel the other watching greedily. They share each other's pleasure, watching you twitch. And when they've screwed you up to the breaking point the daughter springs her abominable revelation—and you go mad and run amuck. And there's one more soul that's damned."

"No, Paco—no."

"What do you know about them? You've only seen them once."

"But I think you're wrong. About the daughter, especially. I think she's just a scared girl, desperately trying to save herself."

"And so she runs around saying she's got two navels—"

"I'm beginning to see it's her way of saying she's got a guardian angel. . . ."

"Oh, you poor sap, Pepe—to be taken in by that little girl act of hers!"

"Well, weren't you?"

"Oh, yes. Oh, yes indeed."

"And you really haven't got over it yet, have you?"

"No," said Paco woodenly and, rolling over, lay very still with his face on the grass.

They were alone in the park. Mary had taken the children home; it was colder, and time for supper. She had told them to follow in a moment: the soup would be waiting. . . . The moment had become hours.

Pepe said: "We had better go. Mary has been waiting and waiting."

Paco did not move. When he felt Pepe's hand on his shoulder he said dully, not lifting his face from the grass: "Oh, leave me alone."

"But Mary will be worried."

"I can't go home."

"Don't be silly, Paco."

"It's no use. She knows I'm just waiting to go back."

"To those women?"

"They're not through with me yet."

"Are you in love with them?"

Paco lifted his face from the grass. "They're waiting for me," he smiled. "They've followed me. If I were in love with them I'd have gone to them by now."

"If you're not in love with them you wouldn't be afraid to go."

"It's not love—how could it be? I know they're vile, I know they're evil. But they've got some kind of a hold on me—oh, a strangle-hold, I know. But I also know that, sooner or later, when they call I'll come running. And Mary knows, too. We're both of us just waiting."

"Paco, you've got your own will—"

"No, I lost that over there, too. . . . *Oh, leave me alone!*"

"It's too cold to stay out here anymore—"

"I don't mind."

"—and Mary's waiting."

"You go and tell her not to wait. Tell her I've got a headache and need this air. I'll be along in a moment."

"Then I'll wait for you."

"Oh, go away—damn you—go away!"

"Okay, man."

Pepe stood up and, after a glance at Paco, who was lying very still again on his face, walked away across the park. The light fog, always a gleaming sheet a step away, made him feel like Alice, stepping through mirrors. But it wasn't I who stepped through the mirror, he thought. It was father and Paco—and the glass broke. They can't step back anymore; not father anyway. . . .

His father would have had supper by now and would be in bed, but not sleeping. He hardly slept at night; just lay there very still, with staring eyes, in the dark room—as Paco now lay very still on his face, with eyes open, down there on the grass. His father had said little about what he had seen on the other side of the mirror. But that was hardly father who came back, thought Pepe, remembering the stranger's footfalls he had been alarmed to hear in his father's room when his father should still have been in Manila.

When the great news came that the flag of his country waved at last in sovereign solitude, his father was ill and could not attend the inauguration of the Republic. It was a year before he could make the momentous voyage home. He had wanted no one to accompany him; this voyage, the great dream of a lifetime, he desired to make alone. Pepe had deferred his marriage— he and Rita Lopez had been engaged since the end of the war—because the old man had expressed the wish that they should be married in their old house in Manila. His father would arrange to have the house rebuilt at once; Pepe was to follow with his bride. The old man, when he set off, looked like a young bridegroom himself: stiff and vigorous; and waving at last to his sons with unconcealed exultation as his ship pulled off from the wharves, bearing him home again after half a century of exile.

Less than a month later, he was back, suddenly and unannounced. Pepe, one stormy afternoon, after a muddy round at the racetrack stables in Happy Valley, came home and heard someone moving about in his father's room. He did not recognize the fumbling footsteps. Without waiting to take off his dripping coat and galoshes, he hurried to the room and found the old man there, shakily pushing a chair around, and looking so frail, so altered, he might have been away for years, not for a month. Pepe, after one look at his father's face, was careful not to express surprise.

"When did you arrive, Papa?" he asked as he kissed the old man's cheek.

"Just this afternoon. I took an airplane."

"You should have cabled."

"I left in great haste."

Pepe, stripping off his rubbers, waited for explanations. None came. His father complained about the dust in his room; hearing the quaver in his voice, Pepe started. Besides, the room was clean.

"I'll tell the boy to tidy up here," he said. "Let's go and have tea."

"I must wash first," said the old man.

But when Pepe came back to the room he found the old man asleep, folded up in a chair, his head fallen on the chair's arm. Pepe called up his brother Tony and Rita Lopez, bidding them to supper but warning them that something was wrong: they must not press the old man with questions.

During supper that night, the old man was silent—not with

the brooding silence of the old days but with a silence as vacant as the look he cast on the bright table, festive with flowers and champagne to celebrate his return. Immediately after dessert, he asked to be excused; he felt tired from the trip, he said, and wished to retire early. He kissed Rita on the cheek, and his two sons accompanied him to his room, where they helped him undress and put him to bed.

When they returned to the living room (which was also Pepe's office) Rita was bringing in coffee. They felt tired, and too shocked to speak—as though somebody had suddenly died. They pulled the sofa up to a window, sat down in a row, and sipped the coffee in silence, watching the rain pouring outside and the ferry-boat lights twinkling back and forth in the storm. When they started to speak they whispered.

"But he must have been writing you boys," said Rita. "What did he say?"

"Nothing that explains *this*," replied Pepe.

"Father's letters are as reserved as his talk," added Tony, with a smile. Tony was in his white friar's habit; he had not had time to change into the black soutane the religious wear in Hong Kong when they go out in public. "But I began to smell something," he continued, "when the first letter came, and then the second, and then the last one—but still no mention about his being able to say at last: '*Nunc dimittis servum tuum, Domine.*'"

He grinned at Pepe over Rita's head as he chanted the Latin words, the opening line of the Song of Simeon, and Pepe bleakly smiled back. When they were kids their father took them every evening to attend Compline—over at the cathedral on Sundays; up at the Dominicans on weekdays—just to hear that song. He told them that the words meant: *"Now let thy servant depart, Lord"*—and he said that when he had at last returned to his own country he would, like Simeon, be able to say: *"Nunc dimittis . . ."*

"That's the Canticle at Vespers, isn't it?" asked Rita, seated between the brothers, sipping her coffee. She used to sing with the cathedral choir.

"The Canticle at Compline," corrected Tony.

"Compline, yes. The Song of Simeon—when everybody stands up."

"But you and I," smiled Tony to his brother, "would peer around and wink at each other."

"We would be thinking," explained Pepe to Rita, "of a river in Manila we had promised each other to go swimming in—because the *Nunc Dimittis* always made us think of going home, and going home always made us think of that river, and of the dead pigs and dogs that father said it was always full of." He paused; then added: "But though we winked and smiled we felt just as deeply, just as seriously about that song as father himself."

He spoke with a sad earnestness, as though defending himself. He felt the emptiness of his father's silence. In their different ways, they had all betrayed and forsaken the old man—their mother had died; he, Pepe, had turned to horses; Tony had turned to God. They had become, as they grew older, more and more restive under the old man's brooding monomania. They had apostatized, leaving the old man to carry on his cult alone. . . . Now the cult had abruptly come to an end; the candles had all been extinguished and removed. There was only a vacant darkness, a vacant silence.

"Oh, I should have gone along with him!" he cried aloud.

"Don't blame yourself, old man," said Tony. "Father wanted to go alone."

"But only because he knew we didn't share his dream anymore."

"There was nothing we could have done."

"We could have protected him from whatever it was that broke his heart. And how can we help him now when we don't even know?"

"But, perhaps," said Rita, rising and collecting their cups, "he's just exhausted from the trip. Let's give him time to rest up. Then we'll find out what happened."

"He won't tell us," said Pepe, remembering the vacant look. "Don't you see he doesn't even want to remember?"

"Take it easy, old man," said Tony. "Our father's a brave man. He'll get over this. He got over harder heartbreaks, didn't he?"

"I'll take these cups out," said Rita, "and then you boys will have to take me home."

"I'll go take a look at him a moment," said Tony.

Left alone, Pepe rose and stood by the window and thought

of his father standing up very straight for the *Nunc Dimittis*, one hand over his heart. . . . When Rita returned from the kitchen he helped her into her boots and coat; they did not say what both of them were thinking: that this might mean they would have to postpone marrying again.

Tony came back and announced that the old man was not sleeping. "I thought he was when I entered, but when I stooped over him I saw that his eyes were open. So I said, 'Papa, Papa.' But he didn't seem to hear me."

"Maybe I shouldn't leave him alone," said Pepe. "Tony, will you take Rita home?"

All that night, Pepe lay unsleeping in his room, conscious of his father in the next room, unsleeping too. Toward dawn he heard the old man moving about. He rose, pulled on a robe, and went to the next room. The old man was rocking himself in a chair, in the dark. Pepe turned on the light.

"You have risen early, Papa."

"I could not sleep."

"The rain has kept me awake too."

"Oh, not the rain—the dust, the dust, the dust. . . ."

"We will make the boy wash this room thoroughly today."

"And crabs. Crabs crawling everywhere. Wherever I place a foot I crush a crab."

Pepe heard his heart pounding.

"Dust and crabs, dust and crabs, dust and crabs . . ." dully intoned the old man to the wooden rhythm of the rocking-chair.

"Would you like a sleeping pill, Papa?"

"No."

"Would you like some coffee?"

"Thank you, yes."

When Pepe returned with the coffee the old man was still dully rocking himself. Pepe pulled up a chair and sat in front of his father while they drank the coffee.

"Tell me about Manila, Papa. How did you find it?"

The old man was silent, rocking himself in his chair; blowing into his cup, then taking a sip, then blowing again.

Pepe slightly raised his voice. "Did you enjoy your stay in Manila, Papa?"

The old man still did not seem to hear, slowly rocking himself up and down.

Pepe put down his cup and leaned forward, placing his hands on his father's lap to stop the rocking. "Listen to me, Papa. It is I, Pepe, your son. You can talk to me. You can tell me everything."

The old man looked up from his cup but there was no expression in his eyes.

"Tell me what happened, Papa. Do you hear me? I pray you to tell me what happened."

The old man leaned back in his chair and shut his eyes.

"Leave me alone," he said woodenly. "Go away, go away . . . Leave me alone!"

And that was how Paco, too, had whimpered, lying on his face down there on the grass, thought Pepe Monson, as he walked up to the rim of King's Park; as he paused on the rim and looked back, trying to see where he had left Paco lying at the bottom of the bowl-shaped park. But he could see nothing in the darkness; and turning around, he saw the street dazzling before him, shadows of dwarf pines lacing the edges, and cars' headlights knifing through the fog. Across the street, behind the fog—its doorways and windows blurrily shining—stood Paco's apartment-house, where Mary and her soup waited.

He knew now what Mary had known for some time: for both of them, though they had stepped through no mirrors, the safe glass had cracked and things from the other side had begun to seep through. Out of the fog, this morning, had come drifting the stylized girl in black furs and a black hat, with gray gloves on her hands and pearls at her throat; had come drifting the madonna-like lady belted up in a white fur jacket, with a polka-dotted scarf round her neck and gold coins swinging from her ears; had come drifting Paco in a dark-blue turtleneck sweater, with a Boris Karloff look in the eye; had come drifting his father, sprawled forward in a chair, unconscious—though his eyes were open and his mouth smiled. . . .

But you've got your own will! he had cried to Paco—and realized now that he had been crying to a ghost; that he was crying to a world of will-deprived ghosts.

—I'm just waiting. Sooner or later, when they call I'll come running.

—And crabs. Crabs crawling everywhere. Wherever I place a foot I crush a crab.

—When I was a little girl I thought everybody else had two navels.

—When I was a little girl people like your father were my conscience, walking around in elegant clothes.

—Dust and crabs, dust and crabs . . .

The mirror's cracked world was safe no longer; was perilous with broken glass, teeming with ghosts; was now the world where Paco waited for the strangle-hold and dear good Mary told lies and the cautious Rita was dazzled by dragons and Tony hid in a monastery and fathers took drugs and mothers had lost their dictionaries and young women had two navels. . . .

Pepe shivered at a sudden gust of cold wind. He tucked up his coat-collar, plunged his hands into his pockets, and hurried across the street—to the lighted doorways and windows, to Mary and her waiting soup.

GUARDIA DE HONOR

In October, a breath of the north stirs Manila, blowing summer's dust and doves from the tile roofs, freshening the moss of old walls, as the city festoons itself with arches and paper lanterns for its great votive feast to the Virgin. Women hurrying into their finery upstairs, bewhiskered men tapping impatient canes downstairs, children teeming in the doorways, coachmen holding eager ponies in the gay streets, glance up anxiously, fearing the wind's chill: would it rain this year? (But the eyes that, long ago, had gazed up anxiously, invoking the Virgin, had feared a grimmer rain—of fire and metal; for pirate craft crowded the horizon.) The bells begin to peal again and sound like silver coins showering in the fine air; at the rumor of drums and trumpets as bands march smartly down the cobblestones, a pang of childhood happiness smites every heart. October in Manila! But the emotion, so special to one's childhood, seems no longer purely one's own; seems to have traveled ahead, deep into time, since one first felt its pang; growing ever more poignant, more complex—a child's rhyme swelling epical; a clan treasure one bequeaths at the very moment of inheritance, having added one's gem to it. And time creates unexpected destinations, history raises figs from thistles: yesterday's pirates become today's roast pork and paper lanterns, a tapping of impatient canes, a clamor of trumpets. . . .

For the young Natalia Godoy they had moreover become emeralds—emeralds from her father, to wear to the procession—a ring, a necklace, a brooch, a comb to crown the veil with, and pendulous earrings shaped like chandeliers. She was eighteen, and would march for the first time with the "Guardias de Honor" of the Virgin. And two suitors waited below with their carriages (as her father now reminded her), each anxious for the pleasure of conveying her to the procession.

"But how can I ride with both of them? And to choose one is to hurt the other."

"My poor baby—but you have already chosen?"

"Yes, father."

"—and not only for this afternoon—"

"For all my life."

"Good. Then ride with that one."

"No . . . No, I shall ride with the other. Oh, please do not laugh at me father!"

"How you girls love to kill with kindness!"

"But I feel I owe him that kindness—"

"Of course, child. Go and ride with this one you have not chosen; and I shall tell the more fortunate one that, only for this afternoon, he is unfortunate."

"But do not betray me to him yet, father."

"Esteban?"

"Mario."

"But I thought that Esteban—You seemed to like him better."

"Oh yes, yes—he is so gentle, so good; and I desire to ride with him this last afternoon. But it is Mario whom I love, father."

Suddenly forlorn—"I love" is a door girls slam in their fathers' faces—he speechlessly turned away. He had always expected, of course, that she would marry some day—but not that she would fall in love. It seemed years before she awoke to the silence, to his averted face.

"Father—?"

At that word the door that had slammed shut opened again; but it was not his baby, not his little girl, that he saw, but a towering, faintly familiar person, a mature woman, before the radiant nakedness of whose passion he felt shy and formal.

"Do you approve, father?" she asked, rather alarmed.

"What need is there to ask?"

"Oh, *why* must people have feelings!"

"But I told you, Natalia, when those young men first spoke to me, that you yourself should decide. Whatever your choice,

I would have approved of it. I believe in the reasons of the heart. Is your heart happy?"

"Yes, father."

"Enough, then—I give my fiat. Mario is a fine fellow, a man of spirit—of too much spirit, I would say; but the years will modify that. And I give you my blessing."

She stared at him a moment, pale and breathless; then ran forward, her skirts rustling, and kissed his hand. He ruefully touched the emeralds that swung down her cheeks: he had given those emeralds to a girl; the girl had evaporated; the jewels remained—but burning now (it seemed to him) with greener fires. The green years of her girlhood now lived in those emeralds.

He said: "There, your mother is calling below. She must have lost all patience." He and her mother and the rest of the family were driving ahead in their own coach; Natalia's mother, a *jefa* of the guardias, desired to be early at the church. Natalia would have her aunt to accompany her.

He said, already at the door: "And so she is in love, too— your Aunt Elisa?"

"We have known Andong Ferrero all our lives, father."

"I see that love is not like lightning."

"Has Andong spoken for her?"

"He and his parents are coming tonight to make the formal petition."

"Oh happy Aunt Elisa!"

"How this house must smell of women in love!"

"Will you tell her to run up here a moment—"

And how it transfigured them, grumbled the old man as he walked away. His old eyes had certainly been opened: I thought her a young, young child; I thought Elisa an old old maid— now I look at the two together, and I cannot tell the niece from the aunt. . . .

"—and remember to tell Esteban that we are riding with him!" called Natalia from the doorway. This last afternoon should be wholly his, she sighed to herself, closing the door and returning in front of the mirror; but, as she gathered up her great black veil, it was of Mario that she thought. Had he read into her quietness of last night? She wondered, picking up the jeweled comb and hand mirror—and suddenly her heart stopped. It will rain! she gasped, turning cold—for the room's image in the big glass had darkened. She stood still, the veil gathered up in her arms, staring at the darkening glass, and waiting for the rain's clatter on the roof; but what she heard, instead, were two voices—unfamiliar, unrecognizable—speaking just behind her.

—Her name was Natalia, and she was the grandmother of my mother's grandmother and her beauty became a proverb in the family. Go on, Josie—put them on.

—How green they burn, mommy! They rather scare me. . . . Are these their old settings?

—The original ones. Natalia's father gave them to her the day she first marched in the Naval procession as a guardia: they have remained unchanged since then. And they have been jealously preserved—through war and plague and poverty. These jewels are more than heirlooms, Josie; they are sacred: the tokens of a vow.

—Mother—

—Yes, dear?

—You feel very deeply about these things, no?

—I have a sentimental fondness for the old traditions, darling. You have made me very happy by wishing to carry them on yourself. When you came and told me that you, too, wanted to be a guardia—

—Oh, why must people have feelings!

—Josie, is something wrong? Is there anything that troubles you?

—And that is why people have hurt you so much.

—Because I feel?

—Too deeply.

—Stop talking nonsense. No one has hurt me. I have had a long full life.

—We have all made you suffer, mother.

—Well, naturally! I am not so saintly as to deserve to have saints for children. But one thing I can say for myself: I have

*always respected your freedom. No, I cannot say I wholly
approve of the lives you lead: but I would prefer you to sin,
being free, than not to sin, because I had tied your hands.*

—*Oh, is that why, mother?*

—*Why what?*

—*Why you lend me these emeralds.*

—*I lend you those emeralds because my mother lent them to
me, and because her mother lent them to her—but it was more
than a lending: it was an entrusting.*

—*Do you trust me, mother?*

—*Is there something you want to tell me, Josie?*

—*No. No, mommy—nothing.*

—*Then come, cheer up! This is your first appearance as a
guardia de honor, remember! I may be nothing to look at now,
just skin and bones—but oh, the first time I marched in that
splendid procession! I felt myself growing up as I walked: I
knew that I carried on my person something far more lovely,
far more precious, than those emeralds. . . . But how they sparkle on you, Josie! Everybody will think you a great heiress. And
then they will say: But why is she wearing only one earring?*

—*Do I look funny with just one earring?*

—*All the women of our family have walked in the Naval
processions wearing that one earring.*

—*Because of the accident?*

—*Because of the miracle, Josie—it was a miracle. You
remember the story? It happened on this day, the Feast of the
Naval—the very day Natalia's father gave her those emeralds.
She and her aunt rode to the procession in the carriage of one
of her suitors, a boy named Esteban. And then, oh, they had
this dreadful accident. The horses became panicky and bolted
and finally broke loose. The carriage was hurled against a wall
and smashed into pieces. The aunt and the boy Esteban were
instantly killed—but Natalia was saved. They found her
standing unhurt amidst the wreckage. Nothing had happened
to her except that she had lost an earring. She firmly insisted
on going on to the procession. She cried that at the very
moment of disaster she had called on the Virgin of the Rosary,
and the Virgin had snatched her away. A votive picture of her*

deliverance hung for a long time at the Dominicans. And forever since then, her descendants have marched as guardias in the Naval processions wearing one earring. . . .

Moveless before the mirror, Natalia Godoy watched the glass growing bright again; but in the room now reflected in it nothing was familiar save her own pale jeweled face and the bells' clamor. Unnoticed, veil and comb and hand mirror had dropped from her hands; the voices continued behind her: she no longer listened—until the voices stopped, when she heard footsteps departing and a door closing; but knew herself not yet alone in that room whose strange image gleamed at her from the glass—an image that fluidly altered again as she turned around to face the staring eyes behind her.

"Hello there," said Josie limply. "You must be Natalia."

The two girls stood close together; white gowns and breathless faces almost touching.

"How you startled me," said Josie. "I dropped my hand mirror."

They both glanced down at the spoilt glass on the floor, between their feet.

"It was I who dropped that," said Natalia.

"—or maybe we both dropped it," said Josie. "We seem to be wearing the same jewels too."

"Only, as you see, I have both the earrings."

"But you heard what my mother said—"

"It will not happen."

"Will *not*? It has not happened *yet*, you mean? But I thought you were—"

"No, Josie: it is *you* who are the ghost here. Look around— You see? This is my room; that noise of bells and ponies and carriage wheels is my world; this afternoon is my today. But you, my dear Josie, are real only for this moment."

"Oh, I assure you: I *have* been real for a long, long time!"

"But how could you be?"

"You see this white frock? Well, I bought it a week ago, shopping downtown with mommy. We got caught in the rain, and that old taxi we took leaked. And a year ago, I was graduating from high school; a month ago, I met a man at the movies; yesterday, I was having lunch with him; and this afternoon,

I received a letter. . . . Are you and I happening at the same time, Natalia?"

"Maybe this explains that odd feeling I sometimes have—"

"—that what is happening has happened before?"

"But you are still in the future, Josie. Everything has still to happen to you all over again."

Josie's eyes grew wide at this. *"Oh, no!"* she gasped, white-lipped.

Natalia felt embarrassed. "Is it so terrible?" she asked, cautiously.

"Where I am?"

"—and what happens to you."

Pushing the hair off her brow, Josie traveled uncurious eyes round the archaic room. "Terrible or not," she said, "things have to happen. I try not to feel about them too much. I just let them happen."

"But you look so worried, Josie."

"These emeralds—"

"Do they frighten you?"

Josie smiled. "Nothing," she said, twisting the ring round and round her finger, "frightens me anymore."

"But I heard you say they scare you."

"As emeralds, no. As emblems, yes."

"And so you accept them only as emeralds?"

"I accept only their market value," said Josie, twisting the ring round and round.

"I feel as if you were *wringing* me out of those jewels, Josie!"

"And I *am*!" cried Josie between her teeth, "—wringing and squeezing and straining you out of them; and not only you but mommy also, and everything else they mean. Nothing must be left except a price tag!"

"But why should you want to do that?"

"Because I have to, because I must. I have gone in too deep; there is no turning back now, and no use struggling: the pressure is terrific! But when was life ever a question of one's wanting or not wanting? Life is just one pressure after another. Whatever one does one was always bound to do, like it or not."

"Oh, nonsense. One can always stop, or do something else."

"If I did something else, it would still be Josie. If I stopped, Josie would still go on. What is impossible is not to be Josie."

"Well, is Josie not good enough?"

"Oh, poor Josie is not good at all, Natalia—and what happens to her should not happen to a dog!"

"Happen, happen, always happen! Why let things just happen?"

"What else can you do?"

"You could *make* them happen."

"How young you are, Natalia! But today you have two earrings, tomorrow you will have only one, and then you will be as old as I am."

Her hands flying up to touch the earrings: "I mean to keep both of these," announced Natalia, smiling, and she turned away, glittering with more than jewels, her chin tossed up.

"There is *nothing* you can do!" gasped Josie, clasping her hands. "I *know* the fate that awaits you!"

"Well, I know nothing of this fate of yours; but I do know that people call me a very stubborn girl! Do you know what it is to love?"

"Oh, God, yes. Who is that coming?"

"My aunt Elisa. She is in love, too—with Andong Ferrero. And she is *not* going to die, Josie!"

"But how can you stop something that has happened already?"

"And where have I put my veil? . . . Oh auntie, auntie—what a long time you were, coming!"

"But I ran up the moment your father told me—"

"Are they still down there?"

"The family?"

"Esteban and Mario."

"Yes, both of them."

"Then please run down at once and tell Esteban that I am very sorry, but I have changed my mind: we are not riding with him. And ask Mario if he will be kind enough to take us to the church."

"Whatever has happened?"

"I have had a premonition."

"What premonition?"

Natalia opened her mouth to speak—and found nothing to say. What, indeed? Baffled, she whirled around, her skirts flying, and found it nowhere. But something fled her round and round the dim fringes of the room; something always just escaped her eye as she spun round and round—until her eyes fell on the cracked hand mirror lying on the floor.

"I broke my small mirror," she said, and listened. The something still hovered, uncaptured.

"And is that all?" asked the aunt, smiling.

"NO!" cried Natalia, and she grasped her aunt's hands. "There *was* something else, Aunt Elisa—something terrible, a feeling of something terrible about to happen! We cannot ride with Esteban—*we must not ride with Esteban!* Oh hurry, Auntie, and tell him so—but hurry! hurry!"

When she heard her aunt scurrying downstairs the pressure on her heart eased; she smiled and thrust her chin up again; and returned before the mirror, where, as she shrouded herself in the black veil and crowned her veiled head with the comb, she kept glancing thoughtfully about her, this way and that, searching (although she did not know that she was searching) for Josie, and finding Josie nowhere; although Josie was just beside her, was standing right there by the mirror, pale and frightened, and growing more frightened still as she watched how Natalia's eyes continually sought and failed to find her, until, numb with terror, she would have leaned forward and shouted, when Natalia, having collected fan, beads, and prayerbook from a table, turned away and strode off to the door; pausing a moment in the doorway to look back; making a gay little defiant gesture with her fan at the darkening room before she stepped out, closing the door behind her, and leaving the bewildered Josie alone in the past.

But was this really the past? Or merely her dream of it?

No, this wasn't the past, and it wasn't a dream either: it was simply, actually "today." Everything here was real, was solid—this awful pair of canopy beds; these funny rocking chairs; those preposterous pedestals bearing lamps and flower pots; the quaint harp poised beneath a framed lithograph of St. Cecilia. . . . At the balconies, the round courtyard coldly welled up, brimming with blue dusk, wheeling with pigeons. Down there: silence, stillness—but not a ghostly silence; not a dead stillness. Life there had merely paused, and the pause was part of a ritual. Emptied of their folk this festive evening, the city's houses waited, as they had waited year after year, generation after generation, while at the city's core, the city's Virgin rode radiant through a cold wind singing with bells. But the procession would end; the crowds would scatter; courtyards would bustle with horses; fires would be lighted; pots and pans would clatter; sleepy children would be carried up crying; families would gather round festive boards—for this is the real today, said Josie—wandering through the dusky room, fingering the room's surfaces—but that other today was only a dream. And she told herself that Natalia had been right: It is I who am the ghost here—I and these emeralds and this white frock, and shopping downtown with mommy, and the leaking taxi, and graduating from high school, and meeting *him* at the movies, and yesterday's grim lunch, this afternoon's letter. . . . As she thought how all those things that were *herself* still lay in the distant future a fierce relief consumed her—not the terror she had felt as Natalia's eyes looked through her "as though I did not exist"—but a relief intense and immediate, a bliss of liberation. No more pressures; no more tensions; and ages and ages, yet, before she would awake and anguish, before this cluttered room would be stripped to provide her a streamlined setting: the modishly bare, coyly hygienic chamber where her flesh would writhe and her young tears flow. But the reality now and "Creep slowly, Time," she prayed: "creep slowly, slowly!" was this harp, these pedestals, these rocking chairs, these huge beds; and she moved among them, a detached ghost; unconcerned, uninvolved, absolved—and if I look in the mirror, she gloated, I will see nothing. But when she looked in the mirror she saw her pale self staring; emeralds smoldering on her breast and flashing in her hair; and on a cheek, the one earring burning like a goblin's chandelier. *But that's my room in there!* she gasped, seeing in the mirror her own streamlined room: modishly bare, coyly hygienic, and aglare with morning sunshine. As she stood puzzling at the sunshine she heard, with a quick chill at the heart, two voices—instantly recognized: her two brothers—speaking just behind her.

—Have you looked through these drawers, Tommy?

—But we ought to go and stay with mother.

—Take it easy, the doctor's not expecting any change yet. How about those boxes in her closet?

—Oh, what's the use, Ted? Those emeralds are probably in some Hong Kong hock shop by now. She was seen at the airport last night.

—Was he with her?

—Hell, no; he left Saturday. I found the letter she got from him. He said he was sorry he couldn't take her along, but if she wanted to follow—well, he couldn't stop her.

—And he won't stop her from following as long as she's got some money.

—Oh, we'll soon be hearing about her, one more local dame with an international reputation.

—Our dear little sister, Tommy.

—The slut.

—Well, she started early.

—You know his wife, Ted?

I wouldn't worry about that one either; she'll take care of herself. He's got some very young kids though.

—It's poor mother I'm worried about.

—Yes, dammit; but she had no business letting Josie make an old fool of her.

—Oh, mother wasn't fooled, Ted. She knew Josie meant to steal those emeralds.

—Did she tell you, Tommy?

—I heard her say so. Saturday morning, mother called me up asking me to get her emeralds from the bank. When I brought them over I asked her was she thinking of walking in the Naval procession, because she never wears those jewels except when she joins that procession, and she hasn't been able to since her heart began to trouble her. When she told me that Josie had offered to take her place as guardia I got suspicious right away. Josie has been thick with that guy this last month, and I felt she was up to something. So, yesterday afternoon, I dropped around again. Mother and Josie were in here, dressing for the procession; I stood just outside the door, it was open a

little, and I could hear them talking. I heard mother say: "I wanted to save you, Josefa." And Josie said, very loud: "Don't say that, mother." But mother said she had to say it and that Josie should listen; and then she began to talk about the Christian life and choosing between good and evil and about glory and all that piety stuff, and Josie kept telling her to stop and not to speak. Then I heard mother say: "I placed those emeralds in your hands because I wanted you to be free to choose." *She said that she knew about Josie's crucial temptation and that she was trying to save Josie by trusting her.* "Whatever you choose to do now," *mother said,* "you will choose deliberately, with full consciousness; knowing what you will do to me and to yourself." *But Josie said it was no use at all, it just happened, and was happening even then; and I heard mother say:* "Did you feel it too? Someone just stepped across my grave." *Then I heard a thud, and I listened but there was only silence and at last I got frightened and pushed open the door and went in. Josie was lying on the floor and mother was bending over her, crying very weakly and trying to call out. I lifted Josie and laid her in bed and she really looked as if she had fainted: she was limp and cold all over, and very pale and sweating. Of course it was all a damned fake. Oh, she had it all planned out—this fainting act, so she could stay behind, in bed, with the jewels, while mother went off to the procession. She had me fooled all right; she did look ill; I stopped being suspicious—and mother kept whispering:* "Maybe I've saved her, maybe I've saved her," *and wouldn't let Josie be disturbed. I took mother to the procession and it was past nine when we came back. I dropped mother at the door and drove on home. Mother went right up to see how Josie was—but Josie was gone already. She had left a note, just one line:* "Dear Mother, I have chosen. Goodbye." *When I reached home, mother's maid was on the phone, frantic: mother had collapsed.*

—And she hasn't regained consciousness since then?

—No, but she still might. We really ought to go and stay with her, Ted.

—What worries me is that Josie didn't say she took the emeralds along.

—*But of course she did. That's what her note meant. And they're probably in hock by now.*

—*Sure they're not in your pockets, Tommy?*

—*I wish I was as sure of your pockets, Teddie-boy. Your wife was in here, at two o'clock in the morning, and ransacking like mad.*

—*Well, look who's talking! She tells me you and your wife were in here ahead of all the ransackers, and that you weren't very nice when she offered to help you.*

—*She would barge in here, sarcastic as all hell, and starting to screech and scream, and mother lying in the next room—*

—*Shut up, someone's coming!*

—*Only that charming wife of yours, Junior, I can smell her from here.*

—*You stop that!*

—*Who'll make me?*

—*Tommy, Ted! how can you be screaming at a time like this! Come quick, both of you!*

—*Is she dying?*

—*She's dead!*

—*Oh no.*

—*Oh, no, no. Oh mother, mother!*

—*Control yourself, Tommy!*

—*It wasn't Josie only. . . . We've all killed her! Oh mother, mother, mother!*

—*Control yourself, I tell you! Tommy, control yourself!*

Moveless before the mirror, Josie heard the wild sobs growing fainter and fainter, as though a radio dial were being turned off, until there was only silence, and the sun-bright room mocking her from the glass. But it wasn't tomorrow yet, she doggedly told herself, fingernails digging into her clenched fists, and "No! No! It's not tomorrow yet!" she cried out at the glass and whirled around—and here was her own room, modishly bare, coyly hygienic; and there, at the windows, was today's late afternoon light still glowing, today's feast bells still calling; and here, where she had left it on her desk, was *his* letter: she snatched it and tore it and crumpled it and flung it away. And there on the floor was the hand mirror she had dropped; as she picked it up she heard the door opening and ran toward it.

"Oh mommy, mommy—it's not true, it's not true!"

"Stop shouting, Josie. Mother of God, you still have not finished dressing, and the procession will start in an hour! Come, start powdering that nose of yours." And Doña Pepita, herself already arrayed and veiled, pulled her daughter back to the mirror.

"But it's not true, mommy—not true at all! You are here and you look so lovely—and *she* defied the fates, she made things happen!"

"What on earth are you talking about, Josie?" asked Doña Pepita, combing her daughter's hair.

"—about Natalia. She changed her mind, mommy—she changed her mind! She did intend to ride with Esteban but she decided to ride with Mario instead."

"Why, who told you?"

"Then she *did* change her mind, mommy?"

"Well, the legend goes that way. They say that on that fatal afternoon Natalia broke a mirror, and felt it to be an omen. Years afterward, Natalia said that it was more than the mirror, that she had had a strange vision she could not remember—but later generations have embroidered on her story until now it is full of phantoms and portents and heavenly monitors. Anyway, Natalia had some kind of a premonition; so, she sent her aunt to tell this Mario that she had decided to ride with him instead. Unfortunately, the aunt did not find Mario, because Mario, unable to bear his disappointment, had stolen upstairs; and when Natalia came out of her room she found him waiting in the hall . . ."

. . . She stepped out of her room (having made her gesture of defiance at the dark) and when she turned around and saw him standing there before her, his dark curls dangling and his eyes wild, she felt her heart go fluid with love and tenderness, felt herself melting and flowing toward him.

"Mario—!"

"Why do you treat me like this, Natalia?"

"Did you see my aunt?"

"She passed by a moment ago; I hid myself: I had to see you, Natalia!"

"Then she has not told you—"

"It is you who must tell me something, Natalia. Why do you torture me so?"

"But do I torture you?"

"Why should you ride with Esteban this afternoon—"

"Listen, Mario—"

"No! No! It is you who shall listen! You do not love him, you only want to make me suffer! You are cruel, cruel!"

"Will you *listen* to me!"

"Why have you chosen to ride with him, ha? Tell me that!"

"And why should I tell you, ha? Why should I give you reasons for what I do, ha?"

"Because I love you, because you love me!"

"Oh, indeed?"

"And you are *not* going to ride with him this afternoon—"

"Oh, truly?"

"—or ever again!

"I shall ride with whom I please, sir!"

"You shall ride with me, Natalia!" he pronounced imperiously.

"And who are you to give me orders? Mother of God! Am I this man's slave?"

"I warn you, Natalia—"

"What, do you think to frighten me!"—and she thrust into his face her own face terrible with ire and emeralds.

"Do not ride with him, I tell you!" he screamed into her mouth, their hot breaths mingling.

"And what right have you to tell me what to do? I am not bound to you, my dear sir—nor to anybody else! I am free!"— and she laughed in his face, her jewels dancing.

"I shall tear you away from his side!" he yelled, maddened.

"Then come and try!" she spitefully taunted, and fled, her body atremble. "Esteban, wait! Wait, Esteban!" she cried as she flew down the stairs. "We are riding with you, Esteban! We are riding with you!" she shouted, shivering, glittering, with fury and hatred and love.

And she was still trembling as she fled in Esteban's carriage, her scared aunt frantic beside her—for Mario had followed, Mario thundered behind them, and the crowded streets cleared in terror as the carriages roared past, one fleeing and the other pursuing. "Faster, faster!" prayed Natalia, clasping her swooning aunt to her breast. "Faster, Esteban!" (For at the first sign of the pursuit Esteban had clambered up beside the driver and had grabbed the reins himself.) And peering out the window, she saw the staggering Mario looming huge against the sky, the whip shrill in his hands as his horses leapt the air, his curls flying, his eyes wild—and it was her heart! her heart!—not the bells—that swung and swelled so loud in her ears. "Faster, Esteban!" she shouted, leaping up in the carriage. "Faster! Faster!"

". . . and suddenly," said Doña Pepita, "the wall reared up, the horses swerved, splitting the poles, and wrenched loose, sending the carriage hurtling and shattering against the wall— Josie! what is the matter!"

"Then she didn't . . . Then she couldn't . . ."

"Are you feeling ill?"

"She didn't! she couldn't! but oh, the gesture was enough, the effort was everything! And I can! I will!"—and the trembling girl drew herself up, glittering with more than emeralds, the cracked mirror gripped tight between her hands. "Mother," she began, in a voice of agony, "there is something I must tell you."

"Yes, Josie?"

"I have been deceiving you, mother."

"I know."

"You knew—and yet you gave me these emeralds!"

"I wanted to save you, Josefa."

The mirror dropped from the girl's hands and crashed to the floor. Her eyes bulged out and her face crumpled like paper. "Don't say that, mother!" she screamed, and her hands shot out as though to stop her mother's mouth.

"But I must say it," said Doña Pepita, her thin face infinitely tired, "and you must listen."

Sweat streamed on the girl's face as she stared, fascinated, at her mother's mouth.

"What makes the life of a Christian so hard," that mouth was saying, "is that he must choose at every step, he must choose, choose, choose, at every moment; for good and evil have such confusing faces—evil may look good, good may look evil—until even the most sincere Christian may be deceived—unless he chooses. But that is one of his greatest glories too—that he chooses, and knows he can choose."

"Oh stop, mother, stop! Don't speak! Don't speak!"

"I placed those emeralds in your hands," wearily continued Doña Pepita, "because I wanted you to be free to choose. I know the crucial temptation that afflicts you, and I wish to help you, to save you, Josefa, by showing how deeply I still trust you—for you know what those emeralds mean to me. Whatever you choose to do now, you will choose deliberately, with full consciousness; knowing what you will do to me and to yourself."

"Oh, it's no use—no use at all! It just happens! IT'S HAPPENING RIGHT NOW!"

At this, Doña Pepita started and turned pale. "Why, did you feel it, too?" she asked, and with a dim smile: "Someone just stepped across my grave. I sensed a—JOSIE!"

But Josie had dropped to the floor.

Doña Pepita felt her every nerve straining as she stooped over her unconscious daughter. She tried to shout but her dry throat choked. The bells' clangor seemed the noise her heart made.

". . . And when that clangorous darkness stopped whirling, I found myself standing alone on a strange street—and yours was the first face I saw."

"And the first thing you said to me was: 'I have lost an earring.'"

"And then I looked around and saw what had happened and I flung myself on your breast and sobbed and you hushed me and lifted me away."

"But when we buried her and I knelt sobbing at her grave, it was you who raised me up and comforted me."

"You loved her very much, Andong?"

"And I still love her, Natalia," smiled Andong Ferrero at his wife, "because she brought us together."

"Ah, but we did not know it then!" she cried, gathering up her great veil. "You went away abroad, never to come back, it seemed; and I stayed here, alone for years; mother dead; father dead; my own life dead. . . . But whenever I thought of that afternoon it was your face I saw—and I felt your arms lifting me up again from the ruins. And I wondered: how did he know it would happen? what made him follow?"

"Being a lover, I had a lover's premonition."

"Like mine?"

"What was yours?"

"When no one asks, I know. When someone asks, I find I have forgotten." And Natalia Ferrero smiled at the mirror as she shrouded herself in the black veil, as she crowned her veiled head with the comb.

"And you never saw Mario again?" he asked, clasping the necklace round her neck.

"Only once. When father died. Father was a Tertiary: and when the Franciscans came to wash and clothe his body I saw Mario among them—very thin and altered, and so strange in that coarse brown smock: he who used to be so elegant. Ah, but I had altered, too; it was years and years since that fatal afternoon; the eyes that shone from under the dark hood did not know me at all. Those eyes had found their true love, they were the eyes of a spirit. He is a man caught into God's heart, Andong—a holy man."

He said, bemused: "Yes, God is a cunning hunter. . . . And what strange things have come out of that wild ride of yours!"

She laughed and mocked: "Oh some very *very* strange things indeed! Listen!"

And listening side by side, they heard, above the gay noise of bells and band music, boys' voices downstairs, furious with impatience. "We had better hurry down to the rogues," he laughed.

"But I shall have a daughter too," said Natalia, offering him on her palm the earring shaped like a chandelier. "And I have vowed to the Virgin of the Rosary," she continued as he clasped the jewel to her ear, "that my daughter, too, shall march as a guardia in her procession."

"—wearing this one earring?"

"And may she never, never lose it!" whispered Natalia Ferrero, her eyes suddenly bright with tears as she stood arrayed in her emeralds: a bowed old woman now, heavy with child—but feeling herself for a moment the young Natalia Godoy again, dancing in this room that afternoon her father gave her these emeralds, the afternoon she first told him she loved . . .

And yes! she should wear that earring as a trophy, as a trophy of battle—thought Andong Ferrero, seeing in the tranced figure bowed before him—heavy with the past, heavy with the future—a Guard of Honor indeed, a warrior scarred but unconquered—for the Fates had won nothing from her save an earring. Tonight she would walk hieratic among hieratic women—women equally scarred and equally jeweled: priestesses bearing the tribe's talisman, the clan's hearthfire. And because of her lost jewel (a jewel dissolving now into myth and the earth's mist), the moss would be greener on the walls; the leaves brighter on the trees; the fine air more silver; and the heart's pang of happiness more poignant, more complex, when, at the city's core, the city's Virgin rode radiant against this cold wind singing with bells.

October in Manila!

DOÑA JERÓNIMA

In the days of the galleons, a certain Archbishop of Manila was called to a council in Mexico but on the way there fell in with pirates who seized his ship, looted the holds, slew the crew, and were stringing up the Archbishop to a mast when a sudden storm ripped up and wrecked both pirate craft and Philippine galleon, drowning all that were on board, save only the Archbishop, who, being bound to the cross of the mast, was borne safely over the wrath of the waters and thus reached the shores of a desert isle, a dry isle that was but a tip of reef in the sea, where, for a burning year, he lived on fish and prayer, on rain water and meditation, crouched day and night in deep thought at the foot of the cross of the mast he had set up on the shore, all alone in that waste of ocean, until a passing ship, mystified by a reflection as of a giant cross shining in the air, tracked the mirage to the horizon and came upon the desert isle, and upon the cross of mast planted on the shore, and upon the bowed, mute, shriveled old man squatting motionless and cross-legged there, stark naked and half-blind and burned black as coal, all his hair turned white and his white beard trailing down to his navel, and hardly able to stand or move or speak or grasp, in which dismal condition he was carried back to his city, arriving there some two years after he had left in glory, having departed a fine blaze of a man, handsome and vigorous, and bidden farewell by all the city to a tumult of bells, banners, fireworks, and music, and returning now in decay, terribly altered, terribly aged, mere skin and bone and wild eye, but still amid bells, banners, fireworks, music, and the tumult of the city, for news

of his rescue had preceded him, the marvel of his sojourn on
the island had grown into legend in the retelling, and he himself had become such a figure of miracle—the man twice saved
by the Sign of the Cross; and fed on the desert isle, 'twas said,
by ravens, like Elijah, and with manna from heaven, like the
Israelites—that the folk who poured forth to welcome him
dropped to their knees with a shudder as he was borne past, a
frail wraith that, however, had power to stun the eye and seize
the soul, that would, indeed, in those days, possess the popular
mind, every traveling bard having but this one ballad to sing,
and no print hawked at the fairs but carried the Archbishop's
picture and a relation of his adventures, by which diverse manners the fame of him spread as a holy man on whom God had
showered such mystical favors that when the Archbishop at last
emerged from a long convalescence, firmer in fabric but never
again to be in his prime, it was to find himself being revered in
the land as a saint.

For the Archbishop there was irony in this: that he should be
honored as holy who now knew himself to be hollow. Naked
on the naked isle, he had, for a Lenten year, pondered upon
himself and had seen what a vanity, what a fraud his life had
been. Youthful ambition had probed where lay advancement
and had picked the Church as the quickest avenue to the high
places of the world; and he had entered religion craving not
piety but power. In the Order whose friar's habit his young
shoulders assumed, he had fawned and fought, steering a pull
here and a push there, to hoist himself up the rungs of authority, which he, whose energies found cloister politics too
cramped a field, had used merely to vault higher, ever higher,
until a height long pursued as goal upheld him, and he sat on
the See of Manila. Anointed, crowned, enthroned, the Archbishop of Manila at last, he had, however, come to no end of
his aspiring but rather found himself more ravenous, more
insatiate, reaching out still farther, hungering still for heights,
and therefore making a most turbulent Lord Spiritual, his days
spent in noisy and incessant quarreling, now with the grandees
of the land, now with the merchants of the galleons, now with
the canons of the Cathedral or the friars in the field or the

officials of his own Order, but oftenest and loudest with the viceroys. Time and again had he led a march on the Palace; and governor after governor had cowered or been broken into submission or been dragged out fighting and chastised and sent yelping back to Madrid, while in Manila the Archbishop seized the reins of government and relished, till a new King's man ventured over, the fullness of a power that fused the spiritual and the temporal. At such times did the Archbishop feel his destiny most fulfilled, being kin in spirit to the medieval prince-bishops. Then did he show himself as mighty a warrior on the field of battle as in the field of politics. Were Moro pirates pillaging some shoreline of his See? The Archbishop rode post-haste to the site, to lead the faithful against the infidel. Had the Chinese in Manila risen in revolt? The Archbishop could be seen on the walls of the city, cassock stuffed into boots, rallying the defenders or manning a canon himself. Were English or Dutch heretics threatening the Bay of Manila? The Archbishop was on the instant at the mouth of the bay, drawing up the battle plans, organizing the armies, sending out the ships, and watching from a campfire at the shore's edge, the progress of the sea battle. Well did he know, when called to that council in Mexico, how far his name had resounded; and he had taken ship with a vision of new horizons unfolding before him. Beyond Mexico lay Madrid; and beyond Madrid—who knew?—waited Rome. Could a man of his kidney be allowed to stay a mere colonial bishop? But God had answered the question with a desert isle, where, for a stark year, stripped of more than his purple, the Archbishop had reigned over a few feet of barren rock. Wherefore, never but with a shudder could he wear the red robes again; and restored to his city, restored to his feet, after having had to learn, like a baby, to walk again, and to talk, and to unlock his eyes, he moved in shame through the crowds that clamored to touch him, asking himself what holy man they thought to reach under the robes. No holy man but the shell of a man, back in spiritual infancy. Yet he suffered the popular veneration, being moved with pity for these folk that came from so far and wide to behold the living icon of a miracle; and knowing also that in time the fervor would wane

and the crowds thin; and this latest masquerade ended—
himself as miracle man, as saint—he could resume the quest
for reality that had started on the desert isle.

Ah, if aught had been learned on that island, it was how he
himself ought to learn. For the vivid figures that he had taken
for a self (the ambitious youth, the nimble friar, the turbulent
archbishop, the unbowed warrior) were, he had realized on the
island, but masks, images, ghosts of himself: vapors released
by the fires of the flesh—by ambition, by the lust for power, by
the craving for glory. On the island, all his appetites stilled, he
had, from day to day, moved deeper into the heart of stillness,
where must reside the reality that was himself, a being undisturbed by the shifts in feeling and fortune of a man's life, as the
island's rock endured, unchanged, amid the flux of the waters
and the alternation of day and night, no transient green to disguise its essential bone, but always itself in very bleakness and
bareness, as hard and fixed (thought the Archbishop) as must be
the being waiting to be revealed at the core of the stillness, the
mysterious being he hunted and pursued unceasingly, day and
night, even as he squatted motionless and cross-legged at the
foot of the cross on the edge of the rock. The rescuing ship had
interrupted the epiphany; had returned him, alas, to the disguises of a man in the process of becoming—to the robes of a
bishop, the aureole of an icon, the sheets of a ghost; in which
absurd apparel, appearance became authority, illusion became
truth, and was hailed as holy in the marketplace, where the
mobs jostled to touch hand to the costume. But the absurdity
was part of the self-knowing (for what's accepted as reality must
be experienced as absurd to be exposed as unreal) and he had
therefore suffered the hollow man to be taken for holy man,
waiting patiently to resume the stillness, the interrupted epiphany toward which he had moved on the island, knowing that
the way inward lay no less through marketplace than desert isle
and that the interruption was itself part of the movement.

Even his old foes were, however warily, ready to cry miracle
when, as time passed, the change all noted in him itself remained
unchanged, and there was, with the return of health, no return
of the furious old fellow and his turbulencies: no reappearance

of the Archbishop leading a march on the Palace, or raging up and down the wharves while a galleon outwaited the tide, or leaping out of his carriage to whack some grandee who had haughtily turned his back on the episcopal entourage. Rather, as time passed, did the Archbishop withdraw more and more from public function, delegating the affairs of the See to his coadjutor and to the Cathedral chapter, while he gradually vanished from view. For when, as he had expected, the curiosity of the populace waned and the crowds thinned, he felt under no more obligation to show himself in public and at liberty to withdraw into the retreat he had prepared: a small palm hut in the native style, on the banks of the Pasig, just outside the city walls, but hid in a grove and distant from any suburb.

Into this hermitage he took along a single companion, his manservant Gaspar, who was also his cook, nurse, driver, courier, and Mass server. On great feast days, the Archbishop celebrated Mass at the Cathedral; and when the duties of his office required it, he made an appearance at his old palace inside the walls; but all the rest of his time was spent in the hut by the Pasig, where, pacing round the deep grove, or squatted on the riverbank, or lying in bed by the window that overlooked the water, he strove to recover the stillness that had been his on the desert isle, and to resume the quest for what was permanent under the flux, being in this a child of his age, the *septimocento*, stunned and stricken (like many another in that city at the end of the world) by metaphysical hungers.

In this Manila of the seventeenth century, folk but a father away from paganism, but a baptism away from the Conquista, were (like their more sophisticated brethren in Europe) already exploring mystical ground, already knew of the dark night whereof St. John of the Cross speaks, already craved a total illumination, probing their souls alone, in self-imposed solitude, or together, in experimental communities, with an anguish that was yet an ecstasy, being (though mostly simple and unlettered folk) informed by the high style of their century: changelings that, in the prime of life or beauty or fortune, abruptly fled the carnival and shut the world out, impelled to a quest for something firmer by a fever in the soul.

Our Archbishop was, therefore, not alone in practice when he

retired into his tiny hut by the river to learn stillness; but the stillness he wooed, in many a trance and vigil, eluded him; uneasiness encumbered contemplation; and the soul that sought silence
but shook with anxiety as the Archbishop grew more and more
aware of eyes watching and feet following—of a something
assaulting his solitude.

He was being haunted.

The intrusion was vaguely sensed at first as a whiteness hovering yonder, just before he looked up or over a shoulder, merely
felt, not seen, though every day closer, and presently, from the
corner of an eye, barely glimpsed as a flash of white vanishing
in the foliage, if he paced his grove, or round a street corner, if
he rode in his carriage through the city, or behind a pillar, if,
while saying Mass at the Cathedral, he wheeled around fast
enough from the altar; by which nervous whirlings, and still
from the corner of an eye, he caught, oftener and oftener at
last, haphazard views of his haunter, undulant fractions he
could not, for a time, so dulled were his eyes, piece together
into a human figure (since he espied no face, no arms, but only
what seemed a headless whiteness) but which began to shape
up, eventually, into something human enough, though whether
man or woman, child or ancient, he was at a loss to say, until,
from such repeated and increasingly longer glimpses, he made
out his haunter to be a woman, a woman in white, and veiled
in white from head to foot, her face hid in the white veil, and
nothing other visible save a hand clutching the veil at the
throat, and thus shrouded, when revealed to his eyes, evading
them no more, standing still to suffer his regard on street corner or in church or even at his river retreat, where once, on a
night of moon, squatting motionless and cross-legged at the
water's edge, he had looked up and beheld her on a rock above,
white and faceless, and not moving till he moved, whereupon
she seemed to dissolve into the moonlight.

Hitherto had he made no effort to apprehend her, not knowing if his haunter be an angel or the devil, but now bade his
manservant Gaspar to lie in wait for her, who could only be a

woman, though a most cunning one, for in vain did Gaspar set traps for this weird woman his master claimed to have seen, in vain did the King's fort, when notified, send troops to scour the city for a trace of her, and in vain, so in vain, were even the inquiries about her that the Archbishop, who himself caught no glimpse of his haunter for a month, began to wonder if he was the sighter of an apparition or merely the dupe of a dream, since the woman he sought had dissolved, not now into moonlight but into the light of day.

Then, on the day he sat in his palace to hear all comers, he glanced up above the crowd and saw her at the end of the audience hall, veiled whitely as before; and he whispered to Gaspar to have a guard placed at the doors. Only when the last of the crowd had left did she move from where she waited, and came walking across the hall to the foot of his throne, but not lifting the veil from her face even when she bowed down before him.

"My lord bishop," said she, on her knees, "I have a complaint."

But he said to her: "So have I! Who are you, woman, and why have you been dogging me all this time?"

"If my lord bishop will hear me," was the answer, "he will learn what he would know."

So he motioned her to continue; and rising to her feet, standing shrouded before him, she said:

"Let me tell His Grace and this court a story, wherewith they can better judge my case. It is the story of a young man who pledged himself to a woman, vowing to love her forever. But this young man sailed away to seek his fortune and coming to an island in heathendom fell in love with the goddess that ruled over the island, and she with him. And when he told her that he was already betrothed she assured him that she, being a goddess, had power to cancel a vow and could release him from his, which she did. And so they were married, and the young man returned no more to the woman he had left in his own country. My lord bishop, was this most rightly done?"

"It was most wrongly done," said the Archbishop, "for even were this a goddess with power to free the young man from his oath, she might not do so, until the other woman had been heard. A goddess would be bound by the justice of heaven to send this young man back to his country, to implore his sweetheart to annul their vows, which, unless he had a lawful charge against her, he dare not break without bringing down on himself the punishment of the gods."

"But hear me, my lord bishop: would not a vow made to such a goddess supersede a vow made to a mere mortal?"

"The gods are law," replied the Archbishop, "and if they themselves will not keep faith, why should mankind? Therefore is every vow between man and man sacred, not to be overthrown by a second vow, though this be made to hell or to heaven."

"But hear me further, my lord bishop: what if this young man I speak of had wedded his goddess with deceit, not revealing to her his previous vow?"

"Then is the man not only false but sacrilegious, and must burn forever, he and all his kind, lest chaos befall the world; and his first vow stands, though he make twice a thousand more to repeal it."

At this, the woman fell to her knees, and cried out in a loud voice:

"My lord bishop, let it be as you have said!"

"But what," asked he in amazement, "is your complaint?"

"The complaint," was her reply, as she rose again from the floor, "even of that woman abandoned by a lover who vowed to love her forever. I spoke in parable what is a true history. And I come to lay claim on the man, that he may at last make good his word."

So earnest was her tone that the Archbishop felt compassion for her, and anger at her betrayer.

"Who is the man?" he thundered. "Can you locate him? For, on my oath, he shall keep his promise and make good his word, if you have found him and can produce him."

"My lord bishop, I have and I can—though he had changed his name, and the manner of his dress, and even the look of his face."

"And have you proof against him?"

"I still keep the material token of his pledge, which he gave to me on the riverbank when he swore eternal love."

And drawing closer, she held out a ring to the man on the throne.

The Archbishop glanced at the signet ring that lay in the palm of her hand and, reading the superscription, turned pale and picked up the ring to study it more closely, his breath quickening, staring with startled eyes from ring to woman and from woman to ring, while she stood shrouded before him, her open hand stretched out till he had put back the ring there, dropping it there with a trembling hand and falling back on his throne, pale and panting, his eyes starting out of his head.

But noting the rising murmur of the people in the hall, he ordered that the hall be cleared and the doors closed. When he and she were alone in the room he pushed himself up from his throne and stepped down to where she was; and the two of them stood face to face, she rigid, he shivering.

"Who are you?" he whispered in dread.

"Am I not," she lightly replied, "the woman whom you lately sought?"

"Where did you get the ring?" he pursued.

"A young man gave it to me on the riverbank saying: 'Let this ring be the pledge that, on my knees, I swear to love you forever and ever; and let the river yonder be the witness to my vow!'"

"The river?" said he. "Where are you from on the river?"

"I come from the woods and hills upriver, my lord, where the river flows from the lake."

"Bats' land!" cried he, more to himself than to her.

"Yes, my lord; they hang thick like fruit from the trees and like clouds from the air."

"And dawn is the clangor of their wings flying homeward."

"The lovers of that woodland, my lord, know it is time to part when the great bats rumble overhead. The bats there are the friends of lovers, announcing the approach of night no less than its end, and hiding with their wings the trysts on the riverbank. The lovers lie all night in each other's arms until the bats warn of the daylight. How many lovers have cursed and blessed them! Such horrid huge creatures, black and vile. But O they were love's angels to me, and the canopy of love, as many a time said I to my lover when the wings rumbled. Has my lord heard the dawn on the riverbank there?"

With a catch of his breath he softly cried out:

"*Jerónima!*"

At that word, she seemed to falter a moment and her proud head drooped.

Shaking, he lifted his hands as though to touch her, but could not, and the stopped hands rose higher, over his head, in a gesture of despair, as, sobbing, he cried out again, louder:

"*Jerónima!*"

She lifted her bowed head at his call and slowly drew the veil from her face; and the sob choked in the old man's throat with astonishment as he beheld a face of the most radiant youthfulness and beauty.

Seeing his unbelief, she smiled grimly and said:

"Yes, my lord, it is I—Jerónima. All these years have I kept my grievance fresh, and it has done no less for me. Did I not promise to wait until you returned, promising also not to alter, not to change? Look on me, my lord, and say if Jerónima has not kept her promise! But where, my lord, is yours? These many years have I waited, waited, waited, with no word from you, not knowing where you were, or whether you be dead or alive, until one day, at a fair, I saw the picture of a man who might be the man I awaited; and therefore came to the city and found him, and followed him, and assured myself it was he."

"But I am not *he!*" cried the Archbishop. "Look on me in turn, Jerónima, and say if this be the young man who vowed to love you. That young man died long, long ago, Jerónima, and whatever hurt he did you I shall atone for. But I bear, as you say, not his name nor his clothes nor his face. I am not he, Jerónima!"

But she thrust the ring in his face.

"Is this not your signet and superscription?" she cried. "Is not this ring yours, and the pledge of a vow you made?"

Shutting his eyes to the ring, he groaned: "Who can keep that pledge who wears the skirts of a man wedded to Holy Church?"

"What," she countered, "did you say a while ago: that the gods are law and must themselves keep faith; and that a vow to them can in no manner supersede a vow made to a mortal? You were vowed to me long before you were vowed to Holy Church; and therefore your first vow stands, though you may have made twice a thousand more to repeal it! Thus you decreed in front of your council. So have them summoned back to this hall to say how you judged my case. Let them decide if I have not a lawful claim on you. And let them testify if you did not say to me: *'On my oath, the man shall keep his promise and make good his word, if you have found him and can produce him.'* I have located the man, my lord; shall I call in your councillors?"

"No! No!" cried he.

"Then come and keep your promise and make good your word!" said she.

"But what can you want with me," moaned the prelate, "who am old and dying and weary of life, and incapable of passion? What can this carcass give you, Jerónima?"

"If you cannot give me love," said she, "you shall give me justice!"

"Then give me time to study this matter thoroughly, till I find how the law may requite you."

"I shall," she replied, "give you time, but only to put your affairs in order, before you lay down this office. A month shall I give you, my lord, from tonight's new moon. But when this moon darkens, I shall return to claim what is mine, and to fetch what was pledged to me, and to carry away what I possess."

As he gazed dumbstruck at her fearful beauty, she smiled and bowed down before him, saying:

"I kneel at your feet, my lord bishop, not for your blessing, which is mine already by right, like all else from your heart, but to remind myself of the years in which I lived on my knees, in hope and bewilderment, in heartbreak and humiliation, till my knees be sore as this heart I nurse. But when next we meet you shall kneel as my lover, even as you swore you would, forever and ever, on the banks of the Pasig!"

Having said which, she rose, flung the veil over her face, and swept out of the room, leaving the Archbishop to his throne.

The moon that was then on the wax too fast increased for his comfort, who counted the days with a sinking heart—a heart

that pulsed, painfully, to the words *Forever and ever!* And he
shuddered to think how himself when young craved the infinite, from a greed that saw no end to youth, love, appetite,
pleasure. Yet that juvenile voracity had, in one matter at least,
been glutted soon enough. Carnal concupiscence fast wilted in
the larger heat of the power lust; and the young man that on
the riverbank prayed for nights without end disappeared so
completely with his itches he had left not even the memory of a
memory, he that was so fond of crying *Forever and ever!* But he
had, it seemed, not died; had been only hiding elsewhere, bid-
ing the hour of return, now hovering close, and all the hot past
with him. And the Archbishop found the old man he was
imperiled by the young man he had been.

The son of a minor conquistador, he had grown up on the
tract of bats' land upriver that was his father's prize, that was
his father's plight, that ate up the unhappy old soldier who
farmed too little, drank too much, and mined in vain, venge-
fully trapping him drunk in one of its steaming swamps and
boiling him so clean only his bones were recovered by his young
son, who, all alone in the world, now learned that the King had
reclaimed the estate, and therefore thought of seeking his fortune in the city. No affections did he leave in the jungle save
one: the girl who dwelt on the opposite bank of the river, to
whom he rowed in the evenings, when the bats rumbled overhead, and from whom he slipped away before daybreak, when
again the bats rumbled. Parting from her for the last time,
promising to return, bidding her wait, he had left her a vow and
his ring and rowed away, in tears, gallant in hose and doublet
and a plumed hat, all the while glancing back at her seated on a
rock on the riverbank, as he had so often seen her, glimmering
in the half-dark of dawn, her lovely face grave and her unloosed
hair all about her, blowing in the wind and spilling the flowers
he had stuck there, while overhead the dark rumble of batwings
echoed his cry of *Forever and ever!* But in the city, entranced by
the glut of trulls and stews, and deeply indulging, he had fast
forgotten what faster fused into profusion, into a confusion of
nameless, faceless female flesh, a vague litter of bodies merging
into one huge hump of pure venery; and all this to be kicked

over into oblivion when, coming up at last from the long orgy of pubescence, realizing how mere lechery could not appease his hungers, he had sought to sate himself elsewhere; and so had sized up the cloth, picked a patron, donned a habit, and started the climb up the cloister to the Archbishop's throne, having discarded the young rake along the way.

Discarded, buried, forgotten utterly, that young rake in whom burned all the fevers of the world had survived in one other person's consciousness, had persisted and endured, and now pressed back, who had power to effect in the present what he had willed in the past, and the ability to unbury himself. And the Archbishop reflected that he feared not so much the young woman out of his past as the young man emerging from there, and all his fevered vitality. It was not that he feared to feel the young man in his old flesh: not from there could he emerge, which had been quelled, by one discipline or another, in the years of continence, its itches discarded along with youth's hose and doublet, and its fires quenched. No, the Archbishop feared no revolt of the senses; and he recalled how, when the woman unveiled her face and he beheld her radiant youthfulness and beauty, he had felt no movement in his body except of surprise.

What he feared was not failure of flesh but of faith. Which was the reality: the temporal or the spiritual realm? What if the world's masks, images, ghosts, were not the illusions they were despised as being? Might not the senses and their transient pleasures be the one permanence after all in a flux of thought and creed? Had he been reading the lesson in reverse? What if the itches of the flesh, its greeds and ambitions, were the true fire that gave off as mere smoke and vapor the sciences of the mind and the metaphysics of the spirit?

He thought in dismay of the woman in the veil, kept hard and fresh by her passions. He recalled his image in youth of the world as a vague heap of bodies forming one huge hump of venery. Yet this vile hump it was that spewed gods and goddesses, arts and cultures, and the other spiritualities that waxed and waned on it, while itself remained constant. Mortal man was not mortal save in the things of the spirit, which sensual man survived. This or that body died; but flesh, and the heats of the flesh, outliving its gods, persisted and endured forever: the bush that burned unconsumed.

The young man in hose and doublet who went sailing down-river had seemed as transitory as his fevers; yet he was still somewhere on the river, still on the move and still fevered with appetite, and therefore more actual now (thought the Arch-bishop) than this hollow old man in bishop's robes, all his appetites stilled, on whom the woman gazed without seeing, seizing at the young man she saw there instead.

On the desert isle had started his pursuit of the reality at the heart of the stillness, which he now feared to pursue—for what if, upon reaching the core of the stillness, he should find that unstill-ness was forever, and flesh the only reality?

His mind gagged at the thought. If in youth he had lusted for the never-ending—the story without a stop; food and drink that never gave out; embraces unlocked by no dawn's batwings—he now recoiled in horror from infinites. And his very vitals cried that no hell could be worse than this, which was, when young, his notion of paradise, but now soured his soul with nausea: to be young forever, steaming in youth's heats and sweats; and to love forever, rooting in perfumed carcass after carcass. That would indeed be damnation! But the young lover knew not what he said when he cried *Forever and ever!*

No more could the Archbishop resume his quest for the heart of the stillness, being doubtful, nor his solitude in the hut by the river, being troubled; and he fled from there at the full of the moon, returned to his palace, resumed the labors of his office, but, finding nothing to his satisfaction, fell into wrangling with his canons, and with the friars, and with the grandees, and with the governor, till all the city laughed that the miracle was over and the old devil back again.

But when the moon darkened he returned to the retreat by the river, stern and fierce, as though again on a battlement, manning a gun against a foe. And peering into the hut, where he had spent so many hours of contemplation, he felt no nostalgia for his time here but rather a deep embarrassment, knowing that the contemplative had been no less an absurdity than the popular holy man—one more masquerade, one more disguise.

The fleer from illusion was himself an illusion; and this hut but one more shell to be shed, like desert isle or cloister or hose and doublet.

Unable to bear the sight of the cell that now seemed a prison, he went out to the grove, and down to the edge of the river, the benevolent river, the brown river that had played with him in childhood and proffered the first love of youth. The water was a mere gleam of ripple to the wind in the dark of the moon. The night was as black as bats' land upriver; and he thought how wise the bats were to shun daylight and choose darkness, when the world drops its mask and lies unguarded, in the innocence of sleep. But he had prayed for light, which disguises, and not for darkness, which unclothes, revealing secrets in lovers' bed or dreamer's cry. Only the bats saw the world naked.

As he pondered the conceit he became aware that the woman stood beside him and, looking up, saw her unveiled and gravely watching him, her unloosed hair all about her, blowing in the wind, and flowers stuck in her hair.

"Is my lord ready?" she asked softly, after their wistful greeting of silence.

"Yes, Jerónima, I am ready," he returned, as soft and hard even as she was.

She waited, baffled, but he said no more, and it was he that now smiled at her.

"Shall we go then?" said she.

"*You* shall go, Jerónima," replied the prelate, "when you have handed me the ring."

But now she, too, began to smile, and drew closer, lifting her lovely face to his cold face.

"The ring, my lord?"

"In this garden, Jerónima, are troops waiting to arrest you. I have but to give the signal."

"Troops, my lord?" she laughed. "Are the King's troops called out for one weak woman and one small ring?"

"So give it to me, Jerónima, for, willing or not, you shall yield it."

"Is this," said she, holding out the ring, "what so troubles His Grace?"

"Jerónima," he groaned, "I beg you to face the facts. There

is nothing I can do to requite you, nor aught you can do to force me. But if you give me the ring, you shall depart in peace."

"And if I refuse?"

"It shall be wrested from you."

"And what would become of me afterward?"

"There are houses here of holy women, where I shall place you, with a dowry, and make sure you are cared for all your life."

"Jerónima in a nunnery!"

"Is that not better than bats' land?"

"Oh, my lord, have I not told you how I love those bats and their river?"

"Will you yield the ring?"

"Is it my lover who begs me?"

"This is your bishop who commands you, Jerónima, who must save you from yourself."

"I cannot yield him the ring, my lord, nor should I keep it, who am straitened on all sides. But yonder is the witness to our vows. Let it take the ring—and if it yield it up again, then shall you be quit of your vow."

And before he could stop her she flung the ring into the river.

He saw it drop with a tiny splash into the water, and he staggered backward, as white as a sheet, his knees buckling under him.

"What have you done, Jerónima!" he wailed as he sank. *"Oh, Jerónima, what have you done!"*

Horrified, she bent over the falling man.

"My lord, my lord, are you ill?"

But he turned his face from her, as he lay, collapsed, on the riverbank.

"Go, go, Jerónima!" he gasped. "Flee, make your escape! The soldiers come! Hasten from here, Jerónima!"

She hesitated, casting a wild look at his agonized face; then ran up the bank and into the woods, the flowers spilling from her hair as she fled.

When Gaspar came upon his master, the old man was hot with fever.

In the days that followed, the Archbishop lay ill in his palace, burning and delirious, and believed to be dying; and public prayers

were offered for him, who screamed in delirium of a wild river he
must pass over. But he crossed the crisis, and rose again from his
bed, though so gaunt and grim even his foes felt, in pity, that they
would rather have had him bellowing than thus bitterly mute.

His physicians advised a vacation in the country; the Archbishop dismissed them. With a vehemence as cold as desperation, he worked all day, prayed all night, though neither activity
brought relief. The river that he could no longer bear to see,
that had roared through his delirium, now rushed through his
mind, through his despair, never still, never stopping, until it
seemed the hemorrhage of the unstaunched wound of his life.
The river that was childhood's friend and youth's matchmaker
had become the old man's fiend.

Late one night, he was praying alone in the Cathedral, swaying in anguish as usual to the enraged rushing of the river, the
malevolent river, when he heard, through the surge of pain in
the darkness within him, a sob of pain in the darkness behind
him. Picking up his taper, he searched through the aisles and,
behind the pillar, came upon a form huddled on the floor, sobbing. As he bent down with his light, the griever lifted face
from the floor and the prelate saw it was the woman.

Her first words echoed his wail on the riverbank:

"What have I done, my lord bishop! Oh, my lord, what have
I done!"

"Jerónima!" was all he could say.

Grief had dimmed her young lovely face; and she had doffed
bridal white for penitential mauve, a white cord round her
waist, a black shroud on her head.

"I have dared come," said she, kneeling up to his crouched figure, "to beg you shrive me, though well I know this be another
outrage I do you, who should curse and not forgive."

"No, Jerónima," said he very sadly, as they thus knelt to each
other. "To forgive: it is all we can do for one another in the
world. So do you say you forgive me and I shall reply I forgive
you, and may God have mercy on the both of us."

As she gazed on his gaunt face, the tears sprang unsobbed to
her eyes.

"Oh, how my lord bishop has suffered!"

"But I cherish the thought, Jerónima, that although all the world should loathe me, who have lived most hatefully, one heart has loved me all these years."

At that, she wrung her hands and rocked her head, wailing:

"No, no, I never loved you, I never loved you! Nothing do you owe me, my lord bishop, for it was not you I loved but my own pride! You were as the river that pleased me because I saw myself in it. God has granted me the grace to see the truth at last of this time when we thought we loved, and thought falsely. For what were you to me but comb and brush and mirror, the tools of my vanity? Being young, I loved the laughter you stirred in me. Being fair, I loved the admiration you mirrored for me. Being proud, I loved the power you revealed in me. And being woman, I loved the pleasure you gave me.

"And when you left, my lord, and did not return, was it my heart that wept or only my pride? When I waited, waited, waited, was it not my own patience I loved, and my own faithfulness, and my own strength? But I thought it was you I continued to love when I but admired myself. This is the truth, my lord bishop, and the love I boasted to have kept through the years is as shallow an illusion as the youngness of my face. For grieving, I have loved my grief; betrayed, I have loved my resentments; humiliated, I have loved my injured pride. On these have I lived and thrived; on these has my young beauty persisted and endured, like a rose growing on charnel ground. Love's passions cloy, my lord, but not these others.

"Ah, if I loved you true, when I found you, when I followed you, when I saw for myself what you were, I would have departed unknown and unavenged, but unresentful. For I saw a holy man that would storm heaven. I saw him weeping, fasting, praying, on his hard bed, in his hairshirt. And I saw him in unearthly rapture. How could any child of God disturb such a labor? But because it was not you I loved but my pride, nothing would do but I must flush you out, to be haled, to be claimed, to be fetched, to be carried away, as though you were a weight of meat I had bought at the market, or property that bore my brand.

"The gods are law, you said; but were they only that, then pettier would they be than men, who know how to wed, rule, and ruth, and to mix maxim with mercy. For to read only the letter of the law, as I did, is not justice but spitefulness. Therefore do I beg your forgiveness, my lord bishop, who prized you as a thing to be possessed, in the name of justice, and not as a soul to love, in the name of charity."

But he said to her:

"I have been the tool of God for your illumination, Jerónima— comb and brush and mirror in his hand to put your soul in order, that it may shine as brightly as your beauty."

But she replied to him:

"I am weary of my beauty, that is the parent of my pride; and this flesh I wear hurts me worse than a hairshirt. Now do I think no curse more terrible than to be young and fair forever. Who shall deliver me from the bondage of this life?"

Wincing a little, the Archbishop spoke again of a possible placement in a house of holy women.

And she, echoing herself, laughed: "Jerónima in a nunnery!"

"Then what is to become of you?" asked the prelate.

And she said to him:

"Let me live again on the opposite bank from you. In a village outside the city, on the east riverbank, is a cave where I could go. Give me leave to dwell there, as a penitent, as an anchorite, to expiate my sins and to grope my way to heaven."

"You have my leave," said the Archbishop, "and I shall order that none may touch you in your cave."

"Then bless me, my lord bishop," said she, "and give me absolution."

Shriving, and shriven as well, the Archbishop, on his knees, heard the rushing river pause in his mind and, wondering over this, listening for the torrent, waiting for its roar, grew bemused and becalmed, unconscious of all around him, as the moment's hush widened into an eternity's rolling chant of *I forgive you, you forgive me*, until, a bell tolling, he started from his trance, from this rapture of forgiving and, looking about him, found the woman gone and himself kneeling alone in the Cathedral, his candle guttering on the floor.

A new phase began for the Archbishop, a meanwhile of serenity, not the cored stillness he had craved but a resigned, relaxed repose in the peripheries of being, where he worked without compulsion, prayed with no greed for epiphanies, and relearned the enjoyment of hot chocolate in the afternoon, a glass of wine at night. He doffed his hairshirt, called on the governor. The river raged no more through him; he was somewhere on its banks, watching and waiting.

He knew this quiet was but a respite. Presently he must descend again into the stream, this time forever, and learn if forever be indeed hell, or heaven—or purgatory? The soul appalled by the vanity of the world and the transience of flesh swung to the other extreme and, in turn dizzied by thought of infinity, rebounded to a cynical acceptance of flesh as the first, the final, the only truth. He had, thought the Archbishop, swung up and swung back, and now waited for, without pressing toward, a further revelation. Whatever that might be, it would not be alien but of himself, something he had willed, caused, created by being this man with these passions—not light dropped from above but light grown below: the light from the burning bush when smoke and vapor had cleared.

Of his penitent in her cave on the Pasig, he heard disturbing rumors but lifted no hand to aid her, knowing these ordeals were stages in her passion. When she took up abode in the cave, wondrous things happened to the villages nearby. The river that had been niggard now gave fish in abundance; rain fell in its season and fell prodigally; field and orchard flowed with fruit; cattle fattened and multiplied; barren women suddenly quickened. But the villagers, instead of exulting, shook with superstitious dread and murmured how all this was too good to be true, and therefore could not be good, since what but evil could spring from the illusions of witchcraft? In no one's memory existed a time when bats haunted this region, but now a swarm of them flocked round the cave of the woman on the riverbank; they came at her call; she had been spied talking to them and fondling the black beasts; and the villagers whispered that the woman herself turned into a bat at night and roamed the countryside, sucking the blood of sleepers. Therefore was her cave shunned by the villagers, and stoned by children; and she dared set no foot outside her grove on the riverbank.

Barely a year had she been in the cave when the villagers seized her. One day, Gaspar came running to his master to say how a great crowd of country folk were marching on the Cathedral, bringing the woman with them. The Archbishop strode out to the Cathedral square and there faced the delegation. The rustics were led by their curate; and the woman they dragged was, with much shouting, flung to the ground at the prelate's feet. She was in the filthiest of rags, her head and face shrouded in sacking; and she was bound all over with ropes, like a pig.

As the Archbishop gazed on her his heart wept, but the face he turned to the peasants and their priest was stern.

"Did I not order that this woman was not to be touched?" he thundered.

"No one touched her," replied the friar, "until her cave became a scandal."

"What wrong has she done?"

"She is a damned witch!" cried the friar; and at that, the crowd behind him clamored: "Witch! Witch! Burn the witch!"

The Archbishop stilled the uproar with a look of wrath and a raised hand.

"This woman," said he, "is a holy recluse praying for all sinners and doing penance for the world."

"She is no holy recluse," spat the friar, "but a witch and a harlot!"

"Can you prove your words, friar?" said the prelate.

The priest gestured toward the crowd behind him:

"Here are honest folk to testify how they have seen a young man come to this woman at night and stay with her all night in her cave, even till the break of dawn."

Again the crowd grew riotous, screaming:

"Burn the witch! Burn the harlot!"

The Archbishop had turned pale. But he said to Gaspar, who stood at his elbow: "Have the woman unbound and brought into the Cathedral, that I may question her privately."

At the altar, on his throne, the Archbishop confronted the woman, who knelt before him in her foul rags, her face shrouded in the sacking.

"Jerónima," said he in anguish, "what is this they report against you? Eyewitnesses have denounced the offense. Do you dare deny it?"

"Oh, my lord bishop," moaned the penitent, "the guiltiest of sinners am I—but not in this matter of their imputation. Before God, here in God's house, I swear no man has come to me, nor have I used the cave for aught save spiritual commerce. Seven times do I rise each day to pray; on my knees am I at midnight and at dawn. I fast, I scourge my flesh, I comb my conscience. What time or what appetite can Jerónima have for venery? But if you will not take my word," said she, "then look on my face and say if it be bait for harlotry!"

Whereupon she wrenched the sacking off her face; and the Archbishop gasped to see what a change had been wrought there in one year. For the face he saw was of an old hag—wan, wasted, withered, woeful; no radiance in it and no beauty; mere skin and bone and wild eye; and smelling of death.

"What young man," said she, "would lie with this foul carcass which can only lust for the grave? But let my lord see the rest of the rot."

And ripping the rags from her back, she bowed down to the floor, and he saw indeed the welts of the discipline on her flesh.

"Are these," sobbed the woman, "the marks of love's caresses?"

But he said:

"Rise up, Jerónima, and give glory to God that has released you from bondage. Your own flesh has testified to the truth of your word. Return to your cave and pray for us sinners."

But she could not rise from the floor.

And going down to her, he said:

"Have they used you so ill you cannot stand on your feet? Take my hand, Jerónima, and rise!"

"Oh, my lord bishop, it is another hand that should lift me, who am weary unto death! But I take your hand in greeting, I take your hand in farewell."

So he called to his men and bade them take the woman back to her cave; and to the peasants and their priest he said: "Let no one touch the woman in her cave till I myself have looked into this mystery."

And he said to Gaspar:

"Have horse and carriage ready; we ride forth tonight."

Riding forth from the city at twilight, the Archbishop shivered with senseless excitement and wondered if revelation was at hand. On the desert isle and in the retreat on the riverbank, he had pressed with might and main for an answer; had stormed (as the woman put it) heaven; and heaven had stalled him, stopped him, staved him off—the heaven that kept its secrets from the wise and mighty and revealed them to little ones. Children accepted the earth with frank pleasure, and lost innocence only in the grief of knowing themselves exiles from elsewhere. Was the quest, then, a relearning of this frank pleasure—and of reverence for the despised flesh, astonishment for the scorned world? Was it this quest which, extending beyond this life, made flesh and its fevers, even if they be forever and ever, not hell but, at worst, a purgatory, a school for lovers? "I never loved you!" the woman had cried; and never indeed had she, who needed more than youth's season or life's term to learn the prizing of the body, not as a minute to possess, in the rush of time, but as a being to love, in the light of eternity. Was this not the awful fate that lovers did not know they embraced when they cried *Forever and ever?* But their vows would stand—"lest chaos befall the world."

Thus musing, the Archbishop sped in his carriage along the river, the apocalyptic river, toward the village of the cave. It was a night of moon but the lonely countryside lay empty. When they reached the grove of the cave, Gaspar half-carried his master through the dark woods and down the rocks of the bank, till they came to a level where they looked down on the mouth of the cave but were hid from it by rock. The cave opened halfway up the steep bank and rocks formed steps from its mouth down to the water.

Hardly had master and servant positioned themselves when the air flapped with huge wings and the moonlight darkened to a swarm of bats wheeling over the cave. As though they were bell or clock sounding, the woman emerged from the dark cave, in her rags and shroud of sacking. Prostrating herself on a slab of stone, she began to pray; and such a keening rent the stillness it seemed that here wailed the whole world's conscience in contrition. The moon rose high, and still higher, and the night chill sharpened, but still the prostrate woman prayed, moaning and groaning, lifting imploring hands to heaven, like some mythic victim of the gods chained to a rock. But at last silence seized her, and more than silence; and the watchers on the rock above saw her as though dragged up by the hair, and dragged up to her knees, her arms opening, and dragged up to her feet, her arms opened wide and her veiled face wrenched toward heaven by a bliss that shook the air. The tremor lasted but a moment, and she fell, as though dropped, on her knees, where she stayed a while, swaying and shivering, her face in her hands. Then she rose and disappeared into the darkness of the cave.

Squatting motionless and cross-legged on the rock above, the Archbishop lifted his face to the moon. But Gaspar said to him: "Truly, my lord, this is a holy woman and one dear to heaven. So do you stay here while I go and upbraid the brutes that persecute her." But the Archbishop, still watching the position of the moon, gestured with a hand for silence.

The moon was now at its noon; and once more there was a sudden flapping of wings and a darkness in the air as the great bats, reappearing, wheeled slowly over the cave.

And all at once the watchers above were aware of a young man in a boat crossing the river toward the cave—a young man gallant in hose and doublet and plumed hat. Reaching the bank, he sprang out, made fast his boat, and darted up the stair of stone to the cave, where radiance awaited him, and a pair of arms that flew to embrace him and to draw him into the cave. From the rock above, the watchers saw lights twinkling in the cave and dimly heard music and revelry.

Rising and drawing his sword, Gaspar said to his master:

"Truly, my lord, this is a damned witch and one near to hell! So do you stay here while I go and slay the noxious dam and her tupper."

And on the instant he was scrambling down the bank to the cave where, marveling, he noted no lights nor sound of music and revelry, but only silence and darkness. And venturing inside with drawn sword, he glanced about and at last made out the form of the woman lying alone on the ground, covered with her rags and sacking, but not stirring to his call nor to the prodding of his sword. Lifting away the shroud with his sword, he perceived, in the beam of moonlight that fell on her aged face, that no breath moved in her. He touched her and felt her flesh as cold as the night wind, and he dropped to his knees and whispered a prayer over her.

Returning to the rock above, he told the Archbishop, who still squatted motionless and cross-legged in the moonlight, what he had seen, but the prelate seemed unsurprised, murmuring only, as he bade Gaspar take him home at once, that he, too, felt his hour upon him. "For tonight," said he, "I have gazed on my own ghost."

Carried, as he had bidden, to the hut of his retreat on the river-bank, he lingered there three days more, in his bed by the window that overlooked the water, his dying eyes never moving away from the river, the eternal river, until, on the third night, as though he had espied something there (and the deathwatchers said there was a fleeting radiance on the river, and a form as of a woman sailing swiftly past on a boat, her face lifted to the moon and her unloosed hair all about her), the dying man started abruptly from his pillows and, raising his hand as though to wave, or to salute, or to say aye, or to submit and accept and surrender, he smiled slightly, closed his eyes and sank back, and gave up the ghost.

From that day, Doña Jerónima has been sharing the Pasig with her lover.

The cave she occupies was, in pagan times ('tis said), the abode of a nymph who was gay and kind. Fishermen who chanced to see this *diwata* sitting outside her cave on the river-bank, combing out her long hair, knew the river would teem with fish for them. At night they often saw lights twinkling in the cave and dimly heard music and revelry (for the nymph was fond of feasting the world of faery). Next day, the gold gleaming under the water would be her plate laid out on the riverbed to be washed (for the lazy nymph let the river currents do her dish-washing). Lovers who lay in the woods often woke up to find their hands jointly clasping a jewel—which, however, turned into stone if they quarreled over it. Brides on the eve of their wedding heard laughter outside the window and, looking out, would find a gift from the nymph at the door. But she who was sensual could also be cruel. If she fancied a young man she lured him into her cave and fed him off her golden dishes; he would be found at dawn dazedly wandering in the woods, and thereafter would wander out of his wits.

When Cross and Conquistador came, the nymph departed forlorn. Her cave fell silent.

No more did fishermen hail it as they rowed past, nor their women come to lay offerings of white chicken there. No more did the cave gleam with lights at night there or tinkle with music and revelry—until Doña Jerónima appeared.

For at dawn of the night the recluse died in the cave, the villagers beheld Doña Jerónima sitting outside the cave, young and beautiful, and they knew she was kind.

Ever since then has the cave been alive again with its new *diwata*, and the river too, for Doña Jerónima and her lover range the whole route of the river, riding as swift as light, in their faery boat, from the dawn country upstream, where the Pasig flows from the lake, to the sunset land downstream, where it flows into the sea. You will know they are riding past if you hear a flapping of wings and look up and see no wings: Doña Jerónima's bats are wheeling overhead. And happy fishing will he have who catches a glimpse of the lovers as they fleet past, she reclining and combing out her hair, he rowing and gallant in hose and doublet and plumed hat, and both gazing into each other's eyes. Therefore do fishermen salute the cave of Doña Jerónima as they row past.

Many a night of moon does the cave gleam with lights and tinkle with music and revelry. Next day, when the river folk see golden dishes shining under the water they wink at each other and say: "Doña Jerónima has been dining with her lover."

Sometimes is she beheld seated on a rock outside her cave, a mere glimmer in the half-dark of dusk or dawn, her lovely face grave and her unloosed hair all about her, blowing in the wind, and her lover on his knees by her lap, looking up at her with eyes in which burn all the fevers of the world, his hands tucking flowers in her hair, while overhead creak the ghost batwings as the air darkens round the lovers.

And thus will it be with them—forever shall he love and she be young!—till the river yield up again the Archbishop's ring.

THE ORDER OF MELKIZEDEK

Toothbrush in raised hand, to tell Customs it was all his gear, Sid Estiva, lately come down from heaven but now unwinged by the general guilt, slunk past the courts of the baggage inquisitors, was thumbed the way to the airport lobby, stiffened to see a thin aisle through a crowd that smiled or smirked as he shambled by, ran smack into a tall woman in green who thrust her mouth at his face as if to kiss him. Were anyone here his welcomer it would be his sister Adela, but this woman was his sister only if Adela had been growing again in middle age. Besides, he and Adela now seldom kissed. The snouting kisser, however, aimed at neither his mouth nor cheek but an ear.

"*Toothbrush!*" she hissed.

His head jerked back in alarm.

"*Drop* the toothbrush!" snarled the woman. "People are *looking!*"

Suddenly aware that his right hand still held the toothbrush aloft, he clasped the shocked hand to his heart. Someone guffawed. He bowed coldly to the woman: "Thank you." But she had seized him by the other arm and was dragging him aside.

"Hey, what's this!"

"Shh," whispered the woman, peaked mouth again in his ear. "Walk out to the driveway and wait on the sidewalk. The car's a green and brown Chevy station wagon. Keep the toothbrush in your hand so the driver can spot you. But you don't have to hold it up all that high, my God!"

"Listen," cried Sid Estiva, "will you tell me who the devil you are?"

"Not here!" gasped the woman, eyeballs shuttling right and left; and indeed they were being engulfed by the two tides of welcomers and arrivals. "*Here!*" said the woman, thrusting a card into his left hand and scurrying away.

He glanced at the card. A toothbrush, bristles up, was sketched in black ink above a typed text. Before he could read the message a cry rang out and the crowd in the lobby swayed toward the entrances. Crushed forward, Sid Estiva shoved card and toothbrush into pockets, then fought his way up against the current. He was panting when he reached the bank of the airline counters. Whatever had driven up at the airport had disappointed the crowd, which was now surging back from the entrances, howling humorously. Sid Estiva could not place the tone: was it praise or protest? This was his first time back in Manila in ten years. The sweat that dewed his eyes like tears bewailed the amount of clothes he had on. His body sweltered that had been wintry only two days ago. He did not remember it was this warm here in mid-December.

"Mr. Estiva?"

The girl at his side was in gray sweatshirt and stretch pants and wore her lank hair down to her shoulders. Sid Estiva recognized the man haggardly peering over her shoulder as a co-passenger on the plane.

"Mr. Estiva, there has been a terrible mistake," the girl was saying. "You were given something intended for Mr. Lao here. He says you met on the plane."

The two men nodded at each other.

"Well, yes," began Sid Estiva, "there was this large female in green—"

"Our Mrs. Mañago," smiled the girl, "is not as capable as she looks."

The three of them looked around as another cry swelled from the crowd; some kind of tumult traveled the farther end of the lobby.

"Tell me something," said Sid to the girl, "what's going on here?"

Her glance back at the crowd was sad.

"A lynching, Mr. Estiva. We're supposed to have been insulted again by some foreign pop singers."

"Those guys over there?"

"No, those are just the managers. The boys haven't arrived yet. Mr. Estiva, do you have the card?"

"I put it in a pocket—" He began to knead this and that bulge on his suit. "I can't remember which one." Every pocket he delved into blocked his fingers with layer upon layer of handkerchiefs, cigarettes, match folders, aspirin, chewing gum, keys, and coins. Who the devil invented pockets anyway. The girl and the haggard man behind her tensely watched. "I can't seem to find it," groaned Sid Estiva, limply producing at last only his toothbrush. His two watchers flinched.

From the street came a wailing of sirens. This time its own roar seemed to blast the crowd away from the entrances and, knocked off balance by the recoil, Sid Estiva found himself falling now backward, now forward, now sideways, but somehow never down, propped up by the crowd that swept him along, his heels crisscrossing. A thickening of the mass slowed down the stampede and stood him up at last; nowhere in sight were the girl in gray and her haggard companion. He dug heels in; the crowd slid past round about him and cluttered up a stairway, leaving him at the foot of what he now perceived to be a stopped escalator. As he eyed that latest enigma he was seized on an elbow and whirled around: the large woman in green once more confronted him.

"The card!" she sputtered in his face.

The heels he now dug in had contacted mother ground; he was no outsider here to be pushed around but a proprietor, native to these shores, rightful breather of patrimonial air. He hardened eyes at the woman as, with thumb and finger, he plucked her hand from his arm.

"Go," said he, "to hell."

Turning his back on her, he marched up the unmoving escalator, not once looking back to see if she had followed.

On the second floor, which was lined on one side with bars and shops, the hunt had caught up with the quarry, or part of it anyway. Sid Estiva saw a white man fallen down on hands and knees to the floor trying to crawl away from the young wags poking at him on rib and rump. Girls in brief skirts and white boots wailed aloud as they tailed the procession, like the Marys on the Via Dolorosa. Sid Estiva had no idea if this sort of thing was as common here in the Philippines as in American cities, but this particular local march against the white man struck him as more downright than the civil-rights demonstrations he had watched—and watched uninvolved—in America. Here, to stop his blood from running with the hounds, he went into a bar, picked out a corner table, ordered a beer, and emptied his pockets.

He found the card crumpled into a handkerchief.

The typed message was about as mysterious as the sketch of the toothbrush:

Tuesday a.m. Appointment with dentist. Must.

Tuesday p.m. Get-together of section managers and trainees. Cocktails.

Wednesday noon. Luncheon meeting. Election.

At the Sign of the Milky Seed. Deck Six.

Sid Estiva amused himself with the card over his beer. What organization man was he ruining the schedule of by not surrendering this piece of pasteboard? That haggard man, Mr. Lao, hardly looked the organization type. Maybe he was only a trainee? On the trip from San Francisco, every time Sid glanced across the aisle, he had seen Mr. Lao huddling on another side in his seat by the window, sweating, it seemed, in spirit, a soul in discomfort. The stewardess had several times paused to indicate where the throw-up bag was.

He should, thought Sid, finishing his beer and a cigarette, return the card somehow and not add to poor Mr. Lao's agonies. He slipped the card into his breast pocket, then tried to catch the waiter's eye until he remembered that one didn't catch Philippine waiters' eyes. One hissed or *hoy'd* at them. The chit paid, he tarried in the dim cool bar, wondering again if he should have responded at all to the urgency of sister Adela's cable. Had he been drawn back by more than brotherly concern? He had landed at noon; it was now mid-afternoon; Adela might be worrying—or had she even bothered to check which plane carried him? As he rose he caught the waiter clearing the table watching him from the corner of an eye.

The escalators were moving now; they had, he supposed, been turned off just to spite the pop singers, now unfaithfully departed. In the lobby below was no sign of the large female in green or the girl in gray or Mr. Lao. Why did the bare lobby look so soft?

A man interrupted his vague searching.

"Taxi, mister?"

Poor Mr. Lao would just have to go on anguishing. Sid Estiva followed the driver to his taxi, crawled into his back seat, and gave him Adela's address. She had a new house in the suburbs. As he leaned back in the taxi Sid fleetingly thought that no beer in the world was quite like San Miguel beer.

When he next opened his eyes his first thought was that the new suburbs of Manila were even lusher than he had been told. To the right of him were rolling meadows fringed by woods: perfectly re-created countryside. But where were the chateaux? Then he glanced to the left. The body of water in the distance, sparkling in the afternoon sunshine, could not possibly be the Pasig or the bay. A sixth sense warned him not to start up. He had recognized the blue sparkle as the lake, which meant they were driving *away* from the city. He lay still, eyes half-closed, memorizing the taxi's name and number, printed on the inside of one door. The driver just glanced around as the taxi turned right into a narrower bumpier road. Sid Estiva caught a glimpse of a large billboard announcing a "memorial park." The American way of death out *here?* He had thought what was happening to him now only happened in James Bond movies. He had been warned against the taxis of Manila—but he was carrying no luggage and no money.

This was no more than a trail they were jolting through, a gothic aisle of boughs. Birds twittered in the green dusk where sunlight was but a neon edge on leaves. Eyes narrowed at the driver's mirror, Sid Estiva crept a finger to his breast pocket, fished out the card in there, crumpled the card up in his fist, then shoved it down an edge of the upholstery.

As though abruptly awakened he sat up and yelled:

"Hey you, where the hell do you think you're going!"

Not even looking around, the driver swung out his right arm. The backhand caught Sid in the face and flung him back against the upholstery. Round a bend appeared a green and brown station wagon parked beside a hut in a clearing. Two men in black jackets stood in front of the car, looking at the arriving taxi. The instant the taxi stopped Sid found himself dragged out by hands and feet and spread-eagled on the ground. He just had time to check on the theory that at such moments one's life passes before one's eyes. Nothing passed before his eyes; the enormous moment squatting down on him was a halt in time, a stoppage of breath and thought, a suspension of feeling. He could not even make himself make a sound, yet was aware of himself as being too stunned to be aware.

He was rolled over on his face and in simultaneous tugs was stripped of jacket and shoes, tie and socks, shirt and trousers, undershirt and shorts. He was naked but not being pressed down anymore and after a while made bold to lift his face from the grass. One of the two men was shaking his jacket by its hems and from the upturned pockets showered down handkerchiefs, cigarettes, match folders, aspirin, chewing gum, keys, and coins. The other man was crouched down on one knee intently sifting the spill. Among his underclothes on the grass lay Sid's passport and plane ticket, Adela's crumpled cable, that goddam toothbrush. The taxi driver stood apart, leaning against his car, smoking a bored cigarette.

The man shaking the jacket threw it away and walked over to where Sid lay. He shoved a shoe under Sid's breast and heaved him over face up.

"Where's that card, *pare?*"

The man's thick shoe was nudging Sid on a shoulder.

"If it's not there," Sid heard himself saying, "I don't have it."

The shoe dashed against his jaw.

"Where's that card, *pare?*"

The shoe loomed huge over Sid's face, dangling from the sky.

"Okay, okay, that's enough," said the other man, the man on his knee in the grass. The huge shoe withdrew from the sky and Sid sat up and felt at his jaw. The two men stood whispering to each other. Sid began to breathe normally, and to itch. *They* were in trouble, not he; and he rose to his feet. The taxi driver flung away his cigarette and swore. The two men jerked heads as one toward the driver. From beyond the clearing drifted a sound of voices. The sound might have been a magnet yanking Sid bodily off the ground.

Joint and muscle, not thought, catapulted him from clearing to shrubbery. His body had become pure speed, unstoppable, crashing into bush and vine, rushing through undergrowth. His limbs acted by themselves, each dash or swerve spontaneous. This being was but movement, instinct, impulse, engine, and could have split a tree. Only when it had torn through a thicket into a second clearing did the brute energy, recovering mind, sputter to a halt, gradually embarrassed, knowing itself naked before people.

Staring at him staggering were a woman in a pink dress and a barefoot old man in white undershirt and khaki pants ripped off at the knees, frayed sombrero in hand.

"I was held up," was all Sid could say. He waited, gasping, now utterly aware that he wore nothing but a watch.

"Well, but don't just stand there," laughed the woman, "cover yourself."

Sid clutched at his groin.

"What happened?" asked the woman.

He told her only about being shanghaied by the taxi driver and stripped by the two men.

"Are they following you?"

He looked back over a shoulder, listening.

"I don't think so."

"Near here, sir, is a constabulary outpost," gravely intoned the old man.

"Near here, sir," giggled the woman, "is my car. Want to wait in the back seat for us?"

Vexed by her giggling, Sid coldly bowed at her and walked away with the dignity of one who rated a *sir* even with no pants on. The car was a small Jap coupé. Sid found newspapers in the back seat and spread them over his lap. The red x's on his body were only scratches. The woman was still giggling when she and the old man got into the front seat.

"We're taking you to the constabulary," she announced.

"If you don't mind," he leaned forward as she started the car, "I'd rather you took me home." He explained he had just landed and gave her Adela's address. This sent the woman into another ripple of mirth.

"My God, I can't drive you in there the way you are. That's a *posh* village. Tell you what, mister—"

"Estiva. Isidro Estiva. I'm called Sid."

"Oh, I think I know you well enough to call you Sid!"

"Please do. And whom have I the pleasure—"

"*Mrs.* Borja. Tell you what, Sid—I live just off the highway; we could stop there and make you decent. Unless you want us to go back to where you say you were held up and see if we can locate your clothes?"

"You think it's only a story. I really don't usually go around without my clothes on, believe me. But, no, we better not go back there. I won't have you and your companion take the risk."

She smiled at the old man at her side.

"Mang Ambo here takes care of my lot back there, Sid. I'm planning to build soon."

"Isn't it rather out of the way?"

"When I first built off the highway I was a voice in the wilderness. But it's too crowded for me now. So off to a new frontier."

They came to where the memorial park billboard marked the mouth of the trail. She stopped the car and repeated instructions to the old man before he got out. He bowed toward Sid: "I commiserate with you, sir. Whatever help is in my power—" They left him bowing at the corner, the car turning left to join the thicker late afternoon traffic on the highway. Sid slid lower on the seat, pulling the newspapers up to his neck. Where the highway ended she turned left on another road, then right into a side street that seemed to be one motel after another, with names like Saratoga, Windsor, Biarritz, Versailles. "One reason I'm moving out," muttered the woman at the wheel, nodding toward something called the Taj Mahal Motel.

They stopped before a gate painted in quadrangles of different colors; she sounded her horn; a girl came running to open the gate; and they drove up to a low-slung house cresting a wave of lawn. She stopped on the carport and looked round at him.

"I'm afraid I can only lend you teenage clothing, my son's."

"I'm smaller than your husband, or bigger?"

"I don't have my husband's clothes."

He hesitated.

"Are you a widow?"

"No." Then she added, as she got out: "We just don't live together anymore."

She left Sid in the car. When she came back she was carrying mustard-colored dungarees and a shirt-jac in bold black and orange stripes. "I'm afraid I can't do anything about shoes." She inspected the shrubbery along the driveway while he dressed in the car. The shirt-jac was too broad in the shoulders for him but he had to squeeze his legs into the tight trousers. Neither shirt-jac nor trousers would button at his waist. Crippled by the trousers, he limped out of the car to show Mrs. Borja the mid-riff gap between man and boy.

"I've sent the maid for a taxi," she was giggling again. "You haven't developed a phobia about them?"

"Is the younger generation really built this way? How old is your son?"

"Fifteen." That would make her around 35, thought Sid. "There's a telephone," she said, "if you want to call up your sister."

"No need, I think."

They were standing where the driveway and a piazza merged and the junction was marked by a bit of rock garden built against a corner of the house. On top of the rocks was an old wooden image of a saint; above it hung a capiz-shell lantern. He glanced toward the piazza; instead of the usual wrought-iron art were wicker chairs with lyre backs in the antique manner, a *perezosa*, even a round marble table with a clawed leg.

"You look surprised, Sid."

"Very. Is the past really this much in fashion?"

"How long have you been away?"

"Ten years. When I went away one was sick if one looked back at stuff like that." He nodded toward the termite-eaten saint on the rocks.

"Oh, everybody's collecting them now. Why, did *you* look back?"

"And got jumped on the neck for it. I thought I was a poet then, or maybe an artist. And I was rather fascinated by old things— folk fiestas, icons, the décor of the past. But being interested in that sort of thing was supposed to be unhealthy, reactionary."

"Well, Sid, you'll be happy to learn that what was reactionary then has become very avant-garde. Do you know we actually organize expeditions now to see old fiestas? I must read what you wrote."

"It wasn't much. And I stopped long ago."

"Because they jumped on your neck?"

"Not entirely. I think I got scared. If you go back into the past it could come back."

"How do you mean?"

"People who said that sort of interest was unhealthy were not wholly wrong."

"And so you gave it up to become—what?"

"I'm with a UN agency, in New York."

"Oh—to save the world."

"But it *has* come back."

He was staring at the saint on the rocks.

"Stop it, Sid. You trying to scare me? And there's your taxi." They moved down the driveway together.

"If you need help," she said, "I'm in the book. Look under interior decorators. Sonya's. That's me and mine. But you'll be shy about us meeting again?"

"Oh, I want you to know me with my clothes on."

Adela's village was the other way up the highway and was entered through a sentinel'd gate, like a fort. The houses here all had low walls and chic front lawns and unbarred windows. Bidding the taxi wait, Sid Estiva hobbled on bare feet up the driveway to the front door, which was actually on the side of the house facing the driveway. Beside the open doorway was a

prop on which stood a small ravaged old wooden Virgin. Sid
stepped into the living room. Adela was parting the drapes at a
window, to let in the last of the afternoon light. Sid planted
himself in the middle of the room: bare-footed, boy-trousered,
shirt-jac'd, arms akimbo—the returned native, escaped from
the perils of passage.

"Ah, there you are, Isidro," said Adela, looking around.
"Plane got in all right?"

The guests that evening were mostly Adela's crowd but she had
dug up two of Sid's old chums, Jing Tuason and Etoy Banaag,
and their wives.

"But before you boys go off into auld lang syne," said Adela,
"Isidro has to meet everybody."

Like most of the women there, Adela was in patadyong and
kimona. The men were mostly in tan or faded-blue business
suits. Sid was in a baro and gray pants borrowed from his
brother-in-law. The brother-in-law, Santiago, Adela's husband,
looked antebellum in white sharkskin, small gold cross on lapel.

"I thought," said Sid to a woman he had just been presented
to, "everybody here now wore black suits at night?"

"To something informal?" The chill in her tone was for what
she clearly assumed to be a New Yorker's irony. "Only the very
young or the very naïve maybe."

Sid noticed how certain phrases recurred like refrains: fashion's current passwords apparently. "Do that" or "Yes, do
that" was what the ladies smiled if he said he would call them
up or get them a drink or have to rejoin Adela. If he asked a
man about the last election or the Vietnam war or any current
event, the cheerful snap was "No comment!" and everybody
listening roared with laughter as though something witty had
been said. Sid supposed that a local significance he was unaware
of had made the phrase funny and he felt himself an outsider
after stopping feeling puzzled each time they laughed.

But he was impressed by the shine of the crowd. This was a
middle-aged collection, not beautiful people really, but they
moved with an ease fibered by money in the bank and food
from supermarkets. Perhaps it was that which, making them

beautiful in each other's eyes, produced their collective aura. Sid was startled, as he circulated, to be told that his sister wore "famous clothes" and was a "glamour matron." As far as he could see, Adela was as doughy and pudgy as ever—but her husband was a bank president and a Papal Knight. Still, Sid had to admit that the shine came from more than the mutual admiration of bank accounts. These were not the top nobs but they were clean, decent, reasonably honest folk: salt of the earth agleam. The prevalence of bald heads and paunches in the men coincided with the cantilevered masses of hair and bosom on the women, for whom couture and coiffure had rashly become architecture. They also now sipped at wine or booze; and Sid waited in some suspense until Adela announced that the buffet table was "ready to be raided." She added that, in deference to the returned native, presumably famished for home cooking, the food was "barrio fiesta." The buffet table offered a sopa de fideos, boiled lobster, stuffed boned bangus, a kari de pata with bagoong, pork and chicken adobo, a coconut-heart salad, and lechon. Remembering the steak and barbecue parties of the fifties, Sid felt he was heaping his plate with the culinary equivalent of the antique Virgin in Adela's portico.

Candlelit tables had been set out on lawn and piazza but Sid found his old chums Etoy and Jing among the folk who preferred to eat indoors, in Adela's den, where furniture from their father's house environed a life-size photograph of the old man himself, in its old baroque frame, on a paneled wall.

"We've been admiring it," said Etoy Banaag, putting an arm around his wife. "Picture of the Founder. He looks quite a fellow."

"Vitality, he had it." Sid waved a fork at the picture. "Born penniless, educated himself, became lawyer, editor, politico. Married three times, all heiresses. Had one child by each wife. Third time a widower when he died."

"Mrs. Ferrer is not your full sister?" asked Mrs. Banaag.

"No, Adela's mother was from Vigan. My mother was from Bacolod. And the youngest of us, Guia, the child of my father's old age—her mother was from Ermita."

"North, South, and Centre," laughed Jing Tuason. "Hey, your

old man was some sexual geographer. And sexual economist, too. Your sister Adela's tobacco money; you're sugar—Guia is real estate?"

"But we used to think," said Sid, "that Guia was the Cinderella. Her mother's Ermita property wasn't worth much after the war, ruined and all. Now Guia could buy out both Adela and me."

"I remember Guia," said Jing Tuason. "That little skinny kid I kept thinking was your niece?"

"Well, Adela used to get so mad when I was mistaken for her nephew. There's a decade between every two of us. Adela's forty, I'm thirty, Guia is twenty. Adela *has* been resurrecting things. She used to think this sort of stuff was hideous—you know, the old Sun Studio life-sizes in gorgeous frames. Had this taken down from our sala and stored away. She said it was vulgar and scared off her boy friends. This was just before the war; I was seven: Father only laughed. Father's having the last laugh, too."

"High, high camp," said Etoy Banaag. "Boy, to hang a life-size pic of yourself in your house, you'd have to have a lot of nerve."

"Which," shrugged Jing Tuason, "we don't have."

"But we don't call it no nerve," said Etoy, "we call it understanding."

"Guia Estiva!" Jing Tuason's wife suddenly cried. "Why, we were in the same school, I was a couple of grades ahead, but we were on one judo team together. Oh, you'll never guess where we last met. At a *fortune-teller's*."

Looking around at Mrs. Tuason, Sid noticed that Etoy Banaag's wife, nestling in her husband's arm on the seat they shared, had sat up.

"A fortune-teller," repeated Jing Tuason's wife, setting her plate down on the floor and licking her fingers. "I don't know what had got into me. This was last year, Jing—when the baby didn't seem to be going right inside me and I felt so rotten? Well, there was this dame told me about this fortune-teller— for my peace of mind, she said. No, not one of those crummy joints in Quiapo where they spit on your palm. This was high-class; I was told the clientele included eminent society matrons.

You had to make an appointment, like at the dentist's, so the clients wouldn't bump into one another, I suppose. One's shy at confessionals. But that day there was a mix-up. Guia and I bumped into each other. Our appointments were for the same time. I told Guia she could have it and scrammed. What a relief. I suppose Guia was doing it just for kicks. She was always rather far out, a kook."

"You didn't see the prophet himself?" asked Etoy Banaag's wife.

"No, as I said I scrammed."

"What did the place look like?" asked Sid. "The fortune-teller's."

"Like any reception hall in a plush office. Carpeted, air-conditioned. This was in that big new building in downtown Quiapo. High priest something, he called himself. Mystic Doctor of the East and all that jazz. Some fiesta-fair swami gone up in the world, I suppose."

"Out of this world, out of this world!" groaned Jing Tuason, shaking his head at his wife.

"Out of this world," said Etoy Banaag's wife, in a careful voice, "could also mean *from* this world, *in* this world, *of* this world. The here and now, I mean—not anything fantastic."

Sid became aware that a woman wearing what looked like a Moro costume—patadyong with a kind of sari—was interested in his group's talk and had detached herself slightly from her own group to listen. She seemed to be trying to catch Mrs. Banaag's eye.

"Oh, the here and now can be fantastic enough," said Sid, raising his voice, on a hunch. "You folks should hear what happened to me at the airport this noon, and all because I waved a toothbrush."

He was looking straight at Mrs. Banaag.

"A toothbrush," she said, and waited. No expression at all. But Sid now found the woman in Moro dress at his elbow.

"A toothbrush, Mr. Estiva?"

"Oh, hello. Yes, just an old mangy green Prophylactic. Gather around, folks, and I'll tell you the horrid story."

"Yes, do that." The woman smiled round at the group. "I must hear this. What happened, Mr. Estiva?"

Sid's watchful eyes caught no flicker of cognizance between the woman and Mrs. Banaag. The latter's blank look now included both him and the intruder.

"What happened? I got shoved a card: somebody's schedule of appointments."

"*What* an anticlimax!" laughed the intruder, rolling her eyes.

"Oh, there was more," said Sid. "I was kidnapped, stripped, almost beaten up."

"And all at the sign of a toothbrush," chortled the woman.

"No," said Sid. "At the Sign of the Milky Seed."

This time he saw Mrs. Banaag start. But the sari'd woman at his side was still chortling.

"That sounds like a health bar," she snickered, "or an ice-cream parlor."

"It sounds to me," said Sid, "like something else."

"Hey, what's all this!" cried Etoy Banaag, sitting up. His wife was doubling over, clasping her hands. The Jing Tuasons frankly stared.

"It sounds to *me*," said the sari'd woman, "like a *very* shaggy dog story. And look what you've done, Mr. Estiva; reduced your audience to stitches." She bent over Mrs. Banaag. "It's not that bad, girl. I've heard worse."

Mrs. Banaag lifted her face. The two women looked at each other, the intruder smiling as she straightened up and drew back, Mrs. Banaag staring.

"What's with you, hon?" asked Etoy Banaag of his wife.

She coughed, shook her head.

"Too much to drink, I guess. Excuse me." She smiled at the company. "I have to go to the little girl's."

She rose, sped headlong across the room, bumped against an edge of table, and sank to the floor. The sari'd woman was first at her side, lifting her head up, whispering in her ear. The chorus of squeals had brought Adela to the doorway.

"What's the fun in here?" she asked eagerly, with her hostess smile.

Etoy Banaag had raised his wife to her feet and was now helping her toward the doorway, the sari'd woman hovering solicitously on the other side.

"Don't tell me someone *else* has passed out!" laughed Adela, hurrying forward and enfolding both the Banaags in her arms.

Watching from in front of his father's picture, Sid Estiva mused that Adela was of the North indeed: she never lost her head.

Santiago Ferrer, with jacket doffed and tie loosened, still looked as correct as when smiling attendance on his guests, the last pair of whom he had just seen to their car. Sid now found the courtliness focused on him. The hired bartender, as he folded up his tent on the piazza, was bidden to mix Mr. Estiva a nightcap, which the host himself carried to Sid in the living room.

"No, *cuñao*, I know little of your friends the Banaags. He teaches, writes a column for one of the weeklies, is said to be a fervent nationalist. She also teaches and, I suppose, follows her husband's ideas."

"How about that Moro lady?"

"But she is not a Moro lady, *cuñao*. She is a distinguished businesswoman, she runs a travel agency."

Adela came in and shooed away the servants picking up plates and ashtrays from the floor.

"Santiago, sit down. Put away that drink, Isidro, and listen."

"Are you going to scold me about the Banaags?"

"Goodness, why? I liked them. No, we have to talk about Guia."

"My dear," said her husband, "at this time of the night?"

"Tomorrow, she may have arrived. She's in the provinces now, with that group of hers, evangelizing I suppose."

"Let me tell him, my dear," interrupted her husband, "what I told her the last time she was here."

"Yes, do that."

"I told her, if she really had a vocation, here was this community willing to accept her as postulant. I warned her that if she continued with this group of hers, which is not recognized by the Church, and I doubt it will ever be, she may find the door of every convent in this country closed to her. But your little sister, *cuñao*, is hard-headed. She believes this group of hers will in time win ecclesiastical approval, which is madness."

"Why, what's wrong with her group?"

Brother-in-law Santiago pressed thin lips together and darted eyes upward.

"Heaven forbid," said he, humorously enough, "that I should ever speak against the Holy See. But it seems to me that the Vatican Council has only wrought confusion. At Mass now, nobody knows when to stand, when to kneel. Everything has been disarranged. Only yesterday a young man came to me at the bank; I almost fainted when I found out he was a *priest:* he was dressed in the style of a *teen-ager.* And with *permission.* Now what is happening here, I ask you."

"Well, then, maybe Guia is right to hope."

"Oh no, no, *cuñao*—with her group it is different. Yes, on the surface, it may look like one more of these modernizing movements. Making Christ meaningful to our times, relating the faith to the world of today. Yes, that is how they talk, her group. And they protest that theirs is not a formal order, not a congregation, not even a cofradia yet—merely an informal club of the devout. But such are the rumors about it that the ecclesiastical authorities have deemed it wise, though also informally, to conduct an investigation. We suspect this is not really a religious movement but a nationalist one. They have rented that old nunnery turned into a bodega in Intramuros and made it their headquarters. I visited it with the commission. They have a kind of chapel. The images there are like Igorot carvings, like primitive pagan art. I saw, let me tell you, a figure of the Virgin pregnant, like those figures dug up in Batangas and Mindoro."

"I am not," Sid laughed out loud, "shocked!"

"Wait, *cuñao*, wait. These people never applied for a chaplain, but we hear they are being served by a *defrocked* priest who sings a Mass to which they *dance.*"

"Dancing in church," Sid was still shaking with laughter, "is not exactly new to Philippine Catholicism."

"Do be serious, Isidro," cried Adela. "Oh, all this is your fault. When Guia asked to have her own apartment I was for her staying under my roof but you sided with her."

"She had turned eighteen."

"She is my and your ward until she turns twenty-one and should be living with you or me."

"Oh, don't be such a fossil, Adela."

"Well, look what has been happening since she went off on her own. One crazy thing after another. This weird New Christian group is just the latest. First there were those awful young writers, then a beatnik gang, then she went into advertising and all those media people, and afterward oh all for nationalism. And now religion. I do not for one minute believe she has any vocation. She just likes fads. I didn't mind the other phases; she made do with her allowance, rarely pestered me for more. But this now is serious, this now is a crisis. That's why I cabled you. And you're to blame, Isidro—egging her on instead of trying to put some sense into her. Now what are we to do? Papa put us in charge of her. Are we to abdicate, declare her of age, turn over the estate to her as she now demands, though we know perfectly well she'll only turn it over to that crazy sect of hers?"

"I'd have to talk to her first."

"But she's in the hands of adventurers, Isidro."

"How did she get mixed up with them anyway?"

"In that world she has run off to, it was inevitable. That's where all the queer birds fly: artists, radicals, beatniks, charlatans, and heaven knows what else. I may be a fossil but I didn't interfere, though the things I *heard*. Let her live her own life, I told myself, as you bade me, but she's not living it, she's ruining it. Well, I do think this prodigal daughter has had a long enough holiday from the real world. Two years. She has had her fling. Now I am putting my foot down. She is not to dissipate her inheritance. She is to come back to this house and stay here, learn the duties of a woman, associate with normal folk, go out with nice boys, marry and have children and a home. Carlota Jones has long had her in mind for her eldest boy, and still does, despite this bohemian silliness, and I am for pushing the match. I can't be at peace with my conscience till I've seen her settled down. She has always been more of a daughter than a sister to me."

"My dear, not so fast," put in her husband. "If the girl is going through a mystical phase the kind thing to do is let her get it out of her system. Which is why I advise putting her in a regular congregation. If the life is not for her she will get out fast enough and then it will be easier to marry her off."

Guia, thought Sid, shouldn't have happened to such a couple as the Ferrers. Looking round the room, he wondered if more than a party had laid it waste. But amid the disorder sat Adela and her husband, side by side on a sofa, alike faces turned to each other, sensibly and politely arguing: she for a quick marriage, he for a temporary veil. Sid smiled at the old-fashioned sense of their expedients, yet marveled that they could remain so practical in the glare of underworlds from which (or so he had heard that night from the party's mothers) no home today was safe. At any moment might suddenly appear at the door, for children "of the best families," a policeman with a warrant of arrest.

No sooner had he thought this than a maid came in to say a policeman was at the door, asking for Mr. Estiva. Brought in, the policeman admitted to having no warrant of arrest. Mr. Estiva was merely being "invited" to headquarters, to answer a few questions. "I'll come with you," said Santiago, already getting into his jacket. Sid stared as Adela, smiling hostess again, offered the policeman a saucer of olives.

"I'll call up Attorney Arranz, Isidro, and send him after you," she said.

"Do that," said Sid before he could think.

In the police jeep he felt himself the Kafka hero, being borne to judgment for he knew not what crime. But I know what my crime is, thought Sid. That goddam toothbrush (what was happening now was, of course, its latest repercussion) had been waved as a banner of non-involvement. If he traveled without luggage it was because buying clothes at the other end was less fuss than opening up to Customs and explaining. If he lived abroad it was because being alien committed you to nothing local. You couldn't read a newspaper at home without upping your blood pressure; abroad, newspapers read like anthropology. Even his job at the UN agency involved him in nothing, save in his group's illusion of being useful: present as relief wherever the world hurt. But the benevolence was magic by remote control:

papers moving from office to office, a figure in a report, a line on a graph. And at the other end the recipients of benevolence were statistics. Because he would bypass Customs he had traveled bearing only a toothbrush, had come home with no gifts for Adela and Guia, for kith and kin, and for that crime was now being harassed by the native gods of custom.

"Don't say anything," said brother-in-law Santiago when the jeep stopped at headquarters. "I'll do the talking."

The first thing Sid saw when he entered the police station was a frayed sombrero resting on knees: the old man of the white undershirt and khaki pants cut at the knees sat patiently on a bench, dignity still intact at that late hour in this criminal porch. Then he saw Mrs. Borja advancing on him, a Mrs. Borja smiling apologetically, as if this were still Adela's party and she were coming in late.

"Sid, oh Sid . . . Hey, *now* I've seen you with your clothes on."

"Not yet, these aren't mine—what are you doing here?"

"Oh, Sid, I had to tell them where you were."

"What's it all about?"

"They haven't told you?"

"No, nothing."

"That taxi you took at the airport—the driver has been murdered."

The driver had been shot from behind, in his taxi, at the wheel, when just about to drive away from that clearing in the woods of the proto-suburb. A constabulary patrol had come upon the body; the summoned police had found their way to Mang Ambo's hut nearby and Mang Ambo had led them to Mrs. Borja.

"I think they rather thought," laughed that lady, "I was a gangster's moll, Sid. Yours."

She and Sid, released from their all-night ordeal after giving statements and the promise to be available, stood beside the tragic taxi, in the taxi company's yard. The taxi had been washed inside and out. Sid had searched the back seat in vain: the card was not there. Now they waited while an employee fetched the boys who had washed the car.

"Your homecoming hack, Sid."

"No, my getaway car."

"Toyota '65. Jap invader number two."

"I was trying to escape as usual."

"Do we look unwashed: your crumpled baro, my crushed coat."

"Because I didn't follow through a kindly impulse—return that goddam card—a man died."

"Oh, Sid, we had this all out at breakfast: it was because they had slipped something in your beer."

"No, it's like I told you: I don't like fuss, getting involved."

"Who does?"

"You are enjoying this, Sonya. You like a happening. I don't. Not to me anyway. I'm not curious, not adventurous."

"How about that young go-go for old things?"

"The safely dead past. Kicks from icons. Yeh, man, we dig. Hah. Daring of me, wasn't it? Besides, that wasn't me really, only my father in me. He was a vulgar adventurer, the kind they say battens on experience. If anything scared me off, it was the thought of him coming back. Like, now, in my sister Guia. I think she's the only one of us who's our father's child."

"We are all of us our fathers," sighed Sonya Borja, "though we don't know it."

"My wife used to say I was like that Quaker who told his wife all the world was mad except him and her and he sometimes had his doubts about her. Now that wasn't fair, as I tried to explain to my wife. But explaining was a mistake. After I had made it clear I didn't object to other people's being mad, she left me. She said it had become a strain: pretending Manhattan was a desert isle where only the two of us lived. Now she's married to a Pinoy old-timer on the West Coast who raises horse feed."

The employee came back to say the "washing" had found nothing.

"I always try not to be where the action is," said Sid as he and Sonya walked out of the sunny, busy, dusty yard so heartlessly moving out its own traffic jams to the glut beyond, "so, now, I'm up to my neck in it."

A greasy girl of about fifteen in shirt and denim pants suddenly blocked the sidewalk.

"Sir, ma'am, you are looking for something?" The accent was southern. "Maybe I found it."

"Are you the washing?" asked Mrs. Borja.

"No, missis. I have a stall inside where they eat, the drivers. There at the back, where they wash the cars. Sometimes I look in the cars first, but not always, no—just to see was something forgotten. Sometimes a magazine, or a fallen coin. Very often, panties. Aie, *por bida man guid*, I would not touch those, no, not even if golden."

"This taxi where the driver was shot—" began Sid.

"Yes, I looked inside but I saw nothing. Then I put my hand down the edge of the seat. Sometimes money drops in there. I found only waste paper. So I threw it away."

"You threw it away."

"Then I heard, sir, you were looking for something there. So I ran to where I had thrown it away."

"Yes?"

"But they had swept the yard already."

"Alas," said Sid.

"This," said Sonya, "is beginning to kill me."

"So," said the girl, "I ran to where they throw the garbage, and I searched and searched." She paused, enjoying it, hands behind her back. "And I found what I had found."

She held out a fist that opened to reveal a crumpled card. Sid picked it up and pulled it flat.

"Is that it, sir?"

"Yes, girl, this is it."

The girl's palm was still up. Sid glanced at Mrs. Borja. She laughed, opened her bag, fished out a peso that she clasped into the girl's hand: "Thank you, Inday."

In the coffee shop across the street they pondered the card together.

"My hunch is that they get at the women through a fortune-teller."

"Milky seed . . . milky seed . . . Deck six . . ." mumbled Sonya.

"You getting warm?"

"And fortune-teller . . . Listen, Sid, there's this prophet, and he's supposed to cater to high society, who calls himself Melkizedek. *Melki-zeed-dek*."

"Mrs. Banaag used that word: prophet."

"And you said the other lady spoke of a big new building in Quiapo?"

"Deck six would mean a sixth floor. Are there many buildings now in downtown Quiapo six stories and over?"

"Only one that I know of, and right on Miranda."

"Elementary, Dr. Watson. Shall we go?"

The elevator that took them to the sixth floor of that "big new building in Quiapo" surprised Sid by being an express. The process of elimination (all the other offices on that floor had names on their doors) brought them to Room 666, which had no name on the frosted-glass door, no lights inside.

"You wait here, Sid. I'll get the building superintendent. He'll open up for us. I've decorated at least two offices in this building."

The superintendent garrulously opened up. Room 666, said he, had never had a name on the door, was leased to a Mrs. Cruz, who had moved out just the night before, leaving no forwarding address. Her people—to the annoyance, said the superintendent, of the watchmen—had spent the whole night emptying the suite. However, everything was in order. Mrs. Cruz had simply forfeited her rental deposit. The superintendent shrugged that, yes, Mrs. Cruz was most probably only a front; he had heard the real tenant was a magician.

The state of the suite—a reception hall and two inner offices—confirmed the hasty evacuation. The floor was littered with crushed newspapers and packing-case straw. But nothing had been left behind save one trash can into which someone had leaked on the ashes of burned papers.

On the way out Sid scanned the door again. Crumbs of pulp indicated where something stuck there had been scraped off. The superintendent scratched his head, then remembered that the nameless door did use to carry a small drawing: of a sheaf of grain dripping, or something like that.

"And so to bed?" said Sonya as they flinched again to Plaza Miranda's glare at Christmas shopping.

"No, to Intramuros. The old nunnery."

This was, thought Sid, jolting through downtown, a Manila his backside did not recall. If I closed my eyes, this could be the dirt road to a childhood summer in the provinces. But how shut eyes as agape now as then at the primitive? Rizal's image of the city as a frail girl wearing her grandmother's finery no longer fitted; this was a dirty old broad got up all wrong in a yé-yé girl's clothes. The old city walls that came into view across the soiled air and a bridgeful of chaos astonished with their look of calm and dignity.

The squatters' shanty town he had left in there ten years ago had vanished, but the new high-rise offices along the muddy tracks looked just as wrong, were still squatters on ground that insisted on being more vivid remembered than seen. Only in the Cathedral, its thin dome widowed by an alien skyline, did memory and appearance converge.

Mrs. Borja slipped her car into the alley the dead end of which was the wall of the fort. To the right was another block of wall: the old nunnery. The door in that high blank wall, Sid recalled, had led to the nuns' chapel, unlocked on great feasts to the world. The war had violated a cloister concealed for three centuries; the nuns had since moved elsewhere; cargo was stored where once God had a bridal suite.

From the stopped car Sid glazed at the closed door. This might still be a nunnery, so silent and secret its walls. Then, feeling Mrs. Borja's eyes on his nape, he alighted, stepped up to the door, and knocked. He could hear the sound echoing back, returning to him deepened by, he supposed, the hollows of cell and corridor. He waited, then knocked again. But the door was deaf to the world as of old. Whoever was in there listening, thought Sid, computed in echoes.

As they backed out of the alley, a thick rain spat through the sunshine.

"The devil's wife is mating," yawned Mrs. Borja.

It was time to go home.

But Sid was for waiting a while, with the car parked across

the street from the mouth of the alley, and the two of them inconspicuous in the back seat.

"There *is* some connection between here and that office in Quiapo, between Guia's group and the Prophet Melkizedek."

"Look, Sid, you haven't seen Guia for ten years—"

"Not quite. Adela took her around the world when she was fifteen and they stopped over in New York. And three years ago, when she finished high school, I sent for her, she stayed a summer with me."

"She already a kook then?"

"Not that I remember. She only went to the Village a couple of times. But very serious. Did all the galleries and museums, even made me take her all the way up the Statue of Liberty, my God."

"And you told her not to be such a square."

"Yes."

"You don't feel guilty about that, too!"

"It's like I told you: I don't mind other people's being mad. I'll encourage them, in fact. Adela thinks I encouraged Guia. Adela was going to give her a debut when she turned eighteen but Guia wouldn't have it. She said what she wanted was to be allowed to live on. I made Adela yield. So Guia took an—"

"Apartment? What's the matter, Sid?"

"The car! There's the car!"

Coming up the street was the green and brown station wagon, a capped chauffeur at the wheel, two women inside.

"Is that one of the men who stripped you?"

"No."

The car had stopped at the corner of the alley. The two women got out, carrying airline bags and guitars. One of them stopped to say something to the chauffeur. Sid could feel Mrs. Borja watching him staring, but he could not move, could not breathe, and knew that to move or breathe would be to feel pain.

He heard Mrs. Borja from far off:

"It's Guia?"

Suddenly the pain was right there.

"That's Guia."

He could feel Mrs. Borja waiting—but what could a stricken man do?

"No, we don't do anything," he said.

The station wagon drove past and the two girls, both in sweatshirts and jeans, scampered up the alley (it was still drizzling through the sunshine), stepped up to the nunnery door, and rapped. The door opened, then closed behind them, and the alley muted up again in the sunny shower.

Sid was still staring.

"Now we know," said Mrs. Borja, "there are people there. Shall we try again?"

"No, not now." Sid had sunk back on the seat. "Take me back to Adela's," he said.

Guia's voice, low-keyed but lively, drew him to Adela's den when, having woken in surprise to darkness (had he slept through noon, afternoon, evening?), having shaved and bathed, and picked a shirt and trousers from the clothes he had ordered, he came downstairs wanting supper.

He paused at the door of the den, dreading the encounter. Adela and Guia sat with heads together, on opposite chairs, softly chattering. Above their heads rose their father in eternal tuxedo. In a rocking chair angled to the sisters' vis-á-vis sat another girl, sipping at a cup—the same girl Guia had been with this morning. The girl glanced around, saw Sid in the doorway, and leaned forward to speak to Guia.

"Sid! Oh Sid! I thought you'd never wake up!"

Guia had sprung up and was running toward him. She kissed him on both cheeks: "You poor dear, I've heard of your *ghastly* homecoming." She linked arms with him and drew him into the room: "Come and meet Sister Juana."

Sid bowed to the girl in the rocking chair, then gave Adela a look. "I'm hungry," he said. He had told her nothing of this morning's detective work. "I didn't want to wake you up," said Adela, and called for a maid.

"You look fine," said Sid to Guia. In the snaps she had sent him during her beat phase she had hair falling down to her elbows. The hair was now cut short, hugging the ears. She wore a simple blue dress with a short skirt and matching sandals. He saw no gleam of her mother's jewels.

"I've been telling Adela she should join me on these trips, if she wants to reduce. Oh, these are fun trips, Sid. I've got a whole new slant on the Apostles when they first hit the road."

"You just got in?" Sid asked very casually.

"No, this morning. But we had to report at headquarters. And *wash* up. I hadn't had a bath in weeks."

"You're burned black," said Adela.

Guia hugged her bare arms.

"Yes, I *am* tanned. But I like myself this way. Hey, you remember Papa teasing us? He said you two were country but I was town. He should see me now!"

She laughed up at the picture on the wall.

"Papa," said Adela, "*should* see what you're up to now. And I a Daughter of Isabela."

"Are you for real? He turned Aglipayan to marry your mother, Adela. *She* was Aglipayan."

Adela looked so put out Sid choked with mirth.

"But," he said, coming to the aid of the Daughter of Isabela, "Papa was reconverted when he married *my* mother."

"Hey, Siddie, remember how you used to make Adelita cry?"

"Said she was a heretic, a heretic, a heretic."

"I," snorted Adela, but beginning to laugh too, "was baptized Holy, Roman, Catholic, and Apostolic, what are you?"

"Anyway," said Guia, "Sister Juana here can tell you we have at least two Daughters of Isabela in our movement."

"Just what do you do?" asked Sid.

The girl in the rocking chair sat up and cleared her throat.

"Well, Mr. Estiva, we try you might say, uh, to bring the Vatican Council to the masses. For example, more public participation in ritual. But our parish priests don't have the time to train all their flocks in the procedure. This is where we come in. Wherever we go we gather a crowd to train. We use the techniques of traveling salesmen: our personnel put on a show. We are usually a combo of four, with guitars. Sister Guia here does an exhibition of the twist or the frug, we sing Beatles songs. But we also slip in the songs now enjoined for Mass. Presently the crowd is joining in. It's the guitars, Mr. Estiva. They make even sacred songs native and contemporary. Especially to the young.

We suspect organ music intimidates; that's why people don't sing in church. In some backwoods parishes that are so poor they don't have organs the priests are sometimes bold enough to invite us to play during Mass, on our guitars, and you should hear the *response*."

"What we do," put in Guia, "we make the hymns such top-ten hits in the barrios when people hear them in church they're so familiar everybody wants to sing."

"And then," said Sister Juana, "it's so much easier to teach them the dialogue portions of the Mass because they're already so eager to know everything."

"Wherever we really go over," said Guia, "you should see the change in attitude about going to church. No longer a deadly bore, or just a duty. Everyone simply dying to go. And when they come out, after all that active worshipping—oh Sid, such a glow on their faces you could cry."

"Your brother will think we're gushing, Sister Guia."

"It sounds harmless enough," said Sid.

"*Harmless*, what are you!" cried Guia. "You should see the chain reaction. I won't go into the civic thing: people becoming a community and all that. You're always so het up about popular taste. Well, let me tell you this new excitement is nerving some priests into throwing away all those awful plaster images and replacing them with decent stuff. We're in this, too. We try to direct their taste. The Philippine look and all that."

"Oh, we don't mean," laughed Sister Juana, "anything so superficial as putting a barong tagalog on Christ or a kimona on Our Lady."

"Just following the line," said Guia, "of our native statuary, from the pagan carvings to the santos. And *that's* our line, Sid: continuation. Electric guitars and Beatles songs and the Tijuana Taxi may not seem to be in the tradition—but they are, Sid, they are. What I mean is, whatever is Mod is God, or can be, but isn't only because we won't use it, thinking it blasphemy. Look, weren't we dancing something like the twist or the frug when Christ first arrived here? And we didn't think it blasphemy to dance our twist and frug when we first worshipped Christ. We still do, don't we, in Cebu, before the Santo Niño? But our processions now—do we have to just file stiffly past carrying candles? Can't we be more . . . more . . . *spontaneous?*"

"You mean," said Adela, "like those savages in the Quiapo procession?"

"Well, why not? At least they worship with the whole of their bodies, with their sweat, snot, phlegm, and all. Which is more than I can say for those pale polite Christians of yours, Adela, who think God is the Establishment. And reading their missals is like reading Emily Post—too, too refined. But we want to put muscle back into worship—frenzy even, violence even. All the limbs and organs in wild prayer. That's how our people used to worship. Look at the holy frugging in Pateros, or in Pakil and Obando. And the tadtarin in Paco, Sid. It's that manner of worship we're trying to revive—not automatons moving in a row, but worshippers leaping, hopping, shouting, laughing—"

"We have this theory," said Sister Juana, "that telling children, for instance, to keep still in church gives them a dreadful idea of God—a grumpy old man who's so sick he's vexed by the least stir."

"And imagine," cried Guia, "giving the impression that God frowns on dancing as sinful when dancing most probably started in worship. It has to be brought back there."

"Yes," said Sid, "I hear your group has its own Mass, where you dance."

He saw the two girls just glance at each other.

"We have," said Sister Juana, "no Mass of our own, Mr. Estiva. We go to the regular kind."

There was a pause in Adela's den. Sid felt Guia at his side not moving, the parted lips breathless. It was a pose he remembered from her childhood. Whenever she was very excited she went still all over, the parted lips breathless. Then he noticed that Adela was crouched forward on her chair, plump hands on thighs clenching. Their father seemed to be leering down at them from his wall.

The maid came in to say that table was laid for the señorito.

"We'll watch you eat," said Guia, springing alive. "Come on, Sister Juana."

"No, please excuse me. Mrs. Ferrer has offered to show me her collection of antiques."

Adela, Sid noted with relief, had sat up and again looked a heap of blessings like a collection plate in church.

"Adela's just being a fogey," said Guia at table, filching bits of food from Sid's plate as he ate. "In nine-ten months anyway I'll come of age and get the caboodle. So what's the dif giving it to me now?"

"We don't want you to commit it to something you may not like as much nine-ten months from now."

"This is my life work, what are you. Be a darling and cut me just a teeny bit of that pork chop? *Uy*, thanks. Excuse my fingers. No, Sid, I've found myself, as they say in first novels."

"You 'found yourself' a number of times before, you know."

"Oh, *those*. Just stops along the way. You never heard of growing up? But everything was leading up to *this*."

"Even fortune-tellers and so forth?"

Again he felt her stiffen but only for an instant; she poked food into her mouth, rubbed her fingers on the tablecloth.

"How I got here, Sid, doesn't matter. Even silly things can become a way. All the roads lead to, you know."

"No, I don't. *Where* exactly are you? If in church, why are the official church people against your group? And what's this group anyway? How is it organized? Who are its leaders? Has it even got a name?"

She leaned back and clowned a gape at him.

"Siddie, I'm shocked at you. You're talking like digging the squares. Organization, my holy fink. When that, dearest brod, is what we've been avoiding like the plague. We don't want to become even a cursillito. Organization has always been the death of things like this. Look at our old beaterios and cofradias: as long as they were the coming together of the devout they were true brotherhoods. Once they organized they became just convents of nuns or status-symbol clubs, with the hermanos only trying to outdo each other in splash. We don't want to end up like that. We'd rather stay outsiders if that's the only way we can remain informal, freewheeling, experimental, spontaneous. Not organization men."

"Your Sister Juana talks like one. Technique, personnel—hah."

"Well, we also say headquarters. We deliberately use current idioms but we resist even thinking of our group as a *name*. It's bound to get one, of course, sooner or later. Beginning to get one right now—"

"Well . . . ? What?"

"Salem, salaam, maybe salamat. Because when we're asked who we are we say we are people of Salem: it means peace. In the barrios that becomes salaam or salamat and they're beginning to call us salamatistas, or salmatistas, especially since we end every show with a psalm in which we say salamat. We catch ourselves already referring to the headquarters in Intramuros as Salem House."

"Wasn't Salem the kingdom of the high priest *Melchizedek?*"

"Yes. What a lot you've eaten, Sid. You must have been *starved*."

"Can you take me there? Now."

"Salem House at this time of the night?"

"It's only eight. Didn't you say you were the spontaneous ones?"

"Well, all right. Somebody has to take us back anyway."

"You girls there don't have a curfew?"

"Goodness, no. On the road we sometimes start our show as late as ten or eleven, because that's when our target audience is free. We tell each other we're The Late Late Show."

"I'll tell Adela to order a car. Or did you girls come in one?"

"In a taxi."

"Salem House doesn't keep a garage?"

"Oh, this morning we were fetched from the train by somebody's station wagon. Very posh. Our glamour members take care of services like that."

"I see." Sid heaved a full breath. "All right, go wash your hands, brat, if you're riding with me."

Adela drew him aside in the living room.

"Santiago called up. He wants you to call back. He's at his club. Isidro, I can see she's beginning to influence you."

"All I'm doing, I'm taking a peek at their set-up. Why don't you come along too?"

She hesitated. Then: "No, somebody has to remain objective."

Sid rang up his brother-in-law.

"We have to meet tonight, *cuñao*," said Santiago. "Will you be long at the Intramuros place?"

"I don't know. And afterward I'm picking up Mrs. Borja."

"An admirable lady. Bring her here. Remember where the club is? But come, *cuñao*, be sure. This is important."

In the car Guia kicked off her sandals and snuggled up against him; Sister Juana had elected to sit in front with the driver. Sid's arm round his sister enclosed again her lonely orphaned childhood.

"Oh Siddie, oh Sid—you smell of puppies and primers and my first bike: the whole of that old house in Paco. If I cry at all now I smell your hair tonic."

"Yes, brat, you were a pain in the neck."

"My young tears on your neck, silly. But you were a darling to baby me when you were a perfect baby yourself. When you went away it was like Father had died again."

"I'm sorry I ditched you."

"Whatever became of your writing?"

"Also ditched. Whatever became of *your* writing?"

"Rite of passage, brod. Like sharing that awful apartment in Cubao with this girl from the U.P. We called it Cockroach Farm."

"The same girl you opened a bookshop with?"

"I don't know what *impelled* us to. Yes, I do, too. This young writers' crowd we were with, terrible, we couldn't always be having them at the apartment, you know. The neighbors were *square na square naman*. Oh, perfect creeps. Always kicking about this and that. And in the *middle* of the night, too. Lacson her name was, my partner, Pomona Lacson, but we called her Lucky. So, the bookshop was called The Lucky Steve. Everybody called me Steve in that crowd. Short for Estiva. What do you know, we hadn't been in business a week yet when here were those stupid cops raiding us. And in broad daylight. Pornography, they said. And Lucky and me only eighteen. I said to this officer, hey, first time I heard of minors corrupting a big grown man like you. Because he said he was so shocked. Lucky was wonderful, she has connections. Had the whole thing hushed up and we reopened. Though we had to junk half the stock. I think, do you know, that did it in, my Steve phase. No,

it had been building up already. Like the time we attended this
writers' workshop and got kicked out when all we did, our
crowd, we slept on the beach. Kicked out. The whole crowd.
Just for sleeping. Imagine! And things like that. Well, anyway,
the writing wasn't going at all. Not mine nor my crowd's. We'd
all been published—a poem apiece, a story apiece. Rimbaud
cum Joyce *cum* Kerouac and Angry Young. But I felt myself
more and more on the outside looking in. At them. The Group.
Young Writers. Which was dingy of me considering the crap I
was guilty of, myself. But I felt they were just monkeying with
words, and helling around, but pretending all the time this was
being *creative*. I said to myself, I said, if I was going to hell
around I might as well do it with people who didn't have to
pretend it was art for art's sake, my ass. Now don't be having
ideas, Siddie. I was taking care of myself. Still intact virgin and
all that. Though there was a time or two, like when the bookshop was flopping and we rented the upstairs to roomers, when
I almost *gave*. Because they were beginning to think I must be
lesbian or something and there was this Pakistani painter rent-
ing an upstairs room, not bad-looking but very secretive about
the stuff he did. So I went up there one day prepared to give
myself to him. I knocked, he opened, I swayed in—'*naks*, real
sexy—but one look at his paintings on the walls and, bo-rother,
I knew if I was going to be deflowered it wasn't going to be by
anyone *that* corny."

"So what followed?"

"The *nagwawala* babies, going for lost. The Young Barbarians, Kamikaze, target society. Not the Group now but the
Barkada. You know: scooters and motors, drag races, combos,
stomping in movie houses at rock-'n'-roll films and squealing in
chorus at the Coliseum at pop singers, jam sessions with gin
and dog on the side, sometimes nude swimming in somebody's
pool if their olds were away, oftener a gang rumble—the whole
teenage routine."

"And no longer intact."

"Still most wonderfully intact, though it took some work. I
was Ginny to my barkada, Stowaway Ginny, because I lived

out. Took a pad with this coed I didn't even know was a call
girl, bless my innocence. The Ginny phase didn't last very long,
you know."

"Too old for that sort of thing?"

"I was still eighteen, what are you, but, yes, something like
that. They looked like *babies*. And another thing: I find I tend
to be zany among squares, square among zanies. Now why is
that? In school I was the Compleat Kalog. But afterward, in
New York, where everybody tries to be so kooky, you said I was
a square, remember? The rebound was to the lit'ry bohemians—
but I still couldn't let myself go. Not all the way. They said it
was the convent school in me. Nerts. They couldn't turn me on.
But I wanted so to let go it shot me right into the teen-age jungle. Now that was better really. Basic. Down to basic things.
Food, drink, sex, action. The primitive. And you begin to see
everything else, especially laws and churches and reading, 'rit-
ing, and 'rithmetic, as just the red tape that's messing up life and
making people so sick. Excess baggage. Often, in rumbles, I'd
get a feeling all this teen-age violence would finally set off one
global explosion hurling out all that trash. The world would be
flat afterward but what was left of it could start clean. Now
that was a good cool feeling. Made you feel dedicated. Like the
feeling you get when the barkada says let's go there and you go,
or says let's do this and you do. You've no will of your own,
you're just part of something on the move. Don't you some
times want to be that, Sid?"

"Then why didn't you stay with it?"

"Because it was bogus, too, like the lit'ry life as a sleeping
around. This barkada of mine, they were basic, they were
primitive, they could afford not to be bothered about anything
except eating and drinking, sex and action, but only because
they had allowances. And whenever they got into trouble they
fell back on mommy and daddy. They said they wanted to be
free, hah—their freedom was just freeloading. And how can
you stage a strike that's subsidized by the company? That's
when I asked Adela to stop my allowance. I had begun to feel
like a crook. So, goodbye to Ginny, Stowaway Ginny. I got this

job with an ad agency, moved in with some media girls, got to know the executive-shirt boys."

"If you can't lick 'em, join 'em."

"But I did show I could do okay copy for the rat race: style-wise, market-wise, offbeat approach-wise."

"And got rechristened once again?"

"Gigi this time. You should have seen Gigi's layout. Pink-rimmed eyeglasses, a pouf, linen suits, a rolled umbrella, an attaché case. Cocktails now, instead of gin and dog. Night-club-hopping instead of motorcycling in a pack up to Baguio on the spur of the moment in the middle of the night. But it was good to be able to talk again. This new crowd I was with was with it, whichever *it* was in: hot jazz, new-wave films, Salinger, the young ones. I felt queer, though, talking about teen-agers instead of being one. *Talking.* That was a *talking* crowd. Com-pulsive punners to a man, to a corporate man."

"But Madison Avenue still wasn't Damascus."

"Know what, Sid—I never did figure it out. There I was so anxious to be *sincere*, ready to wrench my soul if need be to Believe in the Product. But nobody did. Not even in what they said about it. If you praised someone for a catchy slogan he'd say: 'Yes, it's so bad it's good.' And all the time all this murder-ous jostling for position but pretending all the time all they really wanted was to write the Great Filipino Novel. My God, there must have been 359 books in progress in this agency I was with, everything from epic poems to exposés of the Filipino soul. They were the least of the status symbols there but they were supposed to keep the package honest. This guy I was going around with, a soft-sell poet wanting to become a high-pressure executive, he said the copy he did was really a blow against the Establishment. He said the crap he produced helped swell the crap being rammed down the public's throat that at last would have to come out, in one big violent throw-up. A revolutionary, what do you know. But all the time wanting oh most pitifully to make it to account executive—and a house in San Lorenzo with an Impala in the garage."

"Any chance of him getting there?"

"All he has got so far is an ulcer."

"And what did *you* get?"

"I got confused, very. You have to be schizoid to last in there, I think. Even the punning's their urge to split up meaning. I worked mine off by beginning to march with the nationalists, because they were at least trying to integrate meaning. Before I knew it I was a card-holding member of the KKKs: Kami'y Kilusang Kabataan."

"This isn't Gigi anymore."

"No, Gigi had become a split personality and I let her lie where she dropped. For the nationalists I was Guiang: hair in a knot, native fabrics, much poring over Rizal and Recto, demonstrations in front of Congress and the U.S. embassy, the protest marches to American bases, Go Home Yankee, and Come Home Filipino. The pre-Hispanic thing."

"Guiang sounds close."

"But not close enough. Still not radical enough for me. I wanted to *go* back, not just look back in anger, like Guiang and her crowd. College professors, parlor pinks, magazine writers, proletarian poets, rich boys with a conscience and shrewd fathers. Back to native roots, they said, and was I rarin' to go. But every time we started off, where we always ended up was at the American embassy or the American bases or some American firm. I got to thinking the way back to native roots must be through Washington, D.C. And some of them, poor finks, they marched Yankee-ward so often they finally stopped there. Like this poet who was almost my b.f.—always T-shirted and denim'd, unwashed and unbarbered, and in a fury—whom I started a fund for so he could write his angry proletarian poems. Next thing we knew, he was with this American firm. Last time I saw him, he was in a white, white suit, would you believe it, and a silk tie yet, a crewcut yet, but still doing the Angry Young Man bit as he passed cigarettes around in a gold-plated case. Oh, that was sad. I felt it was the PRO world all over again. You could stay honest doing crap as long as you were the first one to admit it was crap and you were really meaning it *against* the Establishment. Oh, too sad. And afterward—that boy did break my heart, Siddie— Guiang with her Marikina shoes and Tondo-boy slang was just window dressing. She had to be swept away, too."

"Steve, Ginny, Gigi, Guiang. Down the hatch. And now Sister Guia."

"Yes."

"On the real road to Damascus."

"Yes indeed."

"But what got you on that track?"

"Magic."

"The Prophet Melkizedek?"

She sat up and passed palms along the sides of her head.

"Here we are," she said, "at Salem House."

The door, one step up from the street, opened into a narrow hall, dark save for a flame floating in oil in a coconut shell, flickering before the figure that had shocked Santiago: an Igorot-style wooden carving of the Virgin pregnant, asquat on her haunches, halo of stars round her head. The rude face stared from the dusk of a niche in the side wall.

Sid paused just beyond the door, waiting for the girls to switch on a light, but they glanced back at him in wonder.

"Haven't you got electricity?"

"Oh, we do, Mr. Estiva, but we prefer candle and oil, for atmosphere."

"Siddie, you're not afraid of the dark!"

He advanced to the middle of the stone-flagged room. It was mostly bare but in the winking twilight he could make out a gallenera bench, a couple of round inlaid tables with clusters of high-backed chairs, and what looked like part of an old retablo now turned into a bookshelf.

"This was the nuns' chapel," explained Sister Juana. "We have made it our common room. That wall where the altar stood separated the sacristy and the chaplain's quarters from the nunnery proper, which was behind this side wall. When this was a bodega, after the war, they tore up what used to be the nuns' choir to make a passage into the interior."

Sid followed the girls through the short passage and emerged into a small square courtyard surrounded on all four sides by the restored edifice, of two stories, the upper story ajutting over the lower one to form a roof for the walk. From each of the four posts at the corners burned a torch leaning from a strap.

"This was the cloister," said Sister Juana. "The arches were completely destroyed during the war but we have been able to rehabilitate the cells."

She waved at the doors that lined the square.

"Come and see my cell," said Guia.

She opened a door and Sid peered in over her shoulder. An oil lamp on a cheap wooden chest revealed a bamboo *papag*, a stool, a small high window without bars.

"How many of you stay here?"

"Oh, usually not more than half a dozen at a time; we're usually on the road. We're growing fast, I think, but we're still not a movement of *hundreds*."

"And what's beyond the cloister?"

"Come, I'll show you."

One door opened into a narrow hallway with another door at the end. Sister Juana unbolted the door and they stepped out into an angle of open space, where a cluster of ruins jagged the moonlight. Beyond darkened a high wall.

"This is how the nunnery must have looked after the war," said Sister Juana. "The nuns' compound was in the shape of a triangle, with the longest side parallel to the city walls. This is the upper angle. The original complex must have extended up to here and you can see that whatever building stood here must have enclosed a small circular courtyard."

"Look what curious ruins the war left," said Guia.

Nothing remained of whatever building had stood here save parts of its wall round the courtyard. Six or seven fragments of this wall, unequal in height but still massive though long moldering and pillaged by weed and shrub, stood in a ring, indicating the shape of the courtyard. Sid walked up to the ring of ruins and stood in a gap between two boulders, gazing into the moonlit circle. Guia and Sister Juana appeared in other gaps in the ring.

"We think," said Sister Juana, "the nuns did their washing here. There must have been a well or pool in the center of this courtyard."

"What's that in the middle now—a barbecue pit?"

"No, you silly," giggled Guia. "Those are adobe blocks we found lying about and didn't have the heart to throw away. They must be centuries old. So we piled them up into a kind of table there."

Sid walked up to the pile. Four longish slabs had been set side by side and another layer of four slabs had been laid crosswise upon them.

"The altar stone?" he called out.

"Well, why not?" laughed Sister Juana. "If we ever get permission to hold the sacrifice of the Mass here."

Standing before the adobe pile, Sid looked up and saw a small light in the boulder directly across. As he approached it he noticed that this remnant of wall had been cleaned of weed and shrub. There had obviously been a tall window in this part of the wall but the hollow was now enclosed by a rounded metal door, silvery in the moonlight. A flame deep in a tall glass burned before the shut door and on the ledge were scattered flowers, a sheaf of grain.

Sid glanced around, skyward, and found Guia and Sister Juana standing behind him.

"It faces east," he said.

"A Philippine superstition," said Sister Juana. "Doors and stairs must face east."

"What is this a door to?"

"Our great devotion. Corpus Christi."

"The Sacrament?"

"No, just an image, Mr. Estiva."

"But it's shut up like a tabernacle."

"Not everybody is ready to understand."

"Oh, primitive statuary."

"And you don't find that shocking."

"Can you open it up for me?"

"No, I don't have the keys."

"Your great devotion."

"Mr. Estiva, shall we go in now?"

"What do you call it?"

"We try not to call anything by name, Mr. Estiva. The basic terms have been so corrupted."

"Then when do you celebrate it?"

Sister Juana merely shrugged but Guia spoke up.

"New Year's Day, you donkey. Now shut up and let's go."

"Why New Year's Day? That's not liturgical. Oh yes, it is. Feast of the Circumcision."

"And you're cordially invited to our patronal festivities, donkey. Now let's go *in*. I'm cold."

Sid turned to follow the girls but stopped, seeing something standing in shadow in a gap in the ruins. As he stared at it the shadow moved, emerged, crossed the ring of stone—walking with an almost imperceptible limp—and stood before him: a tall man with long hair in a black suit. Sister Juana had hurried back.

"Father Melchor, Mr. Estiva."

Sid glanced at the man's throat: he was wearing an ordinary tie, not a Roman collar.

"Are you a priest, Father?"

The man smiled and bowed.

"But not a practicing one, Mr. Estiva."

"Oh, *you're* the —"

"—defrocked priest your brother-in-law mentioned?"

"Father Melchor," said Guia, drawing nearer, "was never defrocked, as we tried to explain to Santiago, who's another *hopeless* donkey."

Not wanting to, Sid found himself meeting the man's eyes. He looked between forty and fifty, very brown, with competitive shoulders and a face deep in ambush in the coarse locks that, hardly graying, dangled to his shoulders. But no Beatles bangs curtained the forehead to hide the birthmark there: a slight swell of skin like a welt, darkly purple, the shape rather like a tree aslant. His voice, pitched low, seemed to be muffling thunder.

"It's a long story, Mr. Estiva. I was ordained in China. I had gone there as a lay brother of this order I had joined, but my superiors thought it fit, despite certain physical defects of mine, to elevate me to the priesthood. I was originally in Fookien province but had been sent to Tibet on a mission and there I found myself stranded during the revolt and the change in regime. Unable to join my colleagues, I stayed where I was, serving in the local parish, until I was permitted to leave the county two years ago. When I arrived in Hong Kong I heard that I was under a cloud for having served with the Church in China after it broke with Rome, and that my order had dropped me. I therefore thought it wise when I came back to the Philippines not to raise the question of my status but to return as a simple layman."

"And you founded this movement."

"I don't think anybody can say he did that. This was more or less spontaneous on the part of different people. I am merely a part of it. Sister Juana and Sister Guia do wrong to address me as father, but I reprove them in vain."

"We hope," said Sister Juana, "the Church will take the initiative in recognizing Father Melchor, so we can have him for chaplain. We are happy to note signs of attention. When your brother-in-law came here with the churchmen they wanted to meet Father Melchor, but he was away then."

"I told your sister here, Mr. Estiva, if you should express a wish to come, to bring you at once and show you everything."

Sid glanced around at the shut shrine in the stone.

"Ah, Mr. Estiva, in every brotherhood there is an ultimate veil past which only the initiate may go. But otherwise we are ready to provide you with the usual information: aims and procedures, statistics. . . ."

Sid heard mockery and turned away to speak to Guia.

"Let's meet tomorrow."

"At Adela's?"

"No, at the office. I hear our corp has a new office?"

"In Makati, very plush."

"I'll be there at—four in the afternoon?"

"All right. I'll bring what data Father Melchor has prepared."

They began to move out of the circle of ruins toward the back door, the two girls walking ahead. Sid paused and looked back.

"Aren't you coming, Father?"

"No, I go in another way. When I'm here I stay in a separate part of the building."

Sid looked at the dark man so tall and shaggy in the moonlight, standing in a ring of stone. The birthmark on his brow glowed vivider now, it seemed. Behind him rose the slab of wall where a flame burned before the shut door.

Sonya Borja said it before he could, on their way to Santiago's club:

"The Prophet Melkizedek and this Father Melchor are the same person."

"How many of the dames you talked to know?"

"Actually only one. But the others who did get to see the prophet describe him the way you did: wears his hair in a long bob and has a remarkable birthmark on the forehead. It seems not all who make an appointment at the Sign of the Milky Seed are serviced by the prophet himself. They have some system of selection. If you're not thought worthy you're only attended to by an assistant."

"Palm reading and crystal balls?"

"The usual hocus-pocus. But not with the prophet. These clients of mine who claim to have had him say there were no gimmicks. Apparently it's like with a psychiatrist: you find yourself Telling All. They all speak of the power of his eyes and the charm of his voice. And a funny thing, Sid. Though they all want to go back they can't. After a session or two, they find they can't get another appointment."

"Few are called and fewer chosen."

"Isn't that a funny way to run a racket?"

"Not if the fortune-telling isn't really the point of it."

"Oh, they can tell fortunes all right. This one lady I turned up who did go beyond one or two sessions and made the transition from Milky Seed to Salem House, but didn't stay, is a rich spinster."

"So, the criterion would be, not just wealth, but wealth that's all your own and disposable. Why didn't she stay?"

"She's herself stumped. There must be a second process of selection. She remembers up to six or seven appointments with the prophet and then he told her she was ready for epiphany and that their next meeting would be at this address in

Intramuros. She showed up there and he revealed his other identity, Father Melchor, and he asked her did she want to find her true self too. So she joined the movement. She was too old to go on the road but she did home-front work, like lending her car and hustling up equipment. She understood she was preparing herself through labor for indoctrination. But one day she went to Salem House and the door was closed. She couldn't get in then or the following days and when she asked around nobody had even heard of Father Melchor. She went back to the Sign of the Milky Seed but she couldn't get in there either. The poor woman says she felt so lost until she gave up mysticism for science. Now she has joined the Andromedans, a society of flying-saucer watchers."

"Maybe she wasn't compromised enough to be usable."

"Oh, rackets like that, they can easily get you into such a hole even if you want out you can be blackmailed to stay, or at least keep your mouth shut."

"Keep your mouth shut about this, will you, Sonya, to my brother-in-law?"

Santiago's club was, thought Sid, the apotheosis of Philippine baroque; a culture lately sneered at as being without grandfathers had, with a vengeance, discovered pedigree; and he was amused by the thought that there the reactionary and the neonationalist met on astonished ground. His brother-in-law's reasons for finding the antique so congenial were surely different from those of the famous lady columnist waiting for her car on the driveway, to whom Sonya presented him. He knew from the outside of the club what he would find inside. An authentic old mansion had been restored to its elegance circa the 1890s: porcelain pedestals for flowerpots, paired seashells on the stairs, capiz-shell shutters in the windows, and on the walls of a main hall furnished like a sala in colonial days two enormous oils by some nonocento primitive: a beamy *Death of the Just*, feathery with angels, and a lurid *Death of the Sinner*, agrin with demons. One room Sid passed was hung with Moro gongs and Igorot wood art. Another room was crowded, like an old-fashioned domestic chapel, with holy images in brocade and smaller ivories under glass—the lares and penates of a frontier tribe.

Santiago was waiting out on the azotea, where a few empty tables stood under trellis and starlight.

"Order your drinks, Isidro, Mrs. Borja, while I fetch this person who has important information for us. I asked for a table out here so we can be alone."

The person he came back with was Mrs. Banaag, still looking as edgy as when she had fainted in Adela's den.

"I don't know if I should be doing this but you're a friend of my husband's and, Estiva, he knows nothing of this, I don't want him to know. But after learning what happened to you at the airport I was shocked and so I called on Mr. Ferrer here, trying to decide what to do. And he told me what I have to say might save your sister. Besides, I had long been trying to close my eyes to it, that they were using force, violence, but now that I know they are resorting to murder—"

Mrs. Banaag, who was speaking fast but in a low voice, with bowed head, darted a glance up at Sid.

"Those thugs around Father Melchor, they killed that taxi driver, they might have killed you too, and I fear they're now about to kill another person. You remember a Mr. Lao? On the same plane you came in on. They're holding him now, they're hiding him somewhere."

"Isn't he *with* them?" asked Sid. "That card I got was meant for him."

"Yes, he came willingly enough, it seems, to join them. But now he has changed his mind."

"I saw him changing it," smiled Sid, "on the plane."

"It turns out," said Santiago, "that this Lao is a priest."

"They're trying to recruit priests," continued Mrs. Banaag. "The fallen-away ones. I think they got two or three in the provinces. That's what the movement mostly is: thugs and women and priests in disgrace. They had heard about Father Lao being stranded in the States—he had been sent there to study but got mixed up with some girl and after she left him he just went to pieces. So they sent an emissary to contact him, told him about this movement he could join where he would still be a priest: he was on skid row, just bumming around then, and they helped him."

"Stealing priests from the old church," observed Sonya Borja, "is standard operating procedure for new gospels."

"Is it a new gospel?" asked Sid.

Mrs. Banaag wildly hesitated, eyes flashing, mouth contorting.

"If it's too terrible to talk about—" said Santiago.

"Oh, we are all adults here," said Sonya impatiently.

"It's supposed to be a *returning*," Mrs. Banaag said at last, herself looking puzzled and looking up to offer her puzzled expression to her listeners.

"A returning to *what?*" pressed Sonya.

"I can't tell much . . . There are degrees of initiation."

"How did you get into it?" asked Sid.

"That was strange too. I've heard they're only interested in rich women, and I'm not. We don't know each other. The staff members who go on the road, yes. But we older auxiliaries, if we recognize each other, it's always by chance. I think they're careful, when they assemble a group, that it's of members who don't know each other and move in different worlds—"

"You said it was strange," interrupted Sid, "your getting in."

"Because I'm not religious. I stopped believing a long time ago. I'm a free-thinker like Etoy, my husband. Early this year he was invited to speak to some civic groups in New York, but he could get neither passport nor visa. When he raised a fuss it almost cost him his job. These schools where he teaches, they almost threw him out when they learned he was supposed to be a Red. Which is absurd. We are nationalists, not Reds. I was so mad I joined pickets and demonstrations and wrote letters to the editors. Then I got a note saying there was somebody, the Prophet Melkizedek, very interested in my problem. An astrologer, oh my. But I was mad enough to do anything.

"We met once, we met again, I found myself going back, no longer to the prophet but to Father Melchor. It seemed to make sense, what he said—that nationalism was not a political but a spiritual problem. Our people had to be renewed in spirit. They were not really political, they had no political ideas: nationalism as a political movement, like Recto's, would never reach them. But they were deeply religious in the sense they believed in magical forces. And the nationalist movement could reach them only if it came in the guise of religion, a magical nature religion, but with the Christian forms familiar to them.

"It made sense then, as I said. So I committed myself to the movement; its nationalist format appealed to me. And besides, I was getting back at all the people who had tried to hurt us."

Mrs. Banaag, beginning to bristle like her words, suddenly drooped again. She shook her head and sighed.

"No . . . I'm sorry but I can't stay much longer, I have to go, it's late . . ."

"What happened?" insisted Sonya.

Mrs. Banaag looked helplessly around.

Then: "I went in quite cynically but found myself drawn deeper."

"Becoming," said Sonya, "a true believer, you mean?"

"It was no longer a question of belief, or doctrine, or ideas. Ideas seemed utterly unimportant compared to this felt wisdom in the blood, in the flesh. . . ."

"A clairvoyance?" Sonya's voice had dropped to a whisper.

"It was more a growing awareness of instincts in oneself, a growing capacity for intuition, insight, impulse, as though feeling were thought."

The two whispering women were now leaning toward each other, gazing into each other's faces, and seemed to have forgotten the two men at the table.

"And they know when you've reached that stage."

"The first initiation?"

"Yes," said Mrs. Banaag.

"An outraging, of course."

"*He* said all shame had to be burned out of us, if we were to recover innocence."

"Dancing in the flesh."

"—in the moonlight. This was last October, the last day, behind Salem House. There's a circle of ruins. And a shrine in one stone."

"A shrine?"

"An image of Christ."

"Oh yes, in the primitive manner."

"More."

"More of the outraging?"

"But somehow not outrageous—"

"Naked?"

"—during that dancing to the moon."

"But it was."

"And in the extremest manner."

"Last day of October, that was Halloween."

"Oh, if only there were not this violence—!"

"Mrs. Banaag," Santiago broke in sternly, "your duty would be to notify the police."

"And what would that do?" She was smiling scornfully, head up. "If they traced that station wagon they would learn it belongs to the wife of a very high official. If they raided Salem House they would only find an innocent girls' dormitory. And whatever is being done in the provinces, all they'd see would be a girls' combo singing hymns."

Santiago leaned toward the woman.

"Mrs. Banaag, do you or don't you want to help expose this gang?"

Shaking her head, she retreated from him, at bay against her chair.

"I can't be involved . . . I'm afraid . . . There are things they can tell . . . But, yes, I suppose I should help. Because I think they want to get at my husband, through me—recruit him, I mean, for their purposes. Listen, I can give you a lead. There's an old man who seems to know about Father Melchor."

"An old man?" prompted Sid.

"Dr. Lagman, Ciriaco Lagman. I know because my husband recently did a piece on peasant movements and he went to interview Dr. Lagman because he's one of the few witnesses left of a peasant religious uprising in Pangasinan in 1900. And Dr. Lagman said why didn't my husband talk to this person who called himself the Prophet Melkizedek, who should know about it, but my husband didn't think the lead worth following. He just happened to mention it to me and I have sometimes thought of going to see Dr. Lagman myself. I'll give you his address."

After they had dropped Mrs. Banaag near her door, Santiago and Sid took Sonya Borja home. She remarked that the Banaags' intelligentsia made up for mindlessness by minding. Sid wasn't sure this was really a sneer.

"But the Prophet Melkizedek intrigues me," she said. "If you're going to this Dr. Lagman, Sid, I want to be along."

"Unfortunately," said Santiago, "I'll be out of town tomorrow."

"I'll pick you up in the morning," said Sid to Sonya. "Dr. Lagman first, then Father Melchor's former friars."

In bed that night, Sid stirred from sleep knowing that something had happened that had not happened to him since young manhood. He tried to recall the dream, in which he had watched a confused procession coming up from darkness; but nothing in the dream explained its effect. It was a long time since he had felt any impulse there and had so approved the UN agency because it seemed to use up the material for such impulses. But he was now as wetly sprawled as any adolescent. The wondering lulled him back to sleep.

Dr. Lagman was a small frail ancient in a wheelchair, hugging a patch of sunlight by his window.

"The Prophet Melkizedek? When I tell people they think my mind is going. You, my dear lady, my dear sir, will think likewise. But you come to me asking. *Bueno*, I will oblige. Two years ago a man came into this room. I had already begun to keep to my bed, having suffered a fall. This man who came here, one look and I recognized somebody I had seen when I was a boy, a boy of ten. This was in 1900, when my parents fled with the landlord's carabao and the landlord's rice, and with all of us their children, to join the New Jerusalem in Pangasinan.

"We were part of a great exodus from the North to this New Jerusalem. Peasants by the thousands, on the move, in the dead of night, fleeing to a world without landlords, without soldiers, without rich or poor. For in this New Jerusalem God had appeared, God resided. The roads were clogged with a peasantry escaping to God. Escaping from the capataces of the landlords and the Yanquis of MacArthur.

"In the New Jerusalem in Pangasinan, my parents turned over the carabao and grain to the common wealth, as did all comers. It was a Christian communism: what was put in was shared equally by all. Meat and grain would never fail, for more and more refugees arrived each day, with the landlord's carabao and the landlord's rice. And every day was fiesta. The adults did not farm, we children did not school. At night there was drinking and dancing—and ceremonies we little ones knew nothing of because we were put to sleep first.

"All houses were equal, but there were special houses. In one dwelt Jesus Christ and the Virgin Mary; in another, the Holy Ghost; in a third, The Twelve Apostles, who were resplendent creatures, booted and uniformed. But one house, a little apart from the settlement, was the most special of all, for in it dwelt God. Few saw him, only the maidens in his service and the small boys called in to husk the floor and empty the chamber pots. But even we boys who served there in shifts seldom saw God. He dwelt in a dim chamber where, when we entered, he was but a bulk and a voice. But I saw him in light three times. Once by sunlight, once by lamplight, once by moonlight. A big man with flowing hair and shining eyes and the Godhead was a red mark on his brow. I did not go blind, as they had warned me, but watching from ambush I felt faint and suffered a fever after each of those three times I spied on God.

"Our New Jerusalem lasted barely two years. In March 1901, General Otis sent a Gringo infantry battalion to occupy the town. The Twelve Apostles and the Virgin Mary were thrown into jail; Jesus Christ and the Holy Ghost were hanged in public. *Pues*, the end. We were driven out of Eden, each family returning contrite to where it had come from or desperately seeking a new home. Mine found its way to Manila, where I had the good fortune of winning the sympathy of an American missionary couple and becoming their protégé. But the mystery here is: what happened to God? He had vanished when the infantry arrived.

"At the trials before the military court it was learned that his real name was Baltazar. He did not seem to have any other name. Nobody could say where he came from. He had simply appeared during the Revolution, in the Central Plain, exhorting the peasants to rise, but in the name of his religion. And the peasants began to follow him until he had an army of his own that would harass both Aguinaldo and the Americans. By 1897 he had established his headquarters in this place that was to become the New Jerusalem. At that time, according to testimony, he was already more than forty years old.

"As I said, his end is as mysterious as his beginning. One day he was there, the next day he was not. But many of those who were in his New Jerusalem believed all their lives that he would return one day and call them back to his kingdom.

"And now I come to the serious part of my story. Two years ago, a man came to visit me, here in this room. That this visitor of mine and the mysterious Baltazar, whom I knew as God when a boy, are the same person, I have not the slightest doubt. He looked exactly as I remembered him: the flowing mane, the slight limp, and that fire on the brow. Ah, but it was I now who was older than he!

"He said he had come back as he promised, under another name, Melkizedek, to start the rebuilding of his kingdom. Would I join him again? I tell you, if I were not crippled, I would have stood up that instant and followed him. But all I could do was try to remember for him where this or that survivor of the New Jerusalem had last been heard from. He thanked me and left. He has not come back. But I hear about him. I hear he has been in the provinces tracking down the children or grandchildren of those who were his followers and that many of these young ones, for whom, of course, he is a family legend, are joining him. In what? A new uprising? A new Kingdom? That, I cannot tell. But sometimes, as I sit here musing, I wonder if they are to come back, truly, again: the great days, the Revolution—and how I wish I were young again!"

"Dotage?" asked Sid, on the way to their next stop: the friar order Father Melchor had claimed.

"Not dotage," said Sonya. "Exultant nostalgia."

"Which an impostor took advantage of."

"An impostor, yes, I suppose, or we'd have to posit a man who's over a hundred years old and looks forty."

"What would the friars say of this?"

"An imposture!" said Fray Calezón, who was young, Spanish and had a sheaf of yellowing documents on his desk. "An imposture, Mr. Estiva. I asked for these papers after you tele-phoned me. We had been gathering them since we heard that this Father Melchor claims to have been of our order. Yes, we had a Father Melchor, but these papers will prove that he could not be this impostor going under his name. No, impossible. Our Father Melchor lived toward the end of the eighteenth century. Look, there's the exact date of his entrance into our order: 6 January 1776. That would explain why he took the name Melchor de la Epifania.

"Let me draw your attention to the notations on the deed, which indicate considerable correspondence on this matter. The reason was that it was rather extraordinary: this Melchor was an indigene—or, as they said then, an Indio, possibly the first to be admitted into our order. Here's a letter from the prior at that time of our house in Pangasinan. You can see he has little infor-mation on this Melchor's origins, no information save that he was attached to our house in Pangasinan, evidently as the per-sonal servant of one of the fathers there, the procurator.

"When this father was assigned to our mission in Fookien he urged that Melchor be sent too, because he had shown such indus-try and intelligence. It was finally arranged that Melchor was to be admitted into our order as a lay brother and sent to China.

"These three documents are the pertinent reports from China, several years later, recommending that Brother Melchor be ordained priest and given full missionary scope, having shown a talent for it. The corresponding answers have, alas, been lost, but again we can deduce considerable debate. Here, read this paragraph where our men in Fookien argue for a dispensation in behalf of Brother Melchor. A dispensation was necessary, not for lack of training—apparently, Brother Melchor had already taken Latin, philosophy, and theology—but for physical rea-sons. Brother Melchor was a bit lame and he had an ugly birth-mark on the forehead. Our rules forbid the ordination of any candidate with ugly physical features. The dispensation was granted and Brother Melchor became Father Melchor, in 1796. After this the record breaks off. All we could find is this report from Indo-China in 1800, where there is mention of the 'Melchor scandal.' Apparently, Father Melchor had disappeared in Tibet, after joining an esoteric Buddhist sect there.

"Here you have the documents before you, Mr. Estiva. On such evidence what else can you conclude save that this man who claims to be the Father Melchor of our order is an impostor? Unless he can prove he is over 200 years old! Yes, yes, we have heard of the limp and the birthmark. But those can be faked. Although we are a bit curious to know how he learned about them. As far as we know, all the information about the real Father Melchor is in these documents; and they are, how do you say, or used to be, 'classified information.'

"But now I still have this book before me. It's one of the volumes of the history of our order in the Philippines. This is personal research now. You can see I want to give you, how do you say, 'all the angles.' When I was told to search for these papers on Father Melchor, the description of him in one of the documents I found—about the limp and the birthmark—rang, as you say, a bell. I had read about them before—but where? I thought back and thought back and finally remembered where: in Avila, at the old convent, while preparing for the Philippines by studying the history of our order here. So I reread the history and located the passage—or, rather, passages.

"Here, I have the first one marked in the book. Read it. Fantastic, no? Yes. Our order was, but not immediately, in charge of evangelizing the Central Plain. You can see whoever was before us did not do a thorough job. There were still these stubborn pockets of paganism. That passage refers to what must have been a very stubborn resistance on the part of the old religion. But note the description of the leader of the uprising: he is a high priest of the old cult, he wears his hair long and dresses in the manner of women, he limps a bit, and he has this remarkable mark on the forehead, which his followers, mostly women, take for a sign of godhood. They believe he has been touched by God—that is, struck by lightning. This resistance to Christianity in the Central Plain—and it was an armed resistance—is suppressed; but unfortunately we are not told what happened to that stubborn high priest with the god mark. This is in the late 1500s, practically toward the end of the Conquista—or should I use that word. But there is more. Now turn the pages to the next mark I have put.

"We are now in the 1690s, a century later. Yes, that passage I have underlined. Can you believe it? Here we have another uprising, but this time not of pagans resisting Christianity but of Christians *regressing* to paganism. The thing here is the leader, a Christian by the name of Gaspar who claims he has all along been a high priest of the old cults. From the evidence, we must assume that the old worship had been continuing all the time, but underground, like a guerrilla movement. This high priest Gaspar declares that the time has come to restore his kingdom, and we have this revolt, again in the Central Plain—oh, quite an uprising. But note the description of the leader. Again he has long hair, he limps, he has a mark on the forehead. The good father who wrote the history, he does not know what to think of the coincidence, save that it must be the work of the devil. The Gaspar uprising is suppressed. His lieutenants are caught and executed, but again we are not told what happened to the high priest who would be king again. Gaspar. King that was and king to be. The 'once and future king'—that is the term, no? More, there is this puzzled note that nothing seems to be known of his origins.

"What are we to assume from all this? One: that there has been a series of impostors copying the message and the appearance of a pagan original, and with a predilection for the names of the Three Kings: Melchor, Gaspar, Baltazar. Or two: that there is a man now among us who must be four centuries old: this man who poses as Father Melchor and leads a group that is beginning to call itself the New Salem. Yes, we have heard the rumor that this man also poses as a prophet under the name Melkizedek. One can see the connection he would establish.

"The *Melchizedek* in the Bible is also priest and king and is said to have had no father and no mother. What do we know of him? He simply suddenly appears in Genesis offering bread and wine, and blessing Abraham. And yet he has a rich legend. He is said to have been in charge of the body of our Father Adam, buried in a cave in Hebron. The Talmud mentions a sect of *Melchizedekians* who worshipped Adam's body. Adam is the only other character in the Bible who had neither father nor mother.

"Ah, all this fascinates me. My Gothicism, it is *fearful*. I was in Sta. Ana when they excavated in the church there and as I watched the artifacts being unearthed my hair stood up. A Christian church standing on a pagan burial site. Heathenism emerging from consecrated ground. How do we know what else we resurrect, what else we bring back? This man who calls himself now Melkizedek, now Melchor—is he an impostor or a pagan priest of old come back across the ages? A preposterous question, no? But there are more things in heaven and earth, as your Shakespeare said. Oh, he is not *your* Shakespeare? Well, anyway, I like the wit of this impostor. Really audacious. Because I know what line in the Bible he is acting out. It is an *awesome* line, the most mysterious, I think, in Scripture:

"*Thou art a priest forever, according to the order of* Melchizedek."

The office that afternoon was an elegant igloo after the journeys in the heat of the day. This new heart of Makati was a transplant of American downtown—from tree-lined curb to penthouse'd roof—but glittered anomalously between the rank provincial decay of Manila and the lordly tin roofs of the suburbs.

Guia, in jeans and plaid, was waiting in an inner room that had drapes at the windows and a shoe-deep carpet on the floor.

"The three tables are one for you, one for Adela, and this one is mine. We should come here oftener, Sid. That side door is the executive washroom, strictly private, but it connects with Santiago's office on the other side. We shouldn't let him do all the work for us; all we do is collect dividendazos. And where have you been? You said four. What are all those packages?"

"Just some items I picked up. Mrs. Borja took me around the bookstores."

"What's up between you and this Mrs. Borja? Adela is titillated."

"Did you bring the data?"

"Here in this folder. Aims and procedures, statistics—all the worldly information about us Christniks."

"Drop the cool, sis. I'm on to your group's nik."

"Are you, Sid?"

Having dumped bundles on a table, he crossed over to the table she sat at and leaned over it, palms propped on the polished wood.

"And," said he, "like Adela I am putting my foot down."

She swiveled back and forth on the chair and pretended to be jawing away at a wad of gum.

"Drop the heavy, brod. What bugs you?"

"Your new gospel. Only it's the oldest one in the world."

"Yes."

"Yes? Just like that?"

"If you expect me to deliver an apologia—"

"Shouldn't you try to convert me?"

"I can't think of anyone who needs it more. Except Adela."

He straightened up.

"Now what is that supposed to mean?"

She sprang up from the chair and strode to the middle of the room, arms hugging each other.

"Oh, don't be so prissy. Just what in this bothers you, Sid? You're not a prude."

"I'm not that alienated either."

"*Alienated*. Man, are you way off. This is for bringing back people."

"All shame burned out of them."

"But that's only where you start from."

"I'll bet."

She was standing still, staring, parted lips breathless. Then she ran toward him.

"Oh Sid, Sid, you've got to understand! You're the one outsider I had hoped would understand."

"But you wouldn't even show me your god."

"Oh, is it only that that's worrying you? An *image?*"

"In religion there's no such thing as *only* an image or *only* a symbol."

"Yes, I know; but only when you know what it means."

"Anybody can be trained to find the most outrageous things meaningful."

"*Outrageous*. Ha, ha. The first Christians thought it outrageous of God to be born a baby, in a cattle shed, among animals."

"I've heard that before."

"And that's why it's no longer shocking to you. And *that's* why there always has to be a new idea of God so different from the old one it's shocking."

"*Your* image?"

"You're shocked, aren't you, just by the idea of it, without even having seen it?"

"Oh, I've seen it. Not there in Salem House, but I've seen it. I have been around. I saw it in India, in the Levantine; I saw it in Greece and Italy; I saw it in Mexico. It's the oldest image of God."

"But so old, so forgotten, so carefully shoved back by civilization, it now emerges as something completely new."

"Because outrageous? But I shouldn't be outraged, should I, unless I'm sick? All things clean save to such as think dirty. . . . Oh, for God's sake, Guia!"

"Yes, Sid. For God's sake. We don't claim to have found a new gimmick. This is the longest tradition in Christianity: presenting a new image of Jesus. The babe in the manger. The suffering servant. The risen victor. And all these images were found shocking in their time. How many centuries before anybody dared put up for adoration that mangled dying body on the cross? A scandal to the classic world, but how it sent the medievals. Or take the Sacred Heart. Rather corny now, I'm afraid: a sentimental Jesus for a sentimental age. But when the idea was first broached, what an outcry of horror. How could God's love be represented by a physical organ? And the pioneers of the devotion had to claim that Christ himself had told them that the idea of the Sacred Heart had been reserved for a late, late age of the world when the world's heart had grown cold. It turns out they were being optimistic. We're in a later, later age, with a colder, colder heart. We have need of a new Christ we can relate to."

"Christ as hip turned on."

"The carnal Christ. Why not? Take the fig leaf off the Incarnation so we can see the man hid by 2,000 years of shame. All we're trying to do is restore to worship what was always central to it before ascetics and puritans drove it out as unclean. How else can we now express Christ as being on the side of life? And if it was all right to worship his heart, why not some other part of his body?"

"Decorum forbids."

"Decorum has been the death of God."

"Decorum, young lady, is what you're going back to, like it or not. I'm giving you twenty-four hours to pack your things, say your goodbyes to Salem House, and return to Adela's. I'm speaking as your legal guardian."

She turned away from him, turned her back on him.

"I'm not a young lady, Sid, and it's not decorum you're sending me back to. It's death. Don't you know why I had to flee from that house? Because it's *sick*. The very air is so unhealthy I had to burst out of there to breathe."

"Oh, come now, sis. I know Santiago and Adela are squares, but they're good decent squares."

She looked round at him over a shoulder.

"What a withdrawn chap you are, Sid. So you don't know about them? After their one child, *he* made a vow of chastity and she had to agree to it. It couldn't have been too hard on her then, she was too busy social-climbing. But now she has got everything she wants, what she hasn't got is making a sickness inside her. It's hard on her now, you can see it. Have you noticed how more like Father she looks as she grows older? And Father never was easy to keep down. Oh, I'm not hinting she cheats, or he neither. I know they both behave—and that's what's so terrible. Whatever they're respectively trying to keep down makes that house *fester*. Even their son prefers boarding school."

"A man and his wife have the right to make their own private arrangements."

"But it's twisting them—or her anyway; he has money to fondle. After I took an apartment, there were these mysterious telephone calls at odd hours of the night. Or I'd see a car parked across the street. I only knew it was her when the family next door told me she paid them to use the room next to my wall. And wherever I have moved I have felt her *hovering*."

"Isn't that natural? She was trying to keep an eye on you."

"No, she craved a taste of my life at second-hand. I was sore

at first, until I thought of the loneliness that must have driven
her to that."

"This doesn't change anything."

"I am to go back there?"

"Right away. Then you're coming with me to New York,
where you can either stay in my flat or have one of your own."

She still had her back to him. He took her by the shoulders
and gently swung her around. Her head was bowed.

"Guia baby, don't be like that, we'll have fun, it'll be like old
times again. Listen, we'll go biking in Central Park."

She rested a quiet cheek on his breast.

"Give me until tomorrow night," she said.

After Guia had gone—Sister Juana came to fetch her—Sid rang
up Adela's. A maid answered. The señora was dining out; Don
Santiago was not expected back till the following day. Sid left
word that he was to be contacted at Mrs. Borja's.

Then he went through Guia's folder and the books he had
bought, mostly history and anthropology, until an employee
poked a head in at the door. All the staff had left; would Mr.
Estiva be staying longer?

"You go on home, too," said Sid. "I'll close up."

Out in the corridor, silent now and deserted, he paused to
recall which way one turned for the elevators. As he tentatively
walked down one hall a door opened and he was yanked in. He
was in a dim room, between two familiar figures: the black-
jacketed goons who had stripped him in the clearing.

"The boss," said one of them, "wants to see you, *pare*."

"Do I keep my clothes this time?"

"*Abah*, he's wise to us already," said the other, finger on Sid's
back steering him toward another door. He was shoved in and
the door pulled shut behind him.

This second room was lit only by a lamp near the door. As
Sid looked around a form emerged from the shadows: black
suit, flowing hair, gleaming mark on the forehead—Father
Melchor.

"Forgive me, Mr. Estiva, for compelling your presence here,

but have no fear, you will suffer no harm. I merely wish to talk to you."

"And give me back my things, I hope."

"Surely. But not now. We were in such a hurry my men did not think to bring them along."

"Some religion you have. Using goons and blackmailing women."

"And did *they* not use violence and women to drive us out? Why should we not use the same means to come back? I am not one of your moralists, Mr. Estiva, who so naively believe that the end is shaped by the means. The end is shaped only by success. Whatever wins is right."

"I see. Smuggle back the pagan in Christian disguise. Use Christianity to restore paganism."

"They used the ground of our cults to implant their faith."

"And deluding young girls with all this talk of a new image of Christ when it's really back to the heathen."

"*Deluding*—tch, tch, Mr. Estiva. You know that's not so. The god is worshipped, the true god. Does it matter if we call him Baal or Bathala, Priapus or Christ? What is the point of that passage in the Bible where Abraham and Melchizedek worshipped together? Melchizedek invoked his heathen god El or Zaduk; Abraham prayed to Yahweh. But the Bible makes no distinction between the deities, calling Melchizedek, too, a 'priest of the most high God.' And when St. Paul placed Christ himself in the line of Melchizedek, was this not a recognition that the pagan priesthood was resumed in Christ, that the old cults were being continued in the new faith? Abraham had already made such a recognition: he paid a tithe to the pagan high priest Melchizedek. It didn't matter to Abraham who Melchizedek was or in what name he worshipped God."

"And it doesn't matter either who *you* are?"

"Yes, I hear you have been making inquiries. No, Mr. Estiva, I don't think it matters. What mattered to Abraham was that Melchizedek was on his side. The important thing here is that I am on your side."

"*My* side!"

"You are of those who called me back."

"I don't think I ever went that far back."

"Ah, Mr. Estiva, if you go back at all it's impossible to set a limit: up to this point and no farther. If you dig up one grave you have also unlocked the ones that lie below. You've heard of the diggings during the Renaissance: how it was feared that with the resurrection of their vessels and icons the old gods that had gone underground had surfaced again?"

"And you think that's happening here now?"

"Oh, I don't pretend to be one of the old gods. Merely to be in their service—as you are, though you may refuse to admit it. And as your sister will be, when she has gone beyond the Christian image and learns by herself what is the question that must be asked: the name of the god she worships. It will be her illumination. Therefore, I ask you not to block her path."

"My sister is leaving your gang, is leaving the country."

"Then I must warn you, Mr. Estiva, that you are invoking forces that are without mercy."

"I hope quite soon to meet those forces, across a police desk."

"Very well, Mr. Estiva, I have warned you. It is all I can do. If you and yours move, so will the furies. My men will show you out. The elevators are at the next bend of the hall. And if you think to raise the alarm I advise you to save yourself the trouble. We will not be here when whoever you call arrives."

Supper was laid on the marble table on Sonya's piazza, somewhat to Sid's surprise.

"I thought I was taking you out?"

She limply grimaced.

"Some other time . . . Not in the mood."

She was in a sleeveless yellow blouse and black palazzo pants, and from her ears dangled concentric gold triangles. He found his eyes following their swing along her neck. They ate to the light of candles in tiny glass lamps; she ate listlessly, an elbow on the table.

"Tired, Sonya?"

"I did my Christmas shopping after we parted."

"And cooked all this."

"It's my maids' day out."

He felt that they were alone within layers of wall—the high walls that enclosed her lawn; the still higher and discreetly blind but whispering walls of the motels roundabout, where air-conditioning eared the mock-adobe with eave after eave of rumor.

"The candles," he said, watching their glint on her earrings, "are proper tonight."

"December 21?"

"The eve of the winter solstice."

"No. Bonfires, I think."

"But candles too. That's why we have the Christmas lantern."

He was now watching the shadows the earrings danced with on her neck.

"Tonight the sun god dies and is born again," he said.

"So they light bonfires?"

"To help him warm up."

She shivered and spread fingers over her naked golden arms.

"It *is* getting chilly," she said "—but why feast the sun's dying?"

"*Rage, rage against the dying of the light.*"

"A rage of food, drink, fire?"

"And love too, and love especially. It was the supreme magic, the magic to ensure that the sun would burn again."

They were looking not at each other but into their glasses of chianti.

She said, after their silence and a bit of wine: "Imagine all that, when they must have thought it the end of the world."

"The late late show."

"Man's bravado spirit, and bravado from the start. Tell you what, Sid—"

"Let's celebrate the bravado?"

"And help the sun be born again. There's that pile of leaves and trash on the lawn."

Kneeling to the pile, he thrust a kindled rag into it, then settled back on the grass beside her and took her in his arms. The fire grew slowly, the heart of flame burning buried by itself, yielding a coiled smoke as it slowly steadily dwindled, almost on the wane, only a smoldering, before it began to spread, gleaming into a line here, leaping into a burst of sparks there, the traveling tongues that swayed toward each other seeming to yearn for each other and for that heart of heat now swelling to include them too, now glowing into a furnace round which the darting sparks, shattering, multiplied, the thicker smoke pushing in between brightening as, let loose, it uncoiled, unrolled, arose, rippling now from one blaze, one bush on fire, one total incandescence that rose, rushed, rustled, roared, raged, until, at last, finally fluently flowering, oh, oh, the burst body of it broke free, in a fountain of fire springing up to the skies; and they clung fast to each other, shuddering to the ascent.

Later that night, waking up in her bed, he saw a redness at her window that said the bonfire still burned, though more gently now, as if because they slept; but becoming aware that, awake, too, she, too, lay watching that glow at the window, he spoke her name and, needing no other word, turning as one, they fell on each other's flesh in gluttony.

When he next stirred, the window stood dark, but her body was a darker shape before it. She glanced around, sensing his awakeness.

"Don't you want to get up and watch the newborn sun rising? After all, we did help it."

Naked together at the window, they saw the first edge of sun above the roof of the Taj Mahal Motel.

"We weren't the only ones helping it," she smiled.

"Come back, Sonya, come back."

"It *still* needs helping?"

"It's only a baby sun yet."

After breakfast he had a taxi called. Sonya seemed to have lost her bravura, was again as listless as when he had arrived the night before, and breakfasted with one elbow on the table, the golden triangles swinging from her ears.

He said: "I thought it was the man who was *tristis post coitum?*"

"Last night always seems last year the morning after."

"It's still around three a.m. to me."

"Don't take too long to wake."

"What *is* up, Sonya?"

"The workaday sun, hon. And look at the mess that bonfire made. We'll have to clean up the whole place."

She stood at the gate to wave goodbye, in the palazzo pants and a turtleneck sweater, the earrings flashing arcs on her neck in the sunshine.

When he arrived at Adela's Adela was at the telephone; it was Mrs. Banaag who ran out to meet him.

"Did you get my message?"

"Good morning, Mrs. Banaag. No, what message?"

"I called you up yesterday afternoon."

"Here?"

"Here first. The maid said to try Mrs. Borja's. So I called up there. She said you were expected but had not come yet."

"What did you want to tell me?"

"*They* had a gathering last night. In Antipolo. The whole group. Including him, yes, the prophet. And those two goons who murdered the taxi driver. Last night was Father Lao's turn. I didn't know what to do. So I called you up. Didn't Mrs. Borja tell you?"

"No," said Sid, "she didn't tell me."

Adela came back from the telephone.

"I couldn't sleep all night," Mrs. Banaag was saying, "and first thing this morning I came here, to hear what had happened. I wanted to call you up again, at Mrs. Borja's, but—"

"But I told her better not," said Adela. She gave Sid a look. "It's all right, Isidro, Santiago was there—oh, very much there. It seems he rescued this Father Lao. *And* captured one of the gangsters who held you up. This was last night, in Antipolo. On a hill there where they were having some kind of ceremony."

"Last night." Sid looked from his sister to Mrs. Banaag.

"The winter solstice," said Mrs. Banaag.

"Oh my God," said Sid.

"That was why I was trying to reach you yesterday," said Mrs. Banaag. "I think they planned to have the ceremony in Intramuros, but Salem House has become hot, so they transferred to Antipolo. And after last night they plan to go underground. All of them. Including your sister. But I told Mrs. Borja all this and begged her to be sure and tell you. Didn't she?"

"No," said Sid again. "No, she didn't tell me."

Father Lao and the captured thug were brought back from Antipolo at noon and Sid went to the police station to identify the thug, who was one of the black-jacketed pair all right. Santiago was in a rapture of excitement. Clothes rumpled, the night's growth on his chin, he looked too happy to be sleepy. He had been on a crusade: *Santiago Matamoros!* Father Lao, too, though as haggard as ever, and even more rumpled in the gray suit he had traveled in, seemed to move in exaltation. He had rejected the forces of evil, he had performed an act of contrition.

"What I did, *cuñao*," related Santiago, "was what we should have done long before but did not do because we are not that kind of people. But after my first interview with Mrs. Banaag I decided to do it. I went to a private detective agency and asked them to trail Guia and her companions. Night before last, when we met at the club with Mrs. Banaag, I had already been told that something was afoot in Antipolo. I had learned from the agents that immediately after your visit to Intramuros Guia and a group drove up to Antipolo and stayed the night there. The place is a very isolated hacienda on a hilltop which belongs to a rich widow.

"So, yesterday I joined the agents in Antipolo. There is a high wall around the hacienda and all about it are woods and very rugged ground, but one of the agents had managed to sneak inside and he reported that a man was being held prisoner in a hut in the orchard, behind the big house. Last night they began to assemble. We saw at least ten cars drive up that zigzag road to the hacienda. I was told that Guia, too, had arrived, with her prophet.

"At first, nothing happened, they were all in the house. We were hiding in the woods outside and had one man up on a tree, with binoculars. Then, around midnight, out they all came to the orchard behind the house. Our man on the tree reported that they were dancing around a bonfire—and they were naked, *cuñao*, all of them, men and women. It was then that our agent on the tree saw Father Lao, gun in hand, hurrying this thug through the dark area along the wall. I had some men climb on the wall to pull them both up. We took them at once to the town police and Father Lao pointed to this thug as one of the murderers of the taxi driver.

"The trouble was, we then had to wake up a judge and all that to get a search warrant. When we returned to the hacienda it was too late. Nobody was there. They had all fled. But it's all right, we know where they are. This thug has been talking all night and he has told us plenty. It seems they have a smuggler's boat waiting somewhere on the Cavite coast to take them away, but the constabulary has gone after them and you can be sure that before this day ends the whole gang will be in the hands of the law. This thug has testified that the girls know nothing of the gang's villainous activities. So, I have asked that Guia be separated from the group and brought home at once. As soon as he has finished with his statement, Father Lao is coming home with us too. He has nowhere to go, poor man. He went astray but has repented. I have promised to intercede for him with the ecclesiastical authorities."

In Adela's den that afternoon, Sid and the Ferrers heard Father Lao's story. The priest was about Sid's age, a gaunt ghost with a glitter in his eyes, and still in such an ecstasy his hands trembled uncontrollably as he talked.

"When they first came to me in L.A., I was waiting for a sign. I walked the streets at night waiting for God to find me again. For two-three years—no, longer—God had been absent. It is terrible not to be able to pray. I tried, I tried, but God was not there, God was not listening. This was in a university town in Kansas, where it was always the dark night for me. And because I felt so abandoned I fell into sin. There was this girl— oh, she was a witch, the scarlet woman, the whore of Babylon. She was evil, evil. But I sinned only from despair, because God had withdrawn. And when I was ruined I fled from that town and hid in L.A. I lived among outcasts and was viler than any of them. But now that God had done his worst to me, I said to myself, surely he would now come back to me? And so I walked the streets in my vile state waiting for a sign.

"Then *they* came to me, with their evil proposition: that I use my sacred priesthood in their service. The service of the devil. Oh, I knew at once it was that, though they talked of history and renewal and the native soul. I knew what I was being invited to. And what a blow it was to me! I had begged God to send me an angel; what he sent me was the devil. And if that was how he wanted it, I bitterly said to myself. Again, if I sinned, it was from despair: God had abandoned me utterly.

"So I went with them to San Francisco and they set me up in a hotel and there they left me to make up my mind. When I flew to Manila I was still not decided. I knew there was hope for me yet as long as I did not traffic with what was most sacred in me. And all through the flight I entreated God to show me a sign, show me a sign.

"Then it came, at the airport—the sign, the sign I had so long awaited, the unmistakable sign that God cared. They had told me to carry a toothbrush in my hand. That symbol of their abomination was to identify me to those who would fetch me. But when they found me I learned that somebody else had gone before me, carrying a toothbrush—somebody who had been mistaken for me and was given the message intended for me. God had sent an angel before me, to deliver me. Yes, I know it was only you, Mr. Estiva—but don't you *see* the miracle of the coincidence? God was *using* you to communicate with me. And at that moment, there at the airport, I felt the presence of God. God had come back. The desert, the dark night, was over. I could pray again. And although still mystified that God should have involved me in the forces of evil, I could no longer doubt that in this, too, was design; in this, too, was purpose.

"When they came to me in my hotel that afternoon I told them that I could not serve their god. I was forcibly taken to their headquarters in Intramuros and kept there all night and I found that I had indeed fallen among thieves and murderers. I heard how they had held you up, Mr. Estiva, and killed that taxi driver, because he was going to the police. Oh, I know they were trying to terrorize me. But they made one more effort to persuade me peacefully. At noon the next day, a girl came to my cell and talked to me of their religion. How innocent it all sounded, coming from the lips of one who looked so pretty and innocent, but was a witch, was the scarlet woman, was the whore of Babylon, and evil, evil. And then it was that I understood why God had brought me right into the fortress of the forces of evil. It was because I had been chosen the instrument to destroy that fortress and to slay the forces of evil.

"That night I was taken to the place in Antipolo and kept under guard in a hut. I knew they meant to liquidate me: I had sworn to expose them; but only yesterday did I begin to realize how they meant to do it. I was to be sacrificed at their abominable rites even as the heathen offered human sacrifices to their gods. I had heard they would be having a ceremony at midnight. I felt no fear. I knew that God would deliver me and destroy them. I had noticed a man sneaking around the grounds who was clearly not one of them.

"Last night, when they began their abominations, I pretended to have fallen asleep. There were always two guards with me in that hut but one guard went off to join the rites and the other who stayed clung to the window, so absorbed in his lecherous watching he had forgotten that his gun lay on the table beside him. I crept up, grabbed the gun—I still have it—poked it in his back and made him lead me through the orchard to the wall. And there was Don Santiago waiting. Ask him what was the first thing I did. I kissed the cross on his breast."

Sid listened as dead-pan as the thought of having been Father Lao's guardian angel would allow. The priest looked so drained after his outpouring Adela bade him retire for the day. Santiago, however, still keyed up, could not be kept from going off to get the latest reports from the constabulary.

Sid rang up Sonya's number. A maid replied, asked him to wait, then came back to say she was sorry, Mrs. Borja was out.

Then Santiago called up from constabulary headquarters. The captured Salemites had arrived but Guia refused to be separated from the group. Would Sid rush over and talk to the girl?

"Did they capture everyone?" asked Sid.

"If you mean that other thug who killed the taxi driver—yes."

"Everyone then?"

"Except the prophet, *cuñao*. They could not find the prophet."

Guia, in jeans and a black cardigan, sat in a room with the sisterhood. They were all there: the large female who had been in green at the airport, the girl with long hair who had been in a sweatshirt and stretch pants, the "distinguished business-woman" who had been in Moro costume at Adela's party, and a softly weeping Sister Juana. Doggedly wearing bafflement like veils, the grouped women might have been the Marys at the equinox, left with the vinegar of their lost Lord.

Sid strode up to his sister. She had been Steve, Ginny, Gigi, and Guiang, and had now come to the end of Sister Guia.

"Come on, baby. Let's go home."

She looked up at him, then rose without a word. He put an arm around her and walked her out of the room, down the hall of the military, and out to the cold December evening. In the car she lay quiet in his arms; and he remembered her as quiet in his arms, not weeping, a mere child, when they returned from their father's funeral. He thought: I should never have left home.

Adela waited in her den: all their gatherings seemed to require their father's tuxedo'd presence, hugely there on the wall.

The sisters touched cheeks, Adela flinging her arms around the girl.

"You poor thing. To have had to go through this at your age. Come and sit here beside me."

The two of them occupied a sofa; Santiago enthroned himself on a high-backed antique; Sid took a rocking chair; their father remained standing on the wall.

"But it's over now," continued Adela, sitting sideways to face her sister. "We won't even mention it again. From tonight you're the debutante you weren't. Carlota Jones is bringing her boy over for lunch tomorrow, and she's only the starter."

"Or," said Santiago, "if you prefer a period of transition, Guia, there is this very nice religious community where you could stay for a time."

"Guia and I have already decided," said Sid. "She's coming to New York with me."

There was a pause, during which the three elders looked at one another while Guia sat still, hands folded on lap. Then Adela protested, Santiago opined, Sid refused to argue and then argued.

Guia abruptly stood up.

Sid hated himself for looking up at her, askance, like Adela and Santiago.

"Don't haggle over me," she said.

Adela threw her hands up.

"But, Guia baby, we're only thinking of your own good."

The girl looked around at the three of them.

"My own good, Adela? Or your spite? You think I don't know? You envy me my angers and my passions. And you'd have me as trapped as you are. Poor Adelita's revenge on life! Isn't that why you want me married to that Jones boy? Everyone knows he's incapable of marriage—"

She veered toward her brother-in-law.

"As incapable, Santiago, as *you* are. Ah, but you can hurdle mountains and climb walls for something else. *Ad majorem Dei gloriam?* Come on, Santiago. Why were you so frantic? Because you might lose my money, lose the corporation? And so you want me tucked safely away in this nice religious community that banks with you. Imagine what my dowry would be and you'd get to handle it all for them—"

"Guia," cried Sid, springing up, "have you gone out of your mind?"

"And how about Siddie boy? What's your cut here, brod? Am I on to your nik? What's this about me and you holing up in Manhattan? With me as what? The baby you wouldn't have, the wife you couldn't keep, the mistresses who have to rape you?"

Sid shook: "You don't know what you're saying."

"Ah, but I do, brod. I'm the one girl you can be sure will have to love you always, and the perfect partner in solitude because I'm almost not another person, I'm almost only you again. Picture the two of us so nicely becoming old maids together—"

Sid moved a hand toward the girl but she backed away.

"Don't touch me, don't any of you touch me!"

She backed out of the family circle.

"I'll make you sorry you stopped me!" she cried, then turned on her heels and ran to the doorway, but halted there and looked around again.

"Remember," she smiled, "there will be nine-ten months of this, nine-ten months of us being together like this, before I let go of you!"

It was then they saw a figure looming up from the dusk beyond the doorway, saw a face glittering into the light of the doorway: Father Lao, in a tremble, popeyed at the girl.

Seeing their stare shift, she whirled about and saw the man in the doorway.

"*You!*" he cried, and now trembled in every limb.

Still standing by the rocking chair, Sid rather leaned forward to catch the words—*witch? scarlet? whore?*—that the man was so wildly mumbling as he lifted his right arm.

The instant of seeing what he had in his hand was the same instant they heard the gun howl once, howl a second time, to his twin shrieks of "*Evil! Evil!*"

Then, the gun dropping from his hands, he clung to a side of the doorway, trying to hold on but sliding down to his knees.

Santiago sat petrified, a stone image enthroned. Adela, collapsed on her side on the sofa, helplessly shudderingly moaned. Conscious of their father leering down at all this from his wall, Sid stiffly walked to where Guia lay prone on the floor.

He turned her over in his arms: the parted lips were breathless.

New Year's Day was cold, almost arctic in the office where Sid had been staying since the funeral. It had been quick, the funeral, with only himself in attendance. Adela was in a nursing home with a nervous breakdown; Santiago had retreated into a monastery. Sid had had to take over at the office, sleeping there too and having his meals sent up. Far below, the holidays had danced by unheard, their mirth muffled by the drapes at the windows.

He stood at the windows, in a bulky sweater, holding aside a weight of cloth to look at afternoon sunshine aslant on the cliff below. Practically no traffic down there, whether human on the sidewalk or vehicular on the street. They were all at home recuperating. He let the drape fall back, extinguishing a streak of pink afternoon. Wintry dusk settled back in the large room, save at his desk, where a lamp floodlit a sheet of paper on the glass top.

He returned to his seat at the table and reread Mrs. Borja's letter, from Baguio.

"*My son is at military school here and instead of him going down for the holidays I came up. I couldn't very well have stayed there. However, I owe you an explanation. You must have been wondering why I did what I did; maybe you've even thought I was one of them?*

"*No, I'm not and I wasn't; but after Mrs. Banaag called up that afternoon I had a visitor. Yes, the prophet. He knew I had information; he told me it shouldn't reach you. We talked only a quarter of an hour or so, but in that short time I knew that this thing of his must not be stopped. No, not from any persuasion of his. This was, as Mrs. Banaag would say, instinctive on my part, something I felt quite strongly. How strongly you can guess when I tell you that what Mrs. Banaag had particularly impressed on me—that a man's life was in danger—suddenly seemed unimportant. I was prepared to be ruthless—or something in me was. Maybe Lawrence's dark gods of the blood? We were theirs that night.*

"*Afterward, of course, I was horrified. One doesn't chuck mind that fast. My husband said he could hear my mind at work even when he was making love to me; so he ran away. Now it's I who am running away. What I do now seems so silly. We play with the past, making chi-chi fashions out of it, or décor for a party. Maybe I'm being punished for having used it so frivolously, as mere bric-a-brac.*

"*But it was madness to come up here. This is their country, their terrain, the dark gods. I was in Bontoc and Sagada and up to Ifugao country and they were all about me. Remember telling me how, as you ran from those goons, you felt your naked body had become pure movement, without a mind, every limb thinking*

*for itself? That's how I feel now, as I run and run but always find
myself where I would run away from. . . ."*

Sid dropped the letter, made aware by a movement of air of a
presence in the room. At the farthest end of the dusk the door
had opened. Someone stood there looking in, someone closed
the door, someone slowly crossed the darkness toward the circle
of light where Sid sat.

Father Melchor stood before the table, a bundle in his hands,
a sadness in his droop, the mark dark on his brow.

"Here I am, Mr. Estiva, if you want to call the police."

Sid had risen to his feet: "You get the hell out."

"As soon as I have returned your things, Mr. Estiva, as I
promised." He placed the bundle on the table. "Your clothes,
Mr. Estiva." He put a hand into his pocket and what he drew
out he laid one by one on the table. "Your passport. Your plane
ticket. *And* your toothbrush. I think everything is there now?"

Sid was staring at the things on the table. Then, ruefully, he
picked up the green Prophylactic with the frayed bristles.

"My symbol of non-involvement . . ." he murmured.

"We made it mean the means to deepest commitment."

"But what a coincidence that I—"

"There are no coincidences, Mr. Estiva. When you called us
back years ago you set in motion certain forces that made inevitable, not only that you should come home but that you should
come home bearing a sign aloft to proclaim a connection you
were unaware of; and that, like magnet or lodestone, or the
smell of blood that attracts the creatures of the deep, you
should draw all about you the other participants in this drama
that you initiated. It was no coincidence when they—But why
do you stare at me so, Mr. Estiva?"

It seemed to Sid that he was noticing for the first time the
stripes of white in the man's hair, the fine lines that webbed his
face, the stoop to the shoulders, the tired eyes.

"You think I have changed, Mr. Estiva? Yes, the weariness
comes when one fails and has to hide again. But I have come
back before, I shall come back again. A faith thrives on the

blood of its witnesses. And we have a new one. Saint Guia, virgin and martyr."

He put a hand in his pocket, pulled out a bunch of keys and dropped it on the table, upon the plane tickets. "The Salem House keys, Mr. Estiva. I want you to take care of the place until I come back."

"*That* is a round-trip ticket, in case you haven't noticed."

"Oh, I did."

"And I'm leaving soon."

"No. Mr. Estiva, you are not going away again. You have come home."

He stood quiet for a moment and seemed to be smiling through his melancholy. Then he turned and moved away, and Sid noticed that the limp was heavier: the man seemed to be dragging his right foot as he hobbled into the darkness. Sid heard the knob turn, the door open, and the cold rush of air in the moment before the door closed again.

His jacket hung on the chair. He pulled it on, over the sweater; pocketed passport, plane ticket, keys, and toothbrush; then turned the light off on Sonya's letter.

It was sunset when he stopped the car before the door of Salem house. He found the right key, opened the door, and stepped into the stone-flagged hall. The archaic furniture stood as he had last seen it but no light burned before the pregnant Virgin. He walked through the passage into the cloister, where sunlight lay level with the roof, past the rows of shut doors and into the second passage at the back. He unbolted the door there and stepped out into the angle of back yard. Behind the high wall throbbed a final blush of light. The rising of ruins stood half in shadow, peaks bathed in light.

He stood in a gap in the ring, the evening sun on his face. Not a breath of wind stirred the air. The adobe blocks were gone from the center; they had been found piled up again into a table in the Antipolo orchard. He crossed the ring toward the shrine in the stone facing east. Gone from the ledge were the scatter of flowers, the sheaf of grain, the tall glass of light. But a gap showed between the rounded metal door and one side of the niche. He slipped a hand into the gap and pushed. The door swung around into the niche that now stood open.

But the niche was empty.

The niche was the void where night had begun, though it was another night he heard.

—*When do you celebrate it?*

—*New Year's Day, you donkey. Now shut up and let's go.*

—*Why New Year's Day? That's not liturgical. Oh yes, it is. Feast of the Circumcision.*

—*And you're cordially invited to our patronal festivities, donkey. Now, let's go in.* I'm cold.

It didn't seem right to go without making a gesture. He put hand to pocket, fetched out the toothbrush, and stood it up in the niche, sticking the handle in a crack of rock.

But something else was needed. He pulled out the plane ticket, crumpled it into a wad, placed it in the niche, and lit a match to it. He waited for it to burn before walking away.

At the edge of the ring he paused to look back, looking back across the still evening at the wedge of wall where the wad of plane ticket burned, a flame tall in the void, steady before the standing toothbrush.

CÁNDIDO'S APOCALYPSE

Telephones are latest in a house to wake up, which they do only after breakfast or in the forenoon. A household is in trouble whose telephone rings before breakfast.

Hearing in her half-sleep her telephone's start of surprise, Ineng Heredia rolled over in bed, on her face, sinking back, back, deeper, deeper, into quicksand—but felt herself yanked up and pulled around by the shoulder.

"*Mommy!* I've shouted and shouted. The *telephone.*"

She groped, stubbornly blind, for the nape of the girl at her ear.

"Happy birthday, darling."

But the girl bridled loose.

"It's Mr. Henson. He's Pete's father."

"Who? Ask what he wants."

"I have. You."

"Where O where's your father . . ."

"Shaving. Mommy, I think it's about Bobby."

Mrs. Heredia opened her eyes but her daughter had run out of the room. Day was a dazzle of grilled window, faceted, like a great diamond. With a toss of legs into air, she swung herself up and over the bed's edge, dragging sheet along, stepped into panties, vainly toed the floor for slippers and, winding the sheet tighter over her breasts, scampered on bare feet to the corridor outside.

This house was split level; and the banistered corridor, three steps up from the living room it overlooked, ran past three doors, two of which were open, revealing books and shoes on the beds, pillows and clothes on the floor. The third door, by looking so shut, looked bereaved. At the other end of the corridor, which here had a wall siding instead of banisters, Totong Heredia was shaving in the bathroom, with the door open, in his pajama trousers, leaning toward the washbowl mirror with exaggerated attention. His pretending to be unaware of everything else made his wife click angry heels as she ran down the three steps and across the parlor to the side table where the telephone lived, among pencils and pad paper.

"Hello? Yes? Mr. Henson? He *where?*"

Her daughter and younger boy, having breakfast standing, refused, by not listening, to be included in whatever crisis the telephone was creating. They were having their own crisis.

"You can sleep at grandmother's!" screamed Sophie, who was fifteen today. "I won't have *stupid* babies at my party! It's *my* party!"

"Dad said I could invite Marilu Pérez."

"Junior, if you bring that *stupid* Marilu Perez to my party—"

Glass of milk in hand, Junior was leaning sideways at the table, an elbow on the edge, a foot upon his satchel on the floor, like a tippler at a bar. He was not quite eleven. He scoffed without looking at his sister, who stooped over the other side of the table, disdainfully pinching off, with thumb and finger, pieces of omelet and bread, her other hand spread protectingly over the fresh blouse of her school uniform.

"Besides," she said, licking her fingers and beginning a smile, "she's old enough to be your *nurse*."

He tossed off the milk as though it were a swig of booze, plunked the glass down, and, his eyes narrowing, now deigned to turn his head slightly to scan his relative.

"You're just jealous of Marilu Perez because she can judo and you can't."

"And I'll bet she *teaches* you, boy."

"What kinda party you having anyway? Beer party? Gin party? Sioktong? But your boy friends would pass out on coke. You having dog meat?"

"Junior, I'll *kill* you!"

"Will you stop that, children," shouted their mother. "I can't hear!"

"Bobby's stowaway," gloated Junior not lowering his voice.

For some reason he now had the satchel on his head and stood with one leg before the other, arms poised at his breast, the elbows crook'd: a black belter about to belch.

Sophie had stiffened up but her glitter of fury was not for the grunts of the judo expert.

"Bobby," she keened, one hand still spread over her breast, as though the heart inside hurt, "would do anything, but anything, to *destroy* me! He went stowaway just to *ruin* my party!"

"Sophie," yelled her mother, "didn't I tell you—No, no, Mr. Henson, I understand perfectly. His father will be here before noon."

At this, the two children at the breakfast table turned to look across the sweep of space that was living and dining room at their mother, in her winding sheet, perched on an edge of divan, clutching the receiver with one hand, the folds of cloth at her breast with the other, and firmly not looking toward, though facing, the banisters, over which, the two children now noted, their father leaned with careful indolence, pondering the safety razor in his hand, the cream now washed off his thinnish, palish, still pretending face.

He was aware of their regard some time before he looked up to wink at them. They stared back, unsmiling; the maid dashed in with their chilled water and flounced out again; their mother put down the telephone.

"What's this about before noon?" asked Totong Heredia, smiling at his wife.

"Bobby's there, at the Hensons'."

"Okay. So did you tell them to tell him to come home?"

"Mr. Henson is delivering him, at around eleven."

"Why around eleven, why not right now?"

"Because Mr. Henson says so. He thinks you should be here."

"Who's this guy anyway giving orders—"

"Only mister lifesaver, in case you don't know. It seems our boy has to be persuaded to come home, and Mr. Henson has volunteered. The least you can do is be here to accept delivery."

"I can't be home at noon, you know that."

"And there's the school yet. You'll just have to drop in there and talk to *them*."

"Oh sure, sure, I can take the day off. It just so happens to be our sales evaluation day."

"Oh, for heaven's sake, Totong."

"It's not our sales evaluation day?"

"Your son won't come home and this man calls me up and not you. Shouldn't this be man to man, father to father?"

"Suddenly it's me that's getting it. *I* didn't run away. All I said was, today at the office—"

"You're supposed to be an executive there, Tong. You don't *act* like an executive. Surely they won't all just fall apart if you took a morning off?"

"Oh no, no, darling. And all I have to do is show up there and tell the bastards I don't feel like working today and would they please get the hell—"

"Children," said Mrs. Heredia, "if you've finished breakfast—"

"No, dammit, Ineng, don't you see? There's this new man there, this younger man, and any time, oh, any time at all I don't—"

"Sophie, Junior, if you're through, wait in the driveway."

But nobody moved. Not even the man at the banisters, head now sulkily slumped. Ineng Heredia, who had been glaring at her children, shifted impatient eyes to her husband. He sort of gave his head a shake but did not look up.

At that, as at a signal, Sophie, all this while clenching tighter, uncoiled.

"Oh, I hate you, I hate you! It's my birthday and nobody cares! Oh, I hate you, Mommy, I hate you, Dad, I hate Bobby, I hate everyone!"

The outburst was swallowed in an intake of breath, a gasp or sob that caught in the throat and was not immediately expelled by a rush of breath. Standing there with held breath, Sophie, too, like her mother, seemed impatient, more expectant than emotional. In the pause the maid bounded in to clear the children's end of the table. She had been with the family too long to create or prolong silences and was therefore unnerved enough by this one to stop bouncing and follow everyone's stare at the man leaning over the banisters.

Ineng Heredia could not but burn. Having done so, she stood up, briskly if grimly, and tucking the cloth in at her breast strode to the center of the room, appearing, so imperative she looked, to be trailing more than a bedsheet.

"Sophie, I told you, wait in the driveway. No, Junior, you are to take that cat out of your bag at once. You can put on the señorito's fish now, Inday. If the children are not to be late, Totong, shouldn't you go and get dressed?"

The room came alive with a jerk. Junior's cat sprang out of his satchel, spitting, and onto his shoulder, scratching. He wailed. Sophie stormed out through the kitchen, shoving Inday aside, who dropped a plate. It broke. Totong Heredia plodded back to the bathroom and, just for the heck of it, slammed the door. The wall shook. As Inday in tears threatened to depart the telephone rang again, and its start of surprise was this time even more justified. Somebody had got a wrong number today before breakfast.

The cake shop later that morning was a mother's meet on teen-agers.

"So it's your Bobby now, Ineng? How old is he?"

"Seventeen."

"Welcome to the club."

"She's lucky. My Joey first went stowaway when he was thirteen."

"But what makes them do it? My God, if we had at their age what we give them. My brother's boy now, only sixteen today— the cake is for him—and he's getting a car of his own, just to keep him in school. Your boy in school, Ineng?"

"Fourth year high."

"Maura Cruz called me up simply hysterical yesterday morning. She lives three doors from the Heredias but she heard the shots distinctively while in the bathroom and almost fell off the you-know-what. It's good she always leaves the door open so she can be heard—"

"Nobody," said Ineng Heredia, leaning forward from her corner, "was hurt. Bobby was not firing at anybody."

"What's this about his aiming at Pompoy Morel?"

"But he didn't *fire* at Pompoy."

"Pompoy Morel," one mother was explaining to another, "is Ed and Shirley's boy that they left with her mother when they split. You must have noticed him, this big boy with the eyes? Handsome as the father and, I hear, just as fast."

"What really happened," said Ineng Heredia, smiling at her own patience, "was that Bobby's combo was rehearsing on our piazza yesterday morning and it seems they didn't want Pompoy there. Well, my boy is rather a practical joker and he thought he would give old Pompoy a scare by pretending to shoot at him."

"Were you there, Ineng?"

"Why, yes, I was there."

"Talking with the Morel boy, we hear, when your boy started shooting."

"I didn't know he had run in to get his father's gun. I mean—"

Whatever suspense might have tensed was fortunately snapped by the shop's proprietress bustling up to beg the ladies to please come and tell her pastry cook how they wanted their respective icings.

"The cats!" hissed Nena Santos. "Come on, Ineng, I'll give you a lift."

"My sister's picking me up here."

"Menchu? Is she back from abroad? Look, what *did* happen?"

"Nena, I wish I *knew!* I almost wish I had been flirting with that awful Morel boy. There would be *that* to see. But I swear to God I didn't flutter an eyelash. All I did was go out there to see if they had cokes and sandwiches. I was being the good mother, you see, campaigning for her son. But Bobby, from the first moment I stepped out there, looked at me in the *oddest* way. Though it's only now I wonder about that, and how pale he became. Then, after all that shooting, I sent him to his room. I was a wreck. So I called up Father O'Brien and he said better get the boy to church. Yesterday was a Wednesday and we have this noon Mass in our parish. Bobby came with me willingly, he looked all right. We got to church some time before the Mass. So I asked him if he wanted to go to confession and he said yes. He was in the box waiting, I was watching, and when the priest opened the window Bobby jumped as though he had seen a ghost and rushed out of the church. So I ran out too and Bobby was on the steps pressing a hand to his eyes and shaking all over. I got him into a taxi and all the way home I was trying to calm him down saying Bobby this and Bobby that. And suddenly he jerked up and yelled at me: 'I'm not Bobby, I'm not Bobby! Stop calling me Bobby!' For a moment I wondered which of us had gone mad."

"Now you take it easy, Ineng. Your boy's just going through a phase."

"I know. And Totong and I have decided the best way to handle this is by not making a fuss. Sophie's having her party tonight as planned and I've convinced Pompoy Morel's grandmother we'd all just make matters worse if we told the police."

"The boy hasn't come home?"

"I should have kept him in. But he looked all right at lunch, after being talked to by his father, which I made Totong do. And as I said we thought it wise to act as though nothing had happened, let him go to school as usual and all that. They had only afternoon classes yesterday. But it seems the moment he got there he insulted his professor and the principal. *And* the prefect of discipline."

"My goodness!" laughed Nena Santos. "Whatever did he say?"

"They're not things one cares to repeat," said the prefect of discipline. "They're bad enough but the implications are worse. Your son, Mr. Heredia, referred to certain, uh, secrets of the persons he insulted, which can only mean he had been spying on us or prying into our private lives."

"That doesn't sound like Bobby," said Totong Heredia,

whose concerned expression kept slipping off his face as he
inhaled, in the prefect's cubicle of an office, a lifetime's steam
of boredom, feeling again, as in baffled childhood, that what
were trifles outside school walls became enormities inside
them. He coughed short a yawn and suggested unthinkingly:
"Couldn't my son have been repeating what was merely common knowledge?"

The prefect flushed hard and shook with rage.

"If you'd only give me a hint of what my son is supposed to
have said—"

"My lips," said the prefect at last, grimly, and yet with a
touch of coyness, "are sealed."

All that Bobby probably said, thought Totong Heredia, nodding gravely at the prefect, is that you're a damn old woman.

Aloud he scrupled: "But don't you think that, if only from a
sense of justice—"

"Ah, Mr. Heredia, that was why we called up your house.
We wanted you to come and question the boy and decide for
yourself if we be right in deciding he is not to remain in this
school."

"Yes, I know. My wife called me up to say you had called up
but I couldn't leave the office just then. Anyway she called up
again to say you had called up again because the boy was
gone."

"I left him right here in this office. I had other matters to
attend to. But I put him on his word of honor to stay here until
you came. In this school, Mr. Heredia, we strictly adhere to the
honor system."

You bastard, thought Totong Heredia, you couldn't bear the
thought of an encore.

But it was time now (and his mouth soured with distaste) for
the comedy, and he leaned toward the prefect in the attitude of
one about to make a clean breast.

"Look, don't get me wrong please, but this is man to man.
You're an educator, you've been with children all your life, and
of course you know they are not complete in themselves.
They're also their homes, their parents, and what's going on at
the moment in their families. I'm not trying to justify my son.

I'm sure he said things for which he should be punished, and punished severely. But you and I are adult, we can make allowances if we understand the background of an act. That's what I want you to do in my son's case.

"About a year ago I fell ill—oh, nothing serious—but it sort of slowed me down. Actually it wasn't just the illness. We men, you know, we also reach a certain period of life when we begin to—I had turned forty then. Bobby and I used to have a pleasant, natural, spontaneous relationship, but I'm afraid I've been too worried of late with my own self. And I think, I just think, all this that's happening to Bobby now, do you know, he just wants me to notice him again. But I don't see why I'm telling you all this. You know more about these things than I do. I bet you saw through at once to what lay at the heart of the matter?"

"Well, I did take up psychology in—"

"You did? No wonder I felt at once I didn't have to explain, thought I must say you rather scared me at first, man—but I sensed at once, I *knew*, you would understand."

"Now wait, Mr. Heredia, I didn't say—"

"Go on, please go on. I'm the father but I must confess I'm just as mixed up as the boy. Somebody has to straighten *me* out. I want to be told. You tell me."

"Well—"

I'm a crook, thought Totong Heredia, oh, I'm a damn crook.

"I'll tell you one thing, Mr. Heredia. When your boy insulted me I wasn't really as shocked as I should have been because I was more engrossed, as a psychologist, in his emotional state. I don't mean he was wild or violent or in any way hysterical. No, he was quite calm and he said what he said to me in a matter-of-fact manner. That should really make it worse, you know, indicating impudence and callousness, but I didn't feel he was being brazen. What so interested me was the way he looked at me, as though he really saw—No, I can't describe it. Nobody has looked at me that way since I was, I suppose, a baby. Were I not a psychologist I might have been terrified—"

Totong Heredia found himself trying to recall how the boy

had looked at *him* during yesterday noon's talk but could not remember anything peculiar, save that the boy had kept his eyes lowered most of the time, which had seemed merely natural in somebody young being talked to by authority. Or, thought Totong Heredia, with a dull ache at the heart, have I withdrawn so far I no longer see the most obvious things in those supposed to be close to me, things even outsiders like this old woman here spot at once?

"Where's the boy now?" the prefect was asking.

"Damned," said Totong Heredia in a burst of honesty, his paternal mission now obviously accomplished, "if I know."

"He was at Pete Henson's house last night," said Sophie. "Right now where, I don't know. Before that where, I don't know. Stop asking where, Minnie. I am not my brother's keeper, whatever Sister Corazon may say."

"I think your brother's *heartless,*" groaned Minnie Mota. "I'll hate him forever for breaking my heart."

"Oh, Bobby's a jerk. You couldn't hate him more than I do. I wish you'd try and stop crying here, my God. And don't say I didn't warn you."

"Have you got a coin, Sophie? Have they got 'In Despair' on this jukebox?"

The waiter set down their banana floats.

"If your heart's broken," observed Sophie curiously, "how can you eat all *that?*"

"I'm learning al*ray*dy . . . It's life, Sophie, it's fate. Look, they didn't put enough chocolate sauce in this."

They were the same age, fifteen, but Minnie was ahead by being in love. This was, to Sophie, no progress. Sophie's boy friends were furniture: what you had to have on outings, in basketball games, at dances, and to make your mark in society. But she couldn't see herself falling in love with any of them, let alone *liking* them. In fact, she loathed most of them, and the few she didn't loathe she despised. Boys were filthy, smelly, sneaky, wild, corny, cowardly things. And dirty-minded, my God. How one's best friend Minnie could have fallen for one's brother Bobby, who was filthier, smellier, sneakier, wilder, cornier, cowardlier and dirtier-minded than any of them, was beyond Sophie. She gazed on her poor friend with rather contemptuous pity.

"So what did he do to you?"

"Oh Sophie, I am *ashamed*, I can't talk about it! He was supposed to take me and Glo Ramos to a movie at 5 P.M. yesterday and Glo and I waited and waited and when it looked like he was going to injun us he showed up and right away he said how come Glo had so much hair at her age, did she keep shaving it off, and she slapped him and swore at me and left. So I asked him why did he do that and he said this is it, I've been kicked out of school. And I said what for and he said because I looked at them and saw."

"He said that? How did he look?"

"Just like always, I think. He wore—"

"I mean, *at* you."

"Oh, the way he always looks at me, maybe more so. Why?"

"I could have killed him the way he looked at me at lunch yesterday."

"Did he really try to kill Pompoy Morel?"

"I hope he *hangs*."

"Yes, he said he might have to go to jail. And I said so what, most boys I knew went to jail and I was willing to wait for him no matter how long because I loved him. You know what he did? He *sneered* in my face. He said what did I know about love, I was still stuck together like a Band-Aid. And other *horrible* things. Oh, Sophie, I'm dead al*ray*dy!"

"I'm not. I'm going to have another float."

"Yes, let's. Look, I'm paying. This is my treat, remember? Happy birthday again, Sophie. And then I'll take you home. You sure Mr. Henson said around eleven?"

"I thought you never wanted to see Bobby again?"

"Maybe he's deadball already," gasped Junior. "You fellows really saw the blood?"

"*Pare*, your brother was flat on the ground and that wasn't ketchup on his face."

"Obet and I saw it all—no, Obet? We were on the patio last

night giving his soapbox a tryout. And first the Vampires came and then the Vultures. This is a rumble, I said to Obet. So we ran to behind the church but it was only Pompoy and your brother Bobby, they were going to square."

"Pompoy's Vampire, Bobby's Vulture," gasped Junior, wide-eyed.

"It was no match, *pare*, but one thing I can tell you, your brother he did not run. You ask Obet."

"And Pompoy, the Vultures they pushed him, and he fell down on Bobby."

"And so the rumble?" gasped Junior.

"No, *pare*, too bad. Because then we heard the whistles and everybody ran. Obet he forgot his soapbox. We went back for it and it was still there but your brother was gone. Maybe they carried him away."

"Maybe he's deadball already," gasped Junior, enraptured with horror, knowing now what Mr. Henson would be delivering at around eleven.

The bell to end recess rang and the grade-schoolers scattered in a spill of short pants.

"Deadball already, deadball already!" they chanted as they ran.

"And if not in the morgue," said Inday to her washline crowd, "in the psychopathic hospital. Aie, he is crazy, that one. There will be more shootings in this house."

"*Naku* these teen-agers. Nothing in their heads but shooting, shooting—if not guns, women. I pity the parents."

"This Petra, she talks as though her son was not a teen-ager."

"But how can I, a washerwoman only, have a teen-ager?"

"Petra is right! We who have nothing, our children are gangsters. They who have, their children are teen-agers."

"Or juvenile what-is-it. This I can boast of: I may be only a washerwoman but I have children too and not one is a juvenile. Just let them try, hah. This Bobby, has he ever bothered you, Inday?"

"Aie, no, no. I do not tolerate that. Not even from the fathers. But yesterday I saw I might begin to have trouble with this Bobby. He was allowed to come down to eat but they made him carry out his plate himself. I was fetching a bottle of water and I saw him looking at me. *Naku*, I nearly shrieked. Really cracked, that boy. I said to him, 'You look at me that way, Bobby, and see if your mother does not know right now. I am a woman who is not just-just a woman,' I told him."

"But has the father never really—"

"And if not with the father how much less with the son. The truth is, he does not seem to have that in his head anymore, the father. Bother me? What he wants now is just not to be bothered. My poor señora, she is still young, beautiful. Can you blame her if—"

Heads bending as the voice dropped covered this intersection of four fences but opened up again at the sound of a car on the Heredia's driveway.

"*Uy*, here comes my señora now. Who is that with her? I must leave you, *pañeras*. They will all be climbing on my back again."

"The washlines," said Ineng Heredia, glancing up her driveway at the dispersing backyarders, "have been getting the latest bulletins from the home front."

"Was that your maid or a kangaroo?"

"A maid, Menchu, and becoming as rare in these parts as kangaroos. But come in, come in, and behold the mansion I possess by the grace of God and mortgage."

"I think it's cute."

The sala the sisters stepped into, where heavy curtains covered shut Venetian blinds, suggested hinterland dusk, because of the smell of bamboos on the front lawn, and seemed at first as desolate. Then they made out two girls on the divan sharing the telephone.

"Hang up, Sophie, and come and kiss your tita. *Inday!*"

"That my cake, Mommy? Oh Tita, what's this?"

"Your happy birthday, of course, sweet. Gewgaws. Who's your friend?"

Sophie introduced a shrinking staring Minnie; Inday vaulted in and bore off the cake box, aloft, on a palm, like a basketball about to be shot.

"Come and see my room, Menchu."

"Mommy, Dad's in there."

"Oh, your auntie can stand *that*."

Fully dressed, Totong Heredia lay across the coverleted bed, shoe'd feet just over the edge. Menchu stepped around to the farther side, bent down and kissed him on the mouth. He opened his eyes: "Oh, you." Then he sat up and vaguely brushed off creases from his sport shirt. His wife, indulgently smiling, arms folded, watched from the foot of the bed.

"So, did you go to school, Tong darling?"

"School?"

"I mean Bobby's. Did you talk to them?"

"Yes."

"Everything's all right then?"

"I don't know."

He rose and walked to the dresser, stooped, propping palms on the edge, and looked at himself in the mirror. They heard him groan. He picked up a comb and brought it up to his hair but apparently thinking better of it dropped the comb and sailed out through the open door. But he came back at once. "Hello, Menchu," he said, "how are you?" And out he sailed again. They heard him in the bathroom, running water, then in the sala, drawing curtains and pulling up blinds.

"The Martians," said Ineng Heredia to her sister, "have landed. I have one in the house."

"He doesn't look too Martian."

"And they say life begins at 40."

"Oh, we all have to stop for inventory—see if we're still as good as the next one and can keep up."

"I'm afraid it's worse than that. This one's asking *why* he has to keep up."

"He's just going through a phase."

"The effect on the children, Menchu, that's what I'm worried about. Like Bobby now . . . What time have you got?"

"Almost eleven. How about the effect on *you*, Ineng?"

"Ah, you have heard them talking. No, nothing, Menchu. Nothing at all. I'm too upset to itch. But I suppose a woman like me now, she gives off heat waves. So everybody assumes—"

"As they assumed with me then, you know. And I was enraged. But here I am now —a divorced woman, an expatriate—"

"I'm not you. *Oh Menchu, I'm sorry!*"

"Don't take over too much, kid. Makes you feel up to anything. That's where the danger starts."

"Someone has to hold the fort. There, it's eleven at last."

To the sound of the clock striking they walked out of the room, along the corridor, down the three steps and back into the sala, where noon glowed now from stripped window and white marbled tiling. The two girls were sharing the telephone again, this time on the floor. Slumped in the middle of the divan sat Totong Heredia, drinking beer from the bottle. The women sat down on either side of him and talked across his annoyed face.

"Do you want a beer, Menchu? Or what would you like? I have vermouth, I think, and scotch. *Inday!*"

"When I went away, people just brought them in, the drinks, always cokes. I come back and everybody's asking what will you have: sangria? martini? I'll have a beer."

"Yes, so much has changed. Two beers, Inday, choose the cold ones. We really weren't drinking yet when you went away?"

"Mid-1946, no. I don't remember there were teen-agers then either."

"Now they're a public calamity. The mystery is why. I can understand it happening to the rich, people with money enough for their kids to run wild on. But people like us . . . This house isn't paid for yet. Totong drives a four-year-old car. I do my own marketing and cooking. Not a stick of furniture in this house we're still not making payments on; but ever since he became an executive we have to have façade, always a bit more than we can afford. We couldn't spoil the children if we wanted to."

"Still, they do have more than you and I did at their age."

"Were *we* ever teen-agers? *What* were we when we were their age?"

"I," said Totong Heredia suddenly, and suddenly smiling, "was Mickey Rooney. I duck-waddled when I walked, I wore balloon pants, I had a tuft of hair standing up on my head, I talked from the side of my mouth like Andy Hardy, and I used expressions like *swing it* and *holy cow*."

"All I remember," said his wife, beginning to smile too, "is the boogie, and dancing to a portable phonograph on Dewey, and those everybody's parties during the war—with calamansi juice for drinks!"

"I was a bit ahead of you two," smiled Menchu. "The early 1930s. Still the jazz age. The real jazz age, in fact, over here. I bobbed my hair and used make-up, which only vaudeville artists did before. And I wore my skirts up to here and danced the carioca. Flaming youth we were, smart, modern. Our favorite words. No stuffy *alta sociedad* for us—Club Filipino or Columbian or the Nucleos. We were the first to go night-clubbing. Trocadero, Tom's, the Ronda. Legazpi Landing for breakfast. And Butch"—her smile did not waver; Butch was the divorced husband—"when we were in college, he drove a crazy topless flivver with things written all over it, like *And How* and *Ask Me Another*."

On the floor, having run out of friends to call up, Sophie and Minnie listened to their elders in amazement, now and then exchanging helpless looks. Their glances said: Grown-ups are *mad*.

"And to be young," chanted Totong Heredia, sitting up and raising the beer bottle as though toasting, "was very heaven."

Then, with a glance to either side of him, he collapsed again. Any moment now he would be expected to measure up again. But how could he cope who was himself a mess? When Bobby appears in that doorway can I say to him: Come in, son, and be domiciled, be domesticated? He and I are equally struggling. But he is on the verge, being drawn in; I am on the outskirts, being pulled back. What could I say to him that wouldn't be treachery there where he is or here where I am? This too-white marble room which the untamed Inday bringing in beer rocked with her rudeness was monument to domestic male, at once his trophy and his tomb. But should one knock what one had still not finished paying for?

A car stopping outside at the gate stopped the breaths of

three adults and one child in the room. Only Inday, to whom nothing her betters did could anymore be a surprise, and Sophie, who knew the world revolved only for her, were undisturbed enough to do what was natural. Inday, having crashed tray on table, straightened up and frankly stared at the open doorway. If this was where she came from the mother would have rushed out and grabbed the culprit by an ear while the father shouted gratitude or abuse at whoever the boy was with. *Here* they just sit and pretend not to be waiting. Rising from the floor, Sophie walked not to the doorway but a window, where, looking out, she felt herself looked at: the scene had become hers; the waiting was now for what she would say.

"It's Bobby all right," she announced, over a shrugged shoulder, "in a taxi, with Mr. Henson."

"Is Mr. Henson," her mother asked evenly, "coming down?"

For answer there was the snort of the car driving away.

The quick steps they heard on the driveway lagged on the steps of the porch. They thought: *Now a shadow will fall in the doorway.* But no shadow fell. This was noontime; sunshine outside might be the overflow of brightness from this white room; and the boy suddenly there in the doorway stood in total light, illuminated in front and behind, impaled by clarity, like a statue floodlit in a park.

He was his generation in heralding a new racial structure: tall and leggy and framed bigger, though currently shooting up so fast he might be a swatch of cartilage being stretched as far as it would go and showing the strain. Tension was drilling out a face that would be sharper than his father's—the nose keener, the upper lip not so bulgy nor the mouth so butted out, and the thrust of the jaw more pronounced, though the brown eyes still slanting to a fold in the outer corners remindingly pointed to pedigree. An X of tape on his left eyebrow marked the spot where the body failed. Atop the brow tottered a fat roll of hair, the teen-ager's panache; behind, the thick mop would be cut in a straight line very low on the nape. The boy had just outgrown a taste for sideburns and ducktails.

He was in a light-gray Beatles shirt with red pipings on

collarless neck and sleeve; tight cuffless beige trousers; red
socks; and cream-colored boosters. A rag of red jacket streamed
from his left hand.

He stood with right hand thrust into trousers pocket and
eyes cast down; and when he finally looked up and at the people in the room, the three adults on the divan, who had, at his
coming, multiplied the motions of pouring out and drinking
beer, just caught his blink of wonder. Whatever he had been
steeling himself to see he had not seen. He gave the impression
of rubbing his eyes. But the askance look was succeeded by
very evident consternation. He stared, and stared around in
panic, apparently unable to recognize a face there. This brought
Ineng and Totong Heredia to their feet, and stumbling forward
with hands held out.

"*Bobby*," they cried as one.

The boy's face recorded a third happening inside him: a wave
of relief that washed all over him, untensing his figure, uncrum-
pling his face.

He pulled the hand out of his pocket and waved vaguely.

"Mommy, Dad," he said.

He had come such a long way home it didn't seem strange he
should not quite be sure this was home.

Halting in the hot doorway, watching what he now knew to be
his parents moving toward him, Bobby Heredia prepared for
speech. *Mommy, Dad* were not words. He had not spoken
them. His body had only made those sounds to avoid fuss and
announce itself, as one snaps a knuckle or stamps a foot. He
had heard that prisoners recognized one another by how they
rapped on walls. *Mommy, Dad* were such rappings. They were
Bobby's sounds and now outgrown, but he had to use Bobby's
old sounds to be understood at all.

Those old sounds, he now saw, had started this. First there
was the becoming aware that they were offkey; there was dis-
cord between the sounds and what they were supposed to refer
to, making them false notes that more and more jarred on his
ears, until it seemed to him that his life had, like a school year

or a basketball game or a combo dance engagement, a first and second half. There was all the time he had accepted the sounds without thinking; and there was the time he stepped back and listened critically.

He had caught himself doing this more and more half a year ago, when he turned seventeen, his father long back from the hospital but still acting sick, and himself, aware of a pause at home, standing back to watch it like a movie. And they had begun to sound like people in movies. Why did they say *Mommy, Dad* when other children said *mama, papa,* or *inay, Hay?* Only children in movies said *Mommy, Dad* and he had started feeling like some awful Canó movie child actor whenever he made those silly old sounds. He never used them outside home; outside home parents were *ermat* and *derpa*.

Then there were the names. Everybody he knew was called Bobby or Willie or Boy or Rene, and Susie or Maggie or Tess or Mari-something. All the children he knew had the same names their parents had picked because those were the current "society" names. He had heard that in the old days you got whatever name was on the calendar the day you were born. That had struck him as cleaner naming. No fuss. No nonsense. *A la suerte.* You got what you had to have. It was yours truly and exclusively dedicated.

But parents who picked your name loaded it with wind. The name was not you; the name was your parents and what they thought they were or had got and whatever else they wanted. A boy named Bobby had to be the sort of boy a boy named Bobby would be. The name was not clean, being sticky with stuff like what kind of house you had got and what kind of complexion and what kind of accent when you spoke English. He had come to hate being called Bobby. When he turned seventeen he had looked up in the calendar what he should have been called. *Cándido, martir.* And from that day he had felt that the real Bobby was named Cándido. Whenever he stepped back now to watch he would think: *Cándido would find that offkey* or *Cándido would call that overacting.*

Overacting had been *the* word in his crowd at that time and he had made it his grading mark. If he now felt uncomfortable at home it was because he saw they all overacted by saying Mommy, Dad and having names like Bobby and a white floor instead of the usual wood. He could do nothing about home but he had been eliminating in himself a lot of things he now saw were overacting, like sideburns and ducktails and pants you had to be zippered into and that hung way above your ankles. Pants should be tight but when skintight were overacting. Hair should be long but the Beatles bob was overacting. Red shirts used to be a badge of courage but were now just overacting, and so were shirts and socks that matched if it was some lurid color like purple or mustard but this was something he still did at times, match sock and shirt, though he knew it was overacting and made Cándido wince. Scooters were fun but motorcycles were overacting, especially if you dressed up for it in goggles and helmet and black leather jacket. Drinking was being a man but asking for scotch on the rocks at a swanky place was overacting. Stick to beer, man; the true drink was gin and a mixer. Passing out could happen to anybody but being drunk movie-style reeling about and talking funny was overacting. Boogie was basic, the twist was standard, but everything else, especially the mau-mau, was overacting. Alone with Junior was biology but doing a group race was overacting. Streetcorner talk like *diahe* and *tepok* and *ayos na* and *'lis d'yan* was natural but Canó slang idiom like *get lost* or *real gone* or *dig that* was overacting. Girls on the telephone, girls in the dark, girls at basketball games, girls riding pillion on scooters, and girls who smoked or squealed at combos, or wore shorts to bowling, jeans and a shirt to the movies, were overacting. Even ponytails were now overacting. Anything you wore or did that yelled "I'm a teen-ager" was overacting and so was the word *teen-ager* itself. And vests were overacting; cowboy boots were overacting; Baguio in summer was overacting; the NCAA was overacting; riding piled up in a car with the top down was overacting, especially if you drag-raced on Dewey; and participating in TV teen-age shows was so hopelessly overacting it was okay to do it for laughs and he and his combo had once blackened out their front teeth and combed down their hair and gone on Teeners Canteen under funny names to do some really corny songs like "God Knows."

But seventeen going on eighteen was not anymore really a time for that kind of ball. Even *boladas* were now overacting, unless really savage, like at the Teeners Canteen. One was too busy now worrying over the score of the home team and the score that Cándido kept on one's family had become embarrassing. There was no team; they were all playing by themselves if not playing against each other. One's father fumbled, making too much of fouls, exaggerating the groan each time he faltered. (Cándido would call that offkey.) One's mother hustled sarcastically, making too much of having to do all the running and passing but not missing any tussle at all. (Cándido would call that overacting.) One's brother Junior was the cute rookie playing to the galleries and concerned only with trying to sound even younger than he was because that was how you got what you wanted, by staying the baby of the family. (Cándido would call that offkey.) And one's sister Sophie was the prima donna player hogging court and ball and despising everybody for being so clumsy because nothing was a game with her, everything was one more step up in the world. (Cándido would call that overacting.) Even one's maid Inday faked it, with all that jumping about as the overworked slave was just overacting too because he knew very well that when nobody was around or watching, which was most of the time, she just sat stretched out flat in the kitchen scratching her pits or had the chauffeur next door in and very much in.

He had not wondered about his merely watching all this when he should be on the team himself until yesterday morning when the combo came to rehearse for Sophie's party and the strange thing happened. But he had not wondered for long; he had realized why he stood apart.

The combo was called the Vultures after their gang, of which they were the originals, and had him on the drums, Pete Henson as lead guitar, Willie Veles as rhythm, and Rene Luna as bass, and they had this style he had stopped calling progressive jazz because going around saying you only liked progressive jazz was overacting and anyway nobody understood what he meant or really liked what he and the combo played. The Vultures were not what you might call popular and never got engaged for really important parties like debuts but what could you expect of ignorant kids. They only liked flashy playing and a lot of noise and the drummer rolling his equipment just to get noticed, my God, and the sort of "stagemanship" that meant gaudy uniforms and everybody jiggling back and forth and sideways all together, my God, like some awful PMT drill. He had taken the uniforms and all that awful stagemanship out of the Vultures; each was to move when and how he liked and not care a damn how the other guys were moving as long as every movement was to an impulse of the music or how the music made you feel and you couldn't help yourself. If it was suddenly all of you being so good together it made you feel like jumping into the air, then, man, start jumping. But the feeling had to be genuine or else it was just overacting and he had to keep a special eye on Willie Veles who got easily carried away but they had now developed into so tight a combo it was oftener a case of feeling the impulse together, not all exactly at the same time, one getting it a bit ahead and sort of infecting the others, the spirit jumping now here, now there, and him rolling the drums, which would be honest rolling then, until they were all jumping together, and glancing around, winking, smiling, singing, hooting, glowing at each other, but their fun was mostly a private fun not appreciated beyond the bandstand. Well, what could you expect from those dumb kids. Those dumb kids were always too busy showing off to each other on the dance floor, not even dancing together, just dancing at each other, and they only squealed at what everybody else was squealing at. If you were an expensive popular name combo you could play any which way and they squealed. Or if it was the song hit of the moment you could play it corny, my God, and it didn't matter a bit, they'd be squealing the moment they heard the introduction. He had had to keep the Vultures from playing high hat, disdaining the dance floor, though you couldn't blame them if they did, what with people saying oh the Vultures are all right only they lack pep. Pep, my God. They wouldn't know pep unless it came in a bottle with a label on it. They thought noise and all that stagemanship was pep. He sometimes wished he could take the gadgets off an electric guitar but still keep the sizzle in.

Well, yesterday morning the Vultures had come to rehearse for Sophie's party. Sophie's mouth had curled when Mommy said why get the Moonstrucks when there's a combo in the house and anyway it's not your coming out yet dear and he had felt like kicking both of them but because it was your sister's birthday he had called a rehearsal so Sophie and her stupid crowd could have their stupid mau-mau. And so Pete Henson had to show up with Pompoy Morel because, said Pete, he might not be able to make it to Sophie's party, having just been circumcised and he had heard the third night after was the toughest but if he couldn't make it, Pompoy, though a Vampire, was willing to pinch-hit. Why anybody should wait till they were seventeen to get circumcised stumped Bobby and if Pete had to have it at last why ever time it to a combo engagement and why, for God's sake, get Pompoy Morel for a replacement?

Pompoy Morel was the exact picture of everything Bobby meant by overacting. Bobby often said all that Pompoy needed was a placard across his breast saying "I Am a Teen-age Teen-ager." Pompoy wore Beatles hair, cowboy boots, vests at the slightest drop in temperature, and the reddest shirts and tightest pants, my God, you ever saw. He had a Honda and he dressed for it, wearing that black leather jacket when it was ninety up in the shade. And he had all these Canó slang terms to crush you with when you said 'Lis 'jan, siga.

But Pompoy was not just a stupid siga to laugh at. Pompoy was mean. Pompoy was the kind of guy who twisted with a girl and when the girl was all set up, twisting away, her head tossed back, her eyes on the ceiling, her motor running, and simply going for lost, would leave her there on the dance floor, jerking all by herself like a damn fool, while he watched from the sidelines and joined in the laughing at her. Many a poor girl had fled from a party sobbing because Pompoy had shamed her that way. Pompoy packed knife and gun, robbed small kids of their school money, used elbow and knee in a friendly game of basket, cheated at billiards, turned ugly after one round of gin, hung around the Rizal Avenue corners to be picked up, and always knew which girls were going for lost because he always claimed to have been first there and he told you their names and what they did and how far they would go for lost. But what made all the guys nervous was what Pompoy knew about boys' mothers because he knew all about that too and would tell you which boy's mother had fiddled with his zippers or let him feel her and whenever Pompoy joined a gin-and-dog session there was always this or that guy there worrying which boy's mother Pompoy would say was now going for lost.

Yesterday morning on the piazza Pompoy had been told not to sit in but listen first so he wouldn't come in right away with that awful *siga* overacting of his and the Vultures were working on the stupid mau-mau tune, Bobby trying to figure how it could be done Vulture style and still be what the kids wanted, which didn't seem possible after they had all crashed against each other during the first run-through, but Bobby said let's try it again this time with my drums coming in after four bars instead of eight when he heard his mother behind him asking was anybody for cokes and sandwiches and he had glanced around and seen her standing there stark naked.

He had gasped and would have run to push her back in when he noticed that nobody else was gasping or acting surprised, Pete and Willie and Rene just shaking hands as usual and nothing in the direction of their look to say they saw what he saw and it was then he realized, realizing it from his mother's gestures—pulling at a sleeve, adjusting a belt, slapping a fold of skirt—that she had clothes on and only he didn't see them, only he saw through them, only he saw only her. She had paused before him still stooped over his drums: "How's it going, Bob?" And he had shot up to see her so close that way but had managed to say calmly enough: "It's not going at all. Let's forget this rehearsal, boys. Everybody go home." But she had smiled and said: "Oh, why? You just started. If it's me, don't mind me, I'm leaving." But she had gone over to the edge of the piazza where Pompoy stood with three or four other Vampires and Vultures. He saw them all dressed, only his mother wasn't, and he had seen Pompoy looking at her, looking up and down and all over her that slow way he had of looking at women, and he had seen her nakedness, though she wasn't then even looking at Pompoy, react to his look, with a twitch, a throb, a kind of thrust, a shiver, and he had run in and gotten his father's automatic from the dresser and run back to the piazza and pointed the gun at Pompoy Morel: "I said everybody go home. That means you, Pompoy. You get out of here!" But they had all just stared at him. So he raised the gun and fired three times. Next thing he knew he was in his room, sitting up in bed, listening to his mother trying to sound calm on the telephone.

He was thinking: God has punished me, God has punished me; and his head sank until it rested on his drawn-up knees. Hadn't he often wished he could see through women's clothes? And the wish had come true as a curse: he had seen his mother naked. He shuddered to hear her step coming and in panic began the Act of Contrition, jumping with each footfall he heard, begging God to take this away. Suddenly she stood in the open doorway of his room. His heart dropped through space. She was still naked. "Bobby, I'm going to Mass. I think you should come along." He rose and stepped into his shoes and followed her out without even stopping to look at himself in the mirror.

"And I think you should go to confession," she said in the church. He had knelt down at the box praying this would lift the curse. He could hear Father O'Brien confessing a girl on the other side who had a shrill voice and long sins. She finished at last and the window opened. "Forgive me, Father, for—" That was as far as he ever got because he had seen the father inside stark naked, and the nakedness in a state of excitement, and he had jumped up and run out of the church.

But now the clothes were falling off everybody. A woman in black came up the church steps with a gay look and suddenly the black dress melted away and he was looking at a body with one breast gone and the other swollen. A man in brown pants and Hawaiian shirt and both hands in his pockets ambled by thoughtfully and suddenly the brown pants and Hawaiian shirt dissolved and he was looking at a naked man playing with himself. He shut eyes to such sights, pressed a hand to his eyes, and trembled, yet heard himself saying: Now, look, this is what I call overacting. And suddenly, standing there on the church steps shuddering, a hand pressed to his eyes, he had noted an odd ring in those words. He had not said: *Cándido would find this offkey* or *Cándido would call this overacting*. He had said: This is what I call overacting.

But that wasn't Bobby: *this* isn't Bobby.

And now he knew what had happened.

He had become Cándido.

Seeing with Cándido's eyes he had looked around at his mother tugging at him by an arm and he had located with a glance the zone where the youth of her face ended and the oldness of her body began but the core of her burned as young as her face though all around it was beginning to be ashes, and he had, in the taxi, sobbed for this division in her, while she comforted him, not knowing it was she he wept for, she who sat so pitifully naked, half-young and half-old, and calling to Bobby, Bobby, until he had shouted in pity: *I'm not Bobby, I'm not Bobby! Stop calling me Bobby!*

So she took him to Dr. José, who was the doctor who had brought him into the world, and Dr. José had peered into his eyes and tested his throat and poked him on the body and listened to his insides, asking questions all the while, and he felt tickled because they were examining Bobby's body but were really looking for Cándido without knowing it and this was like a game of blindman's buff because he could feel Cándido dodging this way and that as Dr. José groped and probed and applied instruments, sometimes suddenly stopping, his eyes glazing, as though he had caught a glimpse of Cándido, or suddenly bending down closer to listen, as though he had heard Cándido, and he had almost shouted to Cándido to be still, being now unable to control his giggling at the puzzled prancing of the doctor, especially since Dr. José had started out with white clothes all over him but was now grayly naked and it turned out he looked exactly like those witch doctors you see in cartoons, a little monkey of a man hopping about and chattering and scrambling all over you as though you were the wire netting in a zoo cage.

Then they went home and he was given a pill and sent to his room and he had woken up to find his father sitting on his bed and his father had said to tell what happened and why did you do it, son, and about appreciating one's advantages and what your parents did for you and, yes, this was a terrible time to be young, nothing's sure in the world anymore, boy, but if anything puzzled or worried one there was one's father to go to because one's father was one's best pal, wasn't he; and looking at his father sitting there on the bed, in a narrow olive suit and white shirt and clay-colored tie, he had at first felt this might really be Dad, the old Dad, come home but suddenly the clothes were not there anymore and he was looking at the naked man and he saw that everything in this man had, like his hairline, receded—the muscle of arms and the bulge of breast and the swell of the stomach and even the dangle of the man stuff— everything had receded and the stoop of his body had a shrink to it like somebody waiting to get hit; and he was reminded about what they said was the difference between *siga* and *rugged*: that some boys thought they were *rugged* and acted *siga* until they got one real thrashing that knocked the wind out of them and after that they could never be confident again, but the real *rugged* could get beaten up till they were half-dead but they would only go for lost afterward and act as though life were just something to throw away—*"Kung mapatay di madeadball!"*— and he saw now that the old Dad, so full of charm and jokes and pep and confidence was not the real man but just a *siga* who burst like a balloon the moment the wind was knocked out of him and the real Dad was this naked stranger with a shrink to his stoop and everything about him so receded you could see from his eyes as he talked he wasn't really there and was just broadcasting a speech and how could you be pals with a man who wasn't there, who couldn't even be pitied as one's mother could be pitied, in the taxi, because she was still divided, while this one was already old all the way and had given up and left everything behind; and feeling left behind and abandoned and alone, completely all alone, and suddenly afraid, he had cried out something like *Oh Dad, what shall I do?* And the man on the bed had coughed and stood up and stepped back and said what about lunch.

Going to lunch, he had paused on the three steps to glance around, at the white floor, the stuffed furniture, the curtained windows, and across at the polished table with yellow curved chairs around it, and it had been funny to see his family sitting all naked at that rich table, as though they could afford marble for their floors and upholstery for their chairs and brocade for their windows but not a rag for their bodies. It had been funny to see things so richly clothed and the people not. The people might have been the things there—his father a post, his mother a clock, Sophie a dummy from a showcase in a dress shop, Junior a toy you wound up, and Inday a very ripe dark fruit that had burst in places and oozed. He had been startled to hear the fruit speak, and speak angrily, when he came upon it bottom side up in the kitchen.

They had said he could go to school and he had gone out into the world and there were no clothes falling off now, there were no clothes to fall off, everybody was naked already, though here and there, mysteriously, alone by themselves, were persons who had kept covering and dignity, but they and himself were the only ones clothed in a naked world. He had seen the world become one big burlesque house and everybody was going for lost.

When he got to school there was some fuss about his being in a Beatles shirt; it was some sort of progressive school that didn't require uniforms but put you on your honor not to wear anything improper; but when those lewdly naked people said he wasn't dressed properly he had felt like retorting: *Why, just look at you!*

In history class Mr. Diaz, writing something on the blackboard, had dropped the chalk and stooped to pick it up and he had seen a rose there and as he looked a drop of blood had formed on the rose and trickled down as another drop formed. And he had stood up and said: "It's bleeding, sir." "What's

bleeding, Heredia?" "Your . . . your behind, sir." And Mr. Diaz
had sent him to the principal's office. Mr. Calalang the principal had a hernia that swelled down to his hips and when he sat
down and crossed his legs, he had cried out: "Oh, sir, you'll
crush it!" And Mr. Calalang had sent him to the prefect of discipline. Mr. Quison the prefect had withered breasts and a
white round belly but only part of his equipment and he remembered having heard Mr. Quison had been in an airplane crash
or something while he was studying in America and he had
asked: "Did you lose it in the accident, sir?" And Mr. Quison
had sputtered and grown black in the face and told him to stay
in the office till his father came. But waiting in the office, with
the door open, he had watched the faculty hurrying back and
forth in the corridor outside and there was this intentness in
their hurrying, this cruelty in their old bodies that made him
think, hearing children screaming beyond, that this was a grim
place, an evil place, a place where children were bought and
sold, and he had felt so sick he had rushed out—out of that cell,
out of that prison, out of that torture chamber.

He had found himself heading for Minnie's place. He had a
date with her. Cándido didn't know but Bobby's body remembered. But when he got there that awful Glo Ramos was spread
out on the porch steps, and all that cogon on her, and when he
referred to it she became hysterical. He didn't know why he
had come at all. Poor old Minnie whom he had loved to feel
was a wet baby he felt like washing now when he took her in
his arms, or putting diapers on. Her nakedness was so nursery
and smelled of bathrooms and he had giggled to hear her say
love when she meant her teething rattle. He had rocked her in
his arms as she bawled and bawled and then had firmly set her
down and left. He was too old now for babies.

It was evening by then but bodies naked looked even worse
in the night's lights than in the day's and he had found himself
running, running through the streets, trying not to look, not to
see, appalled by the ugliness of people which shadows now
made scary—mean bodies, lewd bodies, diseased bodies,
deformed bodies, decayed bodies, broken bodies; with sores,

with palsies, with mendings, with animal hair, with erections, with holes, with tumors; crawling with bugs, oily with sweat, caked with filth, dripping with pus, stained with blood, scarred with suffering; on the go, in a slump, at a standstill, with the shakes, out of order, under a strain, beside themselves, and in despair. But they walked in public as if they were clean and happy and beautiful, believing nobody could see into their secret places, what they really were, and he felt the urge again to tell everybody what he saw they had but couldn't stop running.

Running, he had only paused at shop windows to check on himself and gasped with relief each time he saw his reflection still clothed, still in the Beatles shirt, the beige trousers, the red socks, the cream boosters, the red jacket slung over a shoulder, but would begin doubting again as he ran on, running away from a world that didn't know it was guilty of indecent exposure. He could not go home, he might never go home again, but out on the streets was just as terrible and then he remembered the one possible refuge from a world that had become, my God, repulsive. Grandmother's house. So he jumped onto a bus and kept his eyes shut tight throughout the ride afraid he might throw up as all those awful naked bodies pressed all about him.

The lights were not on downstairs except in the dining room where the table was laid for two and old Sianang the cook had popped a head at the kitchen door. He had run upstairs and into his grandmother's room but she was inside her oratory where the stiff-robed saints were. "Who's that?" "Me, Grandmother." "Bobby? I'm finishing my rosary." He had not gone into the oratory but went down again to the sala and turned a light on and sat down on a rocking chair and listened to his motor stopping running.

Something always went still in him in this funny old house. As far back as he could remember this house had meant being outside what was routine. A week ended on Saturday and began again on Monday; Sunday was outside the week because Sunday was gathering here with all the aunts and uncles and cousins to eat Grandmother's puchero or kari and spending the day yawning. A year was the life at home and in school but holidays were outside the year because they were Grandmother's timeless rituals: her relleno on the Quiapo fiesta, her bacalao on Good Friday, her guinatan on All Saints, her boiled ham on Christmas. This had been, when he was a child, a sort of superhome, and *We're going home to* your *grandmother's* meant going back to something more permanent than the various houses they had lived through. They had been always moving, and always moving up, and this latest house in the suburbs with the white floor was surely not the top yet, but all the time they had been wandering Grandmother's house had stayed where it was, and all through the time of the various houses that one by one stopped being home because they were no longer worthy of them, this house was always home and never changed in value. Now it was only when they came here he could feel them still a family; they all stopped overacting here, under Grandmother's quiet eyes. His father became less nervous in this house where he had been little; Junior became just an ordinary boy; Sophie became more of a child; even his mother lost some of her edge. He had known as a child that his mother disliked this house. "How you can let your mother stay in that dump, with all that junk—" But now her attitude had changed; now she wanted the junk—all these old sofas and tables, and even this funny rocking chair he now sat still on, and the stiff-robed saints upstairs, and the big halo with gold rays all around the crucifix on the wall, and the funny thing beside the front door with a mirror on it and handles and holes where, Grandmother said, hats were hung and canes and umbrellas deposited in the old days. Whenever he saw it he thought of ladies with parasols and gentlemen with canes and whiskers and hats lining up to dump hat or deposit umbrella and look at themselves in the mirror. Wearing a hat in the old days made you out a gentleman; if you wore a hat today you were *rugged*, maybe a gangster.

This was now a rugged neighborhood in Quiapo where the house was, but once inside you knew nothing of what screamed outside affected it and once you saw Grandmother you knew nothing that screamed outside could ever affect her house. She was her house in a way they had never been any of the houses they had lived in, and certainly not this latest one with the white floor. She was genuine because she was *rugged* herself and you could beat her up until she was half-dead and she would just rise up afterward and brush away the dirt and be Grandmother again without even overacting all that. His father was her son; why hadn't he got what she had? Or was he just imagining all this? Was what he felt here just overacting too? What if when Grandmother comes down I should see her just as naked and sick as the world outside? And he thought of himself this noon in bed feeling all alone and suddenly afraid and crying out *Oh Dad, what shall I do?* But he had not been totally alone and afraid then; there had been this house in the back of his mind all along, keeping him company, telling him that though everything else might crash it would stay where it was and never change in value. What if this last refuge, too, should be taken from him?

He had stiffened to hear a door close upstairs, and footfalls on the floor above, but when he heard the first step down the stairs he had jumped up and run out the door and down the dark alley and he hadn't stopped running until he found himself back on Plaza Miranda.

The noise on the plaza was deafening, a campaign *miting* was going on, the politicos were lined up naked on a stage but the crowd that cheered or jeered was just as naked, and he could feel they were aware all right of each other's nakedness but pretended to see something else and covered each other's shame with flattery, the people on the stage saying the crowd was great, the crowd was holy, when all he could see, my God, was muck in armpits and lice in hair, and the crowd hailing the people on the stage as knights and heroes, but his stomach had turned at that line-up of big soft rumps and bellies and balls wagging every which way as their owners violently orated; and he had wondered what if grown-ups could really see each other this way would that be the end of their politics, would they frankly turn away from each other in disgust because, my God, how could you call anybody a savior if you could see that tuft of caked hair hanging down from their hole behind? Maybe everything would be more honest if people had to deal with each other on the basis of frank disgust instead of flattery; anyway they would surely have to stop using all those overacting words; the people on the stage wouldn't call this lousy, scratching, belching crowd holy but just make a face and hold their noses, as they probably wanted to do even now, and the crowd would just die laughing, my God, if anybody called any naked waggling rump a hero.

And he had felt himself aching to be with his own crowd, with the *barkada*, with whom there couldn't be this kind of disgust, because their overacting was not wicked, their nakedness was familiar, and even their dirt was somehow clean. So he had hopped a jeepney back to his suburb and gone looking for the guys. They were at the Elvis Billiard Hall and right away he knew he was right to have come here and he heard, as at his grandmother's, the steamy motor inside him stopping running. Pete and Willie and Rene were playing rotation and Pete had the last ball but hit it for scratch and then he leaned hands and chin on the cue stick and looked serious and said: "I got to talk to you, Bob." And he said: "Feed me first, guy. I'm broke and starving. I've gone stowaway." So the guys looked into their pockets and pooled what they had but it came to only two pesos and some cents after they had paid for the table.

They went to the Chinese restaurant next door and he had a bowl of hot mami and a leg of adobo'd chicken and two servings of rice and the guys watched as he ate. Then, over cigarettes, Pete said he'd just have to make up with Pompoy and they were already arranging it. "I don't want an *arreglo*," he had told them.

"Don't be so *siga*, Bob," said Pete. "It's two months now the Vampires and the Vultures have made peace and formed an alliance, thank God. You want to destroy all that? You want them to declare war again? I'm sick of those goddam rumbles."

"Look, I'm not going to say sorry to Pompoy Morel. I can't even stand to see him."

"What did he do to you?" said Willie. "What was all that shooting about?"

"Nothing! I don't want to talk about it!"

"See? So you were just *detonating*. You're in the wrong here, guy."

"And what about us?" said Rene. "You involve us if you let what happened this morning turn into trouble with the Vampires. Okay with us if there was some real trouble. But you just wanted to make an explosion. So now admit it and be with us. *Pakikisama*, guy."

"Pompoy's behaving better," said Pete. "He's willing to meet you and talk this over."

"That's just a stroke of Pompoy's and an old stroke. He just wants a chance to stab me in the back. He's double-faced."

"We'll be there beside you, ready."

Leaning back till the chair tipped back, feeling the food filling up his stomach and the ache of tiredness dulling in thigh and foot, he had looked at the guys and loved them, loving them all together, seeing them not as funny or sickening or frightful as they huddled naked around the table but rather as the only clean things left in the world, and he had shrugged and dropped his head back and blown smoke up to the ceiling:

"Oh, all right. You guys do what you want."

So Pete and Rene went off to tell the Vampires and he and Willie had gone back to the billiard hall and played carambola and then Pete and Rene came back and said Pompoy wanted the peace meeting behind the church and would be with four Vampires and Bobby was not to bring more than four Vultures. So they told Ricky Gardula to come along and when they got to behind the church, where it was as dark as hell, the Vampires were there already. There was some shouting between the two groups as they stood at first bunched far apart but drawing closer as the taunts and threats became ribbing and laughter and then they were pushing at him and Pompoy to move up and shake hands and forget what was past. So he and Pompoy stepped forward and the moment he saw Pompoy's face, and the smirk on it, he had seen his mother naked and Pompoy looking at her and he had with all his might shoved a fist into that mean, stupid, smirking face and Pompoy had hit back and sprung at him and then he was on the ground and Pompoy was all over him and he had seen Pompoy's fist as big as all the world coming toward his left eye and then the whole world had crashed down on him.

Next thing he knew he was in the back room of the billiard hall and Pete was slapping water on his face but when he opened his eyes Pete stood up and moved away, joining the other Vultures in the room, and they talked among themselves with their backs to him and you could see they were disgusted. His head whirled when he sat up on the bench and he had bent over and buried his face in his hands. He had never been this beaten up, never so beaten he had blacked out, and now just the memory of it loosened his knees and panicked his pulse and all he wanted to do was run home and jump into bed and cover himself up and not go out for the next 359 years. He clenched the hands pressed to his face but couldn't control his body's trembling or the sob in his breath and all the while the guys were there talking in low voices and their backs to him and he was wondering how he could sneak out without them knowing and escape and be safe home and in bed, with the door closed. But they stood right in the doorway. And suddenly he had sprung up and walked right *at* them and shoved them aside and strode out of the room and out of the billiard hall.

Pete had run after him and tried to pull him back by an arm.

"Where you going!"

And he heard himself say:

"I'm going to look for Pompoy."

And Pete had shouted to the Vultures that were coming running:

"This guy's gone mad!"

They had piled up on him but he had fought loose.

"Haven't you had enough for one night?" they cried.

"Don't any of you guys try to stop me again!"

And he had strode on, the Vultures following at a distance.

Pompoy was at neither of the two bowling alleys, nor in the lobby of the Village Theatre, nor in front of the Ritz Supermarket, nor in Sally's pinball parlor, nor among the rollerskaters on the cement of the Village Gasoline Station, nor in any of the beer cantinas, nor up on the mezzanine of Mrs. Lim's *sari-sari* where one swigged gin, nor in the crowd at the Crossing where there was also a *miting*, nor inside the Stag Barber Shop where they were showing sex movies, nor with the stambys at the street corners of the Village's downtown section which he patrolled till past midnight, the Vultures still tailing him.

He could hear the cry running through the night:

"*Bobby Heredia's hunting Pompoy Morel.*"

At around one o'clock he was sitting on the sidewalk in front of the closed-up Ritz, dabbing at the cut on his eyebrow which had begun to bleed again, his handkerchief a bloody rag now, and Pete Henson had approached.

"Give up, guy. Pompoy's gone home."

"Pompoy never goes home this early."

"He did tonight. He heard you were after him."

"Hah."

"But they say he said he's going to gate-crash Sophie's party."

"If he lives till tomorrow. Where are the guys?"

"Joey Perez and some fellows went joyriding and dog hunting and they caught a good one. They're going to roast it in the vacant lot behind the Gatdulas and they have a fine collection of longnecks and *cuatro cantos*. The *barkada*'s there. Come on, let's go too. Everybody wants to see you, Bob, everybody's awed at you. Believe *sila*. They say this has to be your celebration because you're stowaway and hunting Pompoy and really going for lost."

So he wrapped the red jacket round his head and over the bleeding eyebrow and he and Pete went to join the guys in the vacant lot. It was *talahib* jungle but in the center was a clearing where the guys were. They greeted him with cheers—"Here's the *patapon!*"—because anybody for whom life had become just something to throw away had graduated from *siga* to genuine *rugged*. A fire had been got going and the dog, a white one, practically a puppy, had a rope round its neck and whined like mad as Rene Luna pulled at the rope. Then Joey Perez whacked it on the skull with a crowbar; Ricky Gatdula slit the throat with a kitchen knife; Willie Veles caught the blood in a bowl; Pete Henson poured gin in, and everybody had a gulp of the bloody stuff, which was warm and bubbly and salty. Then they burned the hair off the dog and each one cut off his own piece and toasted it on a stick or just threw it into the fire and dug it out as soon as it began to smoke black.

The rum, gin, beer, and coke had been mixed up in a basin with a block of ice in it and because this was Bobby's celebration he was made the *tasador* and he filled up the single glass with a dipper and handed it now to this guy, then to the next, and so on around the ring of dog-eaters giggling under the stars and huddling over the fire as the dark dampened and dew fell and a wind blew cold through the tall weeds in the vacant lot. It was a good dog all right, the meat white and tender and unfatty, and they stripped it right down to the carcass, by which time the sky was brightening and they were all vomiting, some had passed out, two guys had quarreled and were groggily slugging it out on their knees, and he himself was reeling about, still turbanned with the red jacket, and talking funny, quite aware that all this was overacting but thinking what the hell, there are no rules anymore, life is a discard and so am I.

Then Pete Henson was pulling him by an arm and his arm was being slung over Pete's shoulder and he and Pete were staggering out of the clearing and out of the vacant lot and out of the Village and across the downtown section to the other side, because Pete lived on the other side, where there were "apartments" instead of houses, and he remembered his mother murmuring at those apartments: "An *accesoria* by any other name . . ." Pete's family had one of the middle doors, not even a corner door, in a barracks-like apartment building, and they had managed to get inside quietly enough but once inside they had bumped into one thing after another, my God, until something really came crashing down. Then steps came clicking down the stairs, a light was turned on, and there he was, there *they* were, he and Pete, sitting on the floor, a fallen bookcase at their feet, Pete's parents hovering above—and they were (surprise!) *dressed:* Mr. Henson in complete pajamas, Mrs. Henson in a long white gown.

"I miss-s-judged the dis-s-tance," Pete was gaily explaining—and in English yet! "I thought this-s-s was the stairs already and we were trying t-to climb the b-bookcas-s-se."

"Where have you been?" he heard Mrs. Henson say.

"Just happy-happy. Where *were* we, Bob?"

"It's the Heredia boy," he heard Mr. Henson say.

"Is that blood on his face?" asked Mrs. Henson.

"He was-s-s in a fight," he heard Pete explaining. "He's-s-s gonna kill Pompoy Morel."

"And so he's wearing red on his head," said Mr. Henson, crouching down. "Listen to this, Bobby Heredia. Without knowing it you reverted to the etiquette of the race. Our ancestors proudly wore a red band around their heads to proclaim they had killed. And you're still them though you live in that snooty Village of yours."

"Does his family know where he is?" asked Mrs. Henson.

"He's-s-s-s stowaway," explained Pete.

"And I *never* wanna go home!" he heard himself shout.

"Oh my God," said Mrs. Henson. "Darling, put on clothes and call up Mrs. Heredia."

Then they both went away.

He was puzzled and carefully put his perplexity into words: "Why—does—your—father—have—to—put—on—clothes—to—telephone?"

"Has-s-s to go nes-s-s door. We no have telephone, s-s-see?"

Then Mrs. Henson came back with a basin and began to towel his face and he had slumped away until he was lying on the floor.

When he opened his eyes he was in the lower half of a double-decker and he knew he was upstairs in the Hensons' apartment. This room was where all the children slept, six or seven of them, though there was no sign of them now. The other room across from this he could see through the open door would be where Mr. and Mrs. Henson slept. He had seen them dressed; that could only mean they had nothing to hide. And he felt at ease in this narrow cluttered room. It didn't pretend to be other than it was. Pete didn't call his parents Daddy, Mom or Mamá, Papa or even Itay, Inay. He called them by their nicknames. He said that was how they wanted it.

Sunshine from the window at the head of the bed looked late morning and everything in his head was also light but clear, no fuzzy ache at all, and as he lay at ease in this room where Pete slept he had begun to hear Pete and Mr. Henson in the other room.

"So how's it now, boy?"

"I'm all right."

"I wish you had told me before you did it."

"I just went ahead. I've had enough of the teasing."

"Didn't I bring you up to be above the crowd?"

"But I don't want to be different."

"Alas. Since it's your decision I must respect it, but I had wanted to liberate you from the customs of the tribe."

"I can't be always you."

He had stopped listening, had turned over on his other side till he heard Mr. Henson calling to Mrs. Henson as he went down the stairs and then Pete coming into the room, when he had turned around again.

"You awake, Bob? How you feeling, *pare?*"

"Okay. Did you get it from your old man? I heard you and him."

"That wasn't about last night."

"Yes, I know."

"My old man has some crazy ideas. I wish he was more normal, like *your* old man."

"Oh Pete, I *like* your home."

"Hell, I wish we lived in a house like yours."

He saw now that what Pete had done, getting circumcised, was his way of giving his old man a failing mark after believing for years he was smarter than the faculty. Was calling your parents by their nicknames as much overacting as calling them Mommy, Dad? He now felt uneasy in this house, which Mr. Henson called liberated because he could not do better.

"Get up, Bob. He wants to talk to you, about going stowaway."

"Oh, he doesn't have to, I've decided to go home."

He couldn't help a shudder at the thought of how Mr. Henson would word the talk. There would be, as usual, the sarcas-

tic remarks about the Village and the ideals of the herd and
how if your parents wanted to give you the better things in life
the least you could do was be a good herd member like them,
and not question anything, especially if you, too, believed the
better things in life were cars and refrigerators and all those
gadgets. He had thought Mr. Henson the most interesting of
the *barkada*'s fathers and had enjoyed hearing what he now
shrank to hear. The words would be like glass now through
which you would see poor Pete saying *I wish we lived in a
house like yours*. If you were poor and just didn't have it in you
to climb up in the world, well, that was just luck and fate and
too bad, but did you have to *justify* it by pretending to be so
superior and above gadgets? And did you have to tell your children not to want them either because you were afraid if they
did and tried for them they might not fail like you did but
succeed?

When he went downstairs he knew he would see them naked,
and they were. In Mr. Henson nothing had receded, like in his
father, because you could see nothing had ever pushed out; and
Mrs. Henson's body was one high brow wrinkling with worry.
He had quickly said he was sorry to have been a trouble and
thanks for everything and goodbye now: "I'm going home."

"I'm taking you home," said Mr. Henson.

"But I can just go home by myself."

"Oh no, no, Bobby. I promised to deliver you to them. So sit
down and eat breakfast and then we'll go."

There had been no escaping Mr. Henson's talk and it was
just as he thought it would be—about the Village and the herd
and the gadgets and how if you were not a liberated person the
best thing to do was stay with the herd, and he had seen, as he
forced himself to swallow the fried egg and the rice, poor Pete
standing in a corner and silently writhing. Then Pete, who
didn't have classes till noon, was sent to call a taxi.

"But, Mr. Henson, we could just walk across."

"Bobby, people like me cannot *walk* into your Village."

It was Mrs. Henson this time that he saw squirm.

In the taxi Mr. Henson had continued being sarcastic but
he had stopped listening and looked instead at the Village,

wondering why it made Mr. Henson so mad. It looked corny enough, my God, all those tin roofs and exposed plumbing, and certainly like nothing you had been accustomed to in the movies. Then Mr. Henson had said something he heard.

"Your dad's waiting for you."

"Dad is never home at this time."

"He's there now."

And then he knew why Mr. Henson had been so set on delivering him in this condition, his clothes soiled and his face a mess and this stupid tape on his eyebrow, and he had *hated* Mr. Henson for wanting him to be seen this way, by his father, before he could be cleaned up and straightened out. But glancing around and seeing that little naked body that could only hump with malice, like a cat, he had thought wearily: Oh, what the hell . . .

But when they reached his gate he couldn't help being malicious himself.

"Here we are, Mr. Henson. Do come down a moment."

The little naked body had balled up. "No, thanks, Bobby. Mission accomplished. I've delivered you. So long."

"Oh, do come down, Mr. Henson. Mommy and Dad will want to talk to you."

And he had laid a hand on Mr. Henson's arm and had felt the man shrink.

"No, really, Bobby. I have to be at the office."

When everybody knew he was jobless again; he just went from office to office.

After Mr. Henson and the taxi had fled he had hurried up the driveway, eager to be with people not different the way Mr. Henson was, but had slowed down on the porch steps remembering he had been set up as judge of the people waiting inside the house, dreading again to see them exposed, though he now felt he could live with the truth about them and get over this revulsion. Still, he had measured his steps up the porch and into the doorway, stopping there and keeping his eyes cast down, delaying as long as possible the moment of seeing, the moment of judging. But when he looked up there was nothing to judge.

Another layer had dropped off what clothed people and more than a nakedness of the flesh was naked before him in the living room.

What he saw was, he supposed, what pictures in medical books showed: the human anatomy with brain, bone, artery, nerve, ligament, joint, and the internal organs exposed. He had seen many such pictures of the body with the skin off, but what he saw now was like those pictures and yet different because in motion. Movement gave what he saw the look of machines— like a running watch with the case off or a throbbing car stripped down to its chassis.

He could recognize vein and brain, bone and tissue, and the various organs, but only now realized how closely all these together resembled an engine and he saw them as coiled springs, wheels, axles, cogs, tubes, cylinders, valves, ball bearings, pistons, nuts and bolts, wires and batteries, even the dark blood veining the mechanism looking for all the world as practical, as unemotional, as gasoline. And wheels turned, wires flashed, mainsprings whirred, valves pumped, pistons swung back and forth, and the motor throbbed running because that was the effect produced by the different parts of the machinery and not because of love or hate, goodness or sin, or being wise or stupid. The motor might run too fast or too slow or suddenly break down but whatever it did would not be overacting. Machines *were* rules.

He could make out some six machines in the living room, four big, two small. Three of the big machines were fitted to the divan, one stood upright beside the table. Of the small machines, one was propped against a window, the other was folded on the floor.

Surprised but delighted to find here, instead of the scandal of human nakedness, which would have to be judged, the precision of machines, which used no morals, he had yet in the next moment blenched. Some of those machines were his family— but who was who? All the machines were faceless and sexless.

And it came to him that the nakedness of the flesh that so sickened him was yet the shape of the person. Mr. Diaz with a rose in his rump, Mr. Calalang with a bell for balls, Mr. Quison with his mutilated manhood were horrid to see naked but that very horridness helped to identify them as, respectively, Mr. Diaz, Mr. Calalang, and Mr. Quison. If you stripped the skin from a person what remained was anonymous machinery. The big wart on the face of this man made him *this* man; scars and wrinkles and mendings and tumors and all that could mar flesh marked out a character, an identity, *this* life, *this* soul.

Oh, they were wrong, he saw now, oh, they were all wrong. The soul was not anywhere inside—not in the mind, not in the heart, not in the spirit, but here upon the seen flesh that they called carnal: this dirt-prone flesh, this bug-bitten flesh, this animal-hairy flesh, this sexual flesh. The ugliest nakedness was still a holy nakedness because flesh was soul and soul was flesh and if it wasn't there all you had were machines you couldn't tell one from the other.

And he dug hand into pocket, feeling himself, wanting to be himself, wanting to be now not Cándido but Bobby, with Bobby's particular growth of hair and shape of eyes and build of nose and curve of mouth and crop of pimples; wanting intensely to be Bobby in color and height and form, in shoulder and arm and breast and belly and genitals and rump and legs and foot size. He gazed in panic round the machines in the room begging them to be souls and persons, to take on flesh again, however horrid the flesh.

And as if in answer to his appeal, two of the machines on the divan lumbered up and rolled toward him—wheels turning, wires flashing, mainsprings whirring, valves pumping, pistons swinging back and forth, and the motor running—and looking, my God, like those robot toys that walk on sidewalks during the Christmas season.

Who had wound them up or switched on their batteries? Was some invisible giant child playing in this room with those toys? Or were they, like space ships, radio-controlled? Was that what God was: the space scientist at the controls? It seemed silly now to have been judging people when they were only machines being turned on and off, moving mechanically. Like poor Mr. Henson, who thought himself so liberated—how could you blame him for not having the guts to compete? That would be like blaming a bicycle for not being a jet plane. And these two robot toys now jerking toward him—whatever emotion they thought had made them rise from the divan and roll across the room was just their imagining because the real push came from outside: the Scientist had pressed a button.

But as they approached they made a sound that flooded him with relief: a human sound, an emotional sound, a sound made by the flesh of lips.

"*Bobby.*"

From the pitch he realized there might be trouble, there could be a fuss. It was they who were worried, it was they who were appealing to him to recognize them. He recognized them all right from the sound they had made. The machine in high gear at the left was his mother; the one in low gear at the left was his father. He took the hand out of his pocket and waved to them, to dispel their alarm, but saw that more was needed. He would have to communicate. But they would understand only Bobby's language.

He heard his body making Bobby's old sounds:

"Mommy, Dad."

Sparks seemed to fly from the two toys as they rolled closer and now the other machines behind were also making noises that identified them—Sophie at the window, Inday by the table, and on the divan his Tita Menchu, whom he had seen only twice: when they met her at the airport and at a family *bienvenida*. Only the small machine on the floor remained unidentified. It couldn't be Junior; it seemed to be weeping.

He heard his mother's voice:

"Aren't you going to say hello to poor Minnie?"

The machine on the floor unfolded and sped toward him, the mother and father machines drawing apart to let the Minnie machine through.

As he watched it coming he heard himself praying desperately: *Minnie, be flesh again, however nursery, however bathroom-smelling. Minnie, be Minnie again, the Minnie I enjoyed fondling.*

But as if to mock his prayer the wheels, axles, cogs, tubes, cylinders, valves, ball bearings, pistons, nuts and bolts, wires and batteries, began falling off poor Minnie—he could almost hear them clinking and clattering to the floor as she approached—until nothing was left of her but a frame of bone, but a small skeleton lifting a death's-head up to his face as though to be kissed.

"Hello, Bobby."

And seeing the lipless grin on that small, white, smooth, hollow skull he could look into through the big holes of eyes and nose he started and cried out and averted his face and, moaning, fled across the sala and up the three steps and into his room, banging the door shut and leaping into bed. He had seen the ultimate strip.

"The doctor," said Ineng Heredia, coming back to the lunch table where now only Menchu sat, having a coffee and cigarette, "still says he can find nothing wrong, except maybe a touch of flu coming on. However, I've decided he's to go into a hospital tomorrow and be under observation. Dr. José says there's a good psychiatric ward at St. John's."

She did not sit down at once, stood listening to Dr. José's car being started in the driveway. At last it was off.

"Oh, that old quack. Why did I have to inherit him?"

"He sounded," giggled Menchu, "very sensible indeed. 'Oh, oh, what's wrong with my poor boy, doctor, he did this and that.' Sniff, sniff. 'Nothing's wrong with the boy, Irene. What he has is a hangover. He's *drunk*.' My goodness, Ineng, I nearly burst."

"This is no laughing matter, you. All the things for the party tonight that are still to be done—"

"If you have to go anywhere I'll stay and stand guard."

"And that hapless Minnie Mota. I know she's at that age when they're most unattractive. But to offer to be kissed and get a look of *horror* instead, as though you were the young Morticia . . . Why, the girl could be scarred for life."

"Should teach her not to *offer*, from now on."

"If you're staying, Menchu"—this was later, in her bedroom,

as she dressed—"you might as well be comfortable. There's a robe in the cabinet and if you can find my slippers—"

"Was the boy given a pill or something?"

"Dr. José said better not, with all that alcohol in him. But he should be sleeping. I'll look in on him before I go."

"You know what I think, Ineng? Your boy's moving up from little girls to bigger ones. The way he squinted at me—The look that separates the girls from the dames."

"No, he's not sleeping." They were now on the porch and Menchu's driver was bringing the car around for Ineng to ride in. "But he's quiet and he said yes, he was willing to chat with you. Now don't confuse him more than he already is, Menchu."

"I'll be Charlie's aunt, from Brazil—where the nuts come from?"

Returning to the sala the expatriate observed a difference between American and Philippine houses. Doors in American homes were always closed. In Philippine homes all doors were open, even bedroom doors, even bathroom doors. Bobby's door, by being the only one closed on the corridor, bespoke anomaly. She rapped once, then stepped in. The boy was sitting up in bed, propped against pillows, his hands clasped behind his head, the sheet pulled up to the slope of his breast.

"Bobby? Your mommy said I could—"

"Hi, Tita."

She was going to bend down but stopped herself in time, remembering Morticia. She pulled up a chair instead and sat down, pulling down her green skirt as she crossed her legs, shyly touching her jade jewelry.

"You and I don't know each other very well, Bobby."

"You sent me all those toys."

"Oh, that was just to keep up connections. One must belong somewhere, you know, be part of something, especially families. I sort of ran away, Bobby, and cut myself off. Now that was a very wrong thing to do. But, as you can see, I have come home."

"Was there something to come home to?"

"Oh, I should say so! I'll tell you this, boy: I was dead all the time I was over *there;* here I have come alive again. I had forgotten there was so many people I love and who love me. And all that loving has made me feel young, vigorous, excited, lovely. You're amused. I must seem the rock of ages to you?"

"No, Tita."

"How *do* I look to you?"

She was smiling but the query was a quest and she leaned forward and searched his face, begging it to see her, in her green dress and jade trinkets, fearing she did not exist in that face, was not alive enough in those eyes, as indeed she was not, for all he could see was a jeweled skeleton on a chair, one knee-ball propped on the other, the chair showing through the spaces between the ribs, and the teeth in the skull heavily clamping and unclamping.

"I never know how people look," he said.

She tried not to hear his tactfulness. She thought: he sees a fat hag.

"But that's wrong, Bobby! You must *look* at people and *see* them, be *aware* of them. Why, that's half the fun in life, watching your co-passengers. Don't be a snob, boy. At your age is when it's *thrilling* to look around. Girls in their first gowns. Smart women walking past. All this world of charming faces and beautiful bodies. Would you think to look at me now I was once considered a beauty?"

"I can see that, Tita."

Both of them saw a long slender laughing girl with short hair in a square dress without sleeves.

"I've seen old photos of you," he said, and tried to fasten the laughing girl with short hair onto the bald skelton on the chair but could not keep it there nor remember how this pile of bones and jewels looked the two times he had seen it in the flesh.

"I was milk and roses," the skelton was saying, articulating joints, waving spiky extremities, "and the belle of the ball. It seems one long ball now, those days, and myself young. I believe, do you know, we never stop being what we were, young. We don't shed that young self, we just put on other skins, one cover after another, but somewhere in us is still that self we were before we fell, before we started covering ourselves. And all the rest of our lives we're trying to go back, we're looking for it, what we lost. Maybe that's why the creed promises a resurrection of the body, for all those who didn't find what they lost. Maybe that's why I came home, to look for it. And because I sometimes feel I have found it I almost—"

She was talking to herself but became aware of the boy in the bed staring—staring not at her, she could see, but through her, and *not* with horror, and the old pleasure of being eyed for her beauty suffused her.

"Oh, you can see it too, Bobby! Yes, that's what I am—not a fat old wicked woman but *this*. Milk and roses, Bobby, and young and pure and happy and lovely. . . ."

He had hardly been listening to her and was startled to see, in the three gaping holes in her skull, three drops of tears as big as stones. He had been staring at something behind her: something lurked in ambush there, behind bone or chair. He had thought he had seen the ultimate strip but a last cover had still to drop off, a last hid thing was still to be revealed. Only, this one was not just going to offer itself. He would have to go after it, look for it, find it. It was somewhere there on the chair now —and he wished that silly old skeleton would stop rattling about.

But she read insight in his look and was blinded with tears. She groped for handkerchief and blew her nose, then sprang from the chair and whirled around the floor.

"I feel young, Bobby. This is me again young, Bobby. And I could dance and dance . . ."

He saw the skeleton jerking its kneecaps and rattling its claws as it spun around and the something hiding was there now in the whirl of the dance, asking to be chased, bidding to be caught, felt now so intensely he pushed covers away and crawled out of bed and tiptoed panting, in jockey shorts, into the circle of movement, groping for what must be caught but himself gripped instead by hard claws.

"Yes, Bobby, come, dance! Let's dance, Bobby, dance with me!"

And he felt himself dragged round and round, struggling,

trying to break loose, to grab that something felt hovering now here, now there, always just out of sight, and yet within reach, but unreachable, because his hands were being gripped hard by the bony claws, by this screaming skeleton now rattling in every bone, the hovering something ever mocking him as he whirled toward it and was whirled away again, beckoning to be pursued as he and the skeleton waltzed round and round and round, till, in utter frustration, he dropped down and burst into tears.

"*Bobby!* Oh Lord, I've excited you too much."

Whatever music had been spinning in her brain stopped. The boy knelt sobbing and she drew him up and led him across the room and put him into bed.

"Now promise you'll try and go to sleep."

She pulled the sheet up to his chin and the music started again in her head and she smiled and did not fear now to bend over the boy, who, eyes wide open, suffered the huge toothy grinning kiss of the death's-head.

He could hardly wait for her to go out of the room. But when the door had closed on her, on her regrets and her vanity, nothing beckoned to be pursued.

The room was empty.

Waking to dusk in the room he lay a while listening to sounds out in the garden. They would be fixing it for the party. Corridor and sala were dark; open doors showed empty rooms. No one was in the house. While in the bathroom he heard a voice saying *testing, testing* on the piazza. Well, Sophie would have a discotheque instead of a combo. Back in his room he found his cabinet locked and the clothes he had worn gone. He padded into his parents' room but his father's cabinet had been locked up too. Then his eye fell on the laundry hamper. Right on top were the soiled Beatles shirt and beige trousers. He glanced out a window. Several skeletons were setting out tables in the garden.

He stole out of the house through front porch and driveway. Twilight deepened the gloss on lawn and pavement along these polite streets where the insides of houses showed dark save for corners where lamps glowed. A Corvette stopped before a gate and the skeleton at the wheel waved to another skeleton framed between the while pillars of a porch. On a front lawn two skeletons playing badminton hopped about shouting and laughing unhurt though the wind blew as freely through their bones as through their net. Up on a railed embankment a family of skeletons stood in a row at their fence doing nothing and you saw their fine house through their ribs. Maybe they were looking back on the way they had come to get up there. You didn't need the checkpoint to know you were out of the Village. In houses beyond lights lighted up the whole room instead of just corners.

He hurried to the Elvis Billiard Hall hungry for companionship. Three skeletons at a table hailing him were Pete, Willie, and Rene. He told them he didn't feel like playing and just stood around and watched them, just wanting to be with them, but found himself still hungry and lonely. He remembered how last night, at the Chinese restaurant, he had looked on these guys and felt overcome by love for all of them together, but he now could stir up no feeling at all for these three identical skeletons hovering over the green cloth. They were not Pete, Willie, or Rene. They were just things. You could not have companionship with things. Anybody in the flesh now seemed better, even the politicos lined up naked on the stage. He ached with the wish this was last night again and he could bury himself in a crowd of *people* and feel their contact again. No, he would not be horrified now. No, he would not flee from them now. No, he would not loathe them or despise them or judge them or feel sorry for them. His Tita Menchu was wrong. People were not half the fun in life: they were *all* the fun.

He thought of what he had been taught about the flesh being a rotting garment you had to shed before you could become capable of feeling a greater love. But without the flesh you couldn't even *feel*, as he could feel nothing for these three skeletons that were no longer Pete, Willie, and Rene because they had lost, in his eyes, the rotting garment which alone made them Pete, Willie, and Rene. Feeling was of the flesh, personality was of the flesh, companionship was of the flesh, friendship was of the flesh, love was of the flesh, contact was of the flesh.

They had been told in Religion about a saint who licked the sores of lepers and he guessed that saint had gone through what he was now going through, had started out feeling so superior and sneering at people for overacting and all that until he got punished and had to wander about in the night, banished from the world of the flesh and trying to find companionship among minerals or some such "clean" things, and when he had learned his lesson and was forgiven and came back to his senses, flesh had looked so *good* to him that even in its filthiest, smelliest, horridest, rottenest state, like in lepers' sores he saw it still as clean, sweet, beautiful, holy, and he had fallen down on his knees and kissed that leper's sores, my God, in sheer adoration, having found God there. Sarcastic idiots kept saying this about beauty or manners or what-have-you being *only* skin-deep. That was their ignorance. He had learned that skin was the deepest thing of all, deeper than earth, deeper than ocean, deeper than outer space, its depths being the joys of human contact, and if God was to be found at all it could only be in those depths.

God. My God! *That* was what had been lurking in the chair, when Tita Menchu sat there, and in the room, as she danced around. *That* was what had beckoned to be pursued, wanting to be revealed. *That* is what I have to chase, to hunt, to look for, to find. God has blotted out all other faces so I may see *the* face, the ultimate face—the face of God.

And his hair stood on end as he realized that even now God was here, here at this billiard table, beckoning there, and he lunged toward the spot, popping up behind, and he spun around, no, now across the table, and he darted there, he darted here, he ran round and round, bumping again and again into the three skeletons—"Hey, Bob, watcha doing!"—but too intent on pursuit to even hear them, his hair rising, for this was a terrible place, God was here, God was now in the doorway, and he rushed there only to find that God was already down the street, somewhere out on the street, and following, running, groping, calling, stopping every now and then to pick up the scent, he dashed into the lobby of the Village Theatre, where skeletons were lined up at the ticket booth, and into the

Ritz Supermarket, where skeletons clawed at cans on shelves, and across the cement of the Village Gasoline Station, where tiny skeletons flew screaming about on rollerskates, and into one beer joint after another, where skeletons put bottle or glass to their teeth not knowing there was nowhere for the beer to go into, and along the *talahib* fields on the highway, where paired skeletons huddling in the grass embraced and kissed and rattled bones together, and into the split circle of the Crossing, where there was a *miting* again and the scent was strongest, was clearest, was closest, here in this crowd of skeletons scurrying, jostling, chattering, laughing, and shouting at a skeleton on the bright stage hugging the mike, here in this riot of bone and bawl, this mass of grinning death's-heads, through which, panting, sweating, pushing, reaching out weeping, he fought his way frantically, what he hunted always just a skeleton away, just a bobbing skull ahead, fighting his way in a zigzag into the core of the crowd and then round and round again back to its edge, speeding after God, who was now there at the checkpoint, there in the Village, himself panting in pursuit, hot on the heels of God, past the checkpoint, past the belt of park, past the lawns where cars shone huge eyes on driveways, past the dark windows where corners of light showed where the elegance was, past pairs of maid skeletons lugging out the garbage, past a line of cars and the chauffeur skeletons smoking cigarettes, past a final wall and into a gate he didn't know was his own until he was running up the driveway and up the porch and across the dimmed-out sala and toward the lights and noise and action beyond on the piazza, suddenly standing there in the doorway and sort of glowing at all those young skeletons jumping about on the stone floor, at those holed skulls jumping to the giant music and the swing of the colored lights and the joy of the flesh he couldn't see, jumping in surprise now, because he was there, jumping toward him and squealing—"Why, it's Bobby!" "Look, it's Bobby!" "Hey, you there, Bob!"—and he was dragged here, dragged there, swung around, danced around, he was in the thick of it now, half-weeping, half-laughing, for this was no dance of death, though the bones were bare and the skulls hollow, this was God's a-go-go, God was here, God was dancing, and so near now that suddenly reaching out he almost touched God, almost grabbed God, who was now hopping off the piazza, himself in pursuit again, hopping off the piazza too and across the garden, running from table to table, where the startled skeletons clutched at him laughing—"Bobby," his mother's voice, "where have you been!" "Bobby," his father's voice, "who you looking for!" "Bobby," his aunt's voice, "aren't we going to dance?"—clutching at him but in vain, calling after him as he paused now at this table, now at that one, with a smile, with a bow, with a quick look, and then running on, running deeper into the garden now, where it was darker, running toward the bamboo grove, where mosquitoes hummed, and as he plunged into the thicket his flesh tingled, his hair bristled, he was warm now, he was close now, God had been tracked down at last, God has been cornered, God was at bay, God was waiting for him who had to bend away this last prickly bamboo, who was parting this last curtain of foliage, who stepped out now from the thicket and saw the wall before him—and there indeed was God, against the wall, waiting for him, and he had smiled at God, he had glowed at God, he had flung his arms out to hail God, but God held a thunderbolt in his hand, God was raising the thunderbolt in his hand, and then the thunderbolt blazed lightnings and he felt a fire on his shoulder and cried out in joy, for God had hit him with love, God had pierced him with love, God had burned him with love, and he could feel the smile on his mouth as he staggered and swooned with the rapture, seeing, as he touched ground and the dark came swooping, that God had the face of Pompoy Morel.

"Gate-crashers," said Ineng Heredia to her husband, "may be criminals in the eyes of the law but they are artifacts in our culture. No party's complete without them."

"Are they also supposed to shoot down their hosts?"

"Look, darling, our Bobby was, as the young put it, *hunting* poor old Pompoy. And when he spotted Pompoy and cornered him against that wall, what was Pompoy to think? How could he know Bobby only wanted to shake hands?"

"I still want that jerk in jail."

"It was only a flesh wound, Totong. Bobby himself doesn't want the poor boy punished. He's been wanting to have Pompoy visit him here but I thought that might not be wise. Anyway, he's all right now and Pompoy's being shipped to his mother in New York. His grandmother didn't make a fuss the other time; why should we make a fuss this time?"

"How about what my son went through?"

"A week in the hospital? We were going to have him in one anyway. And the shock *has* been good for him. He's back to normal now. Actually, all this has been a blessing in disguise, Totong."

She fixed a look at him standing there in the hospital corridor working his jaw up and down but he refused to meet her eye.

"Is Mamá going to be in there all morning?"

"You have to be back in the office?"

"Not until I have taken the boy home."

"Let them talk, darling. Bobby asked her to come."

"Why don't we just go in?"

"*No.* Come and sit down beside me and stop raging."

But she rose instead, seeing her mother-in-law emerge from Bobby's room. She kissed the old woman on a cheek. Totong kissed his mother's hand.

"Is the boy ready, Mamá?"

"He is up and dressed, yes, and has put his things in his bag. But ready for what do you mean?"

"To go home."

"Ah, I fear there is here a small war of succession. Look, Totong; listen, Ineng: your son called me up very early this morning, insisting he had to see me. I said but was not today when he would leave the hospital? He said yes and that therefore we had to discuss where he was to go. Alarmed, I came in a hurry, you can imagine, and we had our little conference, all very serious. Totong, things are bad. It appears your son does not want to go home with you and Irene. He says he wants to come home to me."

"He said that."

"That he said, my dear, and more. I told him the thing was not for me to decide, I was not his parents. I refused even to wait, as he begged me to. So I rose and kissed him and walked out. Now it is your turn in there. I have fired my shot in the war of succession."

"Could we not," said her son, "all go in there and face him together?"

"No, I should not be there. He would feel there were two sides. Totong, Irene, you talk to the boy. If you should so decide, bring him to me. My house is always open to the children of my children. But if they go there because they feel they have nowhere else to go it would be more than I could bear. Are we clear about this?"

"Very clear," said Ineng Heredia, "but you must not worry too much about this, Mamá. The boy merely feels embarrassed at the moment about going home."

"My children never felt embarrassed about their home. It gave them no reason to be. But it is of the old style, no? Bobby understands style. It may be he is too fastidious about style. He wants the style authentic. He knows that style is having grandfathers. But he must not reject you for them. That would be sad. Talking with the boy has made me sad, do you know? I shall have a temper today."

"Are you not well, Mamá?" asked her son.

"Ah, you know me. A little chill and I take to my bed and call for the sacraments. Next morning I am having chocolate and asada and, well, it is *viva' paña* again. Totong, you will decide carefully?"

"I have already decided."

"And where is the boy going?"

"To the optometrist. Doctor's orders."

Mother and son gravely eyed each other.

"And now I must go," she smiled.

"Let me take you down," said her son.

Waiting on the corridor bench Ineng Heredia pondered the blue door shut between her and her son. Then Totong came striding back, dropping a *Come on, gal* from the side of his mouth, like Mickey Rooney, as he went past so rapidly he was already into the room before she could catch up with him, was already into the room before the boy sitting on the edge of the bed could spring up. When he did spring up his parents were already bearing down on him and there was a flash of panic in his look.

"Dad, Mommy," he said.

And Bobby Heredia knew he was going home.

The problem had been there from the moment he opened his eyes the morning after the party and found himself back in the world of clothes. Everybody was in their clothes again—nurse and doctor, the folks and Tita Menchu, the combo and Minnie and Father O'Brien and the other visitors—and it was great to be back in that world; but how go back to a home he had seen naked? He was Bobby again, yes, but Bobby different, and wondering that morning what had become of Cándido he had looked around and seen Cándido in the crowded room, Cándido still in the Beatles shirt and beige trousers and red socks and cream boosters, Cándido leaning against a corner of the room, arms folded, with a quizzical smile for the visitors and a wink for Bobby, as though saying: Don't overdo it, kid. Cándido was right, of course. This high-pitched love for people he was singing now would have to be keyed lower. One would have to strike a balance between loving people too much and judging them too hard. And through the week in the hospital, Cándido—dodging food trays, peering into medical contraptions, riffling through magazines, or just clowning around—had kept reminding him that one shouldn't lose one's sense of judgment. Cándido raised an eyebrow at a nurse's gush, made a face at the tailor's label on the doctor's pants, wrinkled his nose at Sophie's armpits, wolf-whistled at Tita Menchu's gewgaws.

Cándido there all the time had posed the problem of where to go from here and he could only think of Grandmother's house as a place where one might learn balance. During the talk this morning with Grandmother he had kept glancing at Cándido, but Cándido had stayed out of it completely, leaning

in his corner, arms folded, studying the ceiling, only looking at
Bobby, with a shake of the head, when Grandmother had
walked out. Cándido was right again, of course, and so was
Grandmother. One had to face the music. But he still didn't feel
like going home.

And sitting on the edge of the bed, waiting for his parents,
rehearsing in his mind what he would say, garbed now in plaid
shirt-jac and tan slacks and lemon mocs, his left shoulder bulgy
from the padding of bandages, he had flashed appeals to Cándido, still in his corner, not to stay out of this coming talk, to
back him up and stiffen his morale. The talk would go easier if
Cándido was there to raise an eyebrow, make a face, wrinkle
his nose, purse his mouth.

But his parents had entered in such a rush he forgot all about
Cándido and could only see his father suddenly grinning there
before him.

"Hi, boy. Ready? Come on, we're going home. Got your
bag? Can you carry it?"

"Yes, Dad," he heard himself saying, bending down in a
daze to pick up the bag and sprinting after his parents who
were already on their way out. The nurse coming in to say
goodbye backed out in terror as they burst forth. If she didn't
know better she would have thought this a one-two-three.

Setting the pace, leading the way, Totong Heredia, as he
strode back up the corridor, pulled out his car keys, dangled
and jingled them on a finger, winked at the nurse at the desk,
hummed a tune, hardly glanced at his wife and son trying to
keep in step.

Scurrying between her two men, Ineng Heredia giggled and
slipped a hand round the arm of each.

Linked thus to his parents and borne along, Bobby, the bag
bumping on a leg, could only concentrate on motion and didn't
remember Cándido until they were at the head of the stairs,
when he looked around and saw Cándido down the hall, leaning in the open doorway of the room, raising an eyebrow at the
togetherness, but as they went down the stairs Cándido was
waiting at the foot of it, making a face as they descended, and
he was perched on a chair's arm, wrinkling his nose, as they

crossed the lobby toward the door, he was out on the driveway, pursing his mouth, when they stepped out into the shady grounds, he was sprawled on the lawn, pretending to be languishing, while they were crowded into the front seat, and as the car drove off toward the boulevard and the sea, Bobby, turning around for a last look, saw Cándido on the sidewalk wistfully shrug his shoulders and wave a hand and then, buttoning up Bobby's Beatles shirt, digging fists into Bobby's beige trousers, go off in Bobby's boosters in the other direction, up Taft Way, where the traffic was and the sunshine.

A PORTRAIT OF
THE ARTIST AS FILIPINO

(AN ELEGY IN THREE SCENES)

How but in custom and in ceremony
Are innocence and beauty born?

—YEATS

THE SCENES—

FIRST SCENE: The sala of the Marasigan house in Intramuros. An afternoon toward the beginning of October, 1941.

SECOND SCENE: The same. A week later. Late in the morning.

THIRD SCENE: The same. Two days later. Afternoon of the second Sunday of October.

THE PEOPLE—

CANDIDA & PAULA MARASIGAN, *spinster daughters of Don Lorenzo*
PEPANG, *their elder married sister*
MANOLO, *their eldest brother*
BITOY CAMACHO, *a friend of the family*
TONY JAVIER, *a lodger at the Marasigan house*
PETE, *a Sunday Magazine editor*
EDDIE, *a writer*
CORA, *a news photographer*

SUSAN & VIOLET, *vaudeville artists*
DON PERICO, *a senator*
DOÑA LOLENG, *his wife*
PATSY, *their daughter*
ELSA MONTES & CHARLIE DACANAY, *friends of Doña Loleng*
DON ALVARO & DOÑA UPENG, *his wife* ⎫
DON PEPE   ⎬ *friends of the*
DON MIGUEL & DOÑA IRENE, *his wife* ⎭ *Marasigans.*
DON ARISTEO
A WATCHMAN
A DETECTIVE
TWO POLICEMEN

THE FIRST SCENE

The curtains open on a second curtain depicting the ruins of Intramuros in the moonlight. The sides of the stage are in shadow. BITOY CAMACHO is standing at far left. He begins to speak unseen, just a voice in the dark.

BITOY: Intramuros! The old Manila. The original Manila. The Noble and Ever Loyal City . . .

To the early conquistadores she was a new Tyre and Sidon; to the early missionaries she was a new Rome. Within these walls was gathered the wealth of the Orient—silk from China; spices from Java; gold and ivory and precious stones from India. And within these walls the Champions of Christ assembled to conquer the Orient for the Cross. Through these old streets once crowded a marvelous multitude—viceroys and archbishops; mystics and merchants; pagan sorcerers and Christian martyrs; nuns and harlots and elegant marquesas; English pirates, Chinese mandarins, Portuguese traitors, Dutch spies, Moro sultans, and Yankee clipper captains. For three centuries this medieval town was a Babylon in its commerce and a New Jerusalem in its faith . . .

Now look: this is all that's left of it now. Weeds and rubble and scrap iron. A piece of wall, a fragment of stairway—and over there, the smashed gothic facade of old Santo Domingo . . . *Quomodo desolata es, Civitas Dei!*
[*From this point, light slowly grows about Bitoy.*]

I stand here in the moonlight and I look down this desolate street. Not so long ago, people were dying here—a horrible death—by sword and fire—their screams drowned out by the shriller screaming of the guns. Only silence now. Only silence, and the moonlight, and the tall grass thickening everywhere . . .

This is the great Calle Real—the main street of the city, the main street of the land, the main street of our history. I don't think there is any town in the Philippines that does not have— or that did not used to have—its own Calle Real. Well, this is the mother street of them all. Through this street the viceroys made their formal entry into the city. Along this street, amidst a glory of banners, the Seal of the King was borne in parade whenever letters arrived from the royal hand. Down this street marched the great annual processions of the city. And on this street the principal families had their town-houses—splendid ancient structures with red-tile roofs and wrought-iron balconies and fountains playing in the interior patios.

When I was a little boy, some of those old houses were still standing—but, oh, they had come down in the world! No longer splendid, no longer the seats of the mighty; abandoned and forgotten; they stood decaying all along this street; dreaming of past glories; growing ever more dark and dingy and dilapidated with the years; turning into slum-tenements at last—a dozen families crowded into each of the old rooms; garbage piled all over the patios; and washlines dangling between the sagging balconies . . .

Intramuros was dying, Intramuros was decaying even before the war. The jungle had returned—the modern jungle, the slum-jungle—just as merciless and effective as the real thing—demolishing man's moment of history and devouring his monuments. The noble and ever loyal City had become just another jungle of slums. And that is how most of us remember the imperial city of our fathers!

But there was one house on this street that never became a slum; that resisted the jungle, and resisted it to the very end; fighting stubbornly to keep itself intact, to keep itself individual. It finally took a global war to destroy that house and the three people who fought for it. Though they were destroyed, they were never conquered. They died with their house, and they died with their city—and maybe it's just as well they did. They could never have survived the destruction of the old Manila . . .

Their house stood on this corner of Calle Real. This piece of wall, this heap of broken stones are all that's left of it now—the house of Don Lorenzo Marasigan. Here it stood—and here it had been standing for generations. Oh, from the outside, you would have thought it just another slum-tenement. It looked like all the other old houses on this street—the roof black with moss, the rusty balconies sagging, the cracked walls unpainted . . . But enter—push open the old massive gates—and you find a clean bare passageway, you see a clean bright patio. No garbage anywhere, no washlines. And when you walk up the polished stairway, when you enter the gleaming sala, you step into another world—a world "where all's accustomed, ceremonious . . ."

[*The lights go on inside the stage. Through the transparent curtain, the sala of the Marasigan house becomes visible.*]

It wasn't merely the seashells lining the stairway, or the baroque furniture, or the old portraits hanging on the walls, or the family albums stacked on the shelves. The very atmosphere of the house suggested another Age—an Age of lamplight and gaslight, of harps and whiskers and fine carriages; an Age of manners and melodrama, of Religion and Revolution.

[*The "Intramuros Curtain" begins to open, revealing the set proper.*]

It is gone now—that house—the house of Don Lorenzo El Magnifico. Nothing remains of it now save a piece of wall and a heap of broken stones. But this is how it looked before it perished—and I'm sure it looked just like this a hundred years ago. It never changed, it never altered. I had known it since I was a little boy—and it always looked like this. All the time I was growing up, the city was growing up too, the city was changing fast all around me. I could never be sure of anything or of any place staying the way I remembered it. This was the one thing I was always sure of—this house. This was the one place I could always come back to, and find unchanged. Oh, older, yes—and darker, and more silent. But still, just the same; just the way I remembered it when I was a little boy and my father took me here with him on Friday evenings.

[*The sala now stands fully revealed. It is a large room, clean and polished, but—like the furniture—dismally shows its age. The paint has darkened and is peeling off the walls. The*

*windowpanes are broken. The doorways are not quite
square anymore. The baroque elegance has tarnished.*

*Rear wall opens out, through French windows, into two
sagging balconies that overhang the street. At center, against
the wall between the balconies, is a large sofa. Ordinarily
grouped with this sofa are two rocking chairs, a round table,
and two straight chairs. Right now, the table and the straight
chairs have been moved in front of the balcony at right, its
windows having been closed. The table is set for merienda.
Through the open windows of the other balcony, late afternoon sunlight streams into the room, and you get a glimpse
of the untidy tenements across the street.*

*At left side of the room, downstage, is a portion of the
banisters and the head of the stairway, facing toward rear.
In the middle of the left wall is a closed door. Against back
wall, facing stairway, stands an old-fashioned combination
hatrack and umbrella-stand with mirror.*

*At right side of the room, downstage, against the walls, is
a what-not filled with sea-shells, figurines, family albums,
magazines, and books. In the middle of the right wall is a
large open doorway framed with curtains. Next to it, against
right wall, stands an upright piano.*

*Embroidered cushions decorate the chairs. Pedestals
bearing potted plants flank the balconies and the doorway
at right. On the walls above the sofa, the piano, and the
what-not, are enlarged family photographs in ornate frames:
A chandelier hangs from the ceiling. The painting entitled
"A Portrait of the Artist as Filipino" is supposed to be
hanging in the center of the invisible "fourth wall" between
stage & audience. "Left" and "Right" in all the stage directions are according to the view from the audience. Bitoy
Camacho steps into the room.]*

I remember coming here one day early in October back in
1941—just two months before the war broke out. 1941!
Remember that year? It was the year of Hitler for the people
in Europe—but for us over here, it was the year of the Conga
and the Boogie-woogie, the year of practice black-outs, the

year of the Bare Midriff. Oh, we were all sure that the war was coming our way pretty soon—but we were just as sure that it would not stay long—and that nothing, nothing at all, would happen to us. When we said: "Keep 'em flying!" and "Business as Usual!" our voices were brave and gay, our hearts were untroubled. And because we felt so safe, because we felt so confident, we deliberately tried to scare ourselves. Remember all those gruesome rumors we kept spreading? We enjoyed shivering as we told them, and we enjoyed shivering as we listened. It was all just a thrilling game. We were sophisticated children playing at rape and murder, and half-wishing it was all true.

[*He places himself at stair-landing, as though he had just come up the stairs.*]

That October afternoon, I had come here with my head buzzing with rumors. Out there in the street, people were stopping each other to exchange interpretations of the latest headlines. In the restaurants and barber shops, military experts were fighting the war in Europe. And in all the houses in all the streets, radios were screaming out the latest bulletins. I felt excited—and I felt very pleased with myself for feeling excited. It proved how involved I was in my times; and how concerned, how nobly concerned I was with the human condition. So, I came up those stairs and I paused here on the landing and I looked at this room that I hadn't seen again since my boyhood—and, suddenly, all the people and all the headlines and all the radios stopped screaming in my ears. I stood here—and the whole world had become silent. It was astonishing—and it was also highly unpleasant. The silence of this room was like an insult, like a slap in the face. I felt suddenly ashamed of all that noble excitement I had been enjoying so much. But my next feeling was of bitter resentment. I resented this room. I hated those old chairs for standing there so calmly. I wanted to walk right down again, to leave this house, to run back to the street—back to the screaming people and headlines and radios. But I didn't. I couldn't. The silence had me helpless. And after a while I stopped feeling outraged, I began to smile at myself. For the first time in a long, long time, I could hear myself thinking, I could feel myself feeling and breathing and living and remembering. I was conscious of myself as a separate person with a separate, secret life of my own. This old room grew young again, and familiar. The silence whispered with memories . . . Outside, the world was hurrying gaily toward destruction. In here, life went on as usual; unaltered, unchanged; everything in its proper place; everything just the same today as yesterday, or last year, or a hundred years ago . . .

[*A pause, while Bitoy stands smiling at the room.*

Enter CANDIDA MARASIGAN *at right, bearing a chocolate-pot on tray. Seeing Bitoy, she stops in the doorway and stares at him inquiringly. Candida is forty-two, and is dressed in the style of the twenties. Her uncut hair, already graying, is coiled up and knotted in the old manner. Her body is straight, firm, and spare. Not conventionally pretty, she can, however, when among friends, grow radiant with girlish charm and innocence. When among strangers, she is apt, from shyness, to assume the severe forbidding expression of the crabbed old maid. She is staring very severely now at the grinning young man on the stairway.*]

BITOY: Hello, Candida.

[*He waits, smiling; but as her face remains severe he walks toward her.*]

Candida, surely you know me?

[*As he approaches, her face quickens with recognition, and she advances to meet him.*]

CANDIDA: But of course, of course! You are Bitoy, the son of old Camacho! And shame on you, Bitoy Camacho—shame, shame on you for forgetting your old friends!

[*They have met at center of stage.*]

BITOY: I have never forgotten my old friends, Candida.

CANDIDA: Then why have you never—

[*She speaks this with emphatic gesture that causes chocolate to splash from pot. Bitoy backs away. She laughs.*]

Oh, excuse me, Bitoy!

BITOY: Here, let me take that.

[*He takes tray and places it on table. Her eyes follow him. He turns around and, smiling, submits to her gaze.*]

Well?

CANDIDA [*approaching him*]: So thin, Bitoy? And so many lines in your face already? You cannot be more than twenty.

BITOY: I am twenty-five.

CANDIDA: Twenty-five! Imagine that!

[*She moves away, downstage.*]

And the last time we saw you, you were just a small boy in short pants and a sailor blouse . . .

BITOY: And the last time I saw you, Candida—

CANDIDA [*whirling around: passionately*]: No! No!

BITOY [*startled*]: Huh?

CANDIDA [*laughing*]: Oh Bitoy, when you begin to get as old as I am, it hurts!

BITOY: What?

CANDIDA: To be told how much one has changed.

BITOY: You have not changed, Candida.

CANDIDA: Oh yes, I have—oh yes, I have! The last time you saw me, Bitoy, [*She says this with all the gestures of a lively belle.*]

I was a very grown-up young lady, a very proud young lady—with rings on my fingers and a ribbon in my hair and the stars in my eyes! Oh, I was so full of vanity, so full of vivacity! I was so sure that any moment at all someone very wonderful would arrive to take me away! I was waiting, do you know, waiting for my Principe de Asturias!

BITOY: And he has not come yet—your Principe de Asturias?

CANDIDA: Alas, he has not come at all! And none of our old friends come anymore . . .

BITOY: Not even on Friday evenings?

CANDIDA: Not even on Friday evenings. No more "tertulias" on Friday, Bitoy. We have given them up. The old people are dying off; and the young people—you young people, Bitoy—do not care to come.

[*She turns her face toward doorway at right and raises her voice.*]

Paula! Paula!

[*Offstage, Paula is heard answering: "Coming!" Candida approaches Bitoy and takes both his hands in hers.*]

Bitoy, how sweet of you to remember us. You make me feel very happy. You bring back memories of such happy days.

BITOY: Yes, I know. *You* bring them back to me, too—all those Friday evenings I spent here with my father.

CANDIDA: [*releasing his hands*]: But how is it you remember? You were only a child.

BITOY: But I do, I do! Oh, those "tertulias"—how I remember them all! On Saturday nights, there was the tertulia at the Monson house in Binondo; on Monday nights, at the Botica of Doctor Moreta in Quiapo; on Wednesday nights, at the bookshop of Don Aristeo on Carriedo; and on Friday nights— Listen, Candida. On Fridays, do you know, I still wake up sometimes, even now, thinking: Today is Friday; the tertulia will be at the Marasigan house in Intramuros; and Father and I will be going . . .

[*He pauses as* PAULA *appears in doorway, carrying a platter of biscuits. Paula is forty, also slightly gray-haired already, and also wearing a funny old dress. She is smaller than Candida, and looks more delicate, more timid; like Candida, she is ambiguous—the bleakest of old maids, you would call her, until she smiles, when you discover, astonished, a humorous girl—still fresh, still charming—lurking under the gray hair.*]

CANDIDA: Well, Paula—do you see who has come to visit us after all these years?

PAULA [*as she hurries to table and sets down the platter*]: Why, Bitoy! Bitoy Camacho!

[*She goes to Bitoy and gives him both her hands.*]

Holy Virgin, how he has grown! Can this be our baby, Candida?

BITOY: In the short pants and the sailor blouse?

CANDIDA: He still fondly remembers our old Friday tertulias.

PAULA: Oh, you were a big nuisance in those days, Bitoy! I was always having to wipe your nose or to take you out to the small room. Why did your father always bring you along?

BITOY: Because I howled and howled if he tried to leave me behind!

PAULA [*throwing back her head*]: Oh, those old Friday nights! How we talked and talked!

[*She begins to move gaily all over the room as though a crowded "tertulia" were in progress, chattering to imaginary visitors and fanning herself with an imaginary fan.*]

More brandy, Don Pepe? Some more brandy, Don Isidro? Doña Upeng, come here by the window, it is cooler! What, Don Alvaro—you have not read the new poem by Darío? But, my good man, in the latest issue of the "Blanco y Negro," of course! Doña Irene, we are talking about the divine Ruben! You have read his latest offering?

"Tuvo razon tu abuela con su cabello cano,
muy mas que tu con rizos en que se enrosca el dia . . ."

Aie, Don Pepe, Don Pepe—tell me, do you not consider that poem an absolute miracle? Oh, look everybody—here comes Don Aristeo at last! Welcome to our house, noble soldier! Candida, find him a seat somewhere!

CANDIDA [*acting up, too*]: Over here, Don Aristeo, over here! And may I ask, my dear sir, why you failed us last Friday? Paula, some brandy for Don Aristeo!

PAULA [*offering imaginary glass*]: I forbid you to talk politics tonight! Must we hear about nothing else these days except this eternal Don Q?

CANDIDA: Oh, listen everybody! Don Alvaro is telling us just where this Don Q was, during the Revolution!

PAULA: Oh yes, Doña Irene, we went to all the performances— but we consider this zarzuela company inferior to the one we had last year.

CANDIDA: And next month, the Italian singers are arriving! Alas for us girls! The men will all be lined up again at the stage-door!

PAULA: More brandy, Don Miguel? Some more brandy, Don Pepe? Doña Irene, would you prefer to sit here by the piano? Oh, go on, go on, Don Alvaro! And you say that General Aguinaldo was actually preparing his army for a last assault?

BITOY [*in voice of ten-year-old*]: Tita Paula, Tita Paula—I wanna go to the small room!

PAULA: Hush, hush, you little savage! And just look at your nose!

CANDIDA: And how many times have we told you not to call us Tita!

PAULA: You will call us Paula and Candida.

CANDIDA: Just Paula and Candida—understand?

PAULA: Jesús, we are not old maids yet!

CANDIDA: No, no—we are not old maids yet! We are young, we are pretty, we are delightful! Oh, listen, Doña Upeng— last night we went to a ball, and we danced and danced and danced till morning!

[*She dances around the room.*]

PAULA: Papa said we were the prettiest girls in all the gathering!

CANDIDA: Oh yes, Doña Irene—our papa accompanied us— and he was the most distinguished gentleman present!

BITOY [*still the ten-year-old; gesturing excitedly toward door-way*]: And here he comes! Here he comes!

CANDIDA [*whirling around*]: Oh, here you are at last, papa! [*Raising her voice excitedly*] Don Miguel, here is papa! Here is papa, Doña Upeng!

PAULA [*joyously excited, too*]: Here is papa, Don Alvaro! Doña Irene, here is papa!

[*The sisters gesture toward front of stage as they say: "Here is papa!"*]

CANDIDA: Hush, hush, everybody! Papa wants to say something! [*The sisters stand side by side, directly facing audience, their faces lifted, their hands clasped to their breasts, and their bodies at attention, as though they were listening to their father speaking. Then, clapping their hands, they cry out in joyous adoration "Oh, papa, papa!"*

They hold the pose a moment longer. The PORTRAIT *is hanging on the wall right in front of them; and as they become aware of it, the rapture fades from their faces, their bodies droop, their hands fall to their sides. The game is ended; the make-believe is over. They stand silent, bleakly staring up—two shabby old maids in a shabby old house.*

Bitoy is watching them from upstage. Becoming aware of their fixed stare, he lifts his eyes and sees the PORTRAIT *for the first time. Staring, he comes forward and stands behind the sisters, his face between their staring faces.*]

BITOY: Is that it?

CANDIDA [*expressionless*]: Yes.

BITOY: When did your father paint it?

PAULA: About a year ago.

BITOY [*after a staring pause*]: What a strange, strange picture!

CANDIDA: Do you know what he calls it?

BITOY: Yes.

CANDIDA: "RETRATO DEL ARTISTA COMO FILIPINO."

BITOY: Yes, I know. "A Portrait of the Artist as Filipino." But why, why? The scene is not Filipino . . . What did your father mean? [*He holds up a hand toward* PORTRAIT.]

A young man carrying an old man on his back . . . and behind them, a burning city . . .

PAULA: The old man is our father.

BITOY: Yes, I recognize his face . . .

CANDIDA: And the young man is our father also—our father when he was young.

BITOY [*excitedly*]: Why, yes, yes!

PAULA: And the burning city—

BITOY: The burning city is Troy.

PAULA: Well, you know all about it.

BITOY [*smiling*]: Yes, I know all about it. Aeneas carrying his father Anchises out of Troy. And *your* father has painted himself both as Aeneas and as Anchises.

CANDIDA: He has painted himself as he is now—and as he used to be—in the past.

BITOY: The effect is rather frightening . . .

CANDIDA: Oh, do you feel it, too?

BITOY: I feel as if I were seeing double.

CANDIDA: I sometimes feel as if that figure up there were a monster—a man with two heads.

BITOY: Yes. "That strange monster, the Artist . . ." But how marvelously your father has caught that clear, pure classic simplicity! What flowing lines, what luminous colors, what a calm and spacious atmosphere! One can almost feel the sun shining and the seawinds blowing! Space, light, cleanliness, beauty, grace—and suddenly, there in the foreground, those frightening faces, those darkly smiling faces—like faces in a mirror . . . And behind them, in the distance, the burning towers of Troy . . . My God, this is magnificent! This is a masterpiece!

[*He pauses and his rapturous face becomes troubled.*]

But why does your father call it "A Portrait of the Artist as Filipino"?

PAULA: Well—it is a portrait of himself after all.

CANDIDA: A double portrait, in fact.

PAULA: And he is an artist *and* a Filipino.

BITOY: Yes, yes—but, then, why paint himself as Aeneas? why paint himself against the Trojan War?

PAULA [*shrugging*]: We do not know.

CANDIDA: He did not tell us.

BITOY: Do you know, a visiting Frenchman has written an enthusiastic article about this picture.

CANDIDA: Oh yes—he was very nice, that Frenchman. He said he had long been an admirer of my father. He was thoroughly acquainted with my father's work. He had seen them in Madrid and Barcelona. And he promised himself—[*She pauses. Bitoy has taken out a notebook and is jotting down what she is saying. She and Paula exchange glances.*]

BITOY [*looking up expectantly*]: Yes? He promised himself what?

CANDIDA [*drily continuing*]: Well, he promised himself that if he ever found himself here in the Philippines he would try to locate father. So, he came here, and he saw father, and he saw this new painting, and then he published that article. As I said, he was a very nice man—but we are sorry now he ever came.

BITOY [*looking up*]: Sorry?

CANDIDA: Tell me something, Bitoy—are you a newspaper reporter?

BITOY [*after a moment's hesitation*]: Yes. Yes, I am.

CANDIDA [*smiling*]: And that is why you have come to visit us after all these years!

[*Still smiling, she walks away. Bitoy looks blankly after her. She goes to table and begins to beat the chocolate. Bitoy turns to Paula.*]

BITOY: Paula, what is the matter! What have I done?

PAULA: Oh, nothing, Bitoy. Only, when people come here now, it is not to visit us, but to see this picture.

BITOY: Well, you ought to be glad, you ought to be proud! People thought your father died a long time ago! Now, after all these years of silence and obscurity, everybody is talking about him! The whole country is agog to discover that Don Lorenzo Marasigan, one of the greatest painters of the Philippines and the friend and rival of Juan Luna, is not only alive but has actually painted another masterpiece in his old age!

PAULA [*gently*]: My father painted this picture only for us—for Candida and myself. He gave it to us as a present; and for a whole year it has hung here in peace. Then that Frenchman came and saw it and wrote about it. And since then we have had no peace. No day passes but we must face a reporter from the newspapers or a photographer from the magazines or a group of students from the universities. And we—[*laying a hand on his shoulder*]—we do not like it, Bitoy.

[*She turns away and goes to table where she begins to prepare her father's merienda on a tray. Meanwhile, Bitoy stands where she has left him, staring at PORTRAIT. Then he pockets his notebook and goes toward table.*]

BITOY: Forgive me, Candida. Forgive me, Paula.

[*Paula goes on arranging tray; Candida goes on beating chocolate.*]

Well . . . I suppose I ought to go away.

CANDIDA [*not looking up*]: No; stay and have some merienda. Paula, get another cup.

BITOY [*as Paula goes to doorway*]: Please do not bother, Paula. I really must be going.

PAULA [*pausing*]: Oh, Bitoy!

BITOY: There are some people waiting for me.

CANDIDA [*pouring chocolate into a cup*]: Sit down, Bitoy, and no more nonsense.

BITOY: These people are waiting just around the corner, Candida, and they will be coming here in a moment.

CANDIDA [*looking up*]: More people from the newspapers?

BITOY: Yes.

CANDIDA: Friends of yours?

BITOY: We all work for the same company.

CANDIDA: I see. And because you are a friend of the family, they have sent you ahead to prepare the way—is that it?

BITOY: Exactly.

CANDIDA [*laughing*]: Well! You *are* a scoundrel, Bitoy Camacho!

BITOY: But I will go right down and tell them not to come anymore.

CANDIDA: Oh, why not? [*She shrugs.*] Let them come.

PAULA: After all, we have to accustom ourselves, you know.

BITOY: But I do not want them to come.

PAULA: I thought you wanted us to be glad about people coming.

BITOY: No.

PAULA: Then, *what* do you want?

BITOY [*after a pause: parodying again a small boy's voice*]: Oh Tita Paula, I wanna go to the small room!

[*They all laugh. Bitoy draws himself up and, one arm akimbo, begins to pace the floor, twirling an imaginary mustache. His gruff voice now parodies a gentleman of the old school.*]

Caramba! These young people nowadays, they are so terrible, no? Hombre, when I was young, in the days before the Revolution—Señorita, if you will be so gracious, a little more of your excellent brandy.

CANDIDA [*offering him cup of chocolate on saucer*]: With a thousand pleasures, Don Benito!

PAULA [*waving imaginary fan*]: Oh, please, Don Benito—please tell us about your student days in Paris!

BITOY [*rolling his eyes at the ceiling*]: Ah, Paris! Paris in the old days!

CANDIDA: Doña Irene, come quick! Doña Upeng, hurry over here! Don Benito is going to tell us about his love-affairs with those Parisian cocottes!

PAULA: Were they thrilling? Were they passionate? Were they shameless? Ah, speak no more—speak no more! My head whirls, my heart pounds! I shall swoon, I shall swoon!

[*She claps one hand to her brow, the other to her heart, and waltzes out of the room. Candida and Bitoy burst into laughter. Candida resumes beating chocolate.*]

BITOY [*approaching table*]: I really am very sorry, Candida.

CANDIDA: Oh, sit down, Bitoy, and drink your chocolate.

BITOY [*sitting down*]: Have people really been annoying you?

CANDIDA: Well, you know how it is—reporters, photographers, people wanting to talk to father—and they are offended when he refuses to see them.

[*She looks up toward* PORTRAIT].

 And you know what, Bitoy? That picture affects people in a very strange way.

BITOY: How do you mean?

CANDIDA: It makes them angry.

BITOY [*also looking toward* PORTRAIT]: It is rather enigmatic, you know.

CANDIDA: Well, we explain—we explain to everybody. We tell them: this is Aeneas, and this is his father Anchises. But they just look blankly at us. And then they ask: Who is Aeneas? Was he a Filipino? [*She laughs.*] There were some people here the other day—some kind of civic society—and they were shocked to learn that we had had this painting for a whole year without anybody knowing about it, until that Frenchman came along. They were furious with Paula and me for not telling everybody sooner. One of them—a small man with big eyes—he pointed a finger right in my face and he said to me in a very solemn voice: "Miss Marasigan, I shall urge the government to confiscate this painting right away! You and your sister are unworthy to possess it!"

BITOY [*joining in her laughter*]: I begin to see what you and Paula have had to suffer.

[*Paula enters with extra cup.*]

CANDIDA: Oh, Paula and I do not mind really. It is father we want to spare.

[*She picks up tray and gives it to Paula.*]

 Here, Paula. And tell father that the son of his old friend Camacho has come to visit him.

[*Exit Paula with tray.*]

BITOY: And how is he—your father—[*gazing toward* POR-TRAIT]—Don Lorenzo el magnifico?

CANDIDA [*pouring a cup for herself*]: Oh, quite well.

BITOY: Is he too weak now to leave his room?

CANDIDA: Oh no.

BITOY: But something is the matter with him?

CANDIDA [*evasively*]: He had an accident.

BITOY: When?

CANDIDA: About a year ago.

BITOY: When he painted that picture?

CANDIDA: A short time after he finished painting it.

BITOY: What happened?

CANDIDA: We do not quite know. We did not see it happen, and it happened at night. We think he must have been walking in his sleep. And he . . . he fell from the balcony of his room into the courtyard below.

BITOY [*rising*]: Oh, my God! Did he break anything?

CANDIDA: No—thank God!

BITOY: And how is he now?

CANDIDA: He can move about—but he prefers to stay in bed. Do you know, Bitoy—he has not once come out of his room for a whole year.

[*She suddenly presses her knuckles to her forehead.*]

Oh, we blame ourselves for what happened!

BITOY: But why should you? It was an accident.

CANDIDA [*after a pause*]: Yes . . . Yes, it was an accident.

[*She picks up chocolate-pot again and pours a cup for Paula. Bitoy watches her in silence. Paula appears joyously in doorway.*]

PAULA: Come, Bitoy! Hurry! Papa is delighted! He begs you to come at once!

BITOY [*walking to doorway*]: Thank you, Paula.

CANDIDA: Bitoy—

[*He stops and looks at her.*]

You will be very careful, Bitoy? Remember: you are not a reporter, you are a friend. You have not come to interview him or to take his photograph. You have only come to visit him.

BITOY: Yes, Candida.

[*Exeunt Paula and Bitoy. Candida sits down and begins to eat. The day's mail is stacked on the table. She opens and glances through the letters as she eats. Paula comes back.*]

PAULA [*sitting down and sipping her chocolate*]: Father was really delighted. He even got out of bed to shake hands with Bitoy. And they were talking very gaily when I left them. Oh, father is really getting better, Candida! Do you not think so? [*Candida does not answer. She has propped an elbow on the table and is staring at a letter, her head leaning on her hand. Paula leans sideways to look at letter.*] More bills, Candida?

CANDIDA [*picking up and dropping one by one the letters she has opened*]: The water bill. The gas bill. The doctor's bill. And this—[*waving the letter she's holding*]—this is the light bill. Listen. [*She reads.*] "We again warn you that unless these accounts are immediately settled, we shall be obliged to discontinue all further service." And this is the third warning they have sent.

PAULA: Have you told Manolo?

CANDIDA: I called up Manolo, I called up Pepang—and they said: Oh yes, yes—they would send the money right away. They have been saying that all this month, but they never send the money.

PAULA [*bitterly*]: Our dear brother and sister!

CANDIDA: Our dear brother and sister are determined that we give up this house.

PAULA: Well, they are not going to make us do it. You and I are going to stay right here. We were born here and we will die here!

CANDIDA: But what if they continue not to send us any money? What if they flatly refuse to support us any longer? All these bills . . .

PAULA [*pensively*]: There *must* be something we can do!

CANDIDA [*leaning toward Paula*]: Listen, I have some new ideas.

PAULA [*not paying attention*]: But what can we do? We are two useless old maids . . .

CANDIDA [*rising and looking about*]: Where is that newspaper?

PAULA: Oh, I lie awake night after night wondering how we can make money, money, money!

CANDIDA [*who has found newspaper and is standing by the table searching through the pages*]: Ah, here it is. Now listen, Paula. Listen to this. It says here—

[*She stops. Below, in the street, a car is heard stopping. The sisters listen; then glance at each other. Candida sighs, folds newspaper, places it on table, and sits down. Paula pours herself more chocolate. Footsteps are heard on the stairway. The sisters pick up their cups and sip their chocolate. Enter* TONY JAVIER, *carrying books and his coat in one hand. He glances toward the sisters, pushes the hat off his brow, and calls out: "Good afternoon, ladies!" Then he opens the closed door at left and flings his coat, hat, and books inside. He pulls the door shut again and, smiling confidently, walks into the sala. Tony is about twenty-seven, very masculine, and sardonic. His shirt and tie are blissfully resplendent; his charm, however, is more subtle—and he knows it.*]

TONY: Ah-ha, merienda!

CANDIDA [*very old-maidish*]: Will you have some chocolate, Mr. Javier?

TONY: Tch-tch. That's bad business, ladies. Remember: I'm just paying for room without board.

CANDIDA [*severely*]: Mr. Javier, anybody who lives under our roof is welcome to our table.

TONY: But are good manners good business?

CANDIDA: Mr. Javier, *will* you have some chocolate?

TONY [*picking up a biscuit and popping it into his mouth*]: Yes, thank you! [*He sees Bitoy's cup.*] Oh, you had a visitor!

CANDIDA: An old friend of ours. Paula, get another cup.

TONY: Oh, what for?

[*As Paula rises, he reaches across the table and presses a hand on her shoulder. She starts and looks at him, not angry but wondering. He slowly withdraws his hand, their eyes interlocked.*]

Please do not bother, Miss Paula. I can use this cup. I'm not particular.

CANDIDA [*grimly*]: Paula, get another cup.

TONY: Or perhaps you would like to offer me *your* cup, Miss Paula?

PAULA [*her eyes still innocently fascinated*]: My cup?

TONY [*picking up Paula's cup*]: Do you still want this chocolate?

PAULA: [*shaking her head*]: No.

TONY: Then, may I have it?

CANDIDA [*rising*]: Mr. Javier, I ask you to put down that cup at once!

TONY [*ignoring Candida*]: Thank you, Miss Paula.

[*He lifts the cup above his head.*]

To better business!

[*Then he throws his head back and slowly, deliberately drinks the chocolate, the sisters staring at his throat in horror and fascination. Then he sets the cup down and smacks his lips.*]

CANDIDA [*coming to life*]: Mr. Javier, it is outrageous—

TONY [*picking up and gobbling another biscuit*]: Oh no—it was delicious!

CANDIDA: It is useless to treat you with decency!

TONY [*bowing*]: Permit me to remove my indecent person from your sight.

[*He walks toward his room. The sisters exchange glances. He stops and looks back.*]

Oh—and thanks a lot for the merienda!

CANDIDA: Mr. Javier, you will please come back here. There is something we have to ask you.

TONY [*walking back*]: Okay, shoot.

PAULA [*quickly picking up chocolate-pot*]: I must just take this out to the kitchen.

CANDIDA: Put that down, Paula. You will stay right here.

TONY: Well, what is it? Come on, hurry up. I haven't got much time. I'd like to lie down a moment before I go out again.

[*He yawns and stretches his arms; his brows darken with momentary irritation.*]

God—but am I tired! I never get any sleep! I never get any sleep at all!

[*He goes to table and picks up another biscuit.*]

Studying all day, working all night! Ambition—hah! Everybody has it!

[*Nibbling the biscuit, he goes to a rocking chair and flops down.*] Look at me—a cheap little vaudeville piano-player. Not a pianist—oh no, no—certainly *not* a pianist! Hey, you know what's the difference between a pianist and a piano-player? I

can tell you. A pianist is uh—A pianist is—well—highbrow
stuff. Oh, you know. He had professors to teach him; he went
to the right academies; and he gives concerts for the high society dames. Culture—that's a pianist! While a piano-player—
oh, that's me! Nobody ever taught me how to play. I taught
myself—and I know I stink!
[*He rises and thrusts his hands into his pockets.*]
    A cheap little vaudeville piano-player. Three shows a day
in a stinking third-class theatre. The audience spits on your
neck and the piano rattles like an old can. And you never
know how long the job will last . . .
[*A pause, while he stares at the floor. Then he sighs deeply
and shrugs.*]
    So what do I do? So I get ambitious! So I tell myself I'm not
going to be just a piano-player all my life. No, siree! I'm
gonna be a lawyer—a big, rich, crooked lawyer! So I'm going
to school—yes, siree! Go to school all day, play the piano all
night. What a life! Oh well, it used to be worse . . .
[*He suddenly turns to the sisters.*]
    Can you, ladies, have any idea what kind of a life I've had?
CANDIDA: We are not interested in your private life.
TONY [*looking her in the eye*]: Oh no?
[*Her eyes falter: she looks away. He smiles.*]
    God! You ladies ought to be—
CANDIDA [*interrupting*]: Mr. Javier, when we allowed you to
    rent a room in our house, it was with the condition that you
    would permit no gambling, no drinking, and no women in
    your room.
TONY: So what now?
CANDIDA: You have broken our rules.
TONY: But I don't do my gambling here.
CANDIDA: I was not referring to gambling.
TONY: Well, I bring home a beer now and then.
CANDIDA: Nor to drinking either.
TONY [*his eyes widening*]: Oh, you mean—
[*Grinning, he traces a woman's form in the air with his hands.*]
CANDIDA [*not smiling*]: Yes!
TONY: But when?

CANDIDA: Last night, Mr. Javier, my sister and I heard you arriving with a woman.

TONY: Holy cow, were you *still* awake when I arrived last night?

CANDIDA: We happened to be still awake.

TONY [*bashfully dropping his eyes*]: Were you . . . waiting up for me?

CANDIDA: Mr. Javier, did you or did you not bring a woman here last night!

TONY [*wide-eyed*]: My dear ladies, you must have been dreaming! That was a wonderful, wonderful dream you had last night— and I sure hate to spoil your fun. So, you ladies dream about me, eh?

CANDIDA: No, we were not dreaming—and yes, you had a woman with you!

TONY: Yes, you were dreaming—and no, I did not have a woman with me!

CANDIDA: How can you have the nerve to lie! I distinctly heard a woman laughing—and so, I told my sister to get up and look out the window. Go on, Paula—tell him. Did you see a woman?

PAULA [*timidly*]: Well . . . it . . . it may have been a woman—

CANDIDA: May have been—! I thought you said you were *sure* you saw one!

PAULA: Only because *you* said you were sure you *heard* one! But it was so dark really—and all I could see was something white. It may have been a woman's dress—or it may have been a man's shirt . . .

TONY: It *was* a man's shirt! And the man inside the shirt was— uh— Oh yes, he was the drummer in our band! And he came along with me last night because I had some of his music in my room. So he came up; and I gave him his music; and then he went away. And that's all there is to it!

CANDIDA: Are you telling us the truth?

TONY [*putting up his hand*]: The whole truth and nothing but the truth.

CANDIDA: I wonder!

PAULA: Oh Candida, if we have falsely accused Mr. Javier, the least we can do now is to apologize for having hurt his feelings!

TONY [*instantly pitying himself*]: Oh no—why apologize to me? I'm just an animal! Animals have no feelings! It is useless to treat them with decency!

CANDIDA [*stiffly*]: Mr. Javier, if we have made a mistake, we are sorry—and we apologize.

TONY [*ignoring her; laying on the misery*]: Just a pile of trash . . . Rotten trash. Not worthy even to be stepped on—too sickening, too repulsive. . . Just something the garbage-collector ought to take away quick so I don't pollute the air for nice people!

CANDIDA: Mr. Javier, this is not funny at all!

TONY: You bet it's not funny!

[*He stands scowling at her. Bitoy appears in doorway, carrying tray. Tony's expression changes into surprise.*]

    Why, hello there, guy!

BITOY: Hi, Tony. Paula, where do I put this?

PAULA [*approaching*]: Give it to me.

[*She takes tray and exits.*]

BITOY [*walking in*]: Well, well, Tony!

TONY: Hi, guy.

CANDIDA: Do you two know each other?

BITOY: We used to work together.

TONY: At the piers.

BITOY [*making a face*]: The most horrible memory of my life!

TONY: Not of mine! What are you doing here, guy?

BITOY: What are *you* doing here?

TONY: I live here.

BITOY: No!

TONY: Yes! See that room over there? It's mine. For fifteen pesos a month.

BITOY: Candida, are you taking in boarders?

CANDIDA: Oh, you know how poor we are! Paula and I—we thought we would try running a boarding-house. But Mr. Javier is our first—and so far—our only customer.

[*Offstage, Paula is heard shouting "Candida! Candida!" Candida raises her voice.*]

    Yes? What is it, Paula?

[*Paula appears in doorway, still carrying tray.*]

PAULA: Oh Candida, a rat! A rat in the kitchen!

CANDIDA: [*with a shake of the head*]: Oh Paula, Paula!

PAULA [*pleadingly*]: And such a big, big rat, Candida!

CANDIDA: All right, I am coming. [*To Bitoy and Tony*] Excuse me. [*Exeunt Paula and Candida.*]

TONY [*contemptuously*]: A pair of crazy dames!

BITOY [*rather stiffly*]: They are old friends of my family, Tony.

TONY [*carelessly*]: Well, you better stay away from them. They're man-hungry.

BITOY [*smiling in spite of himself*]: Why, have they been trying to eat you up?

TONY: Ah, they're crazy. If I just look at them, they start shivering. When I talk to them, they get a fever. And if I touch them—

BITOY: So, you make love to them!

TONY: Me? Make love to *them*? Pah! [*He spits.*] I'd sooner make love to the Jones Bridge! Nah—it's them that's crazy, not me.

BITOY: It must be the poverty . . . I didn't know they had become so poor . . .

TONY: Poor? They're desperate!

BITOY: But they still have a married brother, and a married sister.

TONY: The brother and sister have been paying all the expenses— but it looks like they don't want to anymore. They want to sell this house and put the old man in a hospital.

BITOY: And what becomes of Paula and Candida?

TONY: Candida goes to live with the brother, Paula goes to live with the sister.

BITOY: Oh, poor Candida! Poor Paula! They won't like that!

TONY: You bet they don't like it! That's why they're desperate. They've been trying all sorts of crazy schemes—like trying to run a boarding-house—hah! Who wants to live in a house like this? Oh, Intramuros is full of students looking for a place to sleep in. They come here, they take one look, and they go away fast! They're scared! They wouldn't feel at home here.

BITOY: *You* seem very much at home anyway.

TONY: Oh, I like it here. I'm educating myself, you know. Paula and Candida, they've been wanting to throw me out—but they don't dare. They need the money too much. Besides, they like having me around. Oh, they're crazy. Why, they could have some big money if only—

[*He stops and looks toward* PORTRAIT.]

BITOY: If only what?

TONY [*coming downstage*]: See this painting? Well, I know an American who's willing to pay two thousand dollars for it. Dollars, mind you—not pesos.

BITOY [*coming downstage, too*]: And Paula and Candida refuse to sell?

TONY: They absolutely refuse to sell. Just think of it—two grand! Oh, I've been trying and trying to make them sell—

BITOY: *You*, Tony?

TONY: Sure—me. This American, he hired me to put over the deal, see?

BITOY: And no dice.

TONY: Those dames are crazy!

BITOY: Maybe they love this picture too much.

TONY: Love it? They hate it!

BITOY: How do you know?

TONY: Oh, I just do. And I hate it myself!

BITOY: Oh Lord—but why?

TONY [*staring at* PORTRAIT]: The damn thing's always looking at me, always looking down at me. Every time I come into this house; every time I come up those stairs. Looking at me, looking down at me. And if I turn around and face it—then it smiles, damn it! And if I go into my room and close the door, I can still feel it through the door, and through the walls—looking at me, smiling at me! Oh, I hate those eyes, I hate that smile, I hate the whole damn thing!

BITOY: Oh come, come, Tony! It's only a picture. It won't eat you up.

TONY: Who does he think he is? Who the hell does he think he is?

BITOY: Are you referring to the painting or to the painter?

TONY: You were in his room just now, weren't you?

BITOY: Are you speaking of Don Lorenzo?

TONY: Yes, yes! This Don Lorenzo Marasigan—this great Don Lorenzo who has so much damn pride in his head and nothing at all in his pockets. He had you in his room, didn't he? He talked to you, didn't he?

BITOY: He was very friendly.

TONY: I've been living here for months and he hasn't once asked me to his room!

BITOY: But he doesn't know you, Tony.

TONY: He doesn't *want* to know me! He thinks it's shameful I should be living here! He feels ashamed because his house has become a flop-house! And why should he feel ashamed, I'd like to know! What is he anyway, I'd like to know!

BITOY: Well, among other things, he's a scholar, an artist, and a patriot.

TONY: So he's a great man. So he's a great painter. So he fought in the Revolution. And so what? And what's that old Revolution of his to me? I went hungry and I got kicked about just the same in spite of that old Revolution he's so damn proud of! I don't owe him any thanks! And what the hell is he now? Just a beggar! That's what he is now—just a miserable old beggar! And he has the nerve to look down on me!

BITOY: How do you know he does?

TONY: Oh, I know. I've talked to him. I forced my way into his room once.

BITOY: And he threw you out?

TONY: Oh no, no! He was very courteous, very polite. I went there to tell him about this American wanting to buy this painting for two grand—and he listened very courteously, he listened very politely. And he said he was very sorry but it was none of his business. He said: "The picture belongs to my daughters, it does not belong to me. If anyone wants to buy it, they will have to talk to my daughters." And then he asked me to excuse him, he said he wanted to take a nap—and I found myself on my way out. Oh, he threw me out all right—but very courteously, very politely—the damn beggar— But he's going to pay for it! Oh, I'll make him pay for it!

BITOY: Aren't you being rather silly, Tony?

TONY [*grinning at* PORTRAIT]: And I know just where it will hurt him!

BITOY: What has the old man done to you?

TONY: Won't his damn heart break when his loving daughters sell off this picture!

BITOY: Oh, is that why you're so eager to make them sell?

TONY: Besides, this American has promised to pay me a very handsome commission, you know!

[*Enter Candida and Paula. Tony turns away from the* PORTRAIT.]

Well, did you ladies catch the rat?

PAULA [*proudly*]: Oh, of course! My sister never fails!

[*She and Candida begin to clear the table.*]

TONY: She's the champion rat-catcher, eh?

CANDIDA [*modestly*]: Oh no—just an expert.

BITOY: Candida has been the official rat-catcher of the family since she was a little girl.

PAULA: Oh, even at night—even in the middle of the night—if any of us heard a squeak, we would cry out: "Candida, a rat! Come, Candida—a rat!" And Candida always woke up. She would come; we would hear her prowling about, peering here, peering there; and then we would hear a sudden dash, a brief struggle, a faint squeak—and nothing more—only Candida sleepily walking back to her bed. She always got her rat!

BITOY: How do you do it, Candida?

CANDIDA: Oh, I just seem to have a talent for it.

TONY: Yours is a very special talent, Miss Candida.

CANDIDA [*thoughtfully*]: Yes—but I am planning to—well—develop it, you know—to develop it for more general commercial purposes.

[*Tony and Bitoy exchange blank looks.*]

After all, what is the point in having talent if you cannot use it to make money?

TONY: What, indeed?

BITOY: Speaking of money, Tony here tells me there is an American who wanted to buy this new painting of your father's.

TONY: And he *still* wants to buy it.

CANDIDA: We have told Mr. Javier again and again: the picture is not for sale.

TONY: Two thousand dollars! That's not chicken-feed.

PAULA: We are sorry, Mr. Javier. Our father painted that picture very especially for us. We will never sell it.

[*Sound of knocking downstairs.*]

CANDIDA: Who can that be?

BITOY: I think I know.

CANDIDA: Your friends?

BITOY: Shall I tell them to go away?

CANDIDA: You donkey! Tell them to come up.

[*Bitoy goes to head of stairway. Tony wanders over to the piano, opens it, and runs his fingers over the keys, standing up.*]

BITOY [*at stairway*]: Hi, folks—come on up.

[*Enter* PETE, EDDIE, *and* CORA. *Pete looks rather rumpled and disheveled. Eddie is immaculate, very much the man-about-town. Cora wears slacks, looks bored, and is carrying a flash-bulb camera. Pete, Eddie, and Cora are in their middle thirties. Bitoy turns to the sisters.*]

Candida, Paula—these are the people I told you about.

[*To the visitors*]

Miss Candida and Miss Paula Marasigan, daughters of Don Lorenzo.

[*Chorus of "Hello's" and "Good afternoon's" from the visitors.*]

CANDIDA [*coming forward*]: Won't you sit down? Bitoy tells us you have all come to see our painting.

EDDIE: And to see the great painter, too, Miss Marasigan—if possible.

BITOY: It's quite impossible right now, Eddie. Don Lorenzo is taking a nap. He asked me to convey his greetings and his apologies.

CANDIDA: You must excuse my father. He is getting old—and you know how old people are. They just want to sleep and sleep and not be disturbed.

[*She glances toward table.*]

We were just having merienda. Would any of you care for some chocolate?

[*Chorus of "No, thank you's" from the visitors.*]

Then, will you please excuse us? The painting is right over there. Bitoy, you will show it to them?

[*She smiles and nods at visitors and goes back to table. Bitoy, Pete, and Eddie move downstage and stand before* PORTRAIT. *Paula and Candida pick up their trays and go out of the room. Cora parks her camera on the sofa and walks over to the piano where Tony, oblivious of the visitors, has been idly picking out a tune, still standing. The tune is "Vereda Tropical."*]

CORA: Hi, Tony.

TONY [*looking around*]: Hi, Cora.

CORA [*glancing round the room*]: Is this where you live now?

TONY: Very elegant, don't you think?

CORA [*fetching out her cigarettes*]: It looks rather tired to me. Can I smoke here—or would that old bozo [*nodding toward photograph over piano*] drop down from the wall?

TONY [*sitting down on stool; his back against piano*]: Oh, he's an old friend of mine. Here, give me one too.

[*They light cigarettes. Cora sits down on chair beside Tony, facing audience.*]

CORA [*leaning sideways toward Tony and gesturing with her head toward the group in front of* PORTRAIT]: *The* intelligentsia. Speechless with ecstasy.

[*She raises her voice and mockingly declaims:*]

> "*Then felt I like some watcher in the skies*
> *When a new planet swims into his ken . . .*
> *Silent, upon a peak in Darien—*"

[*After a pause*] Well, speak up, boys. Say something. Or should I send out for some aspirin?

TONY: What do you think of that picture, Cora?

CORA: Don't ask me. I'm allergic to classical stuff. Hey, Pete!

PETE: Yes, Cora?

CORA: Well, what do you say, Pete? Is it Art—or is it baloney?

PETE: Oh, it's Art all right—but I feel like brushing my teeth.

CORA: Oh, good! Hooray for Art!

BITOY: How do you like it, Eddie?

EDDIE: I don't like it at all.

PETE: Well, what do you think of it?

EDDIE: My thoughts are unprintable.

CORA: Oh Eddie, I'm just dying to read them!

EDDIE: Ready, Cora?

CORA [*fetching out pencil & notebook*]: I'm all yours, sweetheart.

EDDIE: Now, let me see . . . What do we say first?

BITOY: We? *You're* writing this feature article, Eddie—not us.

EDDIE: But what the devil can anybody say about this picture?

CORA: I'm waiting, genius.

TONY: Just say it ought to be in the garbage can, guy.

CORA: Oh, Tony—don't you like it either?

TONY: I love it! It's worth two thousand dollars to me!

CORA: Hear that, Eddie? Now you can say that a member of the proletariat—You *are* a member of the proletariat, aren't you, Tony?

TONY: What's that?

CORA: Oh yes, you are. Hey, fellows—this is Tony Javier, a darned good piano-player. He and I grew up among the slums of Tondo. And there you are, Eddie! You can bring in the slums of Tondo just like that.

EDDIE: Oh *no*—not again!

PETE: How can you write about Art and not bring in the slums of Tondo?

BITOY: *And* the Ivory Tower.

CORA: *And* the proletariat. Like Tony here. And if he says the picture's worth two thousand dollars to him—

EDDIE: I don't care what he says. This picture's not worth two cents to *me*. I don't understand all this fuss about it. I don't think it's worth writing about at all. Oh, why did I ever learn to write!

CORA: Darling, who said you ever did?

EDDIE: Come on, Pete—help me out.

PETE: It's easy as pie, Eddie. Just be angry with this picture; just pile on the social-consciousness.

EDDIE: I'm sick of writing about social-consciousness!

CORA: And besides, it's not fashionable anymore.

PETE: You could begin with a punchline: "If it's not Proletarian, it's not Art."

EDDIE: Sure . . . Let me see . . . Something like this: "As I always say, Art is not autonomous; Art should not stand aloof from mundane affairs; Art should be socially significant; Art has a function . . ."

BITOY: Like making people brush their teeth?

PETE: Like making people brush their teeth.

BITOY: Then, Don Lorenzo is a highly successful artist.

PETE: He ought to go and work for Kolynos Toothpaste.

CORA: As I always say, the real artists of our time are the advertising men.

BITOY: Michelangelo plus Shakespeare equals a Kolynos ad.

PETE: My dear boy, compared to the functional perfection of a Kolynos ad, Michelangelo and Shakespeare were amateurs.

CORA: Shut up, Pete. Go on, Eddie. "Art has a function." Now what?

PETE: Now he must emphasize the contrast between the wealth of artistic material lying all about us and the poverty of the local artist's imagination.

CORA: Oh Christ—must I hear *that* again!

PETE: Cora, Cora—imagine being a critic and failing to say *that!*

BITOY [*in mock-oratorical manner*]: Outside are the slums of Tondo—and the battlefields of China—

PETER [*same manner*]: And what does the artist do?

CORA [*same manner*]: He dreams about Aeneas—

BITOY: He dreams about the Trojan War—

PETE: The most hackneyed theme in all Art!

BITOY: And he celebrates with exaggerated defiance values from which all content has vanished!

CORA: He looks back with nostalgic longing to the more perfect world of the Past!

PETE: And he paints this atrocious picture—the sickly product of a decadent imagination!

CORA: Of a decadent *bourgeois* imagination, Pete.

PETE: Of a decadent bourgeois imagination, Cora!

EDDIE: Will you idiots stop fooling and let me think!

PETE: But we're not fooling, Eddie, and you don't have to think! Your article practically writes itself. Just compare this [*waving toward* PORTRAIT], this piece of tripe with proletarian art as a whole. Proletarian Art—so clean, so wholesome, so vigorous, in spite of the vileness and misery with which it deals, because

it is revolutionary, because it is realistic, because it is dynamic—
the vanguard of human progress, the expression of forces
which can have but one—only one!—inevitable outcome!

CORA: Paradise!

BITOY: Heaven itself!

PETE: No tyrants, no capitalists, no social classes—

BITOY: No halitosis and no B.O.!

CORA: Freedom from Kolynos! Freedom from Life Buoy!

PETE: And there you are, Eddie—you've got a fighting article!

EDDIE: Oh, I don't know, I don't know . . .

PETE: What's wrong with it?

EDDIE: Well, as Cora says—it's old hat; it's going out of fashion.

BITOY: How can loving your fellowman ever go out of fashion?

PETE: My dear boy, you must distinguish between doing a thing
and writing *about* it. We are all writers here; and it is our privilege to write about things, like loving one's fellowman, or like
organizing the proletariat. But the kind of writing we do—
alas!—*can* go out of fashion. Look at Eddie here. He says he
is sick of writing about social consciousness—which does *not*
mean that he's sick of social consciousness. Or does it?

EDDIE: Oh, no, no. How I love the lower classes!

CORA: If only they would use Kolynos—

BITOY: And take a bath every day—

PETE: And wear a necktie and coat like Eddie here—

EDDIE: And be able to discourse on Marxism and Trotskyism
like Pete here—

CORA: Boys, boys—no bickering.

EDDIE: Cora—

CORA: Yes, darling?

EDDIE: Shut up.

CORA: That's what I like about Eddie. He knows how to deal
with common people. And if you love the common people so
much, Eddie, we've got lots and lots of them right where we
work. They're down among the machines, and they're there
every day—right in the same building with us. They're small
and they smell of sweat and they live on fish. I'm surprised at
you fellows. Here's the proletariat right under your noses,
day in and day out, but I never see you fellows going down to

organize them—or to fraternize with them. As a matter of fact, I have noticed that you actually *avoid* going down to them. You always try to send somebody else to deal with them. Now why? Don't they speak the same language—or are you afraid?

PETE: Cora, Cora, you misjudge us. What you take for fear is not fear at all—merely awe and reverence.

BITOY: Besides, it's so much easier to love the proletariat from a distance.

PETE: A very safe distance.

CORA: From the smell of sweat and fish.

EDDIE: And that's what all our social consciousness amounts to. Just yap-yap-yap from a safe literary distance. Just the yap-yap-yap of a literary fashion . . .

CORA: In other words—

CORA and BITOY [*together*]: Just yap-yap-yap—

CORA: Period.

EDDIE: Remember when all the world was divided between the Boobs and the Bright Young People? *We* were the Bright Young People, and the Boobs were all those little hicks and Babbits who weren't reading Mr. Sinclair Lewis and Mr. Mencken and the beautiful Mr. Cabell.

CORA: And then, suddenly, those little hicks became the Proletariat.

PETE: Yes—and everybody else were just horrid bourgeois and reactionaries.

EDDIE: And of course *we* were the Champions of the Proletariat, *we* were the Spearhead of Progress, *we* were the Revolution! Didn't we know all about cartels and strikes and dialectics!

CORA: And if we never did go to fight in Spain—well, we did go to the Writers' Congresses in New York.

EDDIE: And now we've divided the world into Fascists and Men of Good Will.

PETE: Ourselves being the Men of Good Will.

CORA: And Pink is no longer the fashionable color. We're now wearing the patriotic red-white-and-blue. It's no longer smart to be a fellow-traveler. We've all become Fourth-of-July orators.

EDDIE: One thing you can say for us anyway—when it comes to literary fashions, we're always right out in front—

PETE: Always right out in the field—

CORA: Behaving as the wind behaves.

BITOY: I wonder what the fashion will be tomorrow?

CORA: I hope it won't be loving those so polite and so heroic Japanese, the champions of Oriental dignity.

BITOY: Oh, impossible!

CORA: Because the marines will keep 'em flying?

BITOY: Because our fashions are always made in America—and imagine the comrades in America starting a fashion to love the Japs! Oh, there's going to be a war, fellows—there's going to be a war! And alas for Culture, alas for Art!

EDDIE: To hell with Culture! To hell with Art! I hope the war breaks out tomorrow!

PETE: I hope it breaks out tonight!

EDDIE: A really big, bloody, blasting war that blows up everything!

PETE: The bigger the better!

CORA: You fellows make me laugh.

PETE: Eddie, we make her laugh!

EDDIE [*in falsetto*]: We're Pollyanna, the Glad Girl!

PETE and EDDIE [*joining hands and prancing about*]: We are the happy, happy boys, who bid your lonely hearts rejoice!

CORA [*drily*]: Ha-ha-ha.

EDDIE: There, we made her laugh again!

CORA: Oh, you fellows are funny all right. Praying for a war—just so you won't have to face up to that picture.

PETE: Eddie, don't we want to face up to this picture?

CORA: No, you're afraid.

EDDIE [*in earnest*]: To hell with that picture! With a big war about to blow us up any moment, who wants to bother about pictures? The times we live in are too tremendous to waste on the pretty visions of poets and artists! Over in Europe, young men are dying by the thousands at this very moment! The future of Democracy and of the human race itself is in peril! And you want us to stand here and wrestle with one little painting by one little man! Think of what's happening right now in England! Think of what's happening right now in China! [*He pauses.*]

CORA: Go on.

EDDIE: Go on what?

CORA: Go on piling up more reasons for not looking at that picture. Go on justifying yourself for running away from it.

PETE: Now wait a minute. Why should we be afraid of this picture?

CORA: Because it is a work of art—and it makes us all feel very bogus and very impotent.

PETE: It doesn't make me feel anything of the sort!

CORA: Oh no?

[*A pause, during which they all look toward* PORTRAIT.]

PETE: No . . . No, it doesn't make me feel anything of the sort! Who is this Don Lorenzo that I should be afraid to face his portrait?

CORA: He is the creator, and we are the counterfeiters. He is the Angel of Judgment come out of the Past.

PETE: Well, I'm the Present—and I refuse to be judged by the Past! It is the Past rather that has to be judged by me! If there's anything wrong with me, then the Past had something to do with it! Afraid? Who's afraid? I stand here and I face you, Don Lorenzo, and I ask you: What were you and what did you do that you should have the right to judge me?

BITOY: Pete, Pete—he did what he could! He wrote, he painted, he organized, he fought in the Revolution.

PETE: And so what? How about afterward? Did he have the guts to go on fighting? Did he even go on painting? All his best work was done before the Revolution. What has he produced since then? Just this one picture—and he painted this only recently. How about all the time between? What was he doing during all those years?

[*He looks around at his listeners; no one answers; and he smiles.*]

You see? But Bitoy here will tell us. Bitoy knows.

BITOY: What do you mean, Pete?

PETE: Go on—tell us about their gatherings—the gatherings of these old men, these old veterans, these relics of the glorious Past! You know, you were there. What do you call those gatherings?

BITOY: Tertulias.

PETE: Yes, the Tertulias! And what did they do there? What did these old men do?

BITOY: Well, they . . . they talked.

PETE: About what? But don't tell me. I can guess. They talked about the Past. They talked about their student days in Manila and in Madrid and in Paris. They talked about the old feuds and bickerings among the patriots. And, of course—in tones of hushed adoration—they talked about their General!

BITOY: Yes—but they also talked about poetry and art and the theatre, and about politics, and about religion.

PETE: Oh, I can almost see them—those pitiful old men—gathered in this room and consoling each other; drinking chocolate and fighting over and over again the Battle of Balintawak and the Battle of San Juan and the Battle of Tils Pass! They had to feel important—so, they reminded each other how brave they used to be. They had been thrust aside and forgotten—so, they hated the Present. They thought it rude and vulgar and on its way to damnation. Isn't that right, Bitoy?

BITOY: There were many things they didn't like about the Present.

PETE: But most of all, they didn't like the men now running the government.

BITOY: No—not much.

PETE: And that's how the Revolution ended! *That's* how the Revolution ended! Groups of embittered envious old men gathering in dusty bookshops and bankrupt drugstores and broken-down tenements like this one! Just look around this room—what does it proclaim? Failure! Defeat! Poverty! Nostalgia! And here they would gather—those bitter old men—to sigh over the Past, to curse the Present, and to execrate the men in power! But what had happened to these old warriors? During the Revolution, *they* were the big ones, *they* were the men in power. Why did they lose that power? Why were they thrust aside and forgotten? Because they were not big enough after all to handle the Future! Because they tried to stop the clock! Oh, it's always the same story: the revolutionaries of today, the reactionaries of tomorrow! And so new men arose—new men displaced them—younger and bolder men who were not afraid to be rude and vulgar and damned! Can you name a single top figure of the Revolution who managed to remain on top in the age that followed? No—they were all swept away! Oh, maybe it's just as well that Rizal and Bonifacio and Mabini died young! Who knows? They may only have swelled the ranks of the old and the obsolete; they may only have rotted away in obscurity and resentment; they may only have frittered their lives away going from one tertulia to another, to drink chocolate and to regret. Like Don Lorenzo here. Yes, like this great Don Lorenzo! Look at him! He has been eating his heart away in obscurity and resentment. He wants to comfort his pride, to justify his failure—so, what does he do? So, he paints himself as a hero—as THE hero, in fact—as Aeneas! There he stands—in classic raiment, in a classic pose, and with the noble classic landscape behind him. He has removed himself completely from his native land—because his native land has discarded him. He has placed himself entirely above the rude and vulgar Present—because the Present refuses to recognize his importance. What a pitiful picture! Oh, what a pitiful, pitiful picture! A Portrait of the Artist as Obsolete!

[*A silence. They are all staring at* PORTRAIT. *Unnoticed,* SUSAN *and* VIOLET *come up the stairs and pause on the landing, surprised at the mutely staring people in the sala. They glance at each other and giggle behind their hands. Susan and Violet are "old girls," plumpish, cute-mannered, and thickly painted. They are wearing tight-fitting sleeveless frocks; and they are both quite tipsy.*]

VIOLET [*leaning forward, cupping her mouth with a hand*]: Yoo-hoo!

[*Everybody in the sala gives a nervous start. Susan and Violet giggle wildly.*]

CORA [*tartly*]: Who are you?

TONY [*rising*]: Holy cow!

SUSAN [*ignoring Tony*]: Excuse us for intruding.

VIOLET: Don't you people know us?

SUSAN: I'm Susan.

VIOLET: And I'm Violet.

SUSAN: We're artists.

VIOLET: At the Parisian Theatre. You know, [*wiggling her torso*] vaudeville!

PETE [*hurrying toward them*]: But of course we know you! Certainly we know you! Susan and Violet, the brightest stars of the Manila stage! Why, girls—I'm one of your most avid admirers! I never miss a show!

[*More giggles from Susan and Violet.*]

And what a break! What a God-given break! Come in, girls—come *right* in! Cora, get your camera.

CORA [*rising*]: What are you up to now?

PETE: I said, get your camera.

[*Cora goes for camera.*]

VIOLET: Goodness, do you want to take pictures of us?

SUSAN: Are you people from the newspapers?

PETE: We're from the "Daily Scream"—and we're going to put you girls right on the cover of our Sunday magazine.

SUSAN [*suspiciously*]: Why?

PETE: Because you are great and honest artists.

SUSAN: Quit your kidding, mister.

PETE: Don't you want your picture taken?

VIOLET: Oh, but not now! We look terrible now!

PETE: You look wonderful.

VIOLET [*giggling*]: Frankly, mister—we're *groggy*.

SUSAN: I'm not. I feel just fine.

VIOLET: We met a couple of sailors down the street. We just said to them, we just said: "Keep 'em flying, boys!" And you know what? They took us off with them and bought us all the drinks we could hold!

SUSAN: Oh, they were nice. Real gentlemen.

TONY [*approaching at last; grimly*]: What are you two doing up here?

VIOLET: Hi, Tony.

SUSAN: We just wanted to see where you live.

TONY: Okay, you've seen it. Now, scram!

SUSAN: Now look here, Tony—don't you talk to me that way! We'll stay as long as we like!

PETE: Of course you're going to stay. Come on, Tony—be a pal. We want to take their pictures.

VIOLET: Can you beat it! The man is serious!

PETE: You bet I'm serious! Come over here, girls.

VIOLET [*giggling; hurriedly fixing herself up*]: Oh, but we look awful really! Fine cover girls *we'll* make!

SUSAN [*following sullenly*]: I hope this ain't a gag or something.

CORA: What girlish optimism!

PETE [*posing girls in front of* PORTRAIT; *their backs to audience*]: Now, just stand right there. Ready, Cora?

CORA: I hope you know what you're doing.

BITOY: Pete, lay off for God's sake!

EDDIE: Oh, leave him alone. He's just putting Don Lorenzo in his place.

PETE: Yeah—among his fellow-artists. I'll teach him to act superior. Now look, girls. [*Pointing up to* PORTRAIT] See that picture?

VIOLET [*looking up*]: Hm, very pretty.

SUSAN: What are those two guys doing? Playing leap-frog?

PETE: The young man is carrying the old man on his back. They're evacuating from a war, see?

VIOLET: What happened to their ottomobile?

EDDIE: Oh, it got commandeered by the army.

SUSAN [*still staring up*]: What horrible eyes!

PETE: You mean, the old man?

SUSAN [*nervously adjusting a shoulder-strap*]: He makes me feel naked, he gives me the creeps—
[*Both girls are staring fixedly at* PORTRAIT.]

PETE [*backing away from camera-range*]: Hold it, girls! No, no—don't look at the camera—look up at the picture! That's right. Get it, Cora!
[*Cora flashes picture.*]
And there we are—all nice and pretty. Thank you, girls.

VIOLET [*approaching Pete*]: Will you really put us on your magazine cover?

PETE: Absolutely! And with the fanciest title I can think of. What would you suggest, Eddie?

EDDIE: How about "A Portrait of One Dead Artist and Two Live Ones"?

CORA: Corny.

PETE: Yeah. I want something with more snap to it.

CORA: Why not try a four-letter word?

SUSAN [*who's still standing in same place, staring up at* PORTRAIT]: He really has got horrible eyes!

VIOLET: Can you beat it! She's fascinated with that old bird! Hey, Susan—he won't eat you up!

SUSAN [*her eyes never leaving* PORTRAIT]: He looks like my father . . .

EDDIE: Your father must be a very distinguished man.

SUSAN [*impatiently*]: Oh, I don't mean they look *alike*! I mean they look *at* me in the same way—

EDDIE: Your father must be a very refined man.

SUSAN: Oh yes—*very* refined. That's why I left home. Whenever I did something bad, he never said anything. He just looked at me [*nodding at* PORTRAIT] like that old guy up there. Oh, damn him! He gives me the creeps!

PETE: Why, you haven't been doing anything wrong, have you?

SUSAN: No, I haven't! And even if I have, what right has he to look at me like that? He's not my father!

EDDIE: Nobody says he is.

SUSAN [*suddenly screaming*]: Then why the hell is he looking at me like that!

TONY: [*approaching*]: Now look, Susan—you're dead drunk. And we've got a show in an hour. You go home— [*He lays a hand on her arm.*]

SUSAN: I'll go home when I damn please! And take your hands off me!

TONY: What's eating you anyway?

SUSAN: A lot you care!

TONY: Oh, it's something I did, is it?

SUSAN: Where were you last night? Where did you go after the show?

TONY: I had a head-ache. So I came straight home.

SUSAN: You never bothered to tell me, did you? You didn't even remember we had a date, did you?

TONY: Sorry. I forgot. But I had such a splitting head-ache—

SUSAN: Don't make me laugh!

TONY: Now listen, Susan—the show goes on in an hour. You've got to sober up. Violet, you take her home and give her a bath.

VIOLET: I'll do nothing of the sort. We came here to rehearse.

TONY: Rehearse what?

VIOLET [*singing and wiggling*]: *"A-tisket, a-tasket, a brown and yellow basket—"* It's the new number we do. We were supposed to rehearse it last night after the show but we couldn't find you anywhere.

SUSAN: He had a head-ache, Violet. Hah!

TONY [*striding fiercely toward piano*]: Okay, okay—so let's rehearse!

VIOLET: You won't mind, boys, will you?

EDDIE: We'll be delighted!

VIOLET: Come on, Susan.

[*They go to piano where Tony is already seated and rattling off the opening flourish. Standing side by side, just behind Tony, they go into the "A-tisket, a-tasket" number with all the appropriate motions. The girls being—uh—plastered, their performance is spirited, of course, but hardly melodious. The newspaper folk listen a moment; then resume their talk, being obliged to raise their voices.*]

CORA: Enjoying yourself, Pete?

PETE: I'm thrilled!

EDDIE: So am I! Hooray for boogie-woogie!

BITOY [*grimly*]: I hope the war breaks out tomorrow!

CORA: I hope it breaks out tonight!

PETE: Look around you, fellows! Think of it! This room—those chairs—that classic painting—those pictures on the walls—

CORA: They ought to drop down from the walls!

PETE: But they don't! They can't!

EDDIE: They're helpless! They're dead!

PETE: Hooray!

CORA [*sarcastic*]: But we're alive—hooray! We can do what we please!

BITOY: Like playing boogie–woogie here!

PETE: Exactly! Oh, think of it! The boogie–woogie—in this room—in this house—in this Temple of the Past—where the bitter old men gathered to recall the old days! Oh, look around you! Savor it fully!

BITOY: What? The outrage?

EDDIE: And there's your title, Pete! "The Boogie–Woogie Invades a Temple of the Past"!

CORA: It's an invasion all right! Are we the barbarians?

BITOY: No, we're Nero—with his fiddle!

[*Candida and Paula have appeared in doorway and are looking rather dazedly round the room. Tony, intent on his playing, does not see them. Susan and Violet go on singing and dancing.*]

PETE: And *there* you are, Miss Marasigan *and* Miss Marasigan!

[*Candida and Paula come downstage.*]

We're speechless with admiration for your father's painting!

CANDIDA: What did you say?

PETE [*shouting*]: I said, we admire your father's painting! We love it, we adore it, we are delirious over it! Could we borrow it for a few weeks?

CANDIDA: What was that?

BITOY: Oh, cut it out, Pete!

EDDIE: But that's what we came for!

CORA: Then, dammit, let's shelve the whole idea!

PETE: Will you people shut up and let me handle this!

CANDIDA: But what are you saying? What is all this?

PAULA: *Please*! Just what do you want of us?

PETE: We want you to lend us this painting!

CANDIDA: What!

PAULA: Lend you our painting!

EDDIE: For a worthy cause!

CANDIDA: What will you do with it?

PETE: We are putting on an Art Show—a benefit Art Show!

EDDIE: We belong to the G.U.D.M!

PAULA: What is that?

PETE: The Global Union of Democratic Men—and we are putting on this show to raise funds!

EDDIE: Funds to help the Democratic cause all over the world!

PETE: We need this painting, Miss Marasigan!

EDDIE: You must lend it to us!

PAULA: We are sorry but we cannot do it!

CANDIDA: It is impossible!

PETE: Only for a few weeks!

BITOY: You heard what they said!

EDDIE: But why impossible?

PETE: They can do it—only they won't!

CORA: After all, the picture is their property!

PETE: If it's a Work of Art it belongs to the people!

EDDIE: It belongs to the whole world!

CANDIDA: No, no—*no*! The picture belongs to us! It must never leave our house!

PETE [*thundering*]: Miss Marasigan, your father fought for freedom, he fought for democracy! He is an old man now and can fight no more in the battlefields—but it is merely right and fitting that this picture of his should go forth in his place—to fight for freedom, to fight for democracy—in this dark hour when all over the world freedom and democracy are in peril! He himself would wish it so! Miss Marasigan, it is your duty to lend us this picture for the Cause! It is your duty to help in the struggle to preserve this way of life we all enjoy! This life of happiness, peace, and dignity!

[*Susan and Violet have reached the climax of their number and are now really yelling at the tops of their voices. So is Pete.*]

Think, Miss Marasigan—think of what's going on right now all over the world! Young men dying by the thousands! Women and children shattered into pieces! Entire cities wiped out as bombs rain down from the skies! Death, hunger, murder, and pestilence—and power-mad dictators wallowing in the blood of humanity! This is no time for selfishness! This is no time for private sentiments! We are all involved, we are all in danger! The bell tolls for all mankind! And it is your duty to send this picture to fight! It is your duty to help the Cause of your father! It is your duty—

CANDIDA [*clapping her hands to her ears and screaming*]: Oh stop, stop, STOP! [*The group at piano breaks off abruptly. There is a moment of startled silence. Candida recovers herself.*]

I . . . I am sorry. Please excuse me.

VIOLET: Can you beat it! They're hysterical! What's the matter? Don't you people like our singing?

TONY [*rising*]: Okay, girls—go home.

SUSAN: Wait a minute! Just what did we do?

TONY: I said, go home.

VIOLET: But why? Oh, are those your landladies, Tony? Well, why not introduce us?

SUSAN [*ambling forward; an arm akimbo*]: He's ashamed of us, Violet. He thinks we don't look decent. He thinks we're drunk.

TONY [*hurrying after her and grabbing her arm*]: I told you to get out of here!

SUSAN [*wrenching her arm loose*]: I'll go when I damn please! I've got as much right to stay here as anybody else! You think I don't know what kind of a house this is? Oh, I found out last night, dearie! I saw you and that Shanghai woman—

TONY [*raising a fist*]: SHUT UP! Shut up or, by God, I'll—

SUSAN [*backing off*]: Yes, I saw you! I saw you last night! And I saw you bring that woman in here!

[*She turns to the sisters*] Now, is that the kind of a house you run?

[*She turns to* PORTRAIT]: And is that the kind of a house *you* run?

TONY [*grabbing her arm and dragging her off*]: You're getting out of here if I have to throw you out!

SUSAN [*screaming & struggling*]: Let me go! Let me go! Let me—AOUH!

[*He has slapped her hard across the mouth. She cowers away, holding her mouth.*]

TONY: Now get out! GET OUT OF HERE!

VIOLET [*taking the sobbing Susan in her arms*]: Okay, big boy— keep your shirt on! We're going. Come on, Susan.

[*She leads the sobbing Susan away. At stairway, she pauses and looks back.*]

Hitting a woman when she's drunk—pah!

[*Tony waits until they have gone down the stairs; then he strides off to his room, slamming the door behind him.*]

BITOY: Fellows, I think we had better go.

PETE: Miss Marasigan, about that matter—

CANDIDA [*quietly*]: It is quite impossible. We cannot lend you the picture. We are sorry.

PETE: Well . . . [*He shrugs.*] Well, thanks just the same—and thanks for letting us come. And good afternoon.

[*Chorus of "Thank you's" and "Good afternoon's" from the others as they move to stairway, Candida and Paula accompanying them. Exeunt Pete, Eddie, and Cora. Bitoy lingers behind on the landing.*]

CANDIDA: Well, Bitoy—you said your friends were coming just to see the picture.

PAULA: You said nothing about their wanting to borrow it.

BITOY: I'm sorry.

CANDIDA: Did they really like the picture?

BITOY: No—I don't think so.

CANDIDA: Which is just what we thought. Nobody ever likes that picture.

BITOY [*gazing toward* PORTRAIT]: I do.

PAULA: But you are an old friend. Other people are not so kind. They say that the picture is beautiful but they do not find it enchanting.

BITOY: Why should they? Art is not magic. Its purpose is not to enchant—but to disenchant!

PAULA: Jesús!

CANDIDA: How impressive you sound!

BITOY: May I come again?

PAULA [*smiling*]: Do you enjoy being disenchanted?

BITOY: No—but I need to be.

CANDIDA: Come whenever you like, Bitoy. We are always at home.

BITOY: Thank you—and goodbye till then.

CANDIDA & PAULA: Goodbye, Bitoy.

[*Exit Bitoy. Paula and Candida leave stairway and begin moving back the chairs and table to their proper place at center with the sofa. From this point, twilight starts and the stage dims very gradually.*]

PAULA [*as they shift the furniture*]: What are we going to do, Candida?

CANDIDA: About what?

PAULA [*nodding toward Tony's door*]: About him.

CANDIDA: We must order him to leave this house.

PAULA: Yes—certainly!

CANDIDA: Bringing a woman here—

PAULA: And then *lying* about it!

CANDIDA: Oh, we have been too lenient!

PAULA: Well, we needed the money.

CANDIDA: He can take his money somewhere else—and at once! He shall leave this house immediately!

[*Tony's door opens and he comes out, wearing his coat and carrying his hat. He now looks gentle and rather wistful. The sisters stiffen and assume their coldest expressions. Candida raps on the table.*]

Mr. Javier, please come over here. We have something to say to you.

TONY [*approaching; guiltily fingering his hat*]: Yes, I know. And there's something I would like to say to you too.

CANDIDA: There is nothing you can say that would interest us!

TONY: Look, if a man asked you to save his soul—would you refuse?

CANDIDA: What nonsense!

PAULA: Why should any man ask us to save his soul?

CANDIDA: Who are we—God?

TONY: You are good, both of you.

CANDIDA: We have had enough of your flatteries, Mr. Javier—

PAULA: *Both* of us!

CANDIDA: And of your lies!

TONY: Then you refuse?

PAULA: We refuse to be flattered and deceived over and over again!

TONY: But look here—I'm not flattering you, I'm not deceiving you! Oh, please believe me! This house is my salvation! This is the one place in the world where I've wanted to be good, where I've tried to be good! Yes, you smile—you don't believe me. Oh, I deserve that all right! I know I'm bad, I know I'm wicked—but that's just the point! I know what I am. Isn't that the beginning of salvation?

CANDIDA: That you recognize your wickedness?

TONY: And feel very ashamed of it.

PAULA: Then why do you continue? Why do you do these things?

TONY [*with a shrug*]: The habits of a lifetime.

PAULA: And you do them here, in this house that you call your salvation!

TONY: Oh, I get so disgusted sometimes!

CANDIDA: With our house?

TONY: With myself.

PAULA: You get disgusted with yourself—but it is our house you defile!

TONY: Yes . . . Remember the first time I came here? Oh, I was in a beautiful condition! I had just lost my job and I had been thrown out of the filthy flop-house where I was staying because of a fight. So I came here. I had seen the sign at the door and I thought this was just another Intramuros flop-house. But as I came up those stairs I suddenly felt as if I was coming home at last. Everything looked so clean, everything was so quiet. This was the home I never had; the home that nobody ever gave me. Oh, I was drunk—I had been drunk for a week—and I felt so ashamed of myself standing here in my dirty shoes and my dirty clothes that—you know what I did? I spat on the floor! Now, do you understand?

CANDIDA [*coldly*]: No.

TONY: Of course not! How could you? You were born in this house, you grew up in this house! Do you know where I was born? Do you know where I grew up? Listen: When you were going off to your fine convent-school in your fine clean clothes, I was wandering about in the streets—a little child dressed in rags, always dirty, always hungry. And you know where I found my food? In the garbage cans!

PAULA [*sinking weakly into a chair*]: Oh no!

TONY: Oh yes! And do you know what it's like to go begging in the streets when you're still just a baby? Do you know what it's like to have your own brute of a father driving you out to beg? Can you even imagine that kind of a childhood?

CANDIDA [*sinking down too, on the sofa*]: We know you have had a hard life—

TONY: You know nothing! [*A pause, while he scowls at the memory. Then the scowl fades into a bravado smile.*] Oh, I'm not crying over anything! I never cry! I haven't had a hard time really. I've always been strong and tough, and I'm clever, and I learn fast. Besides, I'm very good-looking, you know, and I've got a lot of charm. Heck, I don't care if that sounds vain—it's the truth! Ever since I was a kid, people have been fascinated with me—they pick me up and give me the breaks. Nice people, too—people with class. Well, just to be completely honest, I'll admit that when they get to know me they drop me quicker than a hot brick! But what the heck—somebody else always comes along and picks me up again. I'm irresistible! All I have to do is smile and look sort of pathetic—you know: very young, very brave, and very broke. They always fall for that. Oh, I've been using my charm to get me places—and it sure has got me far! Before I was twenty, I had been to America.

PAULA [*in admiration*]: To America!

TONY [*his chest swelling*]: San Francisco, Los Angeles, Chicago, New Orleans, Mexico City, Havana, and New York!

PAULA: But how wonderful!

CANDIDA: [*quite impressed herself*]: How did you do it?

TONY: Oh, an old American couple picked me up and took me along. They were nuts about me. They said I looked like the Infant Samuel.

CANDIDA: Did you have a nice time?

TONY: Wow! The time of my life! Until they dropped me. And then—oh, Jesus!—did I have to slave! But I didn't mind. It was all part of my education. I was educating myself; I was running away from home. I've been running away from home, you know, all my life—as far away as I can get. But even America wasn't far enough. [*He glances wistfully around the room.*]

No fooling—this house is the farthest I've got away from my childhood . . .

This house and the piano—any piano . . .
[*The wistfulness darkens again into a scowl.*]
But of course you ladies would say that I never left home!
As far as you're concerned, I'm still vermin, I'm still trash,
I'm still the Tondo slums!
[*He whirls around at* PORTRAIT.]
See how your father looks at me! And you wonder why I
do the things I do here!

CANDIDA: To spite us?

TONY: And to spite this house—and everything in it!

CANDIDA: And you say this house is your salvation!

PAULA: But do you like it or do you hate it? You change so suddenly from one moment to another. How can we know when
to believe you? How can we know when you are serious?

TONY [*suddenly grinning again*]: How can you? I never know
myself!

CANDIDA: Oh Paula, this is all just the same as usual. He is
only making fun of us!

TONY: Oh no—honest, I'm not!

CANDIDA: Were you serious when you asked us to save your soul?

TONY [*clapping a hand to his brow*]: Oh Lord, did I ask you to
do that?
[*The sisters smile helplessly.*]

PAULA: You certainly did!

TONY [*bending down*]: And will you?

CANDIDA: Are you serious?

TONY [*throwing his hands up*]: Maybe I am and maybe I'm not.
Oh, the hell with it! Does it matter anyway? Look, just tell me
what answer will please you and I will give you that answer.

CANDIDA: Is that your sincerity?

TONY: I'm a poor man—I can't afford sincerity. I have to suit
my moods to the moods of my betters. That's one of the very
first things I learned—and now I'm an expert. Oh, it's not
hard. Nothing I feel ever goes deep enough to make me cry
anyway. So, I'll change my moods and I'll change my colors
if it's to my advantage and if it gets me what I want. *That's*
my sincerity! So, come on—tell me: do you want me to be
serious or do you want me to be funny?

CANDIDA: Oh, you are impossible!

TONY: Then, you won't save my soul?

CANDIDA: It is too late.

TONY [*glancing at his watch*]: Oh Lord—yes! And I'll be late for the show! I must rush!
[*He claps his hat on and runs to stairway where he suddenly stops & turns around.*]
Oh, I forgot—you ladies had something to say to me. [*He shrugs and looks pathetic.*] Well, you may as well say it now. [*The sisters look at him; then at each other; and then down at their hands. There is a moment's silence.*]

CANDIDA [*looking up, but not toward Tony*]: We merely wanted to say, Mr. Javier, that . . . that we do not accept the testimony of intoxicated persons.

TONY [*gravely*]: I see. [*A pause.*] And is that all?

CANDIDA [*now looking toward him*]: That is all, Mr. Javier.

PAULA: Good night, Mr. Javier.

TONY [*grinning and lifting his hat high above his head*]: Good night, ladies. Good night, sweet ladies. Good night, good night! [*He puts his hat on with a swagger and runs down the stairs. The sisters burst into laughter.*]

PAULA: Oh, he is funny, is he not?

CANDIDA: It would have been unjust to ask him to leave on such doubtful evidence.

PAULA: And besides, we need the money.

CANDIDA [*rising*]: Oh, money, money, money! We must act, Paula—we must act at once. And I know just what we can do. [*She picks up newspaper.*]

PAULA: Your new plans?

CANDIDA: Yes. Listen to this. "Fifty centavos for every rat caught." Now, I wonder where this Bureau of Health and Science is? I shall go there and offer them, my services. And, Paula—

PAULA: Yes?

CANDIDA: You will give lessons.

PAULA [*horrified*]: Lessons!

CANDIDA: Lessons in the piano, lessons in Spanish. We will put up a sign.

PAULA [*rising*]: Oh no, no!

CANDIDA: Now Paula, remember—we must be bold, we must become women of the world. Did you see that newspaper girl? And she is younger than we are. We, also, can make money. It is the only way we can save this house, Paula. We must show Manolo and Pepang that we can support ourselves, that we do not need their money.

PAULA: But lessons for whom—girls?

CANDIDA: Girls for the piano, and some men for Spanish. So many of these young students are eager to learn the language nowadays. And men have more money, you know.

PAULA: They would only laugh at me.

CANDIDA: Nonsense! Be bold! Drink a little wine before you face them. Talk in a loud voice. If they become fresh, call a policeman. We could arrange to have a policeman nearby during the first days.

PAULA: You will not be here, Candida?

CANDIDA: I shall be working at this [*glancing at newspaper*] this Bureau of Health and Science. If they are so eager to pay fifty centavos for one rat, how they will welcome somebody who is willing to catch as many rats as they want. And you know how well I do it. Oh Paula, imagine being paid to do something you enjoy! They will be amazed to see what an expert I am—and my work will be extended. I shall be appointed to clear the entire city of rats. Of course, then, I would hardly have time to do the actual catching anymore. I shall be just a kind of director—with a desk, a map, and a staff of workers . . .

PAULA [*giggling*]: And they will all be calling you *Miss* Marasigan!

CANDIDA: And I shall make them all wear uniforms. [*She turns wistful.*] Still, from time to time, I should want to do some of the actual catching myself—but only in the more difficult cases, of course . . .

PAULA: And how much will you earn?

CANDIDA: I must consult Manolo on what salary to ask. Oh, they have a sea of money rolling about in the government!

PAULA: Yes indeed. Just look at the newspapers—always talking of those people who made millions!

CANDIDA: Oh, I have it all planned out. We will make money, Paula—we will make money! And we will show Manolo and Pepang that we can keep up this house with our own efforts.

PAULA [*rapturously*]: And they will not be able to turn us out of here anymore! We will not be afraid anymore!

[*She sinks down on the rocking chair.*]

CANDIDA [*sitting down at the piano*]: We shall stay here till we die! You and I and papa. Yes—and papa! He will get well, he will come out of his room, we will be happy again—just the three of us. It will be like the old days again . . .

[*She begins to play, very softly, the waltz from the "Merry Widow."*]

PAULA [*leaning back, and rocking the chair to the music*]: The old days . . . Yes, how happy we were—just the three of us— you and I and papa . . . In the mornings, we went to church, the three of us together. Then, after breakfast, you went off to market; I stayed here to clean the house, while papa read the newspapers. When you came back from market, we would all go down to the patio to take the sun—papa in his rocking chair, smoking his pipe, and you and I walking round and round the fountain, arm in arm, reciting poems or singing, while all about us the pigeons whirled . . . Then papa would fall asleep in his chair, and we would go up and do the cooking. After lunch, the siesta; and after the siesta, the merienda. Then papa would go out for his afternoon stroll, and you and I would do the washing and the ironing. After the supper, the Rosary—and then we played the piano for papa or he read to us from Calderon. If visitors dropped in, we played "Tres-siete." Remember how we would get so excited over the game that we would play on and on till past midnight? Oh, you were a shameless cheater, Candida—and what a riot when you and papa played against each other!

[*She sits still, smiling. Then she rises, humming the waltz, and begins to dance around the room, holding her skirts in her hands. As the music ends, she whirls and slowly sinks down to the floor. There is a moment of silence—Candida at the piano, her face lifted; Paula on the floor, her smiling*] *face lifted too, her hands folded on her lap. The room is dim but not dark, the forms of the sisters and of the furniture and the squares of the balconies being clearly discernible.*]

CANDIDA: Can we bring back those days again?

PAULA [*lost in thought*]: Huh?

CANDIDA: Wake up, Paula!

PAULA: What days?

CANDIDA: Those days before . . . before father had his accident— before he painted that picture.

PAULA: Oh Candida, we were happy enough then—and we did not know it! We destroyed the happiness we had . . . Oh, why did we do it, Candida, why did we do it!

CANDIDA: Hush, hush, Paula—what is done is done. Go and turn on the light.

PAULA [*rising and going to the switch, which is supposed to be on the left corner of the "fourth wall"*]: Oh, why did we do it! Why did father have that accident! Why did he ever paint that picture!

CANDIDA: All this unpleasantness will pass, Paula. We will be happy again. All we need is money—money and security. We will be at peace again—the three of us . . . Father will forgive us for what we did. And we will be all together again, we will be happy together again—the three of us . . .

PAULA [*in voice of alarm*]: Candida, there is no light!

CANDIDA [*looking around*]: What! Try again!

PAULA: I have turned this switch a dozen times. There is no light!

CANDIDA [*rising quickly*]: Try the switch on the stairway—I will try this one in the corridor.

[*Paula goes to stair-landing: Candida steps just inside the doorway at right. After a moment, she comes in again and looks at Paula across the room.*]

No light either on the stairs?

PAULA: None! How about in the corridor?

CANDIDA: None also. And I saw no light in father's room.

PAULA: Oh Candida, they have cut off our light!

CANDIDA: Sh-h-h!

[*The sisters fearfully come to center of stage where they huddle together.*]

PAULA [*whispering*]: Shall we call up the company?

CANDIDA: It would be useless . . .

PAULA: Then call up Manolo, call up Pepang! Tell them what has happened to us! They must send us the money right away! Oh, how could they do this to us! How could they possibly allow us to suffer this horrible, horrible humiliation!

CANDIDA [*bitterly*]: And how shall I call them up, Paula? Am I to go down and borrow the telephone at the corner drug-store?

PAULA: But that is where we always telephone—

CANDIDA: But how, *how* can I go down to the street now! Think, Paula—everybody who lives on this street knows by now that we have no light, that the company has cut off our light!

PAULA [*in mounting horror*]: Oh Candida . . . Oh Candida! [*Trembling, they glance behind them at the open balcony.*]

CANDIDA: Go and shut those windows.

PAULA [*shivering*]: Oh no, no! They would see me! The neighbors, Candida—they will be all gathered at their windows, watching our house, pointing at our house—the only house without light in the whole street! Oh, Candida—they are all there at the windows, pointing and laughing and jeering!

CANDIDA: Yes—and I can just imagine what they are saying. Oh, this is the chance they have long been waiting for! Yes—they will be all there watching—and "Look, look!" they will be saying, "Look at those two old maids, those two proud señoras, who are so delicate, who have such grand manners, who hold their heads so high—and look, look: they cannot even pay their light-bill!"

PAULA [*covering her face*]: Oh, this is dreadful, dreadful! How can we ever show our faces again in the street!

CANDIDA: We must close those windows.

PAULA: No, Candida! They will see us!

CANDIDA: But perhaps no one has noticed yet that we have no light . . .

[*She cautiously tip-toes toward balcony, keeping herself out of street-range. As she closes the windows, she notices something odd in the street and peers out. Then, boldly, she steps*

right out onto the balcony and looks up and down the street.
She turns around joyously and steps back into the room.]

CANDIDA: Paula, there is no light anywhere!

PAULA: No light?

CANDIDA [*with exultant relief*]: All the houses are dark! All, all of them!

PAULA: What has happened?

CANDIDA: Oh, come and look! There is a total darkness all over the city!

PAULA [*approaching balcony*]: Why, yes, yes! There is no light anywhere! [*Clasping her hands in gratitude.*] Oh, merciful, merciful God!

CANDIDA [*suddenly bursting into laughter as she moves downstage*]: But what fools we are! What ignorant fools we are!

PAULA [*following*]: What has happened?

CANDIDA [*laughing uncontrollably*]: Nothing has happened! Nothing has happened at all! Oh Paula, Paula—we must read the newspapers with more interest! It was in all the newspapers! Didn't you read it? Tonight, Paula—tonight is the night of the black-out—of the practice black-out! All the lights have been turned off!

PAULA: Why?

CANDIDA: It is part of all their preparations—they are preparing for war!

PAULA [*sighing with relief*]: Oh, is that all?

CANDIDA [*laughing hysterically*]: And we thought . . . Oh Paula, we thought. . . We thought our light had been cut off!

PAULA: Oh, thank God, thank God, thank God!

CANDIDA: And how frightened we were, Paula! We were almost trembling!

PAULA [*beginning to laugh, too*]: And we were afraid to close the windows! We were afraid to go down to the street!

CANDIDA [*gasping with laughter*]: And we . . . we were afraid that we could never . . . never show our . . . our faces again in the . . . in the street! Oh Paula—how funny! How funny we were! [*She goes off into another wild peal of laughter that ends in sudden sobs. She buries her face in her hands.*]

PAULA [*alarmed; approaching*]: Candida, Candida!

CANDIDA [*wracked with sobs*]: I can bear no more! I can bear no more!

PAULA: Candida, the neighbors will hear you!

CANDIDA [*holding out her hands before her face*]: All the humiliations, Paula . . . All the humiliations we have suffered, Paula . . . All the bitter, bitter humiliations we have suffered!

PAULA [*taking her sister in her arms*]: Hush, Candida! Compose yourself!

CANDIDA [*breaking away and standing with clenched fists before* PORTRAIT]: And there he stands! There he stands smiling! There he stands laughing at us! Oh, there he stands mocking, mocking our agony! Oh God, God, God, God! [*She sinks sobbing to the floor.*]

PAULA [*kneeling down and taking her sister again in her arms*]: Please, Candida! Please, please, Candida!

[*Candida is still sobbing wildly while Paula holds her tight and strokes her hair whispering "Candida, Candida," as*

THE CURTAIN FALLS

THE SECOND SCENE

As in preceding Scene, the curtains open on the "Intramuros Curtain," Bitoy Camacho is standing at far left, in light.

BITOY: After my father died—he died when I was about fifteen—I stopped going to the Marasigan house. I had no more time for tertulias. I had to leave school and go to work. My childhood had been spent in the tranquil innocence of the nineteen-twenties; I grew up during the hard, hard nineteen-thirties, when everybody seemed to have become poor and shabby and disillusioned and ill-tempered. I drifted from one job to another—bootblack, newsboy, baker's apprentice, waiter, pier-laborer. Sometimes I felt I had never been clean, never been happy; my childhood seemed incredible—something that had happened to somebody else. When I was working at the piers, I often passed this way late at night. I would see the windows of the Marasigan house all lighted up, and I would hear them up there, talking and laughing—Don Lorenzo, Candida, Paula, and their little crowd of shabby old folk.

[*The lights go on inside the stage; through the curtain, the sala becomes visible.*]

I would stand out here in the street—tired and dirty and hungry and sleepy—and I would think of the days when father and I went there together—me, in my pretty sailor suit and my nice white shoes. But I never felt any desire to go up there again; I despised all those people—and anyway I was too dirty. I would walk on down the street, without looking back.

[*The "Intramuros Curtain" opens, revealing the Marasigan sala in daylight.*]

I had said goodbye to that house, goodbye to that world— the world of Don Lorenzo, the world of my father. I was bitter against it; it had deceived me. I told myself that Don Lorenzo and my father had taught me nothing but lies. My childhood was a lie; the nineteen-twenties were a lie; beauty and faith and courtesy and honor and innocence were all just lies.

[*Enter* PEPANG MARASIGAN *from doorway at right. She goes to table at center where her bag is. She opens bag, takes out her cigarettes, & lights one.*]

The truth was fear—always fear—fear of the boss, of the landlord, of the police, of being late, of being sick, of losing one's job. The truth was no shoes, no money, no smoking, no loitering, no vacancy, no trespassing, and beware of the dog.

[*Pepang glances round the room, her eyes stopping at* POR-TRAIT. *Looking at it, she comes forward & stands before it, with a half-wistful, half-mocking smile.*]

When the nineteen-forties came along, I had become a finished product of my Age. I accepted it completely, and I believed in it. It was a hard world but it was the truth—and I wanted nothing but the truth.

[*Enter* MANOLO MARASIGAN *from doorway at right. He glances toward Pepang as he goes to table & helps himself to her cigarettes. Having lighted one, he comes forward too, and stands beside her, gazing up at* PORTRAIT.]

I had rejected the past and I believed in no future—only the present tense was practical. That was the way I thought—until that October afternoon—that afternoon I first went back to the Marasigan house, the afternoon I first saw that strange painting. I had gone there seeking nothing, remembering nothing, deaf to everything except the current catchwords and slogans. But when I left that house, the world outside seemed to be muffled—seemed to have receded far away enough for me to see it as a whole. I was no longer imprisoned within it; I had been released; I stood outside— and there was someone standing beside me. After all the years of bitter separation, I had found my father again.

[*The light dies out on Bitoy; he exits. Pepang & Manolo continue a moment longer to stare at* PORTRAIT *in silence.*

Pepang & Manolo have inherited their father's good looks; but in Pepang, those fine features have grown hard; in

Manolo, they have gone flabby. She looks ambitious, he looks dissipated; she is cynical, he is shifty-eyed. They are both very stylish, and becoming too stout.]

PEPANG: The hero of our childhood, Manolo.

MANOLO: Oh, he was more than that to us.

PEPANG: Only children are capable of such love.

MANOLO: He was our God the Father.

PEPANG: And the earth, the sky, the moon, the sun, the stars, and the whole universe to us!

MANOLO: The most wonderful thing that can happen to any child is to have a genius for his father. Oh, the most *wonderful* thing really!

PEPANG: And the most cruel.

MANOLO: Yes.

PEPANG: Having to break one's childhood hero—to spurn one's childhood god . . .

MANOLO: Oh Pepang, we all have to grow up!

PEPANG: Growing up is cruel. The young have no pity.

MANOLO: But look at Mr. Aeneas up there. He's carrying his old father on his back. He's carrying his father forward with him, along with all the family idols.

PEPANG: But you and I are not Aeneas . . . Manolo, is *that* what father meant?

MANOLO [*scowling*]: He always did have a sardonic sense of humor!

PEPANG: And now he has only himself to carry himself . . .

MANOLO [*testily*]: Oh, stop it, Pepang! We haven't abandoned him to die, have we? That's one of father's old tricks—getting everybody to feel sorry for him.

PEPANG [*smiling*]: Yes. Poor father! [*She turns away.*]

MANOLO: Oh, he's still the same old hero up there—still the same old god!

PEPANG: And nobody to worship him anymore. [*She sits down on sofa.*]

MANOLO: He still has got Paula and Candida, hasn't he? [*He turns away, too.*] And where can they be—those two? Haven't they shown up yet?

PEPANG: They've probably gone to market.

MANOLO: They get crazier every day.

PEPANG: We must talk to them, we must make them listen. Now remember, you promised to be firm. Where's the senator?

MANOLO: Still in father's room. And they're still talking away!

PEPANG [*glancing at her watch*]: That makes two hours of the good old days.

MANOLO: Oh, it's a regular reunion of the old boys in there.

PEPANG: With the senator around, we can make Candida and Paula listen to us. You know how they look up to him.

MANOLO: Because he's a senator?

PEPANG: Because he is a poet.

MANOLO: *Was*, Pepang—*was*! He stopped being a poet a long time ago.

PEPANG: Oh, but they still remember him the way he used to be—when he was still coming here to recite his verses—before he went into politics.

MANOLO: And forgot all about us—the old snob!

PEPANG: And besides, he is their godfather, you know.

MANOLO: Well, if the senator can persuade them to leave this house—

PEPANG: If anybody can do it, *he* can. And I've made a bargain with him. He says the government is very anxious to acquire that painting. I promised to help him persuade Candida and Paula to sell it if he will help us persuade them to leave this house.

MANOLO: I've got a buyer for the house.

PEPANG: I told you—I *already* have a buyer.

MANOLO: Now look—you leave all that business to me. After all, I'm the eldest son in this family.

PEPANG [*smoothly*]: That's just it—you *are*. And I have no confidence at all in the business ability of the men in this family.

MANOLO: Poor father! He ought to hear you!

PEPANG: We all have to grow up, you know.

MANOLO [*looking around*]: How about the furniture?

PEPANG [*rising*]: Well, let me see . . . I'll take that chandelier; I need it for my front hall. And I'll take the marble table in the study. You can have all the furniture here in the sala, Manolo—except the piano. I'll take that. And I'll take the dining room set. We can divide the plate and the silver.

MANOLO [*sarcastic*]: Oh, what for? Why not just take everything, Pepang?

PEPANG: Thank you. Maybe I will.

MANOLO [*raising his voice*]: Sure! Take everything! Take the floors and take the stairs and take the walls and take the roof—

PEPANG: Shh! The senator will hear you!

MANOLO [*lowering his voice*]: . . . and take the whole damned house! I'll cram it down your throat for you!

[*Through the ensuing scene, they speak savagely but in controlled voices.*]

PEPANG: Are we going to fight over a few old chairs?

MANOLO: Excuse me—but you have already given me the few old chairs. Do I still have to fight for *them*? You have taken everything else!

PEPANG: You know that my Mila is getting married next year—and she will need furniture.

MANOLO: If your Mila is getting married next year, *my* Roddie is getting married *this* year—and he's *going* to have furniture! I shall take all the furniture here in the sala, and all the furniture in the dining room, and all the furniture in three of the bedrooms, besides all the books and cabinets in the study, the big mirror downstairs, and the matrimonial bed!

PEPANG: Don't be funny!

MANOLO: I don't see you laughing!

PEPANG: I shall take the matrimonial bed for my Mila!

MANOLO: Okay, let's see you take it! Let's see you move anything out of this house without my permission!

PEPANG: And why should I ask your permission? Who has been paying to keep up this house for the last ten years, I'd like to know!

MANOLO: Okay, who? Are you going to tell me I don't pay my share?

PEPANG: Yes—when you remember!

MANOLO: Now listen—just because I forget to send the money now and then—

PEPANG: Forget! I have to call you up and call you up, month after month, before I can squeeze any money out of you! Pay your share! You are the eldest son—this is your duty, not mine! But if I had left you alone to do it, father would have starved to death by now! And do you think it has been easy for me? Month after month I have to ask my husband for money to support my father and sisters. Do you think I enjoy that? Do you think I don't shrink with shame when he demands why it is not *you* who are supporting them?

MANOLO: Oh, so he asks that, eh?

PEPANG: You never have any money to send here—but, oh, you have plenty of money to throw away at the races, or to lavish on your queridas!

MANOLO: Well, you can tell that husband of yours—

PEPANG [*whispering; glancing toward stairway*]: Shut up!

MANOLO: Or, no—I shall tell him myself—

PEPANG: Shut up, I tell you! They're coming!

[*Manolo sulkily throws himself into a chair. Pepang sits down on the sofa. Paula comes slowly up the stairs, carrying an umbrella and a basket full of the marketing. She looks rather bleak; but on seeing her brother & sister, hurries to them—having deposited her umbrella at stand—with a show of animation.*]

PAULA: Oh, are you two here?

MANOLO [*affectionately*]: Hello there, Paulita.

PAULA [*approaching Pepang*]: Have you been waiting long?

PEPANG: Only two hours.

PAULA: I walked all the way from Quiapo. [*She kisses Pepang on the check.*]

PEPANG: Well, how are you, baby? You look rather haggard.

PAULA: Oh Pepang, they cut off our light a week ago! We thought at first it was only the black-out—but we found afterward that it *really* had been cut off!

MANOLO [*after a pause during which he & Pepang look down at the floor*]: Yes, but you have light again now, haven't you? I went over to the company and fixed it up as soon as you called me. You have light again, no? Everything is all right now?

PAULA [*bitterly*]: Yes—everything is just fine!

[*Manolo & Pepang unwillingly glance at each other.*]

MANOLO: We are sorry it happened, Paula.

PEPANG: And where is Candida?

PAULA [*evasively*]: She . . . she went somewhere.

PEPANG [*firmly*]: *Where* did she go?

PAULA: She is out looking for a job.

MANOLO: Good God—where?

PAULA [*rather proudly*]: At the Bureau of Health & Science.

MANOLO: But whatever gave her the idea she could find a job there!

PEPANG: What does she think she is—a scientist?

PAULA: Why not? They published an advertisement, she has gone to answer it.

PEPANG: You two girls are becoming—oh, I don't know what! All these crazy ideas! And what are all those signs you have placed down there at the door? "Rooms For Rent." "Expert Lessons in the Piano." "Expert Lessons in Spanish." Who is giving all those "expert lessons"?

PAULA [*timidly*]: I am . . . I mean, I want to—I am willing—but . . .

MANOLO: But you have no pupils yet.

PAULA [*miserably*]: No—not one! Nobody has even come to inquire. And we have had those signs for a week!

[*She feels herself at point of tears and quickly moves away, toward doorway.*]

I must take this basket out to the kitchen.

PEPANO: Paula—

PAULA [*stopping but not turning around*]: Yes, Pepang?

PEPANG: Don Perico is here.

PAULA: Oh? Where?

PEPANG: In father's room.

PAULA: He has come to visit father?

PEPANG: And to talk to you and Candida.

PAULA: About what?

PEPANG: Well, he feels that being your godfather, and Candida's godfather too, he has a right to advise you two girls about your future.

[*She waits; but Paula says nothing.*]

    Paula, did you hear me?

PAULA: Yes, Pepang—but I must put these things away first. Excuse me. [*She goes out.*]

MANOLO [*rising moodily*]: Oh, the hell with it!

PEPANG: There you go again, Manolo!

MANOLO: But if they want so desperately to stay here—!

PEPANG: But how can they stay here? Do be sensible! We simply can't afford to keep up this house any longer!

MANOLO: Oh, can't we?

PEPANG [*grimly*]: Whether we can or not, I don't want to! This house gets on my nerves!

MANOLO: Yes—it gets on my nerves too . . .

PEPANG: And I refuse to be sentimental over it anymore. It will have to be sold. And you will take Candida to live with you; I will take Paula.

MANOLO: So you can have someone to look after your house while you go off and play mah-jongg with your society friends!

PEPANG: And *so your* wife can have somebody to look after *your* house while she goes off to her clubs and committees!

MANOLO: Poor Candida! Poor Paula!

PEPANG: After all, we have been supporting them all these years. The least they can do now is to be useful to us. And it's about time they learned to be of some use. They're certainly old enough!

MANOLO: They're too old to change.

PEPANG: Oh, nonsense. The trouble with them is this house, this house! They're buried alive here. It will do them good to be pulled out of here. We are really doing it only for their own good.

MANOLO: And besides, good servants are so hard to get nowadays.

PEPANG: And they will learn to be happy, they will learn to live.

MANOLO: They are happy enough here, they have their own way of life.

PEPANG: What way of life? Hiding from the world in this old house; turning over the family albums; chattering over childhood memories; worshipping at father's feet . . . Is *that* your idea of life, Manolo?

[*She picks up her compact, snaps it open, & begins to do her mouth.*]

MANOLO: Well, what's yours—playing mah-jongg?

PEPANG: Now look here—don't you want Candida to live with you?

MANOLO: I suppose you want to take *her* too?

PEPANG: My dear, your wife would never forgive me! Her need is greater than mine. She thinks her clubs and committees more important than my mah-jongg.

MANOLO: Will you stop bringing my wife into this conversation!

PEPANG: Oh, is this a conversation?

MANOLO: And all those fool things you females do!

PEPANG: At least, we females always know what we do with our time—

MANOLO: Here comes Don Perico.

PEPANG [*putting away her compact*]: But you men just sit around and *groan* at your watches.

[*Enter* DON PERICO.]

PERICO: Pepang, has my wife arrived?

PEPANG: Is she coming here, Don Perico?

PERICO: I told her to pick me up here at ten o'clock. [*He pulls out his watch.*] It is almost eleven now. [*He groans.*]

MANOLO: Senator, the women always know what they do with their time.

PERICO: I never know what they are doing, most of the time. And I have to be at Malacañan at one o'clock. The president is expecting me at lunch.

We have to discuss the present emergency. Oh, I hardly have time now even to eat!

PEPANG: Then come and sit down a moment, Don Perico. Paula has arrived. Manolo, do go and call her.

[*Exit Manolo.*]

And how do you find our father, Don Perico?

PERICO [*sitting beside her on the sofa.*]: He has gone to sleep now. [*He pauses, frowning. Don Perico is in his early seventies, a big man with silver hair, handsome & still vigorous; dressed with expensive good taste; and gleaming with success, self-confidence, and that charming democratic friendliness with which the very rich & powerful delight to astonish their inferiors. Right now, however, his frown of concern is sincere; his complacency has been shaken.]*

Pepang, what has happened to him?

PEPANG: What do you mean, Don Perico?

PERICO: Oh, I should have come to visit him before!

PEPANG: Has he changed very much?

PERICO: No—no, I would not say so. He still is the same Lorenzo I remember—very humorous, very charming. And how he can talk! Oh, no one can talk like your father, Pepang. Conversation is one of the lost arts—but your father is still a genius at it.

PEPANG: Yes, father was in fine form today—so gay, so amusing.

PERICO: And yet—something was missing . . .

PEPANG: But you must remember that he is not a young man anymore.

PERICO: About this accident that he had—it was nothing serious?

PEPANG: Oh, it was serious enough—God knows! Imagine a man of his age falling from that balcony in his room!

PERICO: And this happened a year ago?

PEPANG: Right after he finished painting that picture.

PERICO: But he suffered no serious injuries?

PEPANG: We called in the best doctors to examine him.

PERICO: Then why does he stay in bed?

PEPANG: We have long been urging him to come out of his room.

PERICO: Pepang, what has happened to him?

PEPANG: Just what did you notice, Don Perico?

PERICO: He seems to have no will to live.

[Pepang is silent, staring at him. Enter Paula & Manolo.]

PAULA *[approaching]*: Good morning, ninong. How are you?

PERICO *[rising]*: Is this Paula?

[She kisses his hand.]

Caramba, Paula—I hardly know you! You were only a little girl the last time I saw you.

PAULA: Yes, ninong—it is a long time since we have had the pleasure of your company.

PERICO: Oh Paula, Paula, you must forgive me. We people in the government—we cannot call our lives our own. Our days, hours, even our minutes—all, all belong to the nation!

PAULA: Let me congratulate you on your victory in the last elections.

PERICO: Thank you. As a senator, I find myself in a very good position to help you, Paula.

PAULA: Thank you, ninong—but we need no help.

PEPANG [*rising*]: Now, Paula—listen first!

PERICO: I have been told that your father has refused to apply for the pension to which he is entitled.

PAULA: My father will not accept any pension from the government.

PERICO: Of course, no one can force him to do so—and it is only a trifling sum anyway. But listen, Paula—you *do* desire your father's welfare, no?

PAULA: He will never take the money.

PERICO: No—and I quite respect his reasons, even while I deplore them. But he has served his country unselfishly; it is merely just that his country should not forget him in his old age.

PAULA: Ah, but his country has a poor memory!

PERICO: A poor memory—how true! We are always too excited over the latest headlines and the newest fashions. But now there is this painting . . .

[*He moves toward the* PORTRAIT, *and the others follow.*]

Yes, there is this painting . . . Thank God, there is this painting . . . The whole country is talking about it. We can no longer afford to ignore your father. He has forced us all to remember him.

MANOLO: Do you think this a great painting, senator?

PERICO: My boy, it would be impossible for me to judge this picture objectively. It is too much a part of myself. Any opinion of mine would be merely affectionate and sentimental—for this is a picture of the world of my youth, a beautifully accurate picture. Oh, I am amused when I hear these young critics accusing your father of escaping into the dead world of the past! And I pity these young critics! When we were their age, our minds were not so parochial. The past was not dead for us—certainly not the classic past. We were at home in the world of the hexameter and the Ablative Absolute; it was not a closed world to us—nor an exotic one; it was our intellectual and spiritual atmosphere. We had Homer and Virgil in our bones—as well as St. Augustine and Aquinas, Dante and Cervantes, Lord Byron and Victor Hugo. Aeneas and Bonaparte were equally real to us, and equally contemporary. It was as natural for Pepe Rizal to give his novel a Latin title as for Juan Luna to paint gladiators. Oh, you should have heard us—with our Latin tags and our classical allusions and our scholastic terminology—

PEPANG: Oh, we did, we did!

MANOLO: Remember, senator—we had the privilege of growing up in this house.

PEPANG: Father brought us up on the classics.

MANOLO: He tried to, anyway.

PEPANG: Not very successfully.

MANOLO: But, oh, the tears I shed over those Latin declensions!

PAULA: Pepang, our Latin slang, when we were children—remember?

PEPANG [laughing]: Soror mea carissima, give me a piece of your cibus!

PAULA: Nolo, nolo—quia tu es my inimica today and per omnia saecula!

PEPANG: Avida!

PAULA: Pessima!

MANOLO: Pater mi, Pater mi—veni statim! Ecce, feminae pugnantes! [They all laugh.]

PEPANG: And remember all those uproarious games he would play with us?

PAULA: With the blankets!

PEPANG: Yes—we would take the blankets and dress ourselves up in togas. And father would be Jupiter, the king of the gods—and we children would be ancient Greeks and Romans—

MANOLO: And poor mother—how she would groan over her soiled blankets!

PAULA: But father would only laugh at her! He called her the Cassandra of the Kitchen!

PEPANG: Oh, that old laugh of father's!

MANOLO: Like a roll of thunder!

PEPANG: And however angry you were with him, when he laughed at you, you simply could not go on being angry!

PAULA: Remember how poor mother would end up by simply laughing helplessly?

MANOLO: Because father would be sitting here—on an old box—very stern and solemn—Jupiter, the king of the gods!

PEPANG: Oh, father was magnificent at games like that! And you know why? Because he was not stooping down to play with us children. He shared our seriousness. When he played Jupiter, you could almost see the lightnings round his head. You forgot that his toga was only a blanket and his throne only an old box, and his crown only a bunch of old paper flowers . . . You forgot that it was all only a game—you really felt yourself on Mount Olympus . . . Oh, how many times have we all sat here wide-eyed, listening to him—and when we looked around, it was not this room that we saw—not those chairs, nor those balconies, nor that shabby street outside. What we saw was a space of blue waters, a white sail, and oars gleaming in the sunshine . . .

PERICO: Yes, that is your father all right. Oh, he was a magus. You all know what we called him at school: Lorenzo el Magnifico. There was something lordly about him, even as a boy—an air of elegance and extravagance, though he was poorer than most of us—and a marvelous vitality. He was like—But what need is there to describe him? Look— that is your father up there—that radiant young man! That is the young Lorenzo, the true Lorenzo, the magnifico. Not that bony, shivering, naked old man he is carrying on his back!

[A silence, during which they all look at PORTRAIT. Unnoticed, Candida comes up the stairs. She glances disconsolately toward the group in front of PORTRAIT; goes to the hatrack to leave her umbrella; and remains there, her head

*bowed, her back to the audience. Meanwhile, Don Perico,
who has been frowning at* PORTRAIT, *turns resolutely toward
Paula.*]

PERICO: Paula, your father tells me that this picture belongs to
you and your sister. Now listen—would the two of you be
willing to make a patriotic sacrifice?

[*He waits; but Paula is silent. Upstage, Candida turns her
face around.*]

Because if you were to be patriotic enough to give this picture, to donate this picture to the government—the government might, as a token of gratitude, be willing to set aside a
fund—a fund to be administered by your sister and
yourself—a fund sufficient to maintain your father and yourselves while he and you are alive. Your father would then
have no objection to the money; it would not be offered to
him but to you and your sister as a—well—as a kind of
reward for your generosity. Paula, I am in a position to
arrange all this. I ask you to have confidence in me. I ask you
to be generous: give this picture to your country; give this
picture to your people.

[*Paula is still silent, her head bowed. Upstage, Candida has
turned around.*]

Oh Paula, you would be making a noble and unselfish and
heroic sacrifice. As you know, our country possesses not a
single painting by your father. His great works are all
abroad—in the museums of Spain and Italy. That is why the
government is so anxious to acquire this picture. Surely, his
own land is entitled to one of his masterpieces?

PEPANG [*after a pause*]: Well, what do you say, Paula?

MANOLO: But of course, senator, Paula and Candida will want
to discuss this first between themselves. They will want to
think it over.

CANDIDA [*coming forward*]: We have no need to discuss it, we
have no need to think it over!

PEPANG: Candida!

PERICO: Oh, is this Candida? How are you, my child? Do you
remember me?

CANDIDA: I remember you, Don Perico, and I am very sorry—
but you are only wasting your time. You can go back and tell
the government that this picture is not to be had. Paula and
I will never part with it!

PEPANG: Candida, be silent and listen!

CANDIDA: I have heard all I need to hear! [*She turns quickly,
toward doorway.*]

PERICO: Candida, wait! [*She pauses.*] Come here, my child. Are
you angry with your old godfather?

CANDIDA [*turning around*]: You are the last person in the
world who should want to take this picture from us!

MANOLO: Don Perico merely wants to help our father, Candida.

PERICO: I understand how you two girls feel about this picture.
Your father has painted it for you as a last memento—and of
course you find the thought of parting with it very painful.
But if you really love your father, you will not think of
yourselves—you will think of his welfare. Now listen, Paula;
listen, Candida: I am not a doctor but I can see that there is
something wrong with your father.

[*Paula & Candida glance at each other.*]

Oh, I ought to know; I have known him all his life. We grew
up together, we went to school together, we went to Europe
together, and we fought side by side in the Revolution. I have
not seen him for a long time—and I blame myself; yes, I blame
myself! I should have come to visit him before. But, as you all
know, our roads parted a long time ago. I went my own way—
and he . . . he stayed here. When I saw him again this morning
I thought at first that he had not changed at all: he still seemed
the embodiment of grace and charm and intelligence. But we
had been too close once, he and I; we had been too intimate
once for me not to notice that—well—that there was something wrong. I could see it and I could feel it. And I know it.
There is something wrong with your father.

CANDIDA [*dully*]: Yes.

PERICO: He is sick.

PAULA & CANDIDA: Oh no!

PERICO: I think he is. Very sick. And anyway, I agree with Pepang and Manolo: this old house is not the place for him. He

needs light and fresh air and coolness and quiet. He should be under medical care; he ought to be placed in a hospital— some good private nursing-home. Now, *that* will be rather expensive; and I understand that your father—uh—that he has—well—that he has lost his money. But if you accept this offer of the government, Paula and Candida, you will have the means with which to take care of your father as he should be taken care of.

CANDIDA: He is not sick! Oh, you do not know, you do not know!

PAULA: There is no hospital that can cure him!

PEPANG: What do you mean, Paula?

CANDIDA: We mean that we cannot accept the offer.

PEPANG: Are you two out of your senses? Do you value this painting more than father's life?

PAULA: Father is not sick. And he wants to stay here.

CANDIDA: And we shall stay here with him.

MANOLO: But even if he is not sick, you cannot stay here, you should not stay here! Don't you know that a war may break out any day now? And Intramuros is the most dangerous place in the city! Oh, tell them, senator—tell them!

CANDIDA [*smiling; approaching*]: Yes, senator —tell us. What are we to do? Are we to abandon this house? Are we to abandon this house as *you* abandoned poetry? Go on, senator— tell us. Who could advise us better than you? I promise that we will do whatever you say. Do you agree, Paula?

PAULA: We will do whatever you think is best, ninong. I promise.

CANDIDA: There, we have both promised! Our lives are in your hands, senator. Think carefully, think very carefully! Oh, but what need have you to think? You made a similar decision yourself a long time ago. You yourself abandoned this house when you abandoned poetry, when you abandoned our poor little dying world of the past! Did you ever regret your decision, senator? But what a foolish question! One has only to look at you now. You are rich, you are successful, you are important—

MANOLO: Candida, be silent!

CANDIDA: I must talk. Someone must talk, no? The senator does not answer.

PERICO [*dully*]: Candida, Paula—I have no right to advise you—

CANDIDA: But why not?

PAULA: We listened to your poetry once; we will listen to you now.

CANDIDA: Surely, a senator has more authority than a poet?

PERICO: I ask you to think in terms of reality, not in terms of poetry.

PAULA: Oh, poetry is not real?

PERICO: Poetry will not save you from the bombs.

CANDIDA: No—only politics can save us.

PERICO: Candida, Paula—I feel in my bones what you feel for this house; but this is no time for poetic attitudes! If the war should catch you in this house, what would you do? You are two helpless women. And what would happen to your father?

PAULA [*smiling; looking up at* PORTRAIT]: Like Aeneas there, we would carry him on our backs!

PERICO: Yours is the classic piety—the piety indeed of Aeneas! But it is a piety that belongs to Art, not to life! It looks sublime in that picture up there; it would only look ridiculous in the real world!

CANDIDA: The sublime is always ridiculous to the world, senator.

PERICO: Then the world is right.

PAULA: You did not always think so.

CANDIDA: And how fiercely you used to stand against it! In what beautiful words, you used to pour out your scorn of its laws, your anger against its cruelty, your contempt for its malice!

PERICO: Poetry was the passing madness of my youth, a plaything of my childhood.

PAULA: But when you became a man you put away the things of a child.

PERICO: No man has a right to stand apart from the world as though he were a god.

CANDIDA: Then, what do you advise, senator? Shall we surrender—as *you* did?

PERICO [*after a staring pause*]: Why are you so bitter against me? What have I done? I saw my destiny and I followed it. I have no need to be ashamed of what I did! My whole life has been spent in the service of my country; that is more than your father can say for himself! Yes, I have grown rich, I am successful—is that a crime? What would you have wanted me to do? To go on scribbling pretty verses while my family starved? To bury myself alive as your father has buried himself alive? And what can he show for all those lost years? Nothing except this one picture? Look at yourselves, Paula and Candida—look at yourselves, and then tell me if this one picture is enough to justify what he has done to you! Oh, it is not against me that you are so bitter! It is not against me, I know! For what have I done to you?

CANDIDA: Nothing, senator. But what have you done to yourself?

PERICO [*recovering himself; embarrassed*]: I should not have said those things—

CANDIDA: You had to say them. I suppose you have long been wanting to say them?

PERICO: No, Candida—No! I do not resent your father, I admire him. He is a very happy man.

CANDIDA: Because he did what he has done?

PERICO: Because he always knew what he was doing.

CANDIDA: And *you* did not know what you were doing?

PERICO: Oh Candida, life is not so simple as it is in Art! We do not choose consciously, we do not choose deliberately—as we like to think we do. Our lives are shaped, our decisions are made by forces outside ourselves—by the world in which we live, by the people we love, by the events and fashions of our times—and by many, many other things we are hardly conscious of. Believe me: I never actually said to myself, "I do not wish to be a poet anymore because I will only starve. I shall become a politician because I want to get rich." I never said that! I went into politics with the best of intentions—and certainly with no intention of "abandoning poetry." Oh, I dreamed of bringing the radiance of poetry into the murk of politics—and I continued to think of myself as a poet a long, long time after I had ceased to be one, whether in practice or in spirit. I did not know what was happening to me—until it had happened. I thought I was boldly shaping my life according to the ideals of my youth—but my life was being shaped for me all the time—without my knowing it. Too often, one is only an innocent bystander at one's own fate . . .

CANDIDA [*approaching*]: Forgive me, ninong. [*She kisses his hand.*]

PERICO: It is you who must forgive me, Candida—if I have bitterly disappointed you. [*He shrugs.*] But I could not help it—and I cannot help you. I look back on my life and I have no regrets because I know that I would have been unable to live it differently. There is nothing I could have changed. You can choose to go along with the current—or you can choose to stay on the bank—but those who try to stop the current are hurled away and destroyed. I chose to go along with the current; your father chose to stay or the bank—and neither of us can say of the other that he did wrong. Oh I may dream wistfully now and then of the fine pale poet I used to be—but believe me, I feel no remorse for that poet. I did not kill him—he was bound to die.

[*He pauses, smiling, and looks at his hands. When he speaks again, his voice is tender and rather sad.*]

To feel that driving urge, that imperious necessity to write poetry, a poet needs an audience; he must be conscious of an audience—not only of a present audience but of a permanent one, an eternal one, an audience of all the succeeding generations. He must feel that his poems will generate new poets. Well, poetry withered away for the writers of my time because we knew that we had come to a dead end, we had come to a blind alley. We could go on writing if we liked—but we would be writing only for ourselves—and our poems would die with us, our poems would die barren. They were written in a dying tongue; our sons spoke another language. Oh, they say that no two succeeding generations ever speak the same language—but it was *literally* true of my time and of the present. My generation spoke European, the present generation speaks American. Who among the young writers now can read my poems? My poems may as well be written in Babylonian! And who among the writers of my time can say that his poems have generated new poets? No one—no, not even poor Pepe Rizal! The fathers of the young poets of today are from across the sea. They are not our sons; they are foreigners to us, and we do not even exist for them. And if I had gone on being a poet, what would I be now? A very unhappy old man, a very bitter old man—a failure and a burden—and with no respect for himself. The choice before me was between poetry and self-respect; I had to choose between Europe and America; and I chose—No I did not choose at all. I simply went along with the current. Quomodo cantabo canticum Domini in terra aliena? [*He shrugs, and looks up at* PORTRAIT.]

Look at your father up there. He has realized the tragedy of his generation. He, too, has been unable to sing. He, too, finds himself stranded in a foreign land. He, too, must carry himself to his own grave because there is no succeeding generation to carry him forward. His art will die with him. It is written in a dead language, it is written in Babylonian . . . And we all end alike—all of us old men from the last century—we all end the same. The rich and the poor, the failures and the successes, those who moved forward and those who stayed behind—our fate is the same! All, all of us must carry our own dead selves to our common grave . . . We have begotten no sons; we are a lost generation!

Caray, who would have thought we would end so dismally? Oh, we began so confidently, we began so gaily! When we were young it was morning all over the world; it was the Springtime of Freedom! And was there ever a group of young men as noisy and brilliant and boisterous as our own? Your father, and the Luna brothers, and Pepe Rizal, and Lopez Jaena, and Del Pilar—alas for all those young men! And alas for all the places where we were young together! Madrid under the Queen Regent; the Paris of the Third Republic; Rome at the end of the century; and Manila—Manila before the Revolution—la Manila de nuestros amores! Oh, they talk a lot of solemn nonsense now about the Revolution—we were not solemn! The spirit of those days was one of boyish fun, of boyish mischief! Just imagine us—with out top hats and swagger sticks and mustachios—and imagine the secret meetings in the dead of the night; the skull on the table; the dreadful oaths; the whispers and flickering candlelight; and the signing of our names in our own blood! Oh, we were all hopeless romantics! And the Revolution was a wild melodrama in the style of Galdos! And I drank it all up—all the color and the excitement and the romance! I was a poet then; the world existed only that I might put it to music! Even the Revolution was happening only to make my verses more vivid and my rhymes more audacious! I was a poet then—

[*From the stairway comes the noise of feet, and of feminine mirth & chatter.*]

MANOLO: Here come your womenfolk, senator.

PERICO [*the smile fading from his lips*]: But I was hungry and I traded my birthright—

[*Enter* Doña Loleng, Patsy, Elsa Montes, & Charlie Dacanay.]

LOLENG: Who is hungry? Hola, Manolo! And Pepang too! My dear, if I had known you were here, we would have come sooner. And are these Candida and Paula? Jesús, what big girls you are now! And how delighted I am to see you again! Your mother was one of my dearest friends. May she rest in peace, poor woman! You remember me?

PAULA & CANDIDA: Yes, Doña Loleng.

LOLENG: This is my daughter Patsy. She is my youngest. And this is Elsa Montes—*the* Elsa Montes. You have heard all about her of course. She is the girl who brought the Conga to Manila. And this is Charlie Dacanay. Oh, Mr. Dacanay is not anybody in particular—just somebody who keeps following us around, all the time. Oh Pepang, we were all over at Kikay Valero's—the charity mah-jongg, you know—and, my dear, you will never believe how much I lost! Oh, I am *rabid*! But do tell me, Paula and Candida, how is your dear papa?

PAULA: He is quite well, Doña Loleng. Thank you.

CANDIDA: He is having a nap just now.

LOLENG: But how unfortunate for me! I would like to see Lorenzo again. Oh, your father was the great hero of my girlhood! He must let me come and see him sometime.

PAULA: We will tell him, Doña Loleng.

LOLENG: And what were you saying, Perico?

PERICO: I was saying, my dear, that I was hungry—

LOLENG: You must forgive me! I forgot we were to pick you up. Charlie you brute, I told you to remind me!

PAULA: What can we offer you, ninong? What would you like?

PERICO: A mess of pottage.

LOLENG: What on earth is that?

PERICO: Just an old joke. So please do not bother, Paula. I really desire nothing.

LOLENG [*moving forward*]: And is this the painting everybody is talking about?

PERICO: Would you like to look at it, my dear?

LOLENG: We all want to look at it. Come, come—all of you. Study this work of art and be uplifted.

[*Don Perico steps away from in front of* PORTRAIT *to give place to his wife & her companions. Dressed & bejeweled in the grand style, Doña Loleng is, at fifty, still statuesque & stunning—no wrinkles, no gray hair, no baggy flesh—the eyes languid, the nose patrician, the mouth rapacious. Her daughter Patsy is eighteen, pretty, but sullen-looking. Elsa Montes is a sophisticated forty, and strenuously "chi-chi." Charlie Dacanay is around twenty-five, a typical antebellum glamour-boy, rather the worse for wear. All these people stand a moment in silence, looking up at* PORTRAIT— *Doña Loleng, sadly smiling; Patsy, sulky; Elsa, interested; and Charlie, vacant. The senator watches them ironically, standing at left side of stage. Pepang & Manolo are just behind the newcomers. Candida & Paula have quietly left the room.*]

LOLENG [*smiling at* PORTRAIT]: The young Lorenzo . . . The great hero of my girlhood . . .

PERICO: And what does he say to you, my dear?

LOLENG: He says . . . He says that I am an old woman . . .

CHARLIE: Doña Loleng, I protest!

LOLENG: Be silent, Charlie! Who asked for your consolations?

ELSA: I'm wondering myself.

PERICO: Our Charlie was only trying to be gallant, my dear.

CHARLIE: Senator, you and I belong to the days when knighthood was in flower!

PATSY: Oh, shut up, Charlie! You know how mommy loves to go around telling everybody she's an old woman.

MANOLO: Anybody as beautiful as your mother, Patsy, can afford to tell the truth. The truth can do her no harm. She is above reproach.

PERICO: Being Caesar's wife.

LOLENG: Thank you, Manolo. Thank you, Perico. You are both too kind.

CHARLIE: Now wait a minute—how about me!

PEPANG: Poor Charlie! Nobody wants his consolations!

ELSA: He could try me—but I'm not an old woman yet, am I?

LOLENG: Certainly not, Elsa—whatever people may think.

ELSA [*sweetly*]: You mean, whatever *you* may try to make them think, darling!

PATSY: Oh, mommy is a wonderful mind-reader! Talk to her about bicycles, and tomorrow she'll be telling everybody you're having an affair with the postman!

LOLENG: Patsy—

PATSY [*wide-eyed*]: Oh mommy, did I say something wrong?

LOLENG [*studying her fingernails*]: You ought not to play mah-jongg. You do not have the cold blood for it. You get nervous.

PATSY: Oh, I'm not nervous. I'm just hysterical. Charlie darling, do give me a cigarette.

CHARLIE [*fetching out his case*]: At your service, mam-selle!

LOLENG [*shaking her head*]: Uh-uh, Charlie!

CHARLIE [*lightly slapping Patsy's hand as she reaches for cigarette*]: Sorry, mam-selle—but the mamang, she say no.

PATSY [*her hair flying as she whirls around*]: But, mommy, I *must* have a smoke!

LOLENG [*languorously*]: Perico, will you tell your daughter that she cannot smoke in public? She will not listen to me.

PERICO: Charlie, remember to send me a bill for the cigarettes my family consumes.

CHARLIE: The smokes are on the house, senator. May I offer you one?

PERICO: No, Charlie. Thank you very much.

CHARLIE [*putting cigarette in his own mouth & offering the case around*]: Well, does anybody else want one? No—not you, Patsy! Elsa?

ELSA [*taking cigarette*]: Oh yes—yes indeedy!

LOLENG [*as Charlie lights his & Elsa's cigarettes*]: Elsa has been saying nothing but "Oh yes—yes indeedy!" since she came back from New York. She must have had plenty of practice over there.

ELSA: Did you say something, darling?

LOLENG: Do the women in New York say "Oh yes—yes indeedy" all the time?

ELSA: I really couldn't say. I never had time to go out with the women.

CHARLIE: I'll bet!

PEPANG: You must give us your opinion of this picture, Elsa darling. Having been to New York, you must have become frightfully cultured.

ELSA: Oh, the picture is swellegant! It's delovely! And what's more, it's very inspiring!

PERICO [*who can't believe his ears*]: My dear Elsa, did you say—*inspiring*?

ELSA: Yes, senator—it fills me with such *divine* ideas!

LOLENG: Such as what?

ELSA [*moving closer & gesturing at* PORTRAIT *with her cigarette*]: Such as a divine idea for an evening gown—a really eye-stopping evening gown—just like that absolutely stupendous costume that young man up there is wearing—see? The same cut, the same draping, and the same shade of white—no, it's not white really—more like old ivory . . .

[*Pepang, Doña Loleng & Patsy have also gathered closer in front of* PORTRAIT.]

And with those marvelous designs on the borders! Haven't you noticed them? Pepang, you *must* ask your father to give me a sketch of those designs!

MANOLO: And you said, senator, that this picture is written in Babylonian! The women seem to understand it perfectly.

CHARLIE [*staring at* PORTRAIT]: I don't understand that picture!

MANOLO: Just listen to the women, Charlie, and get wise.

ELSA [*with gestures*]: Just imagine those designs in gold embroidery—up here on the bodice—

PERICO: Yes, women can turn Art into Reality.

ELSA: And all around the hemline.

MANOLO: And the sublime into the ridiculous.

ELSA: And just look at that cute belt he's wearing!

PERICO: Naturally. They are the enemies of the Absolute.

ELSA: Will you look at that gorgeous, gorgeous belt! A sort of golden rope with little black figures hanging all around it— Oh, it's different, I tell you! It's *divine*!

PERICO: Divine is absolutely the right word!

MANOLO: The Lares and Penates, senator.

ELSA: Imagine yourself dancing the conga in a gown like that—

CHARLIE: What did you say those little black figures are?

MANOLO: They are the gods of his father.

ELSA: Your skirts flying—

CHARLIE: Then why is he wearing them around his belt?

ELSA: And those ornaments around the belt would go click-click-click—

PERICO: So the women cannot steal them, Charlie.

ELSA: As you whirled and whirled!

MANOLO: The hell they can't!

PEPANG: And what material would you use for the gown?

ELSA: Let me see . . .

CHARLIE: Who are those two guys anyway?

MANOLO: They are a fellow named Aeneas and his old father Anchises.

ELSA: Some kind of rayon velvet, I think.

CHARLIE: Who the heck are they?

PERICO: They are the Artist and his Conscience.

LOLENG: A silk tafetta would do better.

CHARLIE [*grinning at* PORTRAIT]: I don't think they like me much . . .

PEPANG: Or a yellow silk organdie.

CHARLIE: As a matter-of-fact, they don't like me at all!

PATSY: Oh Elsa, imagine a gown like that in white cotton tulle!

MANOLO: Well, Charlie—that shouldn't be a new experience for you.

ELSA]*looking around*]: Charlie, lend me your fountain-pen, will you—and a piece of paper.

[*Charlie, who's still staring fascinated at* PORTRAIT, *does not hear her.*]

MANOLO: As a matter-of-fact, all of us don't really like one another very much.

LOLENG [*looking around*]: But hurry up, hurry up, idiot!

CHARLIE [*blankly*]: Huh?

LOLENG: Pero, qué animal!

ELSA: Your fountain-pen, Charlie, and a piece of paper.

CHARLIE: Oh, sorry, girls. Here.

[*He gives Elsa his fountain-pen & pocket notebook.*]

MANOLO: No, we don't like one another at all. I wonder why we all keep hanging together.

PERICO: So we won't hang separately.

ELSA [*pondering* PORTRAIT; *fountain-pen poised over note-book*]: What I want is that clear classic effect—

MANOLO: Besides, we enjoy tormenting each other.

ELSA: A marble make-up—

PERICO: And being tormented by each other.

ELSA: The arms and one shoulder bare—

CHARLIE: I suppose you mean I enjoy being tormented?

ELSA: No jewels at all—

PERICO: Yes, Charlie—and I sympathize with you very much—

ELSA: And a Greek hair-do.

PERICO: But I cannot help you.

PATSY: And sandals, Elsa?

PERICO: You were born to be a victim—

ELSA: Sandals, of course—

PERICO: You were born to be eaten up.

ELSA: Just like those ones he's wearing. You see his red-and-black sandals? Dramatic is the word for them! Oh, I've got the whole ensemble complete in my mind. Wait—

[*She begins to sketch rapidly, glancing repeatedly at* PORTRAIT, *her companions watching intently & paying no attention to the men's talk.*]

CHARLIE: Well, well, well! And I thought I was doing the eating up! I was beginning to feel really bad about it, senator. Oh, I've got a conscience too—like that guy up there—a conscience riding on my back. I can feel its hot breath down my neck.

PERICO: That, Charlie, is *not* your conscience. It is merely the air, the weather, the climate of our times—the uneasiness of a guilty world.

MANOLO: Oh, we all feel that hot breath down our necks, Charlie, and it makes us all feel very nervous. Maybe that's why we're so damned nasty to each other. We're like vicious brats waiting to be punished and taking it out on each other.

PERICO: Or like the residents in hell, Manolo.

MANOLO: Exactly, senator!

ELSA [*showing her sketch*]: There, you see my idea? And girls, just think of the color-scheme!

CHARLIE: Okay, but who started this hell anyway, senator? Remember: I just came along and found it open for business!

LOLENG: I see your idea, Elsa, and I could use it myself . . .

PERICO: I know that it can always use anyone who just comes along and "finds it open for business," Charlie.

PATSY: I could use a gown like that on New Year's Eve . . .

CHARLIE: I could use a drink!

LOLENG: Oh Patsy! *You*—in a Greek gown?

PERICO: The drinks are on the house, Charlie. I can help you that much.

PATSY: Oh, mommy wants me to stay just a naked little baby!

CHARLIE: I wish I had stayed just a naked little brat!

MANOLO: Oh, you did!

PERICO: And you will still be one when the last trumpet blows.

LOLENG: The style of this picture is much too severe for you, darling.

MANOLO: This picture is entirely too severe on us. We're not heroes—just naked little brats!

LOLENG: Pepang, may I send my dressmaker here to see this picture?

PEPANG: But of course, Doña Loleng.

PERICO: But can the dressmaker cover up our nakedness when the trumpets blow?

ELSA: Now wait a minute—who first thought up this idea anyway?

PEPANG: Darling, *my* father first thought up this idea and anybody who wants to copy him is perfectly free to come here and do so.

LOLENG [*beginning to speak while Pepang is till speaking*]: And surely, my dear Elsa, my dressmaker can come here if she wants to without having to borrow from the lights of your talent?

PATSY [*beginning to speak while her mother is still speaking*]: Oh, mommy thinks this style too severe for me but she's quite sure she can put on some wooden shoes and look like Helen of Troy!

ELSA [*beginning to speak while Patsy is still speaking*]: Now don't think I'm sore when as a matter-of-fact I'm extremely flattered but don't you see how risky a costume like this would be for certain age-groups?

[*The next three speeches are spoken simultaneously while Elsa is still speaking.*]

MANOLO: Will you girls stop bickering over a costume in which, believe me, you would all look equally implausible and extremely uncomfortable anyway!

CHARLIE: Whoever painted that picture had a fine sense of humor all right but did he have to go and hang his damn painting around my neck!

PERICO: *"Dies irae, dies illa,*
Solvet saiclum in favilla,
Teste David cum Sybilla.
Cuanto tremor est futurus—"

[*The blast of an air-raid siren suddenly fills stage, drowning out their voices. They all jump, startled. Then, realizing what it is, they listen with bored annoyance as the siren goes on steadily screaming. Paula & Candida appear running in doorway. Through following scene, the speakers have to shout to be heard.*]

PAULA [*as Candida runs to the balcony*]: What is it? Oh, what is it!

PERICO: The Trumpets of the Apocalypse!

PAULA: Is it War?

PERICO: It is the Day of Wrath!

LOLENG: Stop your nonsense, Perico!

MANOLO: It is only the air-raid siren, Paula!

PAULA: Are we having an air-raid?

PEPANG: Of course not! We are only *pretending* there is an air-raid!

PAULA: Why?

PEPANG: So we can practice what we are to do! This is an air-raid practice!

MANOLO: A sort of rehearsal!

CANDIDA [*at balcony*]: Oh, come, Paula! Come and look! Everybody has stopped moving! All the people, and all the vehicles! [*Paula runs to balcony. After a moment, the siren stops.*]

CHARLIE: Practice black-outs, practice air-raids, practice evacuations! I'm sick of all this practising! When do we get the real thing? I wish the darned war would break out!

PATSY: Shut up, Charlie! How can you be so horrid!

PEPANG: Oh Patsy, there's nothing to be afraid of! The war will be over almost as soon as it starts!

ELSA: Those poor Japs! They'll never know what hit them!

PEPANG: And the sooner it starts—

PATSY: But not before New Year's Eve! Not before the big ball on New Year's! I want to wear my new evening gown and really make a sensation!

LOLENG: Darling, we *are* going to have the usual ball on New Year's Eve, war or no war!

PEPANG: You know what they say: Business As Usual!

ELSA [*flashing the V-sign*]: And keep 'em flying!

LOLENG: Perico, the Manila Hotel will stay open for business, no?—even if a war breaks out?

PERICO: My dear, we will all stay open for business! We will always stay open for business! We are indestructible!

ELSA: *That's* the spirit, senator! Keep 'em flying!

PERICO [*beating his breast*]: This *was* a spirit, Elsa—but, alas, it can fly no longer!

ELSA [*startled*]: Huh?

PERICO: It has lost its wings!

ELSA: Who?

PERICO: However, it has learned to crawl on the ground—oh, very fast!

ELSA: Loleng—

PERICO: And you know what? It now prefers a gutter below to the stars above!

LOLENG [*approaching*]: What do you mean, Perico?

PERICO: I mean, my dear, that we are beyond all change, beyond all hope. Therefore, we have nothing to fear. The earth will quake—but we will hardly notice. We will be too busy playing mah-jongg and talking about whose husband is sleeping with whose wife.

LOLENG: Do you know what you are saying!

PERICO: And the earthquake will affect us in no way at all. Oh, one of your tea-cups may be broken, my dear; and your mah-jongg table may lose a leg; and your dressmaker may be late for a fitting. But do not worry. After the earthquake, you will buy a new cup, you will order a new table, and your dressmaker will arrive at last. And we will all go on as before.

LOLENG: Pepang, what have you people been doing to him?

PERICO: My dear, what can anybody do to a corpse?

LOLENG: A corpse!

PERICO: Yes. I have just discovered something very funny, my dear. I have been dead for the last thirty years, and I did not know it.

LOLENG [*after a pause*]: Oh, my poor Perico! I see, I see!
[*She comes closer and places her hands on his shoulders.*]
    Oh, why did I let you come here! I should have known this would happen!

PERICO: Do you know what has happened?

LOLENG: This house, Perico—this dreadful old house! It always has this effect on you! Now do you see why I have always refused to let you come back here?

PERICO: Yes, my dear—I see.

LOLENG: Patsy, get your father's hat. We are taking him home at once—and I shall put him to bed right away.

PEPANG: Is he ill?

LOLENG: He has had a slight attack of poetry.

PEPANG [*amused*]: Mother of God!

LOLENG: Oh, there is no cause for alarm. I am used to this, I know what to do. Some aspirin, some hot soup, a good night's rest—and tomorrow he will wake up his ordinary self again.

PERICO: Of course I will, my dear.

LOLENG: Of course you will, man! You always do—remember? And you always laugh at yourself afterward, and at all the things you said and did.

PERICO: Poetry is powerless before aspirin.

PERICO: And tomorrow I will wake up my ordinary self again— healthy, wealthy, debonaire, fastidious, elegant, cool-headed, cold-blooded, confident, capable, callous, and contented!

LOLENG: Regret is ridiculous in a man of your position.

PERICO: Tomorrow I shall be thoroughly ashamed of myself for having been so ridiculous.

LOLENG: And for having felt sorry for yourself.

PERICO: And for having felt sorry for myself.

LOLENG: Believe me, Perico—you could no more have endured poverty than *I* could. We were both born for the expensive things in life. Imagine yourself without your gold studs and diamond pins, without your private tailor, without your imported wines! There is nothing of the ascetic in you, my dear Perico!

PERICO: No, my dear—I quite agree. But every now and then, a man tries to assuage his conscience by weeping over what he might have been.

LOLENG [*contemptuously*]: You men never know what you want!

PERICO: You have been very patient with me, my dear.

LOLENG: Oh, I knew I was marrying trouble when I married a poet! But I was determined to make you . . . what you are now.

PERICO: And she is absolutely right! Everything that I am, I owe to my darling wife!

PATSY [*offering hat*]: Here, mommy.

LOLENG [*taking hat*]: All right. Now go on down to the car, all of you.

PEPANG: But listen—you people cannot go now. You will have to wait until the siren sounds again. Nobody can move about in the streets during the alert.

LOLENG: Oh, *we* can. We have the senator with us, you know. [*She puts the hat on his head, arranges his tie, and straightens his coat-lapels, while her companions take their leave & go downstairs. Then, having given his coat a final brush, she steps back & surveys him.*]

There, you look presentable again! Now, say goodbye to everybody.

PERICO: Goodbye, everybody.

LOLENG [*taking him by the arm*]: Now come along. Pepang, do forgive us for hurrying away like this. And remember to give my regards to your papa.

PERICO [*suddenly struggling as his wife leads him away*] WAIT! WAIT A MINUTE! WHERE ARE PAULA AND CANDIDA?

PAULA & CANDIDA: Here we are.

PERICO [*waving with his free hand*]: Paula! Candida! Stand with your father! Stand with Lorenzo—*contra mundum*!

LOLENG [*laughing & dragging him off*]: Come along, come along, señor poeta! You have been delirious enough for one day. Bye-bye, all of you!

[*Exit Doña Loleng with her senator.*]

MANOLO [*sinking into a chair*]: Poor Don Perico!

PEPANG: The old doublecrosser!

CANDIDA: [*smiling*]: We promised to do whatever he said, Pepang—and we will keep our promise.

PAULA [*parodying Don Perico*]: We will stand with father—*contra mundum*!

PEPANG [*tartly*]: You can stand with him against anything you please—but not here, not in this house!

CANDIDA: This house shall be our fortress!

PEPANG: Candida, I have a head-ache. Please do not make it worse.

PAULA: Perhaps you too would like an aspirin, Pepang?

PEPANG: What I would like is a little sense from the two of you! Have you no eyes, have you no feelings? Do you not see what a burden this house is for me and Manolo? Do you not see how unfair it is to our families to spend so much money here—money we ought to be spending on our own homes? Do you not know that I have to fight with my husband, month after month, to get the money to support you and this house?

CANDIDA: We are not asking you nor your husband nor Manolo to support us any longer!

PAULA: We will take care of ourselves!

PEPANG: And what will you do? Take in boarders? Give "expert lessons" in Spanish? Give "expert lessons" on the piano? How very, *very* funny! Just look at yourselves! Are you the kind of women who "can take care of themselves"? You are both completely useless!

MANOLO: Pepang, I think we can discuss this without losing our tempers.

CANDIDA: There is no need to discuss it at all!

PAULA: We will never change our minds!

PEPANG: We have pampered the two of you long enough!

MANOLO: Pepang, will you let me do the talking!

PAULA: Oh, you can both go on talking forever—it will make no difference!

PEPANG: The most stubborn and stupid pair of old women!

CANDIDA: Paula, we may as well go to the kitchen.

MANOLO [*jumping up*]: You stay right here, both of you!

[*The air-raid siren begins to scream again. They pay no heed.*]

PEPANG [*raising her voice*]: Oh, I know why they want to stay in this house! I know why they like it so much here! I know— and so does everybody! I have heard people whispering about it—behind my back!

MANOLO: Whispering about what?

PEPANG: And I'll bet all the people living on this street have been talking about nothing else!

MANOLO: About what? Talking about what?

PEPANG: About these two fine sisters of ours, Manolo! Oh, they have become quite a laughing-stock—the talk of the town really—a regular scandal!

PAULA: Pepang, what are you saying! What have we done?

MANOLO: Just what is all this, Pepang? What the devil do you mean?

PEPANG: Surely you have heard the gossip?

MANOLO: I have more important things to do—thank God!

PEPANG: Oh, the shame I have suffered! Everybody knows, everybody is laughing at them!

MANOLO: WHY? WHY?

PEPANG: Because of this young man! This unspeakable young man! They have a young man living here—as a boarder! A man of loose morals—a vulgar vaudeville musician—and with the worst kind of reputation! A notorious character, in fact! But, according to what I hear, Candida and Paula are completely fascinated with him!

PAULA: *PEPANG!*

PEPANG: And he flirts with them! They allow him to flirt with them!

MANOLO: Pepang, that's enough!

PEPANG: And at their age! To be fooled at their age—and by a man of the lowest type!

MANOLO: Pepang, I told you to shut up!

PEPANG: And that is why they refuse to leave this house! They cannot bear to leave this young man! They cannot bear to be separated from him—

[*She turns away, trembling. They are tensely silent for a moment, not looking at each other. The siren stops screaming. Manolo grimly confronts his younger sisters.*]

MANOLO: Now, do you see why you cannot remain in this house?

CANDIDA: Do you believe this evil talk?

MANOLO: Do you think me so *stupid*?

PAULA: Oh, there will be enough stupid people to believe it!

MANOLO: Exactly! And their tongues will go on wagging as long as you stay in this house!

CANDIDA: The wagging of all the evil tongues in the world cannot drive us away from here!

PAULA: They are not worth our contempt!

MANOLO: And how about the good name of our family? Is that worth nothing to you either? Is our name to go on furnishing entertainment for the malicious? And what about father? Have you considered how this would hurt him?

CANDIDA: Father knows nothing of this!

MANOLO: I wonder!

PAULA: Father knows nothing of this!

MANOLO: You deceive yourselves. Father always knows! Oh, I see now why he is ill!

CANDIDA: Father is not ill!

MANOLO: Yes, he is—and I know why!

CANDIDA: He is not ill—and you do not know, you do not know!

MANOLO: What is it I do not know?

PAULA: Oh, tell them, Candida—tell them! Let them know! Why should we hide it any longer?

MANOLO: Then, there *is* something?

PAULA: Yes! Yes!

MANOLO: What have you been hiding from us?
[*A pause. Then, Candida, gripping herself together, turns around to face her brother & sister.*]

CANDIDA: Father wants to die. He tried to kill himself.

PEPANG [*sinking to a chair*]: Oh, my God.

MANOLO: To kill himself . . . When?

CANDIDA: When he had that accident. It was not an accident, Manolo. He did it on purpose.

PEPANG: But how do you know?

MANOLO: You said you did not see it happen.

CANDIDA: We did not see it happen—but we know he wanted to kill himself, we know he wanted to die.

MANOLO: Why should he want to die?

PAULA: Because of us! Because of us!

CANDIDA: I was to blame, Paula. You merely followed me.

PAULA: Oh no, no—we were in this together. We faced him together, we accused him together!

PEPANG: Accused him of what?

PAULA: Of having ruined our lives!

MANOLO: Paula! Candida!

PAULA: And we blamed him for our wasted youth, we blamed him for our poverty, we blamed him for the husbands we never had, and we blamed him for having squandered away mother's property!

PEPANG [*shutting her eyes tight*]: Poor father! Poor, poor father!

CANDIDA: Yes—we flung it all in his face—all the humiliations we have suffered since childhood because we never had enough money. And we accused him of being heartless, of being selfish, of having lived his life only for himself and for his art. We told him to look at people like Don Perico, who are now rich and successful. We told him that he, too, could have become rich like Don Perico. Why not? He had the same talents, he had had the same opportunities. But he had wasted his talents, he had wasted his opportunities—he had been too cowardly, too selfish—So, now, he must pass his old age in poverty, he must depend on charity, while Paula and I—Oh, we told him we could have made brilliant marriages if only we had been rich! We told him that it was his fault, his fault, that our youth had been wasted, that our lives had been ruined!

MANOLO: And what did he do when you had said all this?

CANDIDA: Nothing.

MANOLO: He should have slapped your faces!

PAULA: He asked us to excuse him.

[*A pause, during which they all slowly turn their faces toward* PONTRAIT.]

MANOLO: And did you never ask him to forgive you?

CANDIDA: Oh, we tried, we tried—in the days that followed. What we had done, we had done in a fit of desperation. We were ashamed of it at once. We wanted to throw ourselves at his feet—to beg him to forgive us, and to forgive all the bitter things we had said. But he would not give us the chance. He kept away from us. He had begun to paint this picture; he was working on it night and day. And when it was finished, he called us to his room and showed us this picture. He said he had painted it very especially for us, that it was his final gift to us. We wanted to kneel down then and beg his forgiveness— but he pressed the picture on us, he waved us away. And when we were at the door he said: "Goodbye, Candida. Goodbye, Paula." And then that night . . . that very night he . . . he fell from the balcony . . .

[*A pause, as she chokes back her tears. When she speaks again her voice is flatter & more desolate.*]

   Do you see? Do you see now? It could not have been an accident . . .

MANOLO [*grimly*]: No, Candida—it was not an accident.

PAULA: And he will never, never forgive us!

PEPANG [*rising & swiftly approaching her sisters & putting an arm around each of them*]: Paula, Candida—do not say that! Of course he will forgive you! He is our father! You must go to him again—

PAULA: We have been trying and trying ever since.

CANDIDA: It is no use. He refuses to forgive us.

PAULA: When we kneel by his bed, he turns his face away.

CANDIDA: That is why we cannot part with this picture. It is our punishment. He painted it to punish us. We cannot look at it without suffering. We can never escape from this picture. It is our punishment.

MANOLO [*sobbing; sinking down to a chair*]: Oh Paula, Candida—how could you have done it! You were all he had—and you abandoned him too, you turned against him too! [*He buries his face in his hands.*]

PEPANG: They were only doing, Manolo, what you and I had done.

MANOLO [*sobbing into his hands*]: Oh father! Oh, poor, poor father!

PEPANG: We all have to grow up, Manolo—we all have to grow up. Oh how we worshipped him when we were children! We were so proud of him because he was a genius, because he was different from all other fathers. We always took his side against mother—remember? Poor mother, with her eternal worrying and her eternal complaints—poor mother did not understand him, of course. Only we, his children, understood him. And we defended him, we justified him, we were willing to be poor, to go without the things other children had, so that our father could go on being just an artist. Oh, we were happy enough, I know—though, even then, I promised myself that *my* children should never suffer what we had to suffer. And when we grew up, Manolo—then what did we do? When he could not give us the things the young people of our age all had—what did you and I do? Did we not face him also and accuse him of cowardice and selfishness? Did we not blame him also for the humiliations of our youth? Did we not berate him also for having squandered mother's property? And did we not also tell him that he could have been a rich man if he had only used his talents to advance himself in the world? Yes, we did, Manolo—you and I! We faced him and we accused him and we rejected him! And how can we blame Candida and Paula now?

MANOLO [*looking up*]: But I thought they were happy together. Candida, Paula—I thought you were contented to stay with father.

CANDIDA: Yes, we were—as long as we were sure of our life together. But you and Pepang had begun to complain about the cost of this house; you were talking of selling it. And we realized how little sure we were of the future.

PAULA: We were desperate.

CANDIDA: And whom could we blame but . . . but *him?*

MANOLO [*rising*]: Well, one thing is definitely settled now. You cannot go on living together, the three of you—not with all this hatred and bitterness among you. This house must be sold. Father must be placed in a hospital.

PAULA: You cannot take him away from us now!

CANDIDA: You must give us time—time to atone for what we did!

PAULA: We must go on working for our forgiveness!

MANOLO: I want no more arguments! Oh, I did not dare sell this house as long as I thought that father wanted to stay here. But now I know he does not want to stay here, he does not want to stay with you! He will never get well until he has been completely separated from the two of you!

PAULA: Manolo!

CANDIDA: Oh, he has a right to be cruel. His conscience is clear!

MANOLO: I am glad I found out about this.

CANDIDA: Yes, you are glad—both of you—very glad! Oh, you are delighted to find that Paula and I have proved unfaithful too—that we have turned against father even as you did! And what a relief you must be feeling now, you and Pepang!

Because, now, we are all alike, we are all the same, we have all destroyed our father!

PEPANG: Candida, control yourself. Manolo, you must give them time.

MANOLO: They can stay until this house has been sold—but they must dismiss this boarder of theirs at once—and I shall arrange to have father transferred to a hospital as soon as possible. I expect to have this house disposed of before the end of this month. You will come to live with me, Candida. Paula, you will live with Pepang. And listen, all of you—this is absolutely the last talk we shall ever have on this matter. Pepang, are you ready to go now?

PEPANG [*going for her bag*]: Yes, Manolo.

MANOLO: Wait a minute while I go in and see if father is awake. [*He exits.*]

PEPANG [*earnestly*]: Candida, Paula—have confidence; everything will turn out for the best. And father will be better off really in a hospital. You must not blame yourselves. Father will forgive you. In fact, he *has* already forgiven you. You say this picture is your punishment. I do not think father would be so cruel. He did not paint this picture to punish you; he painted it to release you, to free you! Do you not see? When you said all those bitter things to him, he was not angry; he understood your predicament; and he took pity on you. He could not give you any money, of course—but he could give you this picture, knowing that you could make money out of it—the money to release you, to set you free! Paula, Candida—your happiness is in your hands. You can have money of your own. You will feel secure and independent. You will not have to worry anymore about the future.

[*Enter Manolo.*]

MANOLO: Father is still asleep. Come on, Pepang.

PEPANG [*kissing her sisters:*] Goodbye, Candida. Goodbye, Paula.

MANOLO: Now remember—you are to dismiss this boarder of yours immediately!

PAULA: Yes, Manolo.

MANOLO: Candida, did you hear me?

CANDIDA: Yes, Manolo.

MANOLO: And take away all those signs from the door.

PAULA & CANDIDA: Yes, Manolo.

MANOLO: Well, goodbye now. And do be more sensible, both of you!

PAULA & CANDIDA: Goodbye, Manolo.

MANOLO: Tell father I shall be around again soon.

[*Exeunt Pepang & Manolo.*]

PAULA [*after a pause*]: Candida, have you no news? Oh, tell me you have news—good news!

CANDIDA: We must go and do the cooking if we are to eat anything.

PAULA: Then, you did not go?

CANDIDA [*bitterly*]: Yes, I did!

PAULA: To this Bureau of Health and Science?

CANDIDA [*shuddering*]: Oh Paula, it was horrible!

PAULA: No place for you?

CANDIDA: They thought I was crazy!

PAULA: Oh Candida!

CANDIDA: They only made fun of me. They sent me from one department to another. Oh, I thought they were serious—and I tried to act very smart, like a woman of the world—I went into every office and told them that I wanted to catch rats, that I was an expert—and they listened attentively—I thought they were really interested—but they were only laughing at me, they were only making fun of me. And then they began to be afraid of me—they thought I was dangerous. They became more and more nervous. They began running about excitedly and shouting and blowing whistles. A crowd began to gather. They thought I was a criminal! I had to run away! They chased me down to the street! I had to run and run!

PAULA [*taking her sister's hands*]: Oh, Candida!

CANDIDA: Pepang is right. There is no place for us anywhere in the world. We are completely useless. We must separate. You go and live with Pepang. I will go and live with Manolo. I will take care of his children and keep an eye on his servants. You will look after Pepang's laundry, brush her hair, and answer her telephone.

PAULA: She will make me wear her old clothes and I must pretend to be grateful.

CANDIDA: And Manolo's wife will make me cut my hair and paint my face.

PAULA: Oh Candida, is there no escape for us?

CANDIDA [*turning her face toward* PORTRAIT]: Did you hear what Pepang said? She said this picture is our release, our freedom... [*As they gaze wonderingly at* PORTRAIT, *a car is heard stopping down in the street. They glance quickly at each other. Candida shudders.*]

   Oh, I cannot talk to him now!

[*She hurries to doorway & Paula follows. Tony Javier is heard running up the stairs & shouting: "Miss Candida! Miss Paula!" The sisters pause in the doorway. Tony appears on the landing, breathless.*]

TONY: Oh, there you are! Come here, both of you! Come and sit down!

   Oh Miss Paula, Miss Candida—I bring wonderful news! This is your salvation!

CANDIDA: Our salvation?

TONY: If you want to be saved—and I know you do!

PAULA: Mr. Javier, what is all this?

TONY: Come here, ladies—and you shall know! Come and listen to me—please!

[*Paula glances at Candida; Candida walks back into the room & Paula follows.*]

CANDIDA: Well, what is it, Mr. Javier?

TONY [*waving toward sofa*]: Oh, sit down, sit down first I don't want you to go running off before you have heard everything.

PAULA: Oh Candida, this is all nonsense!

TONY [*giving her his most appealing look*]: *Please*, Miss Paula!

CANDIDA: [*going to sofa*]: Very well, Mr. Javier—but you must hurry. We still have our cooking to do.

[*She & Paula sit down on sofa.*]

TONY: Oh, you'll forget all about your cooking after you've heard what I have to tell you! And—oh, yes—I know you have forbidden me ever to mention this matter again—but I must disobey you.

PAULA: Is it about that picture again?

TONY: And about the American who has long been wanting to buy it.

PAULA [*rising*]: Oh, Mr. Javier!

TONY: Sit down, Miss Paula—sit down and listen! [*Paula obeys.*] Now, about this American—he's going back to the States. All the Americans are being sent home—evacuated, you know—so they won't get caught here when the war breaks out. Well, this particular American is leaving in a week. He still wants this picture; he wants to take it back with him. Oh, he says he's crazy about it—and so, he's offering a crazy price for it. His last price. Take it or leave it. He simply doesn't want any more bargaining. And, ladies, do you know how much he's offering now for that picture of yours? [*A pause, while he looks at the sisters.*] He is offering ten thousand dollars!

CANDIDA [*after a stunned pause*]: Ten thousand dollars!

TONY: And that's twenty thousand pesos.

PAULA: Twenty thousand pesos!

TONY: Oh, he wants it bad, and he wants it at once! He's leaving Friday. [*The sisters are silent, staring at* PORTRAIT.] Well, what do you say now? But take your time, take your time! Don't let me hurry you! Think carefully, think *very* carefully! Oh, just think of it! Twenty grand! Enough money to last you for years and years! Why, you'll be *loaded!* You'll be sitting on top of the world! And you can snap your fingers at this brother and sister of yours!

PAULA [*after a pause; rising*]: We . . . we are sorry, Mr. Javier. But we told you before that the picture is not for sale. Well . . . it is still . . . still not for sale.

TONY: *WHAT?*

PAULA: Come along, Candida.

[*Candida remains seated, staring at* PORTRAIT.]

TONY: Wait, wait, *WAIT!* Oh, my God! Think, ladies—*think!* This may never happen again! This is the chance of your lifetime!

PAULA [*with a slight smile*]: It seems to be rather the chance of *your* lifetime, Mr. Javier.

TONY: Mine? Why?

PAULA: You are so anxious to make the sale. Has this American offered you a very big reward?

TONY: Just think how *much* he's offering you!

PAULA: And how much is he offering *you*, Mr. Javier?

TONY: Why do you ask?

PAULA: A lot of money?

TONY: Sure! And I need it!

PAULA: We are very sorry you cannot earn your reward.

TONY: But think of yourselves, think of yourselves! Miss Candida, just think what you'll be throwing away!

PAULA: We know what we are doing. Candida, will you tell him he is only wasting his time?

TONY: Miss Candida, will you tell her what a chance you'll be wasting?

[*Candida rises in silence & walks away. Paula, astonished, takes a step to follow her.*]

TONY [*grabbing Paula's arm*]: Oh, stay and listen! Listen to me—*please*!

CANDIDA [*walking slowly toward doorway*]: I must go and do the cooking . . .

PAULA: Oh Candida, do not leave me alone!

CANDIDA [*whirling around; with sudden passion*]: Why? Are you afraid?

PAULA [*startled*]: Afraid? [*Tony releases her arm.*]

CANDIDA [*fiercely*]: Yes, yes—afraid! Afraid to stay! Afraid to find out that it is true after all! Everything they are saying, everything they are whispering and laughing about!

PAULA: Candida! You know it is not true!

CANDIDA: Then why are you afraid to stay? Why do you always need me at your side? Are you a baby, am I your nurse?

PAULA [*grimly*]: I am not afraid to stay. I *shall* stay, Candida. I do not need you.

CANDIDA: Why should you need me? Why should we need each other? Oh it is time that each of us faced facts alone by herself! Alone, Paula! Not together, not always together!

PAULA [*with a shake of the head*]: We are not together anymore, Candida. You have already made your decision.

[*They stare a moment at each other. Then Candida turns away quickly, toward doorway. Paula smiles mockingly.*]

And I know why you are running away, Candida! I know, I know!

CANDIDA [*turning around in doorway; defiant*]: And you are right, Paula! You are absolutely right! Why should I go on suffering? And why should you go on suffering? But you must decide that for yourself, Paula—alone! Yes, I have already made my decision! Oh, you are right, Paula! We are not together anymore! We are not together anymore!

[*She covers her face with her hands and rushes out.*]

TONY [*after a pause*]: I'm sorry, Miss Paula.

[*Paula is motionless, looking at doorway. Tony shrugs.*]

I suppose you know what you're doing . . . But twenty thousand bucks!

[*He whistles.*]

Saying no to twenty grand! Saying no to a chance like that! God, if it was me! If it was only me!

[*He moves toward* PORTRAIT *and stands before it, staring bitterly.*]

What I could do with twenty grand! That's all I need—just the money to start me off. Get away from this hick town, get away from vaudeville, get away from all those bums . . . Oh, I could make something out of myself—they'd see that soon enough! Make a name for myself, make a big-shot out of myself . . . All I need is a little money. Organize my own band and play all over the orient—Hong Kong, Shanghai, Java, India. I'd be making money fast enough. And then I'd go to Europe. Sure, why not? This war won't last forever. I'd go to Europe and really learn to play the piano . . .

[*Paula, at the mention of Europe, turns her face toward him & listens inteutly. He has forgotten all about her.*]

God knows I'm not just a piano-player! I've got ambitions. I've got a lot of big dreams—I've got so much inside me! And I just go wasting what I've got on vaudeville! It's not fair! Why don't somebody come and offer to give me twenty grand—just like that? Oh baby, what I could do with twenty grand! Go to Paris, go to Vienna, go to New York . . .

[*Paula comes and stands beside him. Absorbed in his dreams,
he does not notice her*].

PAULA [*in a sort of trance herself*]: Paris . . . ? Vienna . . . ? New
York . . . ?

TONY [*not really noticing her*]: Yeah—and all those other glam-
orous places over there. Spain, Italy, South America . . . But
I wouldn't be going there just to have fun—no, siree! This
won't be a punk whoopee party like the last time. I'd really
be serious this time. I'd really study, really get educated. And
then we'll see if I'm wrong about what I've got!

PAULA: I used to dream of traveling myself . . .

TONY [*looking at her now*]: Huh?

PAULA [*smiling dreamily at* PORTRAIT]: Europe . . . I've always
wanted to go to Europe. Spain and France and Italy . . .
[*Slightly horrified, Tony steps back, away from her side. She
does not notice.*]
     I've always wanted to go to all those places where my
father lived when he was a young man . . .
[*Tony now looks up at* PORTRAIT. *Suddenly, he smiles.*]
     Do you think it would be possible to go there now?
[*She turns her face toward him & notices his grin.*]
     Why are you smiling?

TONY [*grinning at* PORTRAIT]: Because your father is going to
get it!

PAULA: Get what?

TONY: What was coming to him!

PAULA: What do you mean?

TONY [*turning his grin toward her & stepping forward beside
her*]: So, *you* want to travel, too—eh?

PAULA [*smiling again*]: When I was a girl.

TONY: How about now?

PAULA: And they were just dreams—just the foolish dreams of
a young girl . . .

TONY: You could make your dreams come true.

PAULA [*with a sigh*]: Ah, it is too late now!

TONY [*moving closer*]: Paula—

PAULA [*stiffening*]: It is too late now!

TONY [*softly, tenderly*]: Paula . . . too late?

PAULA [*beginning to shiver*]: Yes!

TONY: But why, Paula—why?

PAULA: I am not a young girl anymore!

TONY [*moving still closer*]: Paula, listen to me—

PAULA [*shivering; rooted to the floor; but keeping her face rigidly averted from his approaching face*]: No, no! It is too late now! I am not young anymore, I am not young anymore!

TONY: Paula, you do like me a little, don't you?

[*She is tensely silent, her face averted.*]

Won't you say you like me a little, Paula?

PAULA: Oh, you must not talk like that! What would people say?

TONY: Who cares what people say? Are you afraid of their big mouths?

PAULA [*with sudden spirit*]: I despise them!

TONY: Then show it! Show your contempt! Do what you like— and to hell with what people say!

PAULA [*her face hardening*]: Yes, you are right!

TONY: And what can they do to you anyway?

PAULA: I am not afraid!

TONY: You can leave them to their nasty talk! Pack up whenever you please, and go wherever you want!

PAULA: Far away?

TONY: Yes, Paula—as far away as you like. You can make your dreams come true.

PAULA [*faltering*]: My dreams are dead.

TONY: Dreams don't die.

PAULA: Mine did. A long time ago.

TONY: But suppose somebody came along and said the right words, do you think they would come alive again?

PAULA: I stopped waiting—a long time ago . . .

TONY: Paula, look at me. [*She keeps her face averted.*] Look at me, Paula—please!

[*She begins to turn her face; but catching sight of* PORTRAIT *she freezes, her eyes widening with horror. He looks at her & then at* PORTRAIT *& he begins to back off.*]

Turn your back on him, Paula! Turn your back on him!

PAULA [*agonized; unable to move; eyes fixed on* PORTRAIT]: I cannot do it, I cannot do it!

TONY [*sternly*]: Yes, you can! Yes, you can! Turn around, Paula! If he wants to rot here, then let him! Why should you rot with him? Turn around, Paula—turn around!

PAULA [*struggling to move her body*]: I *cannot* do it!

TONY: Try, Paula—*try!* Here I am, Paula—here I am behind you! Come to me, Paula!

[*With a supreme effort, she twists around until she is facing him, her back to the audience. He utters a great groan of relief & breaks into a gay smile.*]

There! You did it! Oh Paula, you're not afraid anymore! You have turned your back on him! You have won! Oh, come—come, Paula!

[*Holding out his arms, he begins to step backward slowly, toward stairway, talking steadily. Tranced, she steps forward slowly, following him.*]

Come on, girl—keep moving! You've smashed your shell! No, don't look back, don't stop—just keep moving! That's right! That's the spirit! Atta, girl, Paula! Hooray for you! Oh, you'll join the navy and see the world! Hell, you won't either—you don't have to! You're loaded—you lucky girl! And think of it! All those places you've dreamed about— Spain and France and Italy! You'll see them now! You're still young, Paula! You've got a right to be happy! And you will be happy, Paula! Your dreams aren't dead yet! They'll come alive again! They'll come true at last!

[*He has reached the balustrade, and stops. She stops too. He moves toward her, his arms extended. She suddenly shudders away from his touch.*]

PAULA: No, no! Do not touch me! You must not touch me! Not—[*glancing round the room*]—not here . . .

TONY [*with knowing smile*]: Okay, Paula—not here. [*He goes to stair-landing.*] Come, Paula. [*He waits, smiling. After a while, she walks to his side, her head bowed. He smiles down at her; she looks up at him, her face grave. Looking thus into each other's eyes, they descend the stairs. After a*

*moment, his car is heard starting. Simultaneously, Candida
begins to shout "Paula! Paula!" inside.*]

CANDIDA [*appearing in doorway*]: Paula!

[*The car is heard moving away. She runs to balcony where
she stands, looking up the street. Then she turns around, a
hand pressed to her throat.*]

CANDIDA [*in shocked whisper*]: Paula!

[*Then, resolutely, she strides toward stairway. But she
catches sight of* PORTRAIT *and, with a terrified gasp, she
cowers away. She stands shuddering, her eyes fixed on* POR-
TRAIT, *her breath coming faster and faster as*

THE CURTAIN FALLS

THE THIRD SCENE

As in preceding Scene, curtains open on the "Intramuros Curtain," with Bitoy Camacho standing at far left, in light.

BITOY: The next time I went to the Marasigan house was on a cold cloudy afternoon—the afternoon of the second Sunday of October. A typhoon wind was blowing; the skies above were dark—as dark as the weather in our hearts—for the rumors of war were thickening fast; panic was in the air.

But that afternoon, Intramuros was in a holiday mood. As though knowing that it was about to die, about to be obliterated forever, this old city was celebrating—celebrating for the last time. The streets were decorated, and filled with hurrying people. The bells rang out high and clear. It was the feast of La Naval de Manila.

[*A faint faraway sound of bells and band-music.*]

As I walked down this street, I could hear my footsteps reverberating against the cobblestones; when I talked or laughed, my voice seemed to echo on and on. Aware of the doom hanging overhead, I looked about me with keener eyes; and everything I saw—even the slum-tenements—seemed suddenly very beautiful and very precious—because I might be seeing them for the last time.

[*The lights go on inside the stage; through the curtain, the sala becomes visible.*]

I *was* seeing them for the last time. Two months later, the bombs began to fall. There is nothing left of it now—of the old Manila. It is dead, obliterated forever—except in my memory—where it lives; still young, still great, still the Noble and Ever Loyal City. And whenever I remember it, the skies about are dark; a typhoon wind is blowing; it is October; it is the feast of the Naval.

[*The "Intramuros Curtain" begins to open, revealing the*

sala. It is late in the afternoon and the room is rather dim. The doorway at right and the balconies have been decorated with festive curtains, which are blowing steadily in the wild wind.]

In October, a breath of the North stirs Manila, blowing summer's dust and doves from the tile roofs, freshening the moss of old walls, as the city festoons itself with arches and paper lanterns for its great votive feast to the Virgin.

[*Candida comes slowly up the stairs, carrying prayer-book, rosary, and umbrella. She goes to the stand to deposit her umbrella.*]

Women hurrying into their finery upstairs, bewhiskered men tapping canes downstairs, children teeming in the doorways, coachmen holding impatient ponies in the streets, glance up anxiously, fearing the wind's chill: would it rain this year?

[*Candida pauses in front of balcony and puts out a hand to feel the wind.*]

But the eyes that long ago had gazed up anxiously, invoking the Virgin, had feared a grimmer rain—of fire and metal—for pirate craft crowded the horizon.

[*Candida goes to table at center where she lays down her prayer-book and rosary. She takes off her veil and begins to fold it. She pauses, hearing a sound of distant bells and band-music.*]

The bells begin to peal again and sound like silver coins showering in the fine air; at the rumor of drums and trumpets as bands march smartly down the cobblestones a pang of childhood happiness smites every heart. October in Manila!

[*Candida stands still, listening. The veil drops from her hands onto the table. Candida is wearing her best dress—an archaic blue frock—and her jewels.*]

But the emotion, so special to one's childhood, seems no longer purely one's own; seems to have traveled ahead, deep into Time, since one first felt its pang—growing ever more poignant, more complex: a child's rhyme swelling epical; a clan treasure one bequeaths at the very moment of inheritance, having added one's gem to it.

[*Candida goes to the other balcony, on one side of which she stands, her face lifted, her eyes closed, the wind blowing her hair.*]

And Time creates unexpected destinations; history raises figs from thistles: yesterday's pirates become today's roast pork and paper lanterns, a tapping of impatient canes, a clamor of trumpets . . .

[*Candida bows her head and covers her face with her hands. The distant rumor of bells and music fades out. Bitoy steps into the room and places himself at stair-landing.*]

Hello, Candida.

[*She whirls around, nervously.*]

CANDIDA [*with relief*]: Oh, it is you, Bitoy.

BITOY [*walking in*]: Boy, are you all dressed up!

CANDIDA [*coming forward*]: The fiesta, you know.

BITOY: I saw you and Paula in church.

CANDIDA: Yes, I came home ahead. There was such a crowd. I felt dizzy. Sit down, Bitoy. Paula will be coming in a moment.

BITOY [*remaining standing*]: And how is your father?

CANDIDA: Oh, just the same as usual. Do you want to see him? But he will—

CANDIDA & BITOY [*together*]: —be having a nap just now.

BITOY [*laughing*]: I knew you would say that!

[*Candida smiles. Sound of bells pealing again. They listen, glancing toward the balconies.*]

CANDIDA: Have you come for the procession?

BITOY: October again, Candida!

CANDIDA: Yes . . . Oh Bitoy, the Octobers of our childhood! The dear, dear Octobers of our childhood!

BITOY: Remember how my family used to come here to watch the Naval procession from your balconies?

CANDIDA: And so did the families of all our friends.

BITOY: Year after year—

CANDIDA: And year after year our house stood open to all comers on this day, the feast of the Naval. It was always the biggest fiesta in this house.

BITOY: Lechon and relleno in the dining room—

CANDIDA: And ice-cream and turrones here in the sala—

BITOY: And the chandeliers all lighted up—

CANDIDA: And all our windows and balconies simply crowded with visitors—

BITOY: The procession passing below and all the children shouting continually: "Who is that one, mama?" and "Who is that other one now, mama?"

CANDIDA [*in pious maternal tones*]: That, my son, is the good San Vicente Ferrer—and he is wearing wings because he was as eloquent as an angel.

BITOY [*wide-eyed and craning his neck*]: And who is that one coming now, mama?

CANDIDA: That, my son, is the noble San Pedro Martir.

BITOY: Oh look, look—he has a bolo in his head! Why has he got a bolo in his head?

CANDIDA: Because wicked men killed him with a bolo.

BITOY: And who is that one now carrying a flag?

CANDIDA [*laughing*]: Oh, shut your big mouth, my son! You are a pest and a nuisance!

BITOY: And then you knock me on the head—

CANDIDA: And one more nuisance carried off howling—

BITOY: To be silenced with ice-cream and turron—

CANDIDA: Or dragged off to the small room—

BITOY: And the bells ringing, the bands playing, the crowds clamoring in the street—

CANDIDA: And the rain suddenly falling!

BITOY: Alas!

CANDIDA: Remember?

BITOY: If I forget thee, O Jerusalem—

CANDIDA: Oh, smell that wind, Bitoy! It is the smell of the holiday, the smell of the old Manila—the Manila of our affections!

BITOY [*throwing back his head & singing*]: "*Adios, Reina del cielo!*

Madre, madre del Salvador . . ."

CANDIDA [*suddenly pressing a hand to her eyes*]: Oh, stop it, Bitoy!

BITOY [*laughing*]: Gosh, do I sing that bad?

CANDIDA [*trying to smile*]: Much, much worse!

BITOY: You should have knocked me on the head!

CANDIDA: Shall I?

BITOY [*offering his head*]: Sure. Go ahead. Right here.
 [*Candida disconsolately turns away. Bitoy straightens up.*]
   I'm sorry, Candida. Is anything wrong?

CANDIDA [*bitterly*]: Yes! Everything!

BITOY: What?

CANDIDA: This is our last October here—in this house—where
 we were born, where we grew up!

BITOY: The last October?

CANDIDA: We are leaving this house.

BITOY: Why?

CANDIDA: Because to save one's life is to lose it!

BITOY: Oh Candida, you would have had to leave this house
 anyway, sooner or later. It is too old—

CANDIDA: It is our youth.

BITOY: And when the war breaks out it will become very unsafe—

CANDIDA: There is no safety for us anymore, anywhere.

BITOY: And you must think of your father, you must think of
 this painting—
 [*He looks toward the site of the* PORTRAIT *and, suddenly,
 his eyes pop out, he gasps and steps forward, staring in
 amazement.*]
   Candida, the painting! It is gone!

CANDIDA [*not looking around*]: Yes.

BITOY: Where is it?

CANDIDA: I do not know.

BITOY: Has it been sold?

CANDIDA: No.

BITOY: Stolen?

CANDIDA: No, no!

BITOY: Then, *where* is it!

CANDIDA: I tell you, I do not know!

BITOY: Oh Candida, what have you done with it!

CANDIDA: Paula took it down and put it away. She did not tell
 me where.

BITOY: But why did she take it down?

CANDIDA: She did not tell me that either.

BITOY: But how could you allow—

CANDIDA: Oh, stop asking, Bitoy! I know nothing, I know nothing at all!

[*Sound of rapid knocking downstairs. Candida starts nervously again, and presses a hand to her forehead.*]

Oh God, God! Bitoy, please see who that is. And remember: whoever it is, I am not at home, Paula is not at home, nobody is at home!

[*She turns around quickly to leave the room but Susan and Violet have already appeared on the landing*].

SUSAN: Oh yes—you are home all right!

[*Susan & Violet advance into the room. They are sober this time, and look extremely determined. They have hurried right over from the Sunday matinee, and are still wearing their stage make-up and costumes: very brief gaudy ballet skirts.*]

VIOLET: Excuse us for coming right up.

SUSAN: And don't tell us to go away because we won't go away!

VIOLET: Not till we find out what we want to find out!

SUSAN [*earnestly*]: Look, we'll behave ourselves—honest!

VIOLET: You remember us, don't you? We're from the Parisian Theatre. We were here about a week ago.

SUSAN: And I'm sorry about how I acted that time—and about the things I said.

CANDIDA: What can I do for you?

SUSAN: We want to see Tony.

VIOLET: What's the matter with him?

SUSAN: Is he sick?

VIOLET: He hasn't shown up at the theatre for the last two days. And if he still doesn't show up tonight, the manager is going to fire him!

SUSAN: He'll lose his job!

VIOLET: We came right over from the show to tell him. It's important!

SUSAN: Where is he?

CANDIDA: I do not know. Mr. Javier hasn't come back here either for the last two days.

SUSAN: Oh, where did he go!

VIOLET: Did he take his clothes with him?

CANDIDA: No; his clothes and all his things are still here. Tell me—are you very good friends of his?

VIOLET: Yes, we are!

CANDIDA: Then, will you do me a favor? I have put his clothes and all his things together. They are downstairs.

VIOLET: In those two suitcases?

CANDIDA: Yes. Will you take them with you and give them to Mr. Javier when you find him?

SUSAN: So, you're throwing him out!

VIOLET: Couldn't he pay his rent?

CANDIDA: And please tell Mr. Javier that I beg him never, never to show himself here again!

SUSAN: What did he do?

BITOY: Now look, girls—that's strictly between Tony and Miss Marasigan. It's none of our business. You go and take his clothes with you. He's bound to show up sooner or later.

SUSAN: I won't go away until I find out what's happened to him!

BITOY: Nothing's happened to him. He's probably just out on a binge!

SUSAN: Are you throwing him out because of what I said the last time?

CANDIDA: That had nothing to do with it.

SUSAN: Oh, he's not bad, he's not bad! But *you* make him feel cheap! You make him run wild!

BITOY: I thought you said you were going to behave!

[*Sound of people coming up the stairs.*]

CANDIDA: Oh God, who are those now!

[*They all look toward stairway. Enter Doña Loleng, Elsa, & Charlie. Elsa is wearing a terrific Carmen Miranda costume with a towering head-dress. Charlie is in the costume of a Cuban rhumba dancer. Doña Loleng is in a swanky terno. She hurries forward and grasps Candida's hands.*]

LOLENG: Candida my dear—do forgive us for dropping in like this! But I have been so worried about you, my dear—so very worried! I have been hearing the most fantastic rumors!

CANDIDA: What rumors, Doña Loleng?

LOLENG [*looking around*]: Where is Paula?

CANDIDA [*trying to draw away*]: Won't you sit down? Paula will be coming in a moment. She has gone to church.

LOLENG [*astonished; keeping firm hold of Candida*]: Then, *nothing* has happened to her?

CANDIDA [*lightly*]: Why, what have you been hearing?

LOLENG: That she had eloped with somebody—or that she had been kidnapped!

[*Susan & Violet, who are listening alertly, glance at each other.*]

CANDIDA [*with a careless laugh*]: Oh, but what nonsense!

LOLENG [*incredulous*]: Nothing has happened?

CANDIDA: Paula has *not* eloped—and she certainly has *not* been kidnapped.

LOLENG: Oh, thank God, thank God! I have been *so* worried, my dear.

CANDIDA: We are grateful for your very kind interest, Doña Loleng.

LOLENG [*avidly studying Candida's face*]: And everything is all right with you and Paula? You are quite sure, my dear?

CANDIDA: One hears nothing but wild rumors nowadays.

LOLENG [*disappointed; releasing Candida's hands*]: Well . . .

CANDIDA: Are you going?

LOLENG: Yes, we must be running off again.

CANDIDA: Do stay a moment and have a drink.

LOLENG: How we wish we could—but duty, Candida, duty! Oh, these are serious days for all of us! And so much good work to be done. I hardly have time to sit down anymore. Tonight we are giving a dance for the American servicemen. Those poor boys, Candida—so far away from home and so lonely. We are doing all we can to console them. Elsa here is doing a jungle conga.

[*Sound of knocking downstairs.*]

CANDIDA: Bitoy, will you please see who that is?

LOLENG: Well, goodbye, Candida—and remember: the senator is your godfather and your mother was one of my dearest friends; so, if you and Paula have any troubles, I want you to come and tell me all about them. I shall only be too happy to listen.

CANDIDA: Thank you, Doña Loleng.

BITOY [*at stair-landing*]: Candida, it's the people from the news-papers. Do you want to see them?

CANDIDA [*with a gay laugh*]: Now *what* on earth can they want with me! Yes, Bitoy—tell them to come up.

LOLENG: On second thought . . . I believe we *could* stay a moment, Candida.

CANDIDA [*hollowly*]: Oh, how nice.

LOLENG [*moving to sofa*]: And we are all so exhausted from running around that we would all be grateful for a drink, my dear—if you still care to offer us any.

CANDIDA: Of course, Doña Loleng. Excuse me just a moment. Bitoy, will you tell those people to wait?

[*Exit Candida. Enter Pete, Eddie, & Cora. Pete is in white shorts and polo shirt, and carries a tennis racket. Eddie is in a dinner jacket. Cora is wearing a smart evening gown, and carries her camera.*]

BITOY [*as the newcomers come up*]: Well, what do you people want now!

PETE [*excitedly*]: Bitoy, is it true?

BITOY: What's true?

PETE [*pushing past him into the room*]: Oh Christ—it's true! The painting has disappeared!

LOLENG [*rising*]: Why, so it has!

[*They are all staring toward site of* PORTRAIT.]

EDDIE: What do they say, Bitoy? Have they sold it?

BITOY: No.

PETE: Well, where is it then?

BITOY: They have only hidden it—for safekeeping, I suppose.

CORA: Ho-hum. Another wild goose—that laid an egg.

PETE: Are they here, the sisters?

BITOY: Candida is here.

EDDIE: Then the other one is still missing?

ELSA [*rising*]: You see! What did I tell you, Loleng!

BITOY: Paula is not missing. I saw her at the Dominican church just a while ago.

EDDIE: She was reported missing the day before yesterday.

ELSA: And that was when we saw her with this fellow. They were in his car.

SUSAN: Excuse me—but which fellow was she with?

CORA: Your boyfriend, girls—but, oh, don't worry. He was only teaching her how to drive.

ELSA: A fine time to teach her! It was almost midnight. Charlie, what time exactly did we see them?

CHARLIE: Quarter past eleven.

ELSA: P.M.

CHARLIE [*coming forward*]: Hello, Violet. Hi, Susan.

SUSAN: Charlie, did you really see her with Tony?

CHARLIE: Is Tony the guy who plays the piano at your show?

VIOLET: That's him.

CHARLIE: Then, that was Tony with her all right. They were having a nice long ride in the moonlight.

SUSAN: Tony hasn't come back since then.

PETE: You know what I think? They eloped—and took the picture with them!

BITOY: I tell you—I saw Paula with my own eyes this afternoon!

EDDIE: Then he doublecrossed her! He pretended he was eloping with her—but he just ran off with the picture and left her flat!

CORA: I wish I had your imagination!

PETE: What we have is a nose for news.

LOLENG: And my nose was not wrong either when it led me all the way here.

VIOLET: We smelled something rotten ourselves!

CORA [*aside to Bitoy*]: What's this—a gathering of the vultures?

ELSA: There's nothing so dangerous as an old maid! Oh, I studied all about it in New York. Sex-frustration, you know.

LOLENG: And I'm so glad I found out all this! Oh, this house, this house! Well, it has begun to smell after all!

ELSA: Come on, Loleng—let's go!

CHARLIE: She can hardly wait to spread the good news!

LOLENG: No—I *must* talk to Candida.

CHARLIE: And learn all the details!

[*Unnoticed, the Watchman & the Detective have crept stealthily up the stairs. The detective whips out his gun, his hand wobbling.*]

LOLENG: I simply must know what really has happened to the painting. Charlie, will you—*MADRE MIA!*

[*She has seen the two newcomers and the gun. The others look around & freeze.*]

THE DICK: Hands up, everybody! Nobody moves!

[*They all put up their hands. The Dick & the Watchman advance into the room. The Watchman is a small nervous old man; the Dick is a tall nervous young man.*]

WATCHMAN: Where is she? Where is she?

BITOY: Who?

WATCHMAN: That old woman!

LOLENG [*indignant*]: There is no old woman here!

WATCHMAN: Oh yes, there is! I saw her come in here a while ago!

THE DICK: You should have followed her inside!

WATCHMAN: Are you crazy! I was unarmed, I had to call you up first! She may be carrying a time-bomb!

ELSA: A time-bomb!

THE DICK: She is a spy—a fifth-columnist!

PETE: And you saw her come in here?

LOLENG: Why, she may be hiding somewhere below!

[*Susan & Violet begin to screech.*]

ELSA: We may all be just about to be blown up!

VIOLET [*whimpering*]: Oh Susan, why did we ever come!

SUSAN: Why don't you go and search the house!

LOLENG: Call the police, you boobs! Call the police!

ELSA: Oh Loleng, let's get out of here at once!

THE DICK: Silence! Nobody moves!

EDDIE: Suppose you tell us just who you are.

THE DICK [*flashing his badge*]: I'm a detective!

WATCHMAN: And I'm the watchman at the Bureau of Health & Science!

CORA: Then look—you can put that gun away. We're not spies or fifth-columnists.

VIOLET [*crying*]: We're innocent!

SUSAN: We're peaceful law-abiding taxpayers!

LOLENG [*fuming*]: Will somebody tell them just who I am!

CHARLIE [*to watchman*]: Hey, you—come over here!

[*Watchman approaches; Charlie whispers in his ear. The watchman glances toward Doña Loleng and his eyes pop*] *out. He hurries to the Dick, and whispers in his ear. The Dick's eyes pop out; he immediately puts away his gun.*]

LOLENG [*sinking down to the sofa*]: Idiots! [*The others limply put down their hands.*]

THE DICK: We are very sorry, señora!

WATCHMAN: We are very, very sorry, señora; please forgive us!

THE DICK: We were only doing our duty, señora!

WATCHMAN: We were trying to catch this old woman—

PETE: What does she look like?

WATCHMAN: She looks *suspicious!*

THE DICK: We've been on her track for the last two days. She is a member of the RATS!

CHARLIE: What rats?

THE DICK: The RATS! The R.A.T.S. The Rope And Trigger Society!

EDDIE: Oh God, Pete—that's the band of terrorists!

THE DICK: Exactly! They go around the government offices trying to start a Reign of Terror! This old woman was last seen at the Bureau of Health & Science—and she was *openly* declaring her connection with the rats!

[*Enter Candida with a tray containing glasses & bottles. On seeing her, the watchman staggers backward so suddenly he bumps against the other people, almost falling down.*]

WATCHMAN [*pointing & screaming; terrified*]: *AND THERE SHE IS! THAT'S HER! THAT'S THE WOMAN!*

THE DICK [*whipping out his gun and pointing it at Candida*]: You're . . . you're under arrest!

CANDIDA [*pausing; startled*]: What!

CHARLIE: Oh, rats!

LOLENG: Will you idiots get out of here before I *break* your necks!

EDDIE: Miss Candida, you had better offer these two fellows a drink. They need it.

THE DICK [*looking about uncertainly; lowering his gun*]: Do . . . do you all know this woman?

CHARLIE: Yes! Now go away!

THE DICK: She is not a gangster?

CORA: If *she's* a gangster, so's your grandmother!

WATCHMAN: But she's the woman I saw! She's dangerous! She came to the—

LOLENG: Shut up!

WATCHMAN: I am sorry, señora.

LOLENG: I answer for this woman, do you hear!

WATCHMAN & DICK: Yes, señora.

CANDIDA [*placing tray on table*]: What has happened?

LOLENG: Let them tell you. Go on, idiots! What did you say she was?

ELSA: They suspect you of being a spy!

CANDIDA [*laughing*]: I—a spy! But how exciting! Yes, do tell me all about it! Oh, I feel like a character in a romantic novel! Doña Loleng, do you think I might be just the right— [*She stops short as two policemen appear on the stairway. A silence, while the policemen fetch out their notebooks and glance around the room. Then, as nobody says anything, they move forward. One of them has a black-eye.*]

1ST COP: We want to speak to Miss Marasigan.

CANDIDA [*faintly*]: I am Miss Marasigan.

2ND COP [*glancing at his notebook*]: Miss Candida Marasigan?

CANDIDA: What can I do for you?

2ND COP: Miss Marasigan, the day before yesterday, at around noontime, you telephoned us and reported that your sister had been abducted—

1ST COP: We have been unable to locate your sister but we have found the man who—

CANDIDA [*quickly interrupting*]: Please forgive me—but it was all, all a mistake!

1ST COP: What was a mistake?

CANDIDA: My telephoning you. Nothing had happened really.

2ND COP: Your sister was not abducted?

CANDIDA: No.

1ST COP: And she is not missing?

CANDIDA: I only thought she was.

[*The cops glance wearily at each other and shrug.*]

1ST COP: Then, why did you not call again to tell us?

CANDIDA: I am sorry. I forgot.

2ND COP: You are withdrawing your charges?

CANDIDA: It was all a mistake.

2ND COP [*pocketing his notebook*]: Miss Marasigan, you see this black-eye? I got this because of your mistake. Be more careful next time, will you?

1ST COP: Could we use your telephone?

CANDIDA: We have no telephone.

1ST COP [*to his companion*]: You go down and call up the station. Tell them to release this fellow.

PETE [*as 2nd Cop exits*]: Which fellow, officer?

1ST COP: The fellow she said had run away with her sister. We picked him up this morning.

SUSAN [*approaching*]: Is his name Tony Javier?

THE COP: That's right.

VIOLET: Where did you find him?

THE COP: In a bar—trying to break all the furniture.

PETE: Drunk?

THE COP: And violent. He gave my companion the black-eye.

SUSAN: But they're going to release him now?

THE COP: Oh, sure—after he pays a fine.

SUSAN [*turning on Candida*]: You see! Now I hope you and that sister of yours are satisfied!

THE COP: Just what actually happened, Miss Marasigan?

CANDIDA: Nothing at all really. My sister simply went off for a drive—and forgot to tell me she was going.

THE COP: And this was at around twelve o'clock noon, the day before yesterday?

CANDIDA [*desperately*]: But she came back right away!

SUSAN: Oh no—she didn't!

BITOY: Will you shut up!

SUSAN: She did *not* come back right away, *Miss* Marasigan! You think nobody knows? Oh, we all know, *Miss* Marasigan! Everybody knows! That sister of yours was still out driving with him at midnight, the day before yesterday!

THE COP: What time did she come back, Miss Marasigan?

BITOY: Officer, since no charges are being made, I see no point in all these questions.

SUSAN: Well, *I* do! I want this dirty business dragged out into the open!

VIOLET: Why should they get off free? They started this trouble, they ought to pay for it!

LOLENG: Oh, my poor Candida!

SUSAN: Poor Candida—hell! They get poor Tony in jail, they make him lose his job—and then they laugh and say: "Oh, excuse us please! It was all a mistake!" And then they try to get everybody to hush up! Oh, they got what they wanted from Tony—they've been wanting that a long time—and now they think they can get away with it, just like that! Oh, they think they can keep it all safe and quiet, do they? Well, you don't, *Miss* Marasigan! I'll take care of that!

VIOLET: We'll shout your name all over town!

SUSAN: We'll see everybody knows about this fine ride your sister had in the moonlight!

VIOLET: So, she came back right away, did she?

CANDIDA [*going to pieces*]: NO! No, she did not come back right away! I lied, I was lying, I speak nothing now but lies and lies! No, she did not come back right away; she came back at three o'clock in the morning. I was standing right here. I was waiting for her. No, she did not come back right away . . . I was lying . . .

LOLENG: Candida!

CANDIDA: I was lying, I tell you! I was lying! No, she did not come back right away; she came back at three o'clock in the morning. I know. I was waiting. I was standing right here, waiting for her to come back. And I was going to throw her out. Oh, I felt righteous! I was horrified with what she had done. And I knew just what I was going to say to her—all the bitter, bitter words I was going to fling in her face! I felt justified, I was the virtuous one. And then she came . . . It was three o'clock in the morning. I was standing right here. And she came slowly up those stairs . . . And then she stood there, not saying anything . . . And her face, her face! How can I ever forget her face!

LOLENG: Candida, stop it!

CANDIDA: How can I ever, ever forget her face! And I knew then who was the guilty one! I knew then who was the evil one! Oh, pray for me! pray for me! I have destroyed my sister!

[*She bows down, rocking her head from side to side.*]

CORA: Bitoy, make her go in!

ELSA: Who are those two creatures anyway?

VOILET [*bristling*]: Listen, do you mean us?

PETE: *Yes*, now *shut* up!

EDDIE: Oh, why? They have been a great help. We all came to find out, didn't we?

CANDIDA [*looking up, with a faint smile*]: Yes, didn't you?

BITOY: Candida, why not go in and lie down?

CANDIDA [*smiling*]: You all wanted to know, didn't you? You all came to find out, didn't you? Well, now you know! Now you have found out!

CORA: Oh Bitoy, take her away!

CHARLIE: Why don't we all just go away!

CANDIDA [*wildly*]: Wait, wait! You know where she was, you know what she did, you know what happened to her—but, listen: *I* am the guilty one, I have committed a greater sin, I have committed a terrible crime against my sister! It was I who let her go—who *made* her go! I knew it was going to happen—and I let it happen—I *wanted* it to happen! And do you know why? Because of ten thousand dollars! Oh, I was thinking of my own future safety, my own future security! And no more poverty, no more bickering over money, no more haggling at the market, and no more hiding here in the darkness, the light cut off, the water stopped, the bill-collectors pounding and pounding at the door!

BITOY [*grasping her by the arms*]: Candida!

CANDIDA: Oh, I was thinking of ten thousand dollars in the bank! And so I let her go! And so I let her perish! I have destroyed my father—and now I have destroyed my sister! I am evil, evil, evil—

BITOY [*shaking her*]: Candida! Candida!

CANDIDA [*subsiding*]: And now you all know . . . Now you have found out . . .

[*She turns away from Bitoy's grasp and passes a hand over her brow.*]

And now you must excuse me . . . I . . . I do not feel well . . .

[*Charlie instantly claps on his hat and exits. Doña Loleng, after a glance at the motionless Candida, goes off too, followed by Elsa. The Cop shrugs, pockets his notebook, and, looking embarrassed, departs, followed by the Dick & the Watchman. Pete takes Susan & Violet by the arm and walks them off, followed by Cora & Eddie. Only Bitoy is left. He approaches Candida.*]

BITOY: Candida—

CANDIDA [*dully*]: Go to her, Bitoy. Please go to her.

BITOY: To Paula?

CANDIDA: She is in the church. Go and look for her. Tell her to hurry home. I must speak to her. Oh Bitoy, we have not spoken to each other since she came back! There has been only silence, silence between us. But now I can break that silence. Now, I can look in her face and speak. I know my sin, I recognize it.

BITOY: Candida, you must not blame yourself.

CANDIDA: Don't you see, Bitoy? I lost faith, I lost valor. I turned cowardly. Father brought us up to be heroes—but I refused his heroism. I wanted only to be safe, to be secure. My crime is prudence.

BITOY: It is not a crime, Candida. Everybody wants to be safe and secure.

CANDIDA: And that is why we are all destroying each other—

BITOY: We have to kill—

CANDIDA: And being destroyed by each other.

BITOY: Or be killed.

CANDIDA: Will you go to Paula?

BITOY: What shall I tell her?

CANDIDA: Tell her . . . tell her that we are together again!

BITOY: Only that?

CANDIDA: She has been waiting and waiting to hear me say that!

BITOY: Very well, Candida.

[*Exit Bitoy. Candida stands still a moment; then she turns away, toward table. The bells peal out again; she pauses & listens, gazing wistfully at the blowing curtains. Then she goes to table, intending to take out the untouched tray of drinks. She takes hold of the tray but does not lift it, remaining thus: stooped over the table, her back to the stairway. Tony Javier comes up the stairs and pauses on the landing. He is hatless, uncombed, unshaved, untidy, and unsteady. He sports a black-eye, and looks physically and—yes!—spiritually ravaged. He is still wearing the same clothes as in preceding scene; the clothes being very soiled & rumpled now, the loosening tie still dangling around the unbuttoned shirt-collar. From this point, Twilight starts and the stage dims very gradually.*]

TONY [*at stairway; curtly*]: Where is she?

[*Candida straightens up but does not look around nor reply. Tony raises his voice.*]

   Where is she?

CANDIDA [*still not looking around*]: She is not here.

[*Tony has turned his face toward site of* PORTRAIT; *his eyes blaze.*]

TONY: And where is it? Where is the picture?

CANDIDA [*moving away; wearily*]: I do not know.

[*Tony grabs her by the arm and whirls her around.*]

TONY: I said—WHERE IS THE PICTURE!

CANDIDA [*moaning*]: Go away . . . Please, please go away . . .

TONY: Oh, I'll go away—don't you worry. I'll go as far away from here as I can get! But not till you give me that picture!

CANDIDA [*with a toss of the head*]: I will never give it to you!

TONY [*sneering*]: Well! You *have* changed your mind, haven't you? Oh I could see you were willing enough to sell the last time, Candida!

CANDIDA: And you were right!

TONY [*with a leer*]: And you were willing to let me persuade your sister to sell too!

CANDIDA: Oh yes—yes indeed!

TONY: You were even willing to let me take her out and convince her! You didn't care how I did it—as long as it was effective!

CANDIDA [*mockingly*]: And was it?

TONY: You bet it was! I chose the most effective way in the world to convince her!

CANDIDA [*smiling contemptuously*]: Ah—but *did* you?

TONY [*flushing furiously and giving her a shake*]: You know I did! You know I did!

CANDIDA: All I know is that she came back alone! All I know is that she got away from you!

TONY: Well, she can't back out now! And *you* can't either! I've got the both of you in my hands! Oh, don't worry—I won't doublecross you! You'll get your ten grand; all I want is my commission.

CANDIDA [*jerking her arm loose*]: Your commission! And that is all you ever wanted, wasn't it?

TONY: Sure! Why? Did you think I wanted *you*? Did you think I wanted your sister?

CANDIDA: How could you have the nerve to touch her!

TONY: Remember, Candida—I had your permission! When you walked out of this room that day, you left her completely in my hands!

CANDIDA [*trembling; her fists clenched*]: Please go! I beg you to go at once!

[*Unnoticed, Paula has come up the stairs, carrying prayerbook, rosary, & umbrella; her church-veil draped around her shoulders. She pauses and glances toward the two people in the dim room. Paula, too, is wearing her best dress—an archaic blue frock—and her jewels; and she looks very young, happy, & tranquil. She has fought, she has conquered: now she comes back radiant—merciless as a child; ruthless as innocence; terrible as an army with banners.*]

TONY: I'm waiting for that picture. The American is waiting for that picture. Give it to me and we'll all get what we want. He gets his picture, you get your ten grand, I get my commission. Yes, Candida—that was all I ever really wanted! Just a little money to start me off—to get me away from here! But I wouldn't take you or your sister with me if the both of you had a million dollars! What do you take me for—a nut? I can get younger women, Candida—women to my taste! Not a pair of skinny, screwy, dried-up old hags!

[*Paula goes to set her umbrella in stand.*]

CANDIDA: Will you go—or shall I call the police?

TONY: Will you give me that picture—or shall I go in and tell your father?

PAULA: My father knows, Tony.

TONY: [*whirling around*]: PAULA!

PAULA [*moving calmly forward*]: My father *always* knows.

TONY [*hurrying to meet her; agonized*]: Why did you run away, Paula? Why did you leave me?

PAULA [*passing him by as she goes to table and lays down her prayer-book & rosary*]:
Because there was something I had to do. Something very important.

TONY [*in anguish*]: Oh Paula, I could kill myself! I could kill myself for having touched you!

PAULA [*smiling at him*]: How vain you are!

TONY [*approaching*]: Do you know what I did when I found you gone? I went out and got drunk! I got roaring drunk! I wanted to kill myself! I wanted to kill everybody!

PAULA: Poor Tony! And all he wanted was his commission!

TONY: To hell with it! I don't want it anymore! All I want is . . . that you forgive me!

PAULA: You will never forgive me, Tony, for what I have done to you.

TONY: Oh Paula, don't hate me!

PAULA: Why should I?

TONY: Then listen to me! Believe me!

PAULA: I listened to you before, Tony, and I believed you — remember?

TONY: I was lying then, I was only fooling you! Oh, you know what kind of a beast I am! I'm always out for what I can get! You were there for the taking—so, I took you!

PAULA: And besides, you were thinking of your commission.

TONY: Yes, I was thinking of the money too! I needed the money!

PAULA: And you also wanted to hurt my father.

TONY: Yes, yes—that, also! I wanted to hurt him, to spite him, and to spite this house! I've been wanting to do that for a long time! Oh, I did it for spite, and I did it for the money, and I did it for a lot of other reasons you wouldn't understand because you haven't lived my kind of life! I'm all twisted inside, Paula! Paula, don't hate me for what I did! Try to understand me! Oh, we started all wrong, you and I—but we could start all over again. We could make it right. I want to make it right, Paula; I want to make up for what I did to you. Oh, say you believe me!

PAULA: I believe you.

TONY: I deceived you that time, Paula, but now I speak to you from the heart! I'm on the level now—as I've never been in all my life!

PAULA: I believe you.

TONY: Then, where is the picture, Paula? Give it to me. It is not your salvation alone anymore: it is *my* salvation too. It is *our* salvation—yours and mine! We'll go away, Paula—just like we said. We'll go away together. Spain, France, Italy. We'll start a new life. And I'll make you happy, Paula—I promise! I will learn to be good, you will learn to be free!

PAULA [*with a laugh*]: To be free!

TONY [*horrified*]: Oh Paula, don't laugh, don't laugh!

PAULA: You were laughing the last time, Tony. Now, it is my turn.

TONY [*staring at her*]: Don't you believe me?

PAULA [*gravely*]: Do you . . . *love* me?

TONY: I will learn to love you, Paula—I promise! All we need is to get away from here. All we need is the money so we can run away and be free. Where is the picture, Paula? The American is waiting.

PAULA: Then, you must go and tell him to stop waiting.
[*She turns her face toward the site of the* PORTRAIT.] The picture is no more.

TONY [*his eyes widening*]: What have you done with it?

PAULA: I have destroyed it.
[*A pause, while Tony & Candida stare at her. She is gazing down at her hands.*]

TONY [*stunned*]: OH NO! OH NO, NO!

PAULA [*turning toward Candida*]: Did you hear what I said, Candida?

TONY [*feverishly*]: Say it's not true, Paula! Say it's not true!

PAULA: I have destroyed our picture, Candida.

TONY: No! No! It's not true! It's not true!

PAULA [*exultant*]: I slashed it up and I smashed it up and I tore it up and then I burned it! There is nothing left of it now! Nothing, nothing, nothing at all!

TONY [*bursting into sobs*]: Oh, you are mad, mad!

PAULA: Are you angry, Candida?

CANDIDA [*approaching*]: No, Paula.

[*She embraces her sister. Tony has sunk, sobbing, to his knees.*]

PAULA: Candida, are you crying?

CANDIDA: Oh no—look at me!

PAULA [*looking round the dim room*]: But someone is crying. I hear someone crying.

CANDIDA [*indicating Tony*]: Only Mr. Javier.

PAULA [*approaching the sobbing Tony*]: Oh yes . . . Poor Tony! He has found his tears. He has learned to cry.

TONY: Oh, why did you do it, Paula? Why did you do it!

PAULA: Because I do not want to run away, Tony, like you do.

TONY: I could have made you happy! I could have made you free!

PAULA [*laughing*]: But I *am* free! I am free again, Tony! Oh, there is no freedom in your world. Only nervous people huddled together, distrusting each other, trying to run away all the time. Only frightened slaves trying to buy their way out! But you cannot buy the freedom I have for a million dollars! Oh, I was mad—mad for a moment—infected with your fear, desiring your slavery! When I burned that picture I set myself free again!

TONY [*rising savagely*]: Yourself, yourself! And that was all you were thinking of, wasn't it? Yourself! How about me? Do you know what you did to me when you burned that picture?

PAULA: Now you know *who* is the victim!

TONY [*staring at her*]: And you've got no pity! You don't feel any pity!

PAULA: I told you, didn't I, that you would never forgive me for what I had done to you.

TONY: You could have saved me—

PAULA: But I *have* saved you, Tony. Oh, you do not know now—

TONY: You could have saved me but you didn't want to! Okay, now I'm going to the devil! [*He begins to move backward, toward stairway.*]

I'm through with struggling and trying to be good! I'm going back to where I came from—back to the gutter! back to the life you could have saved me from!

PAULA: You will not go back, Tony. You cannot go back anymore. You will never be the same again. It is the price you pay. And you will not go back.

TONY [*sobbing again; moving backward*]: Yes, I will! Yes, I will! I'm going back—back to the gutter! I'm through with fighting! I just want to rot! You could have saved me but you didn't want to! And I could have saved you, Paula. Well, now you're damned! And I'm glad—yes, I'm glad! Oh, I've done just what I wanted to do: I've damned you and I've damned your father and I've damned this house! Oh, you dug your own grave, Paula, when you burned that picture! You nailed your own coffin! I could have set you free! Well, now you're going to rot here! You're all going to rot in this house, the three of you, and be afraid to look in each other's faces! You're all going to sit here hating each other and rotting away till you die! That's what I've done to you! And I'm glad, I'm glad, I'm glad!

[*He is already at stairway and stops, overcome with sobs. He peevishly brushes his nose with his fist, fighting to control himself.*]

Oh, I'll be rotting myself—but I'll be happy to rot! Yeah—happy! I want to rot, I want to go to the devil! I'll enjoy it, I'll have the time of my life, I'll simply love—Oh, damn you, damn you!

[*He stops again, choked by sobs. Furiously he draws himself up to his full height and makes a final attempt at bravado.*]

So, you think I've got to pay, do you? So, you think I won't ever be the same again, do you? You flatter yourself, Paula! Oh, you never touched me! Look at me! I'm still Tony! I'm still the same old Tony! And believe me, girls, I'm going to—[*It's no use. He breaks down completely; he doubles over, sobbing hoarsely; his face in his hands.*]

Oh, why did you do it, Paula? Why did you do it? Why did you do it!

[*He staggers down the stairs.*]

PAULA: The poor victim of our little sacrifice!

CANDIDA [*approaching; timidly*]: Was it . . . *our* sacrifice, Paula?

PAULA [*turning around; gaily*]: Oh Candida, I merely wielded the knife!

It was you who laid the wood on the altar, it was you lighted the fire!

CANDIDA [*sinking down to her knees*]: Oh Paula, forgive me!

PAULA [*sinking down beside her*]: Candida, tell me you have no regrets!

CANDIDA: About the picture?

PAULA: What would you have done?

CANDIDA [*spiritedly*]: Just what you did! I would have destroyed it!

PAULA: Be careful, Candida! Have you considered to what we commit ourselves?

CANDIDA: To the darkness and the bill-collectors and the wagging tongues!

PAULA: And now they will say we have lost our senses. Remember: we have destroyed a piece of property worth ten thousand dollars. That is something they will never understand. They will say we are mad, they will say we are dangerous! And Candida—they may be right after all—eventually . . .

CANDIDA: I am willing to take the risk.

PAULA: Listen! They are talking about us now . . . They are gathering, they are coming!

CANDIDA [*with a smile*]: Ours is a very special talent, Paula.

PAULA: Alas, yes! We can only catch rats and speak Babylonian. What place is there for us in the world?

CANDIDA: Why should we want a label or a number?

PAULA: And you are not afraid, Candida?

CANDIDA: Of being . . . a Babylonian?

PAULA: And of being exterminated.

CANDIDA: May God forgive me for ever having desired the safeness of mediocrity!

PAULA [*rising & drawing her sister up*]: Then stand up, Candida—stand up! We are free again! We are together again—you and I and father. Yes—and father too! Don't you see, Candida? This is the sign he has been waiting for—ever since he gave us that picture, ever since he offered us our release—the sign that we had found our faith again, that we had found our courage again! Oh, he was waiting for us to take this step, to make this gesture—this final, absolute, magnificent, unmistakable gesture!

CANDIDA: And now we have done it!

PAULA: We have recognized our true vocation!

CANDIDA: We have taken our final vows!

PAULA: And we have placed ourselves irrevocably on his side!

CANDIDA: Does he know?

PAULA: Oh yes, yes!

CANDIDA: Have you told him?

PAULA: But what need is there to tell him?

CANDIDA [*rapturously*]: Oh Paula!

PAULA: He knows, he knows!

CANDIDA: And he has forgiven us at last! He has forgiven us, Paula!

PAULA: And we will stand with him?

CANDIDA: *Contra mundum!*

PAULA: Oh Candida, let us drink to it!

CANDIDA [*as Paula pours the drinks*]: But now we stand with him as persons; we stand with him of our own free will, knowing what we do and why we do it. Oh, we did not know before, Paula. We loved him only because he was our father and because we were his daughters. But now we are no longer his daughters—no . . . And how I shiver with terror! We cannot resume the past, Paula; we must work out a new relationship—the three of us. Something has happened to the three of us—and to father most of all. Paula, do you realize that we do not know him anymore? He is no longer the charming artist of our childhood; and he is no longer that bitter broken old man who jumped out of the window. Something has been happening to him all this year. He has come to terms with life; he has made his own peace; he has found a solution. We will be facing a man risen from the grave . . . Oh Paula, how I shiver! And yet I can hardly wait! I can hardly wait to face him, to show him these new creatures he has made of us! We are no longer his daughters; we are his friends, his disciples, his priestesses! We have been born again—not of his flesh but of his spirit!

PAULA [*offering glass*]: Then, come! Let us drink to our birthday!

CANDIDA [*taking glass*]: And nothing can divide us now! They can drive us away from this house and separate us—but we will still be together, you and I and father. And as long as we stand together, the world cannot be wholly lost or doomed or destroyed!

PAULA [*raising her glass*]: We stand against the world only to save it!

CANDIDA [*raising her glass*]: And to save it, we must stand against the world!

[*They touch glasses.*]

PAULA: Happy Birthday, Candida!

CANDIDA: Happy Birthday, Paula!

[*They drink; then burst into laughter. The bells peal out again, and continue pealing to end of the Scene. From the distance comes a rumor of drums.*]

PAULA: Candida, the procession!

CANDIDA: And why are we standing in darkness?

PAULA: Let us turn on the chandelier!

CANDIDA: Let us turn on all the lights!

PAULA: It is a Holiday!

CANDIDA: It is the birthday of our lives!

[*They fly apart—Paula to the left; Candida to the right—and turn on all the lights as Bitoy appears on the stair-landing.*]

PAULA: Halt! Who goes there!

BITOY [*blinking*]: Why, Paula!

PAULA: Are you friend or foe?

BITOY: Friend!

PAULA: Advance, friend, and be recognized!

BITOY [*walking in*]: I have been looking for you everywhere.

CANDIDA: I sent him to look for you, Paula.

PAULA [*clasping her hands to her breast*]: My hero! And at last you have found me—in this enchanted castle!

BITOY [*laughing*]: What on earth has happened?

PAULA [*whispering*]: The evil spell has been broken!

CANDIDA: The enchantment has dissolved!

PAULA: The princesses will now return to their kingdoms—

CANDIDA: And live happily ever after!

BITOY: Don't I get half of the kingdom?

PAULA: Beware, Bitoy! Our kingdom is a barren land; and the king, our father, an old man.

CANDIDA: Are you willing to carry him on your back?

BITOY: With all his ancestral gods!

PAULA: Candida, our first novice!

CANDIDA: Bitoy Camacho, I am delighted with you!

BITOY: And everything is all right now?

CANDIDA [*her expression quickly changing*]: No! No, not yet!

PAULA: Oh Candida, they are gathering now! They are coming!

BITOY: Who?

CANDIDA [*giggling*]: Oh, what shall we do, Paula? Where shall we hide!

BITOY: What is all this!

PAULA: Shh! Listen!

[*They listen, looking toward stairway. Enter* DON ALVARO & DOÑA UPENG.]

ALVARO: A holy and good evening to everyone in this house!

PAULA & CANDIDA [*hurrying to meet visitors; finger on lips*]: Shhh! Shhh!

ALVARO: Is your papa sick?

PAULA: Oh no, no, Don Alvaro!

CANDIDA: He is in the best of health!

PAULA [*hurrying visitors into the room*]: Come over here, Doña Upeng! Come over here, Don Alvaro! Oh, we are so glad you have come! Candida, some brandy for our guests!

CANDIDA: And of course you remember Bitoy Camacho. He was a regular member of our old tertulias. Bitoy, say good evening to your old friends.

BITOY: Good evening, Doña Upeng. Good evening, Don Alvaro.

PAULA: He, too, has come to celebrate the Naval with us!

ALVARO: You do well, my boy, to honor an old tradition before it disappears.

CANDIDA [*as she offers glasses*]: Disappears?

ALVARO: Yes—there is all this talk of war, war, war!

UPENG: And that is why we have come tonight. We wanted to salute the Virgin again from your balconies—as we used to do in the old days. Oh Paula, Candida—this may be the last time!

[*Enter* DON PEPE.]

PEPE: Yes, Upeng—this may well be the last time!

UPENG: *Pepe!* Pepe, you old carabao—where have you come from?

PEPE: Practically from the graveyard, Upeng. But I felt I had to come tonight—

PAULA [*hurrying to meet him*]: Shhh! Come over here, Don Pepe!

PEPE [*as he is hurried into the room*]: My dear Paula, what is happening?

ALVARO: Yes—just what is wrong, girls?

PAULA: Listen—we are in trouble—Candida and I.

CANDIDA: We need your help!

PEPE: Candida, Paula, we will do anything for you!

CANDIDA: Oh, thank God, you have come tonight!

PAULA: We need our old friends tonight!

PEPE: Well, here we are! [*He glances toward stairway.*] And here come some more of us! [*He goes to stairway as* DON MIGUEL & DOÑA IRENE *come up; greeting them with finger on lips.*] Shhh! Come over here, you two! Candida and Paula are in danger!

IRENE [*kissing the sisters*]: My dear Paula! And dearest Candida!

MIGUEL: What is it, girls? Can we help?

PAULA: Don Miguel, you have already helped us!

CANDIDA: Simply by coming tonight!

IRENE: Oh, we simply had to come tonight!

MIGUEL: They say a war is coming—a big war!

IRENE: Nothing will be left of what we have loved so much!

UPENG [*taking the other woman's hand*]: Aie, Irene—not much is left—even now!

IRENE: No, Upeng. Not much is left even now . . .

PEPE: The wind is left anyway. Look at it blowing! It is the same wind, the good old wind of October! Oh, feel it, smell it—all of you! It is blowing from the old days, from the days of our youth! It is blowing from the old Manila—*la Manila de nuestros amores!*

MIGUEL: And here we are—gathered again—relics of the old dispensation . . .

[*A pause, while they watch the blowing curtains of the balconies and listen to the sound of bells & approaching drums. The visitors are all very old, very frail, & very faded—but still talk & carry themselves with an air of grandeur, being impoverished gentlefolk. They are poorly but neatly dressed—canes*

*& the "Americana Cerrada" for the men; fans & the starchy
"saya" with train for the women; old shawls draped under
their pañuelos.*]

ALVARO: And what memories, eh? Personal memories, ancestral memories . . . That wind, those bells, this feast . . . *La Naval de Manila!* How the words ache in one's heart!

MIGUEL: Ah, but you speak only for ourselves, Alvaro.

ALVARO: Yes. In this, we are the last of the generations.

MIGUEL: Already, for our children, these things awaken no special emotion, no memories, no filial pieties . . .

IRENE: The old traditions are dying . . .

PEPE: There is no need for a war to kill them.

[*Enter* DON ARISTEO.]

ARISTEO: Alas, no! And there is no need for a war to kill us either!

VISITORS: Aristeo!

ARISTEO: Caramba, you are all here!

VISITORS: Shhh!

ARISTEO: Huh?

PAULA [*approaching; whispering*]: Welcome again to our house, noble soldier!

ARISTEO [*in booming voice*]: Paula, I have dragged my dying bones up here to salute the Virgin for the last time!

VISITORS: Shhh!

ARISTEO: But what is the matter with all of you!

UPENG: Stop your shouting, Aristeo! Paula and Candida are in great peril!

IRENE: Their lives are threatened!

ARISTEO: Girls, is this true?

CANDIDA [*smiling*]: Will you defend us?

ARISTEO: Oh, I should have brought my pistol!

PAULA: We need only your presence, Noble Soldier! Candida, some brandy for our champion!

ARISTEO [*taking her hands*]: Wait a minute, Paula—let me look at you. Caramba, your hands are cold!

PAULA: Oh, truly?

ARISTEO [*looking her in the eye*]: Paula, all this is not. . . just a joke?

PAULA: Oh no, no!

ARISTEO: You are actually in grave danger?

PAULA [*bending her face toward him*]: Surely you can feel the floor trembling beneath us?

ARISTEO: I can feel your hands trembling, yes.

[*She withdraws her hands, still smiling.*]
　　What is it, girl?

PAULA [*with a shrug*]: Oh, this may be the last time, the last night, we shall stand here—Candida and I—in our own house.

ARISTEO: I see.

CANDIDA [*offering him a glass*]: But of course we mean to be stubborn!

PAULA: And listen—I am not afraid.

ARISTEO: Why should you be? Am I not here?

UPENG: And we will all stand with you, Paula and Candida!

ALVARO: You *must* remain in this house!

IRENE: We *need* you here in this house!

PEPE: To continue us—

UPENG: And to preserve us—

ALVARO: And as a symbol of permanence!

PEPE: This house is our assurance that life will go on!

MIGUEL: Exactly! Why, just look at us now. Terrified by rumors of destruction, we have all come running here as to a rock! Even so, for those great warriors of Thermopylae—

ARISTEO: My dear Miguel!

MIGUEL: My dear Aristeo!

ARISTEO: We are in no mood for orations! Candida, pass the brandy! *Animo, amigos! Sursum corda!* We all have no money in our pockets—but we are not dead yet! We can still drink!

CANDIDA [*laughing*]: Don Aristeo is always right! Come on, everybody—more brandy!

PAULA: Yes, let us all drink and be merry!

IRENE: And to whom shall we drink?

CANDIDA: To the Virgin! To the Virgin, of course!

ARISTEO: Amigos, let us drink to the Virgin. We are gathered here in her honor.

ALVARO: And this is our feast—

PEPE: And the feast of our fathers!

ARISTEO: And they still live—our fathers. Something of them is left; something of them survives, and will survive, as long as

we live and remember—we who have known and loved and
cherished these things . . .

MIGUEL: And we will live for a long time yet!

PEPE: We will live to be a hundred!

UPENG: Oh, what old fools we were—to be so timorous, to be
so terrified!

IRENE: This time is not the last time!

UPENG: And tonight is not the last night!

ALVARO: We will live to be a thousand!

MIGUEL: We will live forever!

EVERYBODY: Viva!

PAULA: And listen, everybody—tertulia on Friday! Tertulia
again on Friday!

CANDIDA: Yes, yes! Our house shall be open again as usual—
next Friday—and every Friday! We must continue, we must
preserve!

EVERYBODY: VIVA! VIVA!

PAULA [*raising her glass*]: Don Aristeo?

ARISTEO: Amigos y paisanos!

[*He raises his glass.*]

A la gran señora de Filipinas en la gloriosa fiesta de su Naval!

EVERYBODY: *VIVA LA VIRGEN!*

[*They drink. Enter Pepang & Manolo, and advance grimly
into the room, Paula & Candida are standing side by side at
center. The visitors are grouped solidly behind them. Bitoy
is standing a little apart at left, a worried on-looker.*]

PAULA [*gaily*]: Pepang! Manolo!

CANDIDA: Have you also come to salute the Virgin?

MANOLO [*grimly*]: You know very well why we have come!

PAULA: Have you come to confess at last?

PEPANG: To confess!

MANOLO: Are you crazy? Is it we who—

PAULA: Confess, Manolo! Confess, Pepang! Oh, you will feel so
happy afterward! You will be free! Look at us!

MANOLO: Yes, look at yourselves! Just look at yourselves! What
a fine public spectacle you have made of yourselves!

PEPANG: Oh, this shameful, shameful scandal!

MANOLO: Go and get some clothes! You are both leaving this house at once!

CANDIDA: Where are your manners, Manolo? Do you not see we have visitors?

PEPANG: How can you have the nerve? You should be hiding your faces—if you have any shame left!

MANOLO: Tell these people to go away!

[*The procession is now approaching: and the drums rumble ever closer, ever louder.*]

ARISTEO [*coming forward*]: Caramba, it is Manolito! I hardly recognized you, my boy—you have grown so fat!

MANOLO: Don Aristeo, I am sorry but I must ask you to leave. My sisters and I have family matters to discuss.

ARISTEO: And is this Pepita?

MANOLO: Don Aristeo, did you hear what I said!

ARISTEO: Aie, Pepita—what an exquisite child you were: so tender, so affectionate! And how you loved to ride on my back, round and round this room—remember?

PEPANG: Don Aristeo, we have no time to—

ARISTEO: No time, no time! Always no time, always in a hurry! Relax, both of you! Here, sit down—have a drink—and let us talk about the old days!

MANOLO: Candida, will you send these people away!

ARISTEO: Tch! tch! And you used to be such a quiet boy—very thin, very dreamy—

MANOLO: Don Aristeo—

ARISTEO: Upeng, do you remember how you used to scold him for being so bashful?

UPENG [*laughing*]: Oh, he was always blushing—especially in the presence of the fair sex!

IRENE: And you blushed very charmingly, Manolito, when you were a boy!

MANOLO: I ask you politely—all of you—for the last time—

ALVARO: And always reading, always off in a corner with a book—

PEPE: Or playing his violin down there in the patio—

MIGUEL: Or directing a zarzuela, with Pepita here as the prima-donna—

MANOLO [*shouting*]: Will you let me speak!

ARISTEO: Oh, they were the most intellectual children I have ever known!

MANOLO: Don Aristeo, I beg you—

PEPANG: Oh, why do you waste your time, Manolo! It is useless to talk to them!

IRENE: And, Pepita, I will never forget how you used to recite the "Ultimo Adios" when you were hardly seven!

PEPE: It was I who taught her that poem!

UPENG: And it was I who taught you to dance, Manolo, on the night of your fifteenth birthday—remember?—right in this very room!

ALVARO: What gay memories this house holds for all of us!

MIGUEL: And how Manolo and Pepang must love this old scene of their childhood!

PAULA: Alas, no!

MIGUEL: They do not love it?

CANDIDA: They want it sold!

THE VISITORS: *SOLD!*

UPENG: *Que horror!*

IRENE: But why?

PAULA: That is something they refuse to confess, even to themselves!

ARISTEO: But, perhaps, they cannot afford this house any longer.

PAULA: Oh, it is not the expense!

CANDIDA: Although *that* is the reason they give!

PAULA: But they deceive themselves!

PEPANG: Paula! Candida!

PAULA: It is not the expense. Why, they throw money away right and left, night and day, at the gambling tables, and think nothing about it!

PEPANG: Manolo, are you going to stand there and let these—

PAULA: No, it is not the expense! They simply cannot stand this house, they cannot bear it!

CANDIDA: It haunts them, it spoils their fun!

PAULA: It is always rising before their eyes at the most inconvenient moments—

CANDIDA: When they are gossiping with their friends—

PAULA: Or playing mah-jongg—

CANDIDA: Or having a nice time at the races or at the Jai-Alai—

PAULA: Or when they cannot sleep—

CANDIDA: Suddenly—*cataplum!*—the shadow of this house falls upon them!

PAULA: And then their hands falter—

CANDIDA: Their blood turns cold!

ARISTEO: You mean, they are afraid of this house?

CANDIDA: And they want it destroyed!

ALVARO: But why?

PAULA: *Because it is their conscience!*

MANOLO & PEPANG: *PAULA!*

[*The drums are now rumbling right under the balconies.*]

PAULA [*advancing slowly*]: Yes, Manolo! Yes, Pepang! This house is your conscience—and *that* is why you hate it, *that* is why you fear it, *that* is why you have been craving so long and so desperately to destroy it! No, you can not afford it! You cannot afford to have a conscience! Because you know you will have no—

MANOLO [*stepping back*]: SHUT UP! SHUT UP!

PAULA [*standing still*]: You know you will have no peace as long as this house stands here to rebuke you!

MANOLO: [*raising his fists*]: SHUT UP—or, by God, I'm going to—

[*The balconies light up dazzlingly as the procession passes below.*]

PAULA: And you will not rest—no—you will never rest until you have laid waste this house; until you have stripped it naked, and torn down its walls, and uprooted its very foundations!

PEPANG: Manolo, this is beyond endurance!

CANDIDA: Confess, Pepang! Confess, Manolo!

MANOLO: They have gone mad!

PAULA: Confess, confess—and be free!

PEPANG: Are you going to let them frighten you?

MANOLO: They are leaving this house this very moment!

PEPE: Oh no, Manolito—nobody can leave now!

UPENG [*waving toward balconies*]: Look! The procession!

ALVARO: The streets are closed!

IRENE: The Holy Virgin herself has come to save them!

MANOLO [*advancing*]: They are leaving this house right now if I have to throw them down the stairs!

ARISTEO: Then, you will first have to throw me down those stairs, Manolito!

PEPE [*stepping forward*]: And me!

UPENG [*stepping forward*]: And me!

IRENE [*stepping forward*]: And me!

MIGUEL: You will first have to throw all of us down those stairs, Manolito!

[*Manolo stands still, staring.*]

ARISTEO: Well, my boy—what do you say now?

CANDIDA: And that is not all, Manolo. There is father as well. Are you prepared to throw him also down those stairs?

PEPANG: Father hates you!

PAULA: Father stands with us!

CANDIDA: And we stand with father!

BITOY [*suddenly shouting; with astonished gesture toward doorway*]: AND HERE HE COMES! HERE HE COMES!

PEPANG [*staring; gripping Manolo's arm*]: Manolo, look! It's father!

[*Chorus of "Lorenzo!" and "Here comes Lorenzo!" and "Hola, Lorenzo!" from the visitors as they all gaze, amazed, toward doorway. Candida & Paula, who have their backs to the doorway, turn around slowly & fearfully. But, suddenly, their faces light up & lift up; they gasp, they smile; they clasp their hands to their breasts.*]

PAULA & CANDIDA [*in ringing, rising, radiant exultation*]: OH PAPA! PAPA! PAPA!

[*From the street comes a flourish of trumpets as the band breaks into the strains of the Gavotta Marcha Procesional; and as Bitoy Camacho steps forward to his usual place at left front of stage, the "Intramuros Curtain" closes in on the sala scene, everybody inside remaining frozen.*]

BITOY [*speaking exultantly through the sound of bells and music*]: October in Manila! The month when, in full typhoon season, the city broke out into its biggest celebrations! The month that started the display of hams and cheeses among its grocers, and of turrones among its sweet-shops; when her markets overflowed with apples, grapes, oranges, pomelos—and her sidewalks with chestnuts and lanzons! The month when, back in our childhood, the very air turned festive and the Circus came to town and the season opened at the old Opera House!

[*The lights die out inside the stage; the sound of bells & music fades off. The ruins stand out distinctly.*]

Well, that was the last October the old city was ever to celebrate. And that was my last time to see it still alive—the old Manila; my last time to see the Naval procession advancing down this street, and to salute the Virgin from the balconies of the old Marasigan house.

It is gone now—that house—the house of Don Lorenzo el Magnifico. This piece of wall, this heap of stones, are all that's left of it. It finally took a global war to destroy this house and the three people who fought for it. Though they were destroyed, they were never conquered. They were still fighting—right to the very end—fighting against the jungle.

They are dead now—Don Lorenzo, Candida, Paula—they are all dead now—a horrible death—by sword and fire . . . They died with their house and they died with their city—and maybe it's just as well they did. They could never have survived the death of the old Manila.

And yet—listen!—it is not dead; it has not perished! Listen, Paula! Listen, Candida! Your city—my city—the city of our fathers—still lives! Something of it is left; something of it survives, and will survive, as long as I live and remember—I who have known and loved and cherished these things!

[*He stoops down on one knee and makes a gesture of scooping earth.*]

Oh Paula, Candida—listen to me! By your dust, and by the dust of all the generations, I promise to continue, I promise to preserve! The jungle may advance, the bombs may fall again—but while I live, you live—and this dear city of our

affections shall rise again—if only in my song! To remember
and to sing: that is my vocation . . .
[*The lights die out on Bitoy. All you can see now are the
stark ruins, gleaming in the silent moonlight.*]

FINAL CURTAIN

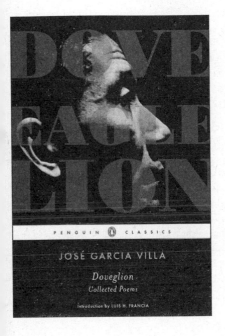

ALSO AVAILABLE

JOSÉ RIZAL

NOLI ME TANGERE (TOUCH ME NOT)

Introduction and Notes with a Translation by Harold Augenbraum

A love story set against the ugly political backdrop of repression, torture, and murder, *Noli Me Tangere* was the first major artistic manifestation of Asian resistance to European colonialism and has become widely known as the great novel of the Philippines.

JOSÉ RIZAL

EL FILIBUSTERISMO

Introduction and Notes with a Translation by Harold Augenbraum

In this riveting continuation of his masterpiece, *Noli Me Tangere*, Rizal departs from previous themes of innocent love and martyrdom to present a gripping tale of obsession and revenge. El Filibusterismo is a thrilling account of Filipino resistance to colonial rule that still resonates today.